PRAISE FOR LARA ELENA DONNELLY'S AMBERLOUGH DOSSIER

Amnesty

"A fitting finale for the series; the experience of reading it is somewhat like watching an elegant train wreck in progress and wondering if there will be any survivors."

—*Booklist*

"A triumph of craft."

—Tor.com

Armistice

"Bracing [and] timely . . . Donnelly has successfully built upon her intricate, lush world of passionate spies and turncoats, and each character leaps off the page in this satisfying novel that succeeds on both grand and intimate scales."

—*Publishers Weekly* (starred review)

"Evoke[s] a smoky, lustrous Art Deco atmosphere reminiscent of a 1930s theatrical production."

—*Booklist*

"Donnelly is attempting to reimagine the spy novel free of heteronormative, patriarchal, Eurocentric restrictions. The result is highly entertaining."

—Historical Novel Society

Amberlough

"James Bond by way of Oscar Wilde."
—Holly Black, *New York Times* bestselling author

"Donnelly blends romance and tragedy, evoking gilded-age glamour and the thrill of a spy adventure, in this impressive debut. As heartbreaking as it is satisfying."
—*Publishers Weekly* (starred review)

"Donnelly's striking debut brings a complex world of politics, espionage, and cabaret life to full vision."
—*Library Journal* (starred review, Debut of the Month)

"*Amberlough* grabbed me from the first page. It is beautiful, all too real, and full of pain. Read it. It will change you."
—Mary Robinette Kowal, winner of the Hugo Award

"Sparkling with slang, full of riotous characters, and dripping with intrigue, *Amberlough* is a dazzling romp through a tumultuous, ravishing world."
—Robert Jackson Bennett, winner of the Shirley Jackson Award and the Edgar Award

BASE NOTES

ALSO BY
LARA ELENA DONNELLY

The Amberlough Dossier

Amberlough
Armistice
Amnesty

BASE NOTES

LARA ELENA
DONNELLY

THOMAS & MERCER

Published by Thomas & Mercer, Seattle

www.apub.com

Amazon, the Amazon logo, and Thomas & Mercer are trademarks of Amazon.com, Inc., or its affiliates.

ISBN-13: 9781542030700
ISBN-10: 1542030706

Cover design by M. S. Corley

Printed in the United States of America

BASE
NOTES

BASE NOTES SOLIFLORE DISCOVERY SET

THE HEROES

Vic Fowler
Unavailable at this time and, at any rate, irrelevant.

Giovanni Metzger
Cool, dry cornstarch. Aldehydes and white balsamic. A bitterness almost like gunpowder.

Beau Singh
Hot asphalt, sweat lather, nutty ambrette. Clean, green whiff of witch hazel. A complex sweetness reminiscent of healing myrrh.

Jane Betjeman
Sweet hay and unwashed hair. Warm, wet wool. Horse stalls and sticky lanolin.

THE VILLAINS

Joseph Eisner
Old book must, dry leather. Powdered latex gloves.

Reginald Yates
Sour milk and little boy. The spermy scent of decorative pear trees.

Conrad Yates
Sour milk and old man. Petroleum ointment tang.

Gerald Pearson
Salty sweetness of bad bourbon, smoker's breath. The pipe-smoke fug of an OTB.

THE INCIDENTALS

Pippin Miles
A sour new pack of playing cards. Antiperspirant, plastic sneakers, dandruff shampoo.

Barry Baptiste
Cocaine sweat and the astringent earthiness of copaiba balsam. Salt, salt, salt.

Iolanda Ríos
Metallic curler smoke. Crisp hair. Something powdery beneath it, flowery but sharp.

AN INTRODUCTION

Notes de Tête: Ozone
Notes de Cœur: Burnt Bacon
Notes de Fond: Wet Earth, Gasoline

Let's try something. As a quick proof of concept before we get started.

Imagine you are me. You are parking a Zipcar at the border of a field upstate. It is early spring, and cold, but the windows are down. Still, everything reeks of ethanol: like twisting the cap off a bottle of Everclear and pressing your nose to its open mouth. Less a smell than a physical sensation.

The sedan has new-car smell: plasticky and fresh. The open windows let in a breeze, and the rich aroma of wet dirt, turned by the plow and soaked with rain. Upwind there is a hog farm. The manure scent carries for miles.

It is very dark out here, which is good for what comes first but bad for what comes next. You are nervous, though you have done this many times before. You can smell your own sweat, and the sourness of fear collects behind your molars, tainting each breath. Taste and smell are near enough it does not matter if you breathe through your nose or mouth: either way you stink of trepidation.

Opening the trunk reveals a plastic tarp, its inside edges wet with condensation. Alcohol burns inside your sinuses and makes you weep.

The body is heavy, but you have practice at this and get it out if not with ease, then at least without undue awkwardness. The tarp crackles on the fallow ground.

There is a metal barrel in this field, not far from the fence, where someone burns their garbage on occasion. You have never actually seen it smoldering, but the scent of melted plastic and scorched Styrofoam is always present, if faint.

Bent in half, Caroline fits neatly over the ashes of last month's trash.

You are sweating now with exertion, and that smells cleaner. The wind shifts and the hog shit fades, replaced by fresh green growth and ozone. A storm is coming. But hopefully not until the fire has burned out.

Though Caroline is pickled, absolutely soaked with alcohol, you have still brought gasoline. You open the can and the metallic tang of it blooms across the back of your throat, summoning memories of filling stations in deep summer.

You pour gas from the can—not too much or the barrel will explode—and add brush from the edge of the forest to get things started. You will add more later as things progress. It takes a long time for a corpse to burn in these conditions, even saturated with accelerant. In the best case, the fire will still leave teeth and bits of bone for you to bury. The sacrum, after all, is so-called for its indestructibility. The holy bone, unscathed amidst the ashes.

The match sends up a thread of sulfur. The wet wood, when it catches, smokes. And as the fire grows, the smoke begins to smell of hair and rendered fat. Someone else might put their shirt across their mouth, sip the charnel air only with reluctance.

But you are me, so you breathe deep.

Yes. Like that.

1

Notes de Tête: Whiskey, Jasmine, Oakmoss
Notes de Cœur: Old Cigarettes and Stale Coffee
Notes de Fond: Mildew, Charcoal, Barbicide

For the aesthetically and culturally inclined, there are few places in the continental United States—or the full fifty, for that matter—as apt to satisfy as Lincoln Center. Unfortunately, for those of us aesthetically and culturally inclined people who are perpetually skint, Lincoln Center is a stretch, financially.

I always made it to the Met's season premiere, where I bought a single drink to nurse and supplement via flask in the bathroom, breathing through my mouth and trying not to smell the Sauvage and White Linen, the Santal 33 and Coco Mademoiselle.

It was all in order to be Instagrammed, of course, and I sometimes managed to get my ticket comped. I knew enough things about enough people to engineer that, at least. I had learned my trade at the elbow of Jonathan Bright, a notorious extortionist and iconoclast of the perfume world; I understood the value of kompromat. And Bright House, now under my dubious stewardship, had just enough brand recognition that the Met Opera interns could find us to tag when they posted.

Besides, I was comparatively young, passingly attractive, and trendily androgynous. Just the right ornament for Last Night at the Met, and the social-media team knew it. Opera couldn't cater to fossils anymore—the Met needed young blood who would inherit their grandparents' money.

Good luck. For most of my generation, it would just go to student debt and cocktails. If anything came to me (an impossibility), I would dump it into a poorly managed career in edgy luxury items. You can't make opera money on perfume that smells like cunts and gasoline.

At any rate, I didn't usually make an appearance beyond the gala. Or, I hadn't until recently. But Joseph Eisner had promised me a fortune, and now he wouldn't take my calls. He did, however, like his chamber music.

It had been an acquired taste for me. In my distant undergraduate past, when circumstance sat me in front of an ensemble, I spent the first five minutes of each concert deciding which musician I would fuck if I had the chance, and the rest shifting minutely in my seat.

I still couldn't stand Chanel. And while I had learned to appreciate—indeed, enjoy—chamber ensembles, orchestras, and on occasion even the opera, I retained my former habit as a dirty amusement to add some private savor to the proceedings. Tonight, it was the violist, weaving and bobbing his way through Dvořák's Terzetto in C Major like a sinuous dancer.

I prefer the romantics—fewer hair-raising harmonies than modern fare, and certainly more engaging than funereal baroque. The intriguing arrangement of the terzetto kept me engaged, in that slightly detached and floating manner engendered by instrumental performance.

Moreover, the woman to my left, one row ahead, was wearing Salome by Papillon. The simple fact of anyone wearing such a scent in public pleased me. So few people dared wear anything at all these days, and when they did, it was inevitably staid: an inoffensive classic or antiseptic citrus-and-powder. But this perfume was one I might have worn myself. Jasmine, yes, but more indolic than your average floral. People sometimes say it smells like dirty panties.

As the trio wrapped up for intermission, I took a steadying breath of musk and straightened my lapels. The music was only a means to an end, after all.

Haunting the lobby of Alice Tully Hall like a well-dressed revenant, I watched ghostly reflections play across the glass. Headlights slid along 65th, slicing through the spectral intermission crowd.

My sex-addled spy, Eisner's personal assistant, had assured me he would be at this evening's performance. She was sweet, and apt to sing like a canary post-coitus. But she still wouldn't put my calls through. In this instance, however, she had been more a help than a hindrance: Eisner appeared from the shadowed staircase leading up from the restrooms like wealthy Pluto rising from the underworld. I moved to intercept him.

"Mr. Eisner," I said, extending my hand. His, when we shook, was wet. From washing; I would have noticed the scent of urine. Instead, I smelled my own concoction, and that added insult to injury. Iris, cotton, iron rust. Dark threads of sweat and blood underneath a greener, cleaner, sparkling surface. A liminal accord, not quite chypre, not quite fougère. I quashed fury and kept smiling.

"Vic," he said. "What are you doing here?" He didn't even have the grace to sound discomfited.

"I enjoy Dvořák as much as anybody."

"Of course, of course." His laugh was expansive, showing ortho-dontically straight teeth yellow with years of coffee and nicotine. Light bounced off his baldness.

A much younger man approached us, holding two plastic flutes of sparkling wine with heavily ringed fingers. "Jojo," he said, lifting one drink and giving it a perilous waggle.

Eisner smiled indulgently. "Andrew, meet Vic."

"Your son?" I asked, because I knew it would annoy him. I should have been polite, but I could hardly bear it. I'm not a polite person, when all is said and done, and less so when I'm pressed or peeved. At times, my displeasure can be downright violent.

Eisner's smile was thin. "Andrew, Vic is a perfumer. Absolutely charming little enterprise called Bright House. Here, smell."

He lifted his wrist to the young man's face in a way no blood relation would dare outside a particular subgenre of pornography. Andrew wrinkled his surgically delicate nose, and my annoyance swiftly solidified into hatred.

"It's so nice to see *young* people taking an interest in the arts," I said.

"Vic," purred Eisner. "You're hardly out of high school."

"I'm twenty-eight," I said, icy. "And I run my own company."

"Well, you don't look it." It was not a compliment. "How is your little cottage industry these days?"

He knew exactly, because he had seen the financials. When our initial off-the-books association led to the perfume he had the gall to wear tonight after breaking his promise, he had offered to act as an investor. He knew I only needed a little push—little by his lights—for a boost in production. With that, I could lock down a European distribution deal I hoped would put Bright House's feet back under us. Then I could stop making spreadsheets and return to making perfume. But I couldn't pull it off without his cash.

The money had not been forthcoming. It was either cruelty or caprice. What did Bright House matter to him? He could wear Frassaï, Frédéric Malle, Fueguia. He could finance his own damn line of aftershave and eau de toilette and never feel the squeeze. And yet he wouldn't cut a check for me, no matter what I had done for him. Despite the specter of scent that hung around his throat and everything I had put into it. There was more in that bottle than iris and aldehydes, and we both knew it.

I wanted to wrap my hands around that wattle where he'd sprayed my scent and strangle him.

The lights rose and dimmed. We all went back to our seats. Throughout the final quartet, I smelled Salome working through its middle notes, decaying to the stink beneath. My mood grew fouler to match until the final chord rang out, and I slipped away under cover of applause.

◆ ◆ ◆

My landlady had not lit the boiler yet, which meant that it was cold. Autumn had come to New York at last and was making its presence felt. I checked my mail—junk, junk, bills, and junk. A cold draft slithered through the mail slot and raised hairs on the back of my neck. The lights of Lincoln Center felt very far away.

My company might have been operating in the red, but I still paid myself enough to live alone. You might think this was an extravagance. Given the lucrative criminal sideline I pursued outside of office hours, I assure you it was not.

I had no projects steeping at the time, and no raw materials to prepare. My basement studio felt empty, my prospects devoid of potential. I was not in a mood to accept this with grace. With more than necessary force, I flung my coat across the armchair and, from the bar cart, drew a dwindling bottle of Longrow I could ill afford to replace. It reeked like seaweed, smoke, and iodine. Before drinking I drew the smell so deep into my lungs they burned. I was in a mood to set most things on fire, including myself.

Fuck Eisner, anyway.

I was tired. I could finally admit it to myself, five years on from that first fateful day in the lab. As protégé to the illustrious Jonathan Bright, founder of the eponymous House, I had been eager to surpass him. As his lover, I had fought for power along every axis of our relationship. And I had finally won it, albeit in an . . . unorthodox fashion. Now that I was—nominally—on top, it was a scramble just to stay in place.

While Bright House shone in the press for some time following Jonathan's tragic disappearance, sales slacked off when our name slipped from the headlines. The company came to me after a little bit of cursory legal paper pushing; I was second-in-command and nobody else wanted it. Peers appreciated Jonathan's craft but wouldn't touch the business with a ten-foot pole. I didn't do much to remedy the situation.

In truth, I was too ambitious out of the gate. A rookie mistake. I spent more money on R & D than I could spare and not enough on marketing, compliance, personnel. Our production of staples faltered—I was not interested in scents just *anyone* would wear. My flaw, like Jonathan's, was an abiding passion to produce perfume that made people think. Or that bypassed the brain altogether and went straight to the gut and groin.

Unfortunately, sex and shit make most Americans uncomfortable, and few of them really enjoy introspection or intellectual exercise. Yourself excepted, of course, or we wouldn't have gotten this far.

It was lucky, then, that Jonathan's death—because *I* know he did not "disappear"—led to one of the most interesting craft discoveries of my career. And my most lucrative, ounce for ounce. Unfortunately it's not something I can advertise. So while I very occasionally made—and still make—a comfortable sum committing or at least abetting an array of unsavory acts in the service of creating inimitable scents with certain arcane attributes, it was not enough to run a company. Besides, the IRS would ask too many questions.

Bright House was floundering. I had hoped we would do better in Europe, before Eisner crushed that dream. The last several years had been a slog. I was exhausted from trying to balance unbalanceable books and, when I stopped to consider it, quite bored. Perhaps even lonely. I missed having someone to snarl at who would snarl back—none of my employees dared, and I dared not snarl at my clients. I wanted a whetstone for my edge. I wanted to get laid, at least. And I wanted to pursue my art outside business or commissions.

All in all, a sorry state of affairs upon which I preferred not to dwell. The Scotch helped a little, but I had something stronger stored away. Several somethings.

In my refrigerator was a battered pink leather jewelry box with a tarnished clasp: a flea market find when I was first stumbling through the world of perfume and needed somewhere dark to keep my new obsession safe.

Then, I had stored samples in the tiny earring brackets in the top shelf. The bottom had been given over to the few full-size bottles worth my money and my time. The box had sat on my dresser in London during my study-abroad semester. It had steadily filled after I dropped out of college to pursue my certificate in perfumery arts. And it came with me to New York when I landed a product dev assistant job at the only place I had bothered to apply: Bright House.

I had gotten the job on the strength of several sterling faculty references. The references in turn I had wrangled by means of flirtation, blackmail, natural precocity, and filthy sexual favors, though not necessarily related to one another or in any particular order. I sometimes wonder if it was whispered word of mouth, and not the written letters, that really recommended me to Bright.

Now that I was more serious about my craft, the jewelry box was crammed full of sample-size atomizers. I kept them as close to inert as I could, at morgue temperature in my mini fridge. Beneath them, on the shelves proper: larger glass bottles labeled with letters and numbers. Absolutes, left over from previous projects.

I set the jewelry box on the small square of counter space and popped it open. Thoughtfully touching the top of each small atomizer, I finally selected one. Applying expert pressure to the atomizer's top, I sent a cool mist across my throat.

A sudden suffusion of coffee, leather, cigarettes, brine.

The AeroPress drip-drying by the sink was ruthlessly clean, as was everything in Jonathan's apartment, but the plastic had been impregnated with arabica and its scent could not be scrubbed away. Somebody in the building was smoking, and the HVAC system carried it to us. Leather for his shoes and mine, set side by side, flush with the wall. His were much nicer, by a margin of several thousand dollars. The brine was for our sweat. Cèpes might have been more appropriate, or musk, but I had needed something clean to balance the unwashed base of this perfume. My Jonathan perfumes were all like that: elegant at the top, voluptuous in the middle, cruel and filthy at their core.

It was warm, in the memory. Hot, even. I had mostly chosen it for the temperature, the play of sun on my bare skin. There were other lovers or memories I might have revisited. I hadn't been a saint outside of my commissions, when I still had time to pursue independent projects. As an artisan and a professional, I needed to experiment in order to refine my technique. As an aesthete, I sometimes met moments, scents, and personalities I wanted to preserve at the expense of the other people who had experienced or produced them.

But besides the sunlight, I needed a reminder of where I'd come from and how far I'd clawed. I wanted to remember my ruthless mentor, and my own ruthlessness in getting ahead of him. I wanted to feel, for just a moment, that there was someone in the world I understood.

When I say "revisit," I do not mean "remember." I mean I was *there*, sweat prickling on my naked skin. I could see Jonathan at the counter, drinking his coffee, checking his phone. He needed a shave. The raw skin across my jaw was marked by the bristles on his.

I did not move, because I hadn't then. I lay across his bed, on his memory foam mattress and creamy Swiss-made sheets, chin resting on my bare arms. Looking down from the loft, I traced the patterns of marble in the countertop, the whorls of coarse, dark hair against his scalp. I took a deep breath of all the faint and mingled smells of the moment, let it out in a sigh.

Jonathan looked up. "What?" he asked, and I could *hear* his voice: its uneasy timbre, artificially low and edging toward nasal, always teetering on the edge of a juvenile crack. His voice, like everything about him, was pretending to be something it was not. I admired his constant performance, because in large part he succeeded. I learned this skill from him carefully, through stealthy observation. Much like I learned the art of perfumery. Since his passing, I have made discoveries and innovations in both arenas. Including *this* discovery, one of my most intriguing.

Scent is the strongest link to our memories. What I do just makes a deeper connection. Brain chemistry or black magic—it's unclear. People pay a lot of money for it, though.

To the best of my knowledge, I'm the only person who knows how to do what I do. Jonathan certainly didn't teach me, except through his unwilling participation in my first experiments. Perhaps it was something he had dreamed of, in concept. In execution—as it were—the product was all mine. Except, of course, for the components that went into it.

Then again, he was a secretive bastard, and I don't exactly shout about my talents from the rooftops. There could be other perfumers offering the same services, but I have as little idea of them as I hope they do of me.

The memory began to swim, growing indistinct as the brighter elements of brine evaporated. The leather and coffee would linger through the last of my Scotch. If I didn't shower, I would go to bed with Jonathan's ghost beside me and wake in sheets that smelled like he had stayed the night and slipped away before I woke.

I finished my whisky and went to the windowless bathroom, turning the water on so hot the whole apartment filled with steam. When I came out my skin was pink and I only smelled like soap. Castille, unscented.

◆ ◆ ◆

My assistant, Barry, found me doing inventory in the lab at half past nine. I had not slept well—unsurprising, given my straits—and was grateful that there were no mirrors in the cold, white space save the shining surface of stainless steel. The walls were unadorned, scrubbed clean. The freshly mopped linoleum floor squeaked beneath my shoes. I had cleaned the drain out with a brush myself, last night, and snaked it not so long ago. The whole place smelled of alcohol and little else.

"You're late," I said, weighing a bottle of benzaldehyde in one hand.

"No," said Barry, ignoring me and checking the arrangement of his free-form locs with his phone camera. "*I* was on time for staff meeting. You know, upstairs? In the office? *And* I brought doughnuts."

I set the bottle back on the shelf and kept myself from cursing. "Anything interesting?"

"Binh's quitting. She got offered a job at Lanvin."

"They're welcome to her." One less person on payroll. And knowing the big names wanted to poach my employees gave me a modicum of satisfaction. We were good at what we did. We just couldn't make any damn money.

"Okay, we'll see how you feel when my sponsorships start coming through and I drop your raggedy ass." Barry was gaining some notoriety as a perfume YouTuber. I had watched a few of his videos, and they were good. I would rather have died than admit this to him.

"I wish you only the best," I said.

"You look tired," he said, with false concern. "Have you been moisturizing?"

"Barry." I used That Tone.

He held up his hands, elegantly uncurling his fingers like the tops of ferns. "Right, right. Don't be such an auntie. You got it all under control." Though he weighed approximately ninety-five pounds when he'd been fasting, Barry could pack twice his weight in sarcasm.

"Joseph Eisner left a message on the office phone last night," he added. "Kind of late."

"About eleven o'clock?" I asked, adding enough time to the end of the concert for a cab ride and a drink. I wondered if he'd kept the boy around after that, only because I couldn't quite picture Eisner making a business call en déshabillé.

Barry raised an eyebrow that asked *What were you up to?* but gave me a nod nonetheless.

"What did he want?"

A shrug. "He said it was 'such a pleasure' to run into you. Like, used-car-salesman status. I had to run home and jump in the shower after I listened, it was that skeevy."

"Not catty?"

At this, a vigorous shake of the head, despite his earlier preening. "No. Slick as hell. Like silicone lube."

"*Thank you*, Barry." I snatched my phone and folio—the former in imminent need of repair or replacement, the latter a lucky thrift store find. "Did he ask for a callback?"

"'Whenever it's convenient,' he said."

Change of heart? Jerk on the chain? Who could say? I'd let him stew for a while. If he called me again, I'd know who had the power.

"Any other calls?" I asked, heading for the stairs. "And is there still coffee in the break room?"

"Yes. Also, Clairfield & Amos." The European wholesale company. "They want to know when you can commit."

"How much longer can we stall?"

"They need numbers next week."

"Fuck." I knew exactly what I'd sell them, but I didn't have the staff or the raw materials to make it happen. Or the cash to acquire them. And no sane bank would lend me money. I was going to have to call Eisner. Eventually.

But not today. I wouldn't fawn or beg. Maybe that made me stupid. But when you haven't got a lot, you hang on to your pride with teeth and nails.

"Are we good to do it?" Barry asked. "I mean I know we're not, but . . . are we *going* to be?"

"Of course," I said. Lying came easily to me. Less easy would be turning this into the truth.

I had a haircut scheduled that evening after work. My mood brightened considerably once I stepped out of the lab, though my hands were raw at the knuckles from cleaning beakers, my skin cracked by high-proof spirits. I didn't mind that so much as the persistent crick in my neck, remnant of long phone calls, or the whisper of tendinitis in my forearms. I thought longingly of the secretary I had let go last year and wondered if an unpaid intern might be worth the trouble.

I always looked forward to haircuts, as they were luxurious but cost me very little. Giovanni Metzger had been carrying Bright House colognes since I first took the reins. I respected his work, so I gave him wholesale prices on small orders that ought to have gone for retail. He responded in kind. My cuts had been steeply discounted for the last several years.

Even if they *had* cost more, I would have tightened my belt. Very few things in my life have made me feel as much myself as a haircut from Giovanni, and these days I miss his ministrations sorely.

He ran a minuscule shop of exceeding quality: a white-tiled Italian barbiere steeped in the scents of Proraso and Barbicide. The front desk was staffed by a rotating cast of smudgy-eyed burlesque performers, sexier somehow for their sleepiness, still smelling of sweat and powder. The man himself was small and ruthlessly neat, with wavy hair parted in the middle and an ambiguous olive complexion. I had never seen him without a scrupulously groomed mustache.

There were three chairs: two manned by barbers who satisfied Giovanni's stringent standards and one by Giovanni himself. His dream, he once confessed to me, was to find a third barber, install an espresso machine, and act solely as host to his customers. A tonsorial maître d'. I hoped in this eventuality he'd still consent to cut my hair, but I didn't waste time worrying. Rents kept going up, and I doubted his profits kept pace.

"Vic," he said, in an affable monotone. Quick eye contact, and then back to the comb and scissors. His hands never stopped moving while he was at work. No hair clung to his immaculate white coat that I had ever seen, nor to the three-piece suit beneath it. Giovanni didn't cut corners. Not on his personal appearance, nor his commitments, nor his vocation. It made him an excellent barber, though ill-suited to life in late capitalism.

One sympathized.

I settled onto the bench to wait, under the smoky gaze of some Slipper Room siren who looked like she'd rather be in bed. A chorus of jackhammers on Christopher Street crescendoed, ebbed, then grew again. I thought of last night's Dvořák and felt angry acid at the back of my throat.

Money. What a hindrance to our arts.

The Indochino ad who had been shorn before me paid and tipped and left, trailing a wake of Old Spice Swagger that almost made me gag. Giovanni swept briskly around his chair and then stepped forward to shake my hand. His morning aftershave had faded, but a pleasing hint of citrus and vetiver still hung in the air around him. Not one of mine, but I wasn't so vain as to begrudge him that.

"Have a seat," he said. "Same as last time?"

"Same as always. Thank you."

Giovanni didn't talk as he worked, unless his client talked first. Normally, this suited my desires. But today I had a vat of bile at a rolling boil behind my ribs, and as he ran a comb through my hair, I sighed and said, "I'm at the end of my fucking rope. And I'm not even the one who should be strangling." Then, embarrassed, I added, "How's business for you?"

I felt the comb pause at the nape of my neck, and that stillness froze the boiling acid in my gut to ice.

Giovanni's hands were never still.

"Ups and downs," he said, and resumed his work.

"Mm." More down than up, if I had to bet. "If you start charging me full price, I'll have to go back to Astor Place."

It won me a brief bout of laughter: a single "ha," mostly through the nose. He did have a sense of humor, if one knew where to dig for it.

"Really," I said. "That cattle chute of clippers is all I can afford, and I'd much rather come here."

He snipped and snipped, swept his hands through my hair, snipped again. The rhythm didn't falter, even when he said, "My lease is up for renewal."

"How much this time?"

He didn't answer. I lifted my eyes in time to catch his reflection shake its head. Refusal to name a figure? Or maybe just despair.

"The Village pricing you out?" I asked. "Welcome to the club." Bright House had kept a storefront on MacDougal for a year but had to fill that particular money pit before the whole enterprise slid in.

"I've been looking around for a cheaper space, but I'll lose a lot of clients if I move uptown or out to Queens or wherever." A shrug in the mirror. "Head down." He gently pushed against my skull. "There are a lot of good shops where I could get a chair, if it came to it."

After a few thoughtful snips, he said, "This place would have been operating in the black in the first two years if they hadn't raised the rent on me every time the lease was up. I'd be in a bigger spot now, and I'd be up front. I'd be fucking franchising." His hands whisked around my head, sorting which pieces of my hair to snip. "Oh well."

The rest of the cut proceeded silently. My fury had at this point bubbled over and left me empty and smoking, acrid with upset. After Giovanni brushed stray hairs from my neck and swept the smock away, I tried to hand him twice my usual tip. He refused.

"Fine," I said. "But at least let me buy you a drink."

2

Notes de Tête: Lime Juice, Burnt Orange
Notes de Cœur: Amaro Sfumato Rabarbaro
Notes de Fond: Stale Urine, Cold Concrete, Spilled Snapple

The cocktails at the bar he picked were more expensive than the tip I'd tried to leave, but the bartender on the happy hour shift clearly recognized Giovanni and greeted him with a smile that said we wouldn't be paying full price.

"Jane." Giovanni leaned across the bar to kiss her cheek. "How's it going?"

It was strange to see him out of his white coat. Stranger still to hear him say four words together without prompting.

"It's going," said Jane. "You know."

"Don't I. This is Vic. Old friend. Works in perfume."

Even stranger than the coat and small talk was hearing him call me a friend. He seemed to realize it, and smiled at me sheepishly.

I wasn't sure how I felt about Giovanni out of his element. I held my counsel on the matter and offered my hand to Jane. Her fingers were slightly sticky, and when I pulled mine back, they were sticky too, and smelled of lime.

"Nice to meet you," said Jane. "What are you drinking?"

Giovanni wiped a hand across his face, smearing on a smile. "Corpse reviver."

"Dealer's choice," I said. "But don't go out of your way."

"I usually don't." We eyed each other, neither willing to back down. Finally she said, "But you're a friend of Giovanni's, I guess. So what do you like?"

"Spirit forward," I said. "Bitter. Dark."

"I got you. Hang on."

Two glasses on the bar, two beakers beside them. The clatter of ice and the ring of a spoon on crystal. As she worked, her brows drew together in a frown. She was pretty, pale and freckled, but the fragile bluish skin beneath her eyes told me she was tired. And the smell of old sweat and dried sugar on her work clothes—she had not washed them in a while. No time, maybe. No days off. No spares to wear on shift while these were at the drop-off laundry.

There was an elegance and concentration to her movements, despite her exhaustion; she could have done this in her sleep, and done it well. I wondered how long she had been behind the bar, and whether she had learned her grace that way or in some other pursuit.

"How do you two know each other?" I asked.

"Jane used to be the assistant to the guy who framed all the art in the shop."

Eyes on her work, she nodded. In between her thumb and forefinger, an orange peel flexed before a match, spitting oil that caught in a burst of aromatic flames.

"She took some of the photos she framed for me."

Jane made a face. "You didn't pay me shit for them either."

"You didn't ask me to!"

"You're a photographer?" I asked.

"Not anymore." My drink landed in front of me, without any of the finesse I had come to expect from her performance. Still, she didn't spill it. "I'm in school now."

"For?"

"Radiology. Associates degree." No wonder she looked tired. She slammed the top half into her shaker and preempted further conversation with a racket of ice on metal, ice on glass.

Giovanni caught my eye and shook his head. Jane pretended not to notice.

"How's Beau?" he asked when she put his glass down—more gently than she had placed mine. "Picked a date yet?"

Her finger was bare, but I imagined she wouldn't wear a ring on the job—apt to scratch or lose it, and tips would be better if she looked single. "No way we're getting married until I'm out of school. We can't afford it."

"There's always city hall," I said. She shot a glare at me and I retreated to my lowball, touching my nose to the ice. It was more to hide my grin than show my shame—I always appreciated people who would fight me and draw blood.

The door opened and a group of men in suits came in, already laughing. Jane looked up from carbonating a bottle of some house-made mixer.

"Shit," she said, and all the combative energy drained from the set of her shoulders. The circles under her eyes seemed to darken.

"What?" asked Giovanni. "Them?"

The group of men settled at the opposite end of the bar, around one corner. Their ringleader was obvious: slightly better dressed, obviously going to pay. He was the focal point for all his toadies, who may as well have been panting, or giving him a hand job.

"Reg," said Jane, and looked down at her shoes. When she managed to lift her head again, she had pasted a smile across lips bright with smudge-proof lipstick. "What can I get you?" she asked, and made her way down the bar.

"You're smiling!" said the ringleader, eating Jane with his eyes. Reg, at a guess. "She *never* smiles, guys. Is it me? Gotta be me. I don't see anybody else in here worth smiling over. No offense." He clapped a jovial hand on one of his confederates' shoulders, and the other man smiled and laughed, at ease with the insult and grateful for the favor of the touch.

Jane tried and failed not to look back at Giovanni, less like a plea than an apology.

"That guy?" Reg snorted. "Babe, come on."

Giovanni almost stood from his barstool. I put a hand out to stop him because this seemed like a familiar scene, a problem Jane could deal with even if she didn't want to. Besides, he looked like a big tipper.

"What can I get you *to drink*?" she asked firmly, smile cemented in place.

He ordered a whisky—they all ordered whisky. Boring Speyside labels too, and overpriced. Reg's hungry eyes followed Jane from bar to bottle to glasses, and she knew it. Her expression was a flat mask worn in the face of humiliation.

When her back was turned, he flipped the lid of the caddy that held slices of lemon and lime, sticky globes of cherries. He picked one of these up by the stem and flipped the lid closed just before she turned to catch him. Too late to stop the crime, she only narrowed her eyes.

He smiled and put the cherry in his mouth, pulling it out slowly so it emerged, obscene, from between his lips. His toadies stilled, watching him in fascination.

With a smile like a workbench vise, Jane approached with a tray of glasses. One by one she set them down. She could have tried to avoid what was coming, sneaked by quickly, risked spilling Reg's drink and spoiling his plans and turning the whole scene into a painful amateur farce.

But she knew exactly how this was going to play out, and she leaned into it. She plunged into it, because like a barbed arrowhead buried deeply in muscle, the only way out was through.

When she leaned forward to place his glass on a coaster in front of him, Reg dropped the spit-slick cherry squarely between her breasts.

His toadies howled and slapped his back. Jane stared at him a moment, then turned away and came back down the bar. A stippling of pink marked the skin of her décolletage. Discreetly, she untucked the tail of her T-shirt from her apron. The cherry fell to the floor.

Reg threw back half his drink, grunted, and then said, "Gotta piss. Back in a sec."

As he passed my stool on his way to the restroom, a wave of recognition struck me. It hadn't been his face, his height or posture, even the sound of his voice. But his perfume: that I knew, and intimately.

You would have thought that kind of man would wear whatever *Forbes* prescribed. Look at him and you'd expect a sterile, bitter citrus. But this was floral, almost feminine, and certainly no mainstream brand. Beach roses, a hint of cloves. Sun-warmed earth and sand. Coppertone. Sweat and skin-scent. The opening notes had all gone, but I remembered them from mixing: seaweed, watermelon, ocean spray.

It was late autumn outside, but this boy smelled like Labor Day on a private Long Island beach.

"I know him," I said to myself, still loudly enough that both Giovanni and Jane heard me. What I meant was, I knew that perfume. And I knew what he remembered when he wore it.

"You know Reg?" asked Jane, hostility creeping back into her manner. "How?"

"He's a client," I said.

The hostility wavered. "No shit."

I nodded and finally sipped my drink. It tasted like tar and cough syrup—agreeably so. I sipped again, then looked up to see both Jane and Giovanni staring. "Or rather, his father is."

Jane blanched. "God, his dad is a nightmare."

Giovanni's eyebrows rose further. "How would *you* know?"

Misery came down across her face like a glacier shearing. She sighed deeply. "Reg was looking for someone to do his suits and I mentioned Beau." Here, she explained to me: "He's a tailor." Then, to Giovanni again: "I mean, he's an asshole, but Beau needed the work. *We* needed the money. God, though, I wish I never had. It's like he thinks a bespoke suit will take twenty pounds off. You can't convince him it's not the cut, and then it's Beau's fault for being bad at his job."

"And he referred his dad?" asked Giovanni, incredulous.

"Worse." Jane glanced over one shoulder to check the toadies' glasses, and then over the other to check for Reg. Her voice dipped low when she spoke again. "His dad found out, and now he's micromanaging everything. Like, Reg will come in, and then two days later his dad calls and demands to see the sketches or the fabric. And it's like, Beau already cut the fucking pieces, but this guy will veto it. And then Reg will cave and do what his dad wants, and then there's fucking wasted fabric and wasted money and Beau's pissed for days. They pull that shit on you too?"

This last to me. "They tried."

Now she looked impressed instead of pissed and gave me a limp salute. "You've got bigger balls than I do."

I accepted this without comment and took another sip of my drink. What I did was so intensely personal that a meddling father's wishes couldn't be taken into account. Besides, it was unseemly to squabble over your dead wife, your son's dead mother. Even if she had been estranged. Even if you had hired someone to trap her ghost in an atomizer for your son.

◆ ◆ ◆

"Sorry about Jane," said Giovanni once we'd left. "Things are kind of rough for her right now."

I shrugged. "They are for all of us, I think. Or at least for me and you. Maybe not for Reg. Which train are you taking?"

"The PATH, at Christopher Street. I gotta get to Jersey. What's up with you?"

It took me a moment to realize he was asking what difficulties I'd alluded to, not what train I needed. "Money, of course. An investor pulled out, no reason. Won't even take my calls. I spend all my time plugging numbers into Excel, and everything always comes up red, no matter what. I'm wasting hours. Days. I should be in the lab, not at the computer."

He shrugged. "That's business."

"It's bullshit." I tucked my scarf into my jacket, swept an angry hand through my freshly cut hair. "It's not why I got into this." .

"Why did you?"

"To make the art."

"So hire a business manager."

"With what cash? And anyway, that's not . . ."

"I know." He buttoned his jacket against a sudden bitter wind. Low clouds around the apex of One World Trade caught light pollution and turned the sky the color of a jellyfish, a bruise. The scent of cold, dry concrete hung brittle in the air.

We had come to West Fourth. I caught the railing at the top of the stairs, palm tacky against drippy green paint. "This is me."

"Thanks," he said. "For the drink."

"Anytime. Or, anytime I come to get my hair cut."

"Here." He took a card from his wallet and a pen from his pen pocket and wrote a second number below the printed one. "That's my cell."

"What for?" I asked, suddenly wary. First "friend," now this?

"When I lose my place and get a chair at Astor." Rue broke his smile, made it crooked. "Or just whenever. I owe you a beer."

"At those prices, you owe me two."

"Maybe if you come across the river." He lifted his hat. Because he was Giovanni, and he wore one. "Have a good night."

"Better than last night, anyway." Eisner's sneering smile appeared to me as vividly as if I'd sprayed a memory of the expression onto my skin. My sigh was more a growl; I was already mad at myself for what I was about to say. "It shouldn't be like this. It isn't fair."

Leaves susurrated on the pavement, curling past our feet. "I don't know what to tell you, Vic."

"Tell me you're angry, at least."

"Furious. But what am I supposed to do?"

What, indeed? I waved and descended past the piss-smelling turnstiles into the rusty, echoing underworld of the subway.

What *were* we supposed to do? What tools were at our disposal, arrayed against management companies and millionaires?

I chewed on this, all through the long ride uptown. Outside the window, arc lights caught the faces of MTA construction crews pressed into oubliettes to avoid the train as it passed. The car stank like shit and spilled Snapple.

When I got home, the radiators had come on, and I slept fitfully in a sweat. At three o'clock I woke to a racket of poltergeist bangs, air bubbles in the steam, and realized I had missed a vital connection.

My studio was small enough that the laptop lit it like a lamp. I filled the kettle to make a pot of tea—I had bags and bags of loose leaf, left over from a brief obsession with the scents of Assam and Lapsang and gunpowder green. We had done a release called Thé Parti not so long

24

ago. Barry named it. I hate naming things; the scent, I feel, should speak for itself, tell its own story. But I've found that's tough to market. These days, luckily, I needn't name anything. My clients don't often ask me to title their scents.

As the iodic steam of sencha curled toward the ceiling, I opened my browser and began to search. First I looked up Eisner and found the page for his asset-management company. Some deeply buried piece of information, previously discarded as irrelevant, had surfaced during my fitful sleep. My research now confirmed it: Conrad Yates and his son, Reginald, were partners at Eisner, Pearson, Yates & Yates.

I had dealt with Pearson too. Eisner had come to me first—found me through a boy who'd modeled for him. He was a dilettante photographer who appeared with sickening regularity in Chelsea shows, coddled by gallery owners who wanted to ensure his future patronage. You couldn't blame them, really. But I did.

Briefly I wondered if Jane knew him, or knew of him. New York could be an awfully small town, once you started tightening the social nooses of your special interests. And god forbid you shit where you eat. I avoided most of the other perfumers in the city now, except as necessity warranted.

This model of Eisner's had fucked another one of my special clients, heard a little bit of peculiar gossip in a moment of indiscretion, and passed it on as unbelievable but interesting. Eisner, analytical aesthete that he was, couldn't resist the lure. That was how I hooked about half of them. Not nubile models, necessarily, but something of the kind. The other half came through direct referrals. Eisner sent me Pearson, who in turn gave me the Yateses.

I had forgotten the referrals; I rarely think of my clients after their payments clear. Unless, like Eisner, they make themselves unforgettable. Unless, like his confederates, they resurfaced from the depths of my memory like bloated corpses rising after a storm.

I had crafted memories for all four of them, undertaking all the risk and difficulty that my process entailed so that they might be rid of a nuisance and possess a treasured moment in time. And now they were fucking me over.

Reg and Connie were making life hell for Jane and her fiancé. Eisner had me stretched out on the rack and had walked away to let me wail. But it was Pearson who controlled the real-estate division of the firm. And according to publicly available records, that division owned a certain mixed-use building on Christopher Street.

Pearson was ultimately in control of Giovanni's rent, and he was going to put my barber out of business.

It wasn't even hostility; hostility I would have understood. Enmity I could engage with. It had a pleasing symmetry, a give-and-take. If I knew that Eisner, Pearson, Yates & Yates had some vendetta against me, against Giovanni and Jane and Beau, that would have been logical, acceptable, worthy of some respect. But this was apathy, and apathy I could not stand. Especially not from people who ought to be impressed by arts of which they had no mastery. But they could barely be persuaded to pay what those arts were worth, let alone give artisans the autonomy and breathing room to work as we were wont.

Setting my cup of tea aside, I took my pink leather jewelry box out of the fridge and pulled the four applicable sample vials: small portions of properly mixed perfume retained for reference, each put aside before the final product went home with its owner.

Eisner's was bronze in color, while Pearson's was nearly black. Both Yates projects were pale gold with the same base, though Conrad's floral had a greenish tinge while Reg's was warmer, an almost orange gourmand.

Trial, error, and long years of experimentation had already taught me that smelling these would give me nothing out of the ordinary. The way my art worked, I could re-create a person's memory, but only they could experience it when they smelled the scent.

Still, one by one I uncapped them and drew a deep breath, recalling my interviews with each man, and the memories they had gone to the utmost extreme to preserve. I knew what moments these men most wanted to remember, and the lengths to which they would go to ensure they did. It seemed to me I should be able to use this knowledge to effect a change in their behavior.

As to how . . . there, alas, I was at a loss.

3

Notes de Tête: Chai Spice, Coffee
Notes de Cœur: Cork Grease, Key Oil, Scotch
Notes de Fond: Warm Wood, Paint Dust, Asafoetida, Petrichor

"Eisner again," said Barry when I walked in the door.

In the midst of sipping my coffee, I raised an eyebrow over my thermos.

"Voice mail's still there, if you want to listen. No details. Just his number. Time stamp was nine thirty last night. That's like old-man two a.m. Is he trying to booty-call you or what?"

"I don't think I'm exactly his type." I set my coffee aside and fell into the creaking office chair behind the desktop. Our headquarters consisted of the office proper: one resident computer, one actual desk (mine), and a landline phone. The break room functioned as an open-plan office for Barry and the two other employees, Binh and Leila. Soon it would just be Barry and Leila. And then, likely, only Barry and the coffee machine. I had seen Leila editing her résumé during her lunch hours.

Downstairs was the lab: a white concrete cube with a stainless steel utility sink, stainless Metro shelves, and a stainless island running nearly the length of the narrow room. I preferred its sterile glare to the cheap and mildewed squalor of our office.

But here I was, hauling the ugly cordless phone to my face to listen to Eisner's latest voice mail. What could he possibly want so badly? And what had changed?

"Hello, this is Joseph Eisner calling again. I'm hoping to reach Vic Fowler. I apologize for all this phone tag, but please, if you could return my call at the earliest possible convenience, it's a matter of some urgency."

Goddamn it. He was going to make me ask. I don't ask for things easily. I have tried to improve upon this character deficit, as I understand asking sometimes yields favorable results. Frankly, I have failed. I can force satisfactory results in myriad other ways.

Eisner repeated his number slowly enough that I had time to snatch a pen and write it down, though I didn't. I had him in my contacts. His cell phone too, not his office. By this time we were what you might call "associates."

"I'm running out for coffee," I said.

Barry looked pointedly at my carafe.

"Fancy coffee," I added. "From that place around the corner. What do you want?"

Judging by his expression, this offer only increased his skepticism. "You're paying?"

"What do you *want*, Barry?"

"Get me that white-girl thing. Large, extra shot. With soy milk."

I had on one occasion sampled the caramel pumpkin concoction to which he referred, and my pancreas convulsed in sympathy. "Disgusting. I'll be back in ten. Fifteen."

I had my phone to my face before I was out of the building. It rang, and rang, and by the time I came to the corner, I had gotten Eisner's voice mail.

"Mr. Eisner," I said. "Vic Fowler. Call me back."

I cursed the rest of the way to the coffee shop, spat Barry's order at the barista, and moodily shredded a croissant as the milk steamer shrieked. Even the rich potency of freshly ground beans couldn't soothe my apprehension.

I had just walked out when I felt my phone vibrate in my back pocket. Juggling pastry bag and pumpkin thing, I managed to answer before it went to voice mail.

"Mr. Eisner."

"Vic," he said. "I'm glad I caught you. Is it a bad time?"

I sat on a convenient bench in a bus shelter. "Of course not." Barry's latte would get cold. I didn't care. Eisner could buy him another one. Ten more. One for every day of the next three months. The next year. If he'd just cut me a fucking check.

"I was wondering if you're free tomorrow evening."

This gave me pause. I leaned into the plastic wall of the bus shelter and watched a man bend down to scoop his chihuahua's shit off the sidewalk. "Why?"

"I'd like to speak with you about a potential commission. And I have an extra ticket to *Scheherazade*."

I was torn. An Eisner commission would bring in some cash. I'd have to launder it a little if I wanted to funnel it into Bright House, but even if I didn't go that far, at least I could cut my own salary and still pay rent in hundred-dollar bills. Iolanda wouldn't mind, and wouldn't ask any questions.

Eisner was unreliable, and I didn't want to reward his fickleness, his treachery. But I enjoyed the music of the Mighty Handful, Rimsky-Korsakov most of all. And I had never heard *Scheherazade* in the flesh.

"Fine," I said. "What time?"

Eisner texted to say he was running late, trapped in the office, wouldn't make the first half. So I listened to a series of increasingly elaborate and ethereal Berlioz art songs on my own, wondering what he wanted. I looked forward to intermission with equal parts dread and intrigue.

About halfway through the interval, I spotted Eisner in the lobby: a miracle in the milling crowd of Q-tips and successful young professionals, salted with student rush and last-minute bargains. Gold Bond, bad breath, Bath & Body Works.

What did they think when they saw us, I wondered. My best guess was father and child. I kept a careful distance from his side as we ascended toward the mezzanine. I didn't want to be this evening's grave-robbing arm candy, even in the minds of strangers.

"It was a surprise to see you at the Dvořák earlier this week," he said. He motioned me through the double doors ahead of him. "I suppose you didn't seem like the kind of young person who enjoys these things."

I wanted to say, *You have no idea what kind of young person enjoys these things. Every young person you've ever invited has been trying to impress you, or at least get you to pay for dinner.* I wanted to say, *You don't know me at all.*

But I wanted him to pay for dinner too. Or at least a drink. I wanted him to pay for my life's work.

Our seats were very good: nestled in the belly of the center orchestra, with just enough elevation to look slightly down on the stage. The musicians rustled and shifted, ran through scales. I smelled cork grease and key oil.

We didn't have to wait long until the conductor appeared in a rain of applause, stepped up, and cued the oboe for a long, clear tuning note.

The oboe doesn't tune to the orchestra, one of my paramours had told me. *The orchestra tunes to the oboe.*

She abided in my leather box now, alongside Jonathan. She had not been a particularly interesting person. Beautiful, yes, and very talented. But it was no sacrifice for me to lose her presence in order to preserve her music in a bottle. Many of my independent pursuits arose when I became involved with people who had a single attribute that captivated, or with whom I had shared one moment of the sublime and several others of the deeply unpleasant. She was one of these: better recalled only in flashes, for the talents she possessed. No lost potential there. Not to say there hadn't been, with others.

If I wanted, when I got home, I could listen to her play Mozart, the two of us alone in the submarine gloom of her ground-floor apartment in South Slope, all the windows facing the courtyard. The boiler just beneath the floor filled the rooms with a low hum like the engine of a ship.

Mildew, lavender, hot metal, spit. And her own smell, unique, inimitable. I could almost conjure them now, but I knew my remembrance, unaided by the true accord, was fallible. Memory is treacherous territory. My scents are maps, guides, pathways, landmarks that will bring you safely to your intended destination.

Silence fell in the concert hall. Several hundred breaths drew in. The baton came down, and the brass exploded.

How can I describe this symphony to someone who has never heard it? I cannot hope to do it justice if you are unfamiliar with the piece, and even then, to hear it performed live by the Philharmonic is another matter.

The music *painted*. It *danced*. It inhaled and exhaled and wove a narrative just beyond language, just behind the veil of comprehension. It moved so lightly from bombast to lullaby that I felt dizzy. And in the end, when all that was left was a single violin singing over the final chords, I felt my soul strain at the bounds of my body as though it would break through my ribs and follow that sound wherever notes went when they died.

Applause did not explode immediately—the audience was stunned. But once it had begun, it would not end. It was like another movement, its dynamics rising and falling as if this paean too had been penned by Rimsky-Korsakov.

"What would it take," asked Eisner in the aftermath, eyes half-shut, "to preserve that sound forever? Just that single note, that moment in the dark."

"Not forever," I said. "Only as long as the perfume lasts, as long as it remains unspoiled, and doesn't oxidize."

He sighed, waved a hand. "You know what I mean. Could you bottle it for me? The last notes of tonight's *Scheherazade*. What would it take?"

I looked around David Geffen Hall, the crowd already streaming out. Bright lights, warm wood, the strange geometric shapes of dampeners. I closed my eyes and took a deep breath, conjuring not the image but its outlines in the air, the way the currents of scent eddied around them.

Warm wood, still: baked by stage lights. Hot dust. Rain carried in on the clothes and shoes of the audience, present in the draft from out of doors. Menthol from a hundred unwrapped cough drops. Old cigarette smoke. New cigarette smoke. The mingled traces of a thousand different colognes, perfumes, shampoos. The smell of the audience. The smell of the orchestra.

"You're not asking about the elements," I said. "Not the absolutes, or the accord. You want to know how many people have to die."

He said nothing, only arranged his purple lips into a thin and crooked smile, eyes fixed on something far away.

"Is that the commission?" I asked. Was that why he had brought me here? "I've never even tried something like that. It just isn't feasible."

"A pity," he said, and even I felt cold. "But no. I have something more practical in mind. Still a challenge, I think, but one more suited to your talents. Join me for a drink, and I'll explain."

◆ ◆ ◆

We went to a whisky bar on the Upper West Side. It unnerved me that he knew what I preferred to drink. Even more so when he said, "And it's close to your trains, I believe."

I doubted Eisner ever took the subway, and the fact he knew enough about my public transit habits to deposit me within easy walking distance of three convenient train lines made me leery.

I tried to ignore the feeling, until I had a heavy tumbler of Caol Ila in hand. (I didn't want to tax his generosity too grossly, not at this juncture.) Once the notes of pepper and lemon rind had seared my sinuses clean and the booze was settling warmly in my stomach, I finally asked, "What is all this?"

Eisner traced the edge of his coaster with one finger. Made no eye contact, except with the meniscus of his Scotch. "It's a commission, as I said."

"But nothing to do with *Scheherazade*. So why the symphony?"

He drank, smiling into his glass. But the smile was grim. When he put the whisky down, he smoothed his hands along the creases in his trousers and said, "Consider that an apology, of sorts. For . . . what is it called? For ghosting you?"

"About your investment."

He nodded.

"I just need a yes or no, Mr. Eisner. That way I can make my plans."

"Unfortunately," he said, "it's a little more complicated than that."

Christ. He was going to be coy. "Don't tell me you're hurting for money." Unease put me on the offensive. "That's a line you'll have a hard time selling."

"No," he said. "Not that."

A worse thought occurred to me. "Is someone onto you? About . . . our work together?"

"No, thank god." Then, sharply: "Why? Have you . . ."

I sipped my Scotch first, just to make him sweat. "Not yet."

Eisner looked relieved. I was unused to seeing anything on his face besides self-satisfaction. My sense of alarm increased.

"So you took me out as an apology," I said. "You can't tell me yes or no, but you still want to hire me for another commission. And you think I'll agree?"

"When you hear my terms," he said.

All my sphincters twisted tight. This sounded very like an entrée to extortion.

"Your perfumes," he said. "They let people relive memories. Their *own* memories. But what about memories of moments they never lived? Can you do that?"

"Fantasy?" I asked. "Imagination? People can certainly extrapolate from scent, but that's not under my control."

He shook his head. "No. Real moments. But ones in which we weren't present. For instance, things that happened behind closed doors."

I shook my head in turn. This wasn't whatever ax I had expected to fall, which meant that one was likely still suspended. "It wouldn't work. As I understand what I do"—I barely did—"it's based on the way our brains retrieve memory, and our associations of particular scents with a moment in the past. If your brain hasn't already built those pathways . . . I can't *trail blaze*, as it were."

"Have you ever tried?"

He had me there. I covered by drinking. The smell made me think of Jonathan, the bottles on his bar cart. The man who had first served me single malt. How many of the scents I had concocted from his absolute relied on some kind of whisky note? How many times had I sat across from him with the smells of smoke and malted barley in the air between us, before that last night, that last drink?

What might he have done in my absence that I would want to know? If Eisner's impossible dream could be made to work, what knowledge could a new memory of Jonathan pass on about this business?

But that wasn't how this worked. I couldn't make something out of nothing. Could I?

"If you can do what I ask," said Eisner, "I'll cut a check. Not just for the perfume, but for the sum I offered to help bump production. You'll get your European distribution in time for the latter part of the holiday season. You'll be in the black. You'll be safe, or nearly."

That invocation of safety didn't sit well with me. "And if I refuse?"

"How shocking, when they tell me my dead father was made into perfume, sold to me by a twisted sadist, a serial murderer."

The Scotch had dried the fat from my tongue, and now it sat rough and awkward in my mouth. "You wouldn't."

"I would."

Only very occasionally had clients threatened me thus—most were dissuaded by the idea of mutually assured destruction, and by the simple fact that what they had hired me to do could just as easily be done to them. Still, it had happened once or twice, though the stakes had been much lower then. I could not take it on the chin if I dealt with Eisner in the usual gruesome way: he held the future of my business in his hands, rather than a few months' rent.

"You're only safe because you're very good at avoiding scrutiny," he said. "Once somebody figures out what rocks they should be turning over . . ."

"Then they'll find you down there squirming right beside me."

"It will come down to hearsay in a court, and I have much better lawyers."

"And who points to the rocks, Eisner? You won't want to be within a thousand miles of all this."

"I learned the importance of middlemen long ago. You'd be well served, in the future, to use a few yourself. The more footprints in the mud, the harder to find the trail you'd like to follow."

"Too many cooks," I said, "tend to ruin the soup." The truth was, I couldn't afford it. He could pay whoever he liked to do whatever he wanted. I couldn't afford a fifteen percent cut, even to cover my ass. I made do with a keen sense of judgment and the occasional threat, which I *occasionally* made good on. This time, it had not been enough.

"What if I try, and fail?" Because I would try—I had to, now.

He shrugged. "I'm sorry. I only have one contingency plan."

I licked my teeth, cleared my throat, and asked him: "What's the job?"

I wrote the email on the train home, confirming Bright House could make the minimum numbers Clairfield & Amos had set for wholesaling. At 125th we stopped for a sick passenger and I had the time and the service to send it, so I did. In London they'd wake up to the terms.

I had asked Eisner for half the money up front. We agreed on twenty-five percent. Enough to start ordering materials and paying import taxes, et cetera. So even if it did all go to shit, at least I'd have inventory for the holidays.

I would put his money to work as soon as it hit the account. Now that I had committed to production, I was inextricably bound to order a suite of expensive raw materials, not to mention some wallops when it came to customs fees and shipping.

Meanwhile, I had never tried to scale the business model for my sideline. I had equipment and capacity to make one peculiar perfume at a time, and the complex preparations ate up hours and days and money and materials I might have used to bolster Bright House. Of course, if I could make Eisner's perfume happen, that would be the biggest bolstering of all.

This was not how I usually worked. I took on one task, one small order at a time. There was one bathtub in my basement. I only owned one tabletop still.

If I was going to attempt what Eisner had asked of me—and I was—I would need to make some changes. Expensive ones.

Two more tubs—I could get them cheapish, probably, from Demolition Depot in East Harlem. But then there was the expense of movers, and getting the tubs downstairs some day when Iolanda was out. Whenever I had a commission, I skimmed a barrel or two of perfumer's alcohol from the lab. I'd need a few more for a project of this size. The stuff was regulated, but the DEA wouldn't look askance at a slight increase in our orders, especially since our production would rise around the same time. The feds didn't give a shit about niche perfume.

I would splurge for new stills. Good ones, handblown crystal that weighed about as much as a soap bubble filled with breath. It was Eisner's money. And I deserved a treat right now, in case everything went to shit later.

Then there were the logistics of sourcing the ingredients. For this particular type of perfume, it took extremely careful planning and execution. It's dangerous to take on too many commissions in a short span of time. It draws less attention to space them out. Something like this, with three people so closely linked to each other and to the client? I might have managed it if I put a year or two between them. Even that seemed like asking for trouble.

Say everything went smoothly, and I got my hands on all the equipment and ingredients I required. I still had no idea how I'd meet Eisner's demand. What he had outlined was impossible.

The controlling shareholders of Eisner, Pearson, Yates & Yates had never trusted him, he said. He was better at the job. But they were Cape Cod, pink shorts, and the Knick, and no matter how much money he made, he would always be a Jewish boy from Brownsville. It didn't help, he said, that he was gay. They seemed to think it might be catching.

For his part, he thought they were bad businessmen: born into their fortunes, and so unfamiliar with growing and maintaining one. And though the whole enterprise was built on the crooked apparatus of late-stage capitalism, Eisner asserted that his colleagues were crooks by the letter of the law as well as the spirit, and liable to get the whole company into hot water if they weren't careful. Which, he said, they wouldn't be. He spoke of their scheming in veiled terms, and of his own resistance much more clearly. He was the last roadblock standing in their way.

And so they were going to push him out. They had held a closed-door meeting while he was away on a business trip. He believed that in this meeting they had made decisions behind his back, plans about the future of the company that they would never share. He wanted to know how much damage control there was to do, how much of what he had tried to prevent had already been pushed through. He had a plan to put them out of the way and simultaneously reveal their secrets. And that plan was me.

Surely a good lawyer could solve these problems better than I. And less illegally. But when I asked, Eisner shot it down. It wasn't just about solving this problem. It was about making sure he had no more problems in the future. And maybe it was also about petty vengeance for years of slights. I could empathize. Grudgingly.

"I made a mistake," he said. "I thought I had arrived. I thought I had *won*. But if you're not standing alone at the top, it turns out you're still in the fight."

Perhaps it's hypocritical that I found this all a bit extreme. But then again, the blackmail he had leveled was no piddling matter either. He was going to force me to extremity alongside him. And I had no idea how to follow. Still, I sent the email. Because I would either get his money or go to jail, and if the former, I wanted to be ready for the windfall. I preferred to avoid the latter, if possible.

4

Notes de Tête: Damp Concrete, Rosemary Shrub
Notes de Cœur: Mint and Coconut
Notes de Fond: Cumin, Musk

I slept badly and came back to consciousness crusty-eyed and peevish. I am not and never have been a graceful morning person. After staggering around and shoving my corpus into clothes, I had just finished pouring viscous coffee into a travel carafe when I heard the buzzer go upstairs and Iolanda's footsteps as she shuffled to answer it.

Out the small, barred window between my refrigerator and my bookshelf I saw a shadow across the pavement. A conversation ensued on the doorstep, which immediately caught my attention and raised some concern. I couldn't hear the words, but if Iolanda was keeping them out, I probably didn't want them to come in either.

It went on, and on, and on. My coffee steamed at my elbow. I tucked myself against the refrigerator and tried to listen in, wondering if it was the city or just a concerned neighbor.

Perhaps I should mention at this point that my studio was fantastically illegal. Iolanda's brownstone, on a street of similar houses in the upper reaches of Harlem, did not actually belong to her. She was a sort of unofficial super, though if anything broke, all she could do was take the cost of the repair off your rent that month—she was old, and not exactly handy with a wrench. I had never been apprised of the house's true ownership, nor had I asked. Iolanda sublet the second and third floors off the books, as well as my subterranean studio. The basement was utterly unfinished except for the single room where I lived. It was neatly whitewashed, and I'd made it habitable, but the damp meant a constant threat of mold, and there was no fire exit. I had never signed a lease.

Still, it was cheap as any place comes in New York, and Iolanda's bad hip meant she never used the basement. Which meant I could, and did. She had gotten the occasional scare from the city, but so far none of the warnings had stuck. That didn't mean this one wouldn't. If it wasn't something worse.

Iolanda's voice rose, and the walls shook when she slammed the door. I dared to move an inch from the refrigerator but darted back when the shadow crossed my window. Footsteps went with it, fading into the distance.

I was fully awake now, and clearheaded enough to realize I could do a little tinkering on my new commission in the lab. I selected a few absolutes from my stash and nestled them carefully in the bottom of my folio, then capped my coffee carafe and went on my merry way, believing Iolanda had sent the interested party packing.

The sense of escape lasted only as long as the journey from studio to street. A white-haired, bearded man in a blue windbreaker was leaning against a streetlamp halfway down the block, and when I passed him he peeled off and started to walk beside me.

I did not run. But only because running implies guilt. I wanted to, and dearly.

"Vic Fowler?" he asked.

I didn't answer.

"You're Vic Fowler." This time it wasn't a question. I subtly increased my pace. "I'm Pippin Miles, private investigator. I want to ask you some questions about Caroline Yates."

I made myself look at him. I told myself it was easy. "I'm sorry?"

"Mrs. Caroline Yates. She's been missing for several months." Now that we were face-to-face, his breath smelled faintly like a dirty crisper drawer. "I've got a couple sources that say you might know something about it. Might have met with her husband once or twice."

"I may have." I conjured the same tone I used when patiently evading questions about my finances. "I see a lot of prospective clients in a given week." Then, a little laugh. "Well, I used to see more. Business isn't exactly booming right now. But she didn't commission anything. I'd remember that."

"You make perfumes, right?"

I nodded, checked my phone for the time, for the next train. Anything but taking flight. Anything but screaming. How had this happened? How had this man found me? I was careful. I had never had a problem like this before.

But there is, as they say, a first time for everything.

"So, did you? Talk to the husband. Conrad. Conrad Yates."

"Maybe," I said. There wasn't anything on the books to prove it. "But you know: perfume is more a girl thing." I threw in a demure and flirty shrug for good measure, looking up from beneath my lashes. He wasn't much taller than me.

He nodded thoughtfully, unmoved. "Mind if I refresh your memory? You had a meeting with him, in early April. Does that sound right?"

"I'd have to check my calendar."

Silence. He was waiting.

I *had* met with Conrad in April. And with Reg. Separately, you understand. The meeting with Reg had been an interview about his mother, aimed at crafting a perfume that recalled that perfect beach picnic, the last time Reg remembered his parents happy together. He had cried. It was very touching, once we got past the notion this perfume should be what he called "beast mode." He was pleased with it, when it was finished.

43

Conrad, on the other hand, knew full well what was in that bottle. And that final meeting with him had been a quick one. We had already gone over the memory he'd like to keep; I had a profile built and was ready to start blending as soon as I had my final element in place. This was purely logistical—where she lived now, whether there were neighbors nearby, or home surveillance. He said that he would call her about some small legal matter, or a detail of his estate, or whatever trifle he needed as a pretense to confirm that she was home. I would take a Zipcar up to Mamaroneck as soon as he called me, and come back the same night.

"Yes . . ." I said, drawing it out as though I had only just remembered. "Yes, I did have a meeting with him." Then a gamble, because I knew who had talked to this man. Whether Reg had hired him or not, he had certainly spilled a can or two of beans. "And another meeting with his . . . son? I could check if you want." I started to unlock my phone again, trying to look helpful. "I'm sorry, the name didn't jog any memories earlier."

"No problem. I didn't mean to play with you." A lie? "I just wanted to see if you remembered them on your own. If there was anything about either of them—Conrad, in particular—that stuck with you. But no dice I guess. You're sure he wasn't acting . . . *odd* at all?"

"April was a long time ago," I said, injecting as much skepticism into it as I could muster.

"I know," he said. "Again, I'm sorry. But anything at all could really help me out."

"I apologize, Mr. Miles. As I said, I meet with a lot of clients. And some of them are very odd indeed." Not an ounce of falsehood there. "I'm afraid Conrad Yates doesn't particularly stand out."

"Well," he said. "If you do remember anything, let me know." He gave me a card.

"Of course." We shook. Leather gloves with a cashmere lining kept my sweaty palms a secret. Paul Smith, sample sale. Marked down from too much to barely affordable. A treat for myself when I had a little extra in the bank. Caroline had paid for them.

On the platform, I nearly tore up the detective's card. But I worried putting him out of sight and mind would give him room to grow, to fester and become a larger problem. Instead, I slipped his card into the back of my wallet and caught the crowded downtown D.

"Vic, what the *fuck*?" Barry brandished his phone at me as soon as I walked in. His eyes looked like they might pop out if his blood pressure rose another notch.

I had spent most of my commute feeling about the same. But I couldn't afford to feel it now, not at the office. Not now that it was time to get to work.

Barry tailed me down the stairs, into the lab, watched me take out each of my little vials of absolute. "I had an email this morning from the distributors, and they think we're doing this thing. Clairfield & Amos. We told them yes?"

"We did." I took a fistful of pipettes from a box on a Metro shelf and filled a beaker with perfumer's alcohol. It looked innocuous, like water. The fumes gave it away.

"What do you mean? We can't afford it." And as I set out vial after vial on the shining stainless table: "What are all these?"

I uncapped one vial and left his second question unanswered. "We can. Afford it."

"You locked down Eisner?" His mouth dropped open.

"Yes," I lied. No, it *wasn't* a lie. It wouldn't be.

I began to add absolute to alcohol, keeping one eye on the scale. Diluted, the odors opened up. The room began to reek. "Turn on the exhaust," I said.

He flipped the switch and the fans started running, a dull roar that would drive me slowly to distraction over the course of the morning.

Shaking his head like he wanted to clear his ears, he asked, "How?"

"Personal charm." When Barry raised an eyebrow, and then kept raising it, I relented. "He asked me to fulfill a difficult commission."

"So that's what all this is?" He dropped onto the opposite stool to peer at my supplies. Without asking, he unscrewed the cap from another absolute and waved a hand to waft its aroma toward his face. "Where'd this stuff come from? Smells . . . animalic." He wrinkled his nose, and I saw his eyes slide from the bottles and beaker to my face, though I pretended not to notice. "This is for Eisner's thing?"

"Yes."

"So I guess the rest of us had better get to work on the stuff for Clairfield & Amos?"

I slid my notebook across the table.

Barry picked it up. "Orders?"

"Put them in."

He was silent a moment, scanning the list. Tallying the breathtaking total, I imagined. "Are you sure Eisner's—"

"Put the orders in, Barry. Now."

After he'd gone I looked at the beaker before me, the single thread of swirling copper within. I wanted to see if I *could* do what Eisner asked, somehow, though I was running mostly on intuition. If I could do it straight off the bat, it would save me a lot of time and worry. With Pip Miles sniffing around my ankles I had a paucity of the first and a surplus of the second. Besides, an accomplishment would make me feel clever.

I had done an impossible thing once, operating only on my intuition. And then I had done it again, and again. What Eisner had asked me to do was outside my wheelhouse . . . and yet it wasn't. Not really. I conjured moments that no longer existed, out of the people who had inhabited them. The issue was that whatever I did, however I did it, the memory that lived in the client's mind was an integral ingredient in the perfume. The difficulty, in Eisner's case, was that the ingredient didn't exist.

There were synthetics on the market these days that credibly, beautifully took the place of highly regulated or impossible-to-find elements. That conjured the same scent, and the same scent memories, as the real thing. Or near enough as might make no difference to an untrained nose. Surely there was something comparable, some feat of reverse engineering that could create a facsimile of the absent thing.

Except substitute ingredients I could sniff, compare and contrast. When it came to this kind of substitution, I had no notion of where to begin. I could source synthetics. I could not source moments in time.

The puzzle of the perfume's formula was a piece of fat to chew on. And this I could devote my own research to, whereas the accelerated logistics of acquiring materials would require resources I didn't have. I longed briefly, absurdly, for an intern. But even for a desperate college grad grasping any chance at advancement, this kind of thing was slightly beyond the pale.

"Vic!" Barry's voice echoed down the stairwell. "Do you want this orange blossom from Scott or PCC?"

Irritated, I lifted my head from my work and shouted back. "I don't give a damn. They source it from the same provider." He ought to have known the answer. Some people needed so much direction. Still, it was easier to have Barry make those calls. It gave me time to . . .

A drop of absolute trembled on the tip of my pipette.

I had been waiting for inspiration. Well, here it came. It helped me with the nuances of perfumery not at all, but formulas were a tenth of a percent of what went into running a successful house.

I couldn't handle the grunt work on my own this time. I didn't want it all leading straight back to me, if anyone started looking. And somebody already had.

Delegating gave me space and time. It freed me up to write formulas and draft test batches—to tackle the elusive elements of my craft.

It protected me from drudgery and frustration and dealing with other humans. If something went wrong with this order of orange blossom, it was Barry who would be on the phone with customer service, not me. In this case, delegating the sourcing and the legwork would give me extra hours and energy to devote to the technicalities of this unprecedented project.

The idea of an intern I had dismissed as impossible, absurd. I could talk people into all kinds of things—lower prices, petty crime, compromising sex—but this was on another level. This required commitment, and backbone, of considerable strength. Did I know anyone possessed of those qualities, yet still susceptible to my favored manners of manipulation? Who just needed a little push before they plunged over the edge from anger into action?

And suddenly, I thought: I might.

I let the droplet fall and watched the essence wend its way down through the beaker of alcohol, twisting around itself like a serpent. Like a noose.

◆ ◆ ◆

I dropped by Jane's cocktail bar once I had cleaned up in the lab. Threads of blood spread across my knuckles, where my spirit-scoured skin was split along the grain. The small pains itched fiercely. You know the feeling—an unrelenting minute agony that wears at you like a tight shoe on a blister.

My experiments had not been successful, and if I had been a blister, I would have been ready to burst.

Early in the morning, I had successfully re-created the memory of meeting my oboist for the first time, at an afterparty following a guerrilla performance inside an abandoned nightclub in Long Island City. I tried to stretch beyond that, to the moment before she walked in the door, to her rehearsals for the concert, to the story she had told me about getting stuck on the G train on her way to the concert. I knew the smell of the subway. The oboist, I had in a bottle. But I created strange-smelling concoctions that got me nowhere. My hypothesis had so far not borne out.

I desperately wanted a drink, and stimulating conversation. And I wanted to meet Beau.

Perhaps this nascent plan would be more successful than my experiments had been so far. To gauge the likelihood of that success, I needed to assess all the potential participants' attitudes toward Eisner's unfortunate colleagues. Giovanni seemed resigned, but I could work on that. Jane's fury and despair might meet my standards, but I didn't entirely trust her assessment of her fiancé.

That was unfair of me, but I didn't know her as well then as I would come to in the months that followed. She knew Beau better than he knew himself.

But that comes later. Now, the bar. Faint disinfectant. Spilled liquor and the ghost of evanesced dry ice.

I was lucky—she was working happy hour again. Reg was nowhere in sight. The place was slow so early, and I had my pick of stools.

"Hi there!" she said: chirpy midwestern charm with which my unhappy childhood lent me a passing familiarity. I wondered where she was from, and if she had grown up as miserable as me. Then a flicker of recognition crossed her face. "Oh. We met, right?"

"Vic Fowler," I said, and offered my hand again. "Jane . . . ?"

She seemed impressed I had remembered, but parted with her surname reluctantly. "Betjeman."

We shook. Not limes, this time, but vinegar, or some kind of shrub. Still sweet and sticky, with an herbal undertone. When she let my hand go I lifted it to my lips, close enough to smell when I inhaled.

She raised an eyebrow and I feigned a blush. "Sorry. I smell things. Bad habit."

"Right," she said. "Perfume."

"Do you wear it?" I asked, knowing that she didn't. I could smell Dr. Bronner's (peppermint) and some kind of coconut-based lotion. But she hadn't put anything else on.

"Not usually," she said. "Maybe for a wedding, or a date."

"Ah," I said, and nodded, wondering who she dated if she was affianced.

She put the nozzle of a gas tube against the neck of a bottle and discharged carbonation into a mixer. I thought for a moment she would stop speaking to me, but once she had capped the bottle and wiped her hands, she admitted, "Beau does, though."

"Your fiancé."

She nodded, looking tired. "Yeah. Sometimes it's the only way I know he's come to bed at all. When I wake up and smell him." Her eyes closed, and I watched her swallow, hard. Her next inhalation juddered like a car failing to fall into gear, but when she spoke at last her voice was steady. "Sorry. I'm supposed to listen to *your* problems. That's the job description."

"No," I said, and firmly. "The job description only says you're supposed to make me drinks."

Her laugh was a hoarse bark, as though someone had surprised her with a kick in the stomach. "Sure. You had . . ."

"Something you invented. And I'll gladly have the same again."

"I don't remember." She didn't try to pad it with apology, which reassured me. I wasn't a customer anymore.

I shrugged, unperturbed. "Then fernet is fine."

"Fuck that. Try this instead." She poured two shots of some amaro I had never heard of. "Sorry. It's just been a rough week."

"Relatable." We clinked our glasses. "Reg again?"

"Sure Reg. And everybody else. Drunk assholes with too much money. Bad first dates. Angry baby boomers."

"And school?"

She rolled her eyes. "Why do you think I don't see Beau? I'm working late and he's already in bed, or I have the night off but I need to study, and he goes straight from work to a show or a party. Client hunting. I'm too tired to get off my ass and out of my sweats, anyway." She wiped her forearm across her face, keeping her hands clean for her work. "I have so many beautiful clothes, and I never wear them anymore."

"Speaking of," I said. "I meant to get Beau's information from you. I'm thinking of commissioning a suit."

"Don't you dare take him up on the friends and family rate," she said. "He'll offer, but I'll kill you."

I couldn't afford not to. Then again, I wasn't so sure I'd really be commissioning a suit. If that was what it took to keep us in touch . . .

Then I remembered Eisner's money. "I would never. I know what that kind of work is worth."

Jane's sharp edges softened a little. "Unlike most people."

"Where can I find him?"

She searched in her apron and found a pen but no paper. I held out the palm of my hand. When she took it, hers was bigger than mine. Fingers long and square-tipped, nails clipped brutally short. I felt the folds of her palm against my roughened knuckles.

"God," she said. "Your poor hands."

The cracks had reopened and smeared a little blood onto her skin.

"Sorry," I said. "Hazard of the trade. A lot of washing."

"Same," she said. "I miss manicures. I used to get stilettos."

Her handwriting was spiky, the ballpoint pushing deep into my skin. She bit her lip as she wrote and it went pale around the imprint of her tooth, a promise of later swelling. I didn't bother to quash the twinge of interest at the seam of my pants. Such things could prove useful, one way or another. And she was very pretty.

When she'd finished scratching down Beau's number and email, I asked for my check. She glared at me—affectionately, I think—and told me to get out.

5

Notes de Tête: Geranium, Rain Clouds, Cedar
Notes de Cœur: Fresh Mulch, Cardamom, Concrete
Notes de Fond: Bourbon, Sweat, and Myrrh

Beau and I set up a meeting in his atelier, a cramped and overheated studio space several stories above Union Square. The elevator was broken, so I walked six flights, arrived in a sweat, and took a moment to catch my breath before I knocked. Outside it had smelled of almost-rain. In here, the corridor had the dusty, mildewed air of floodwater long gone. A leaky radiator, or the roof. Ghosts of halal cart lunches lingered in the corners. The steam pipes ticked, ticked, ticked, and banged.

Through the door of the atelier, I could hear the syncopated strings of a western swing band. When it opened, the live recording coincidentally collapsed into applause.

Beau Singh, bespoke tailor, was a solid man, rather tall, with an impressive beard. He half wore a three-piece suit of outrageous Harris Tweed; the jacket lay abandoned on the worktable behind him. Perspiration had made rings under his armpits. His sleeves were rolled to the elbows, showing wrists hung heavy with jewelry. Jangling strands of tarnished coins. Preppy leather straps fastened with stylized anchors. A dangling golden fish with jeweled green eyes, articulated at each joint. The plain steel kara of a Sikh. Not practicing, though; the bracelet was an heirloom, dull with age, and he wore no turban. His hair—longish, curled, and streaked with gray—fell across his forehead and almost obscured the black eye patch tucked below his right brow bone.

"Vic Fowler?" he asked, and offered up his hand. The fish swung through the air, flopping frantically, a little too lifelike. His rings were hot against my palm. This close I could smell his sweat, and his perfume of cedar and geranium, cardamom and myrrh.

"Beau," I said. "A pleasure to meet you."

"Come on in." He ceded some space and I entered the atelier. A corkboard on the far wall, behind his worktable, mixed fabric swatches with stills from *A Clockwork Orange* and *Jodorowsky's Dune*. In the far corner, a turntable rested on top of a low midcentury bar cart, which held both records and bottles. The window over Union Square was open for a cold draft. Rather than mitigating the heat, this meant the room contained two temperature extremes: hot at the worktable, freezing by the squat love seat upholstered in turquoise velvet. Its arms were stuck through with a multitude of pins, giving the impression of rainbow eye stalks, as if the sofa were an inquisitive sea creature watching Beau at work. A dressmaker's dummy stood by the sofa, supporting a pumpkin-colored overcoat in a herringbone mohair blend. Chalk and basting marked the fabric for alterations.

Beau shut the door behind me, then went to the bar and knelt to take stock of his liquor.

"A little too cold for Campari," he said. His accent was flatter than Jane's: faintly Iowa, or Illinois, at odds with his eccentric attire. "Bourbon? Rye?"

I opened my palms in surrender.

"Have a seat," he said, and poured.

The love seat had gone soft through the ties and sagged when I settled my weight onto it. Beau brought over two lowballs balanced on a notebook and sat in the red-painted patio chair just across the coffee table. When he crossed his legs, lifting one ankle to the opposite knee, I saw he wore white snakeskin boots.

"So," he said. "You're a friend of Jane's?"

"Not yet," I said, and smiled. "But I can dream, can't I?"

I had been developing some suspicions about their relationship based on Jane's mention of dates, on the slightly flirtatious tone of Beau's email replies. I have always had an excellent nose for other people's offbeat sexual predilections. Among other things.

He smiled back: the self-satisfied smile of a man who knows that what he's got is good. There was no jealousy in it that I could see. The corner of his eye showed crow's-feet. "You'd be lucky."

"Does she often send you clients?"

He flipped his notebook open. "On occasion. And usually the people she sends have interesting taste."

Was that innuendo? "Really? Not boring business types?"

His cocked eyebrow was incredulous, and I thought of Jane giving me the same look. A strange sort of pang pinched behind my ribs as I realized they had been together long enough to pick up each other's mannerisms.

Incongruously, it made me think of Jonathan Bright. Someone had asked us once, at a trade show, if we were twins. Fraternal, of course, but close enough in looks and manner that they made the blunder. We laughed at the mistake, not kindly. If nothing else, it added a novel element to our activities that evening.

It was true that we spent so much time together that we began to grow indistinguishable in some ways. We had never been in love, I think, but close proximity and shared ambition could certainly be mistaken for it. And now he was dead and I was all that was left of him, beyond what I kept in vials and atomizers and my own faulty memory.

"Jane told me about Reg," I said.

That snuffed the smile. He turned his whiskey glass ninety degrees, considered it, and said, "I thought you weren't friends."

Was *that* the jealousy? Or was he just confused? "Recent acquaintances. But Reg came in while I was at the bar, and he's an old client of mine as well."

It caught him sipping bourbon, which he swallowed too fast to keep from choking. It made his voice go raspy. "No shit?"

"No shit."

"Perfume," he asked, "right? Jane doesn't usually let me go into this kind of stuff blind."

I wondered what else she had told him. And what she hadn't. "She warned me not to take you up on the friends and family discount."

"She warned me not to offer it."

I didn't know what to say to this; I could feel some kind of tension strung between us, drawing tighter with every moment I remained silent. He was testing me, I thought: Was I worthy of her? Would *we* get along? Something along those lines. I could feel the unsteadiness of his appraisal like the wobble of a settling scale.

And then, miraculously, Beau laughed. "That woman," he said, no venom in it, smiling and shaking his head.

It seemed the needle had come to rest at an agreeable number. "Yes," I said. "She's certainly something."

◆ ◆ ◆

The rain that had been threatening outside began to fall, and Beau got up to close the window. The sounds of Union Square grew suddenly distant. "So Reg," he started, then shook his head again. "Perfume? Really?"

"He insists on calling it cologne." Technically incorrect, as true eau de cologne has a much lower concentration of scent than the stuff I made for him. But masculinity can be terribly fragile.

"He would." Beau made to sit, then realized the record had reached the end of its A side. "You're all right with this?" he asked, raising the disc between his hands and waggling it. Something in the atmosphere of the room had changed. Without the cold draft at my back, I relaxed into the broken-down love seat. Beau flipped the record and dropped the needle. It was an old radio show, recorded live, and opened with an advertisement for Royal Crown Cola. Beau topped up his drink and lifted the bottle toward me. I demurred.

Instead of returning to the red chair, he wedged himself onto the second cushion of the love seat, one knee up. "What's it smell like? Reg's thing."

"His mother," I said. And smiled, showing teeth.

Beau laughed again, and he did it beautifully: head thrown back to bare his throat beneath the beard, his open collar, the gold chains nestled in his chest hair. The sound bounced around the room, and for a moment the space seemed much larger.

Whatever scent he wore—D.S. & Durga, I had begun to think, but it could be something older, or odder, ordered from an Etsy shop I had never heard of—when he laughed, a current of the air caught some of the volatiles, and I in turn caught them.

"Of course it does." He pinched the bridge of his nose. "Christ."

"Out of curiosity," I asked, "does *he* have interesting taste?"

"If by 'interesting,' you mean 'bad.' I'm sure he thinks he's being very avant-garde, with a tight cut and red thread around one button-hole." The sweep of Beau's palm across the box pleat of his orange-and-pink plaid trousers was perhaps unconscious, a sort of automatic self-soothing. A reassurance of his own aesthetic achievements. One sympathized.

"And his father?" I asked.

57

Beau's eyebrow came back up.

"Jane and I got to talking."

"Oh yeah," he said, nodding. "You're friends."

"It didn't exactly feel that way."

"She's a hard-ass to everybody. Even me. But Jane doesn't really 'get to talking' with customers. If she was talking, she thought you were worth talking to."

"I'm flattered."

"You should be." Again there was a subtle shift in the air between us. Not tension this time, but a suggestive opening of Beau's posture. Consideration.

"Reg's father," I reminded him, though a part of me was noting the subtext of our conversation and comparing it to my interactions with Jane. She wore perfume for dates. She often sent him clients. He had seemed on edge until our conversation turned to business complaints, or to secret signals Jane had given for which I had no key. And now that he knew I had her approval, something else was going on.

"Conrad," said Beau, like it was a curse word. "I could *kill* that son of a bitch. I wouldn't even pick up the phone, except I know I'd lose Reg as a client. Reg wants to look like some Suitsupply mod fascist, and Dad wants him to look like the Arrow Collar Man."

"Does he know about Charles Beach?" I asked. Leyendecker had done those paintings of peak American manhood using his lover as a model.

"No. And don't you fucking tell him." Beau grinned over his glass, then finished it off. "Christ, he's cost me so much money. I'm lucky this place is a sublet, or I'd be sunk."

"I was wondering," I said, looking around the atelier. "It's nice. Good location."

"It's a friend's. He's in Singapore for the next year or two. Subletting it at a loss, thank god. Or I'd still be doing fittings in people's apartments. Which"—he jabbed his pointer finger at me for emphasis—"has its charms. But you've got to admit the space lends an air of credibility to the whole enterprise."

I thought longingly of my storefront on MacDougal. "How's business?" I asked. "Outside of Reg."

He shrugged one shoulder. "Passable, I guess. Not great. If I can snag two big commissions a month, I break even. Three and I get a little to spend. And that's not counting what I should save for taxes. But people just don't give a shit, you know? It's too expensive, why is it so expensive? They can get it cheaper off ASOS. Does this look like fucking ASOS?" He curled his thumb beneath the lapel of his waistcoat. "Fuck you. I know my shit. That's what you're paying for."

"God, that sounds familiar."

Grinning, he asked, "You sure you don't want another drink?"

"I shouldn't." Then, inspired: "Not tonight, anyway. I have some work to do when I get home. Speaking of . . . what time is it?"

There was a watch tangled in the bracelets on his right wrist—scuffed gold, rectangular face, clearly an antique. "Quarter past seven."

"I should go. I haven't eaten yet. And we didn't even get to talk about a suit." I was privately relieved, as it delayed the question of whether I would commit to one. Having seen his work, I was sorely tempted. As you might imagine, it has always been difficult to find clothes off the rack that fit both my aesthetic and my frame.

He waved away my concern. "Not a problem. I'm not exactly drowning in appointments, and this was fun. Come back anytime. Here." He snatched his jacket from the worktable and fished out a notebook and fountain pen. "My cell. Text me if you're in the neighborhood."

I pocketed the page he tore out, thanked him, and took my leave.

I didn't really have much work to do at home, and I wasn't particularly hungry. But I had what I'd come for, which was a sense of Beau's frustration, and I didn't want to push things beyond what I'd planned.

Windswept, rain-soaked Union Square gave off a cold breath of concrete and mulch. Before I descended into the subway, I looked up at the window I thought might be Beau's. Reflections obscured any movement behind the glass. Beneath the ugly flying-saucer awning of the subway entrance, I entered his number into my phone and sent a text:

It's Vic. Thanks for the bourbon and chat. Hope to see you soon.

Now he had my number. And when I came up at Eighth Avenue to transfer to the A, he had replied with two thumbs up and the promise that:

You will

6

Notes de Tête: Five-Spice Powder, Lemon Peel
Notes de Cœur: Lavender, Juniper, Clary Sage, and Bergamot
Notes de Fond: Labdanum, Vetiver, Oakmoss, Leaf Mold

He wasn't lying. Just a few days later, in the middle of unloading a carefully packed shipment from one of our suppliers, I felt my phone buzz in my back pocket. I had to wait to check the text until I squeezed down the basement steps past Barry coming up and set the box on one of the lab tables. A deceptively small package, given what I'd paid for it, but anything to do with perfume is like that: outsize impact for its size. Jonathan Bright had barely cleared five foot six.

Even sealed and wrapped in layers of packing, I could smell labdanum coming off the box, unfurling like tendrils of burnt sugar smoke, sweet spice rising on a breeze. Nothing broken—the scent would be much stronger—but just enough to tease, to titillate.

We were back in business. Or nearly. Hopefully, if I moved at a good clip, I could wrap up this whole fiasco before the end of the next fiscal year. My creditors could be strung along until then, if I summoned sufficient charm.

Hopefully. I didn't like that word. I had made no progress on the technical end, though I had continued to meddle with mostly foul-smelling failures. It did seem like I might be closing in on a solution to my logistical problems, though the process would take finesse.

The text message showed a number, not a name. Not strange; I didn't have many names in my contacts. When I swiped to open it, I saw it was a continuation of the short chain of texts I had shared with Beau. Below his last—You will—there was now a link. I clicked through, and as I read, another text came in.

I'll be late, but please come play!

He'd linked me to a calendar event for a pop-up launch party in SoHo: a well-regarded Savile Row tailor had partnered with an Instagram-famous fetish model to create a line of accessories aimed at spicing up classic English styles. The copy in the event description implied there might be . . . actual fetish activities. Which explained Beau's innuendo but made me wonder if there was intent behind it or only amusement.

It wasn't any different than some of the parties I'd attended early in my tenure at Bright House, when I was still trying to impress my employer. At first, I found them exciting. Eventually I realized they were only ever for showing off: a press of people all desperately trying to shock one another, and nobody having a particularly good time. Jonathan had gone to this kind of thing but rarely and, when he did, remained aloof. Once I found myself under his dubious wing, the events took on a new savor: the pleasure of derisive voyeurism, of self-assurance underscored by everyone else's mess.

I could use a little boost to my confidence. It might be fun to watch other people strive desperately, even if just for an evening.

Sure, I said. How late?

Fashionably!!!!

"Vic!" Barry's voice echoed down the stairwell. "Will you come sign for these?"

I sent a thumbs-up back to Beau and spent the rest of the afternoon with my nose to the grindstone. There was hardly time to worry about the Eisner commission in the flurry of prepping for our European launch. I lost myself in scent, surfacing occasionally to notice Barry across the table with his tongue peeking out of the corner of his mouth. The phone upstairs rang once or twice, but Leila answered and if she came down to fetch me I must have snapped at her automatically, because I didn't remember doing it. Not until Barry broke me from my reverie by putting on his coat.

"Leaving already?" I asked.

"It's six o'clock, Vic." He wound a scarf around his neck. "Leila left an hour ago. And if you keep treating her like you did today, she's not gonna come back. And I'm not trying to do her work too."

"You're always welcome to leave."

"Yeah, well, you pay better than babysitting my cousins. Barely." He gave me a funny look—not quite a smile, with his face screwed up like that. "I won't say that it's *good* to have the old Vic back, but . . ."

"Go home, Barry." I capped some clary sage and rubbed my streaming eyes. When I had blinked the tears away, he was gone.

I wondered briefly if Barry liked me. I couldn't think why he would. But I have never cared much about being liked; still don't. I expect the deeper we get into all this, the less and less you'll like me. I'm not bothered. That's not the point.

What is the point? We'll get there, if you can stick it out through the foul bits. Think of it like a dry down: to experience a perfume fully, you have to let it work through every note.

By the time I had everything put away and cleaned up, it was going on seven fifteen. From the unfortunate part of the Lower East Side where the lab was located, it was going to take me twenty minutes to reach the party. I stopped for a cheap steamed bun just outside East Broadway and ate it waiting for the uptown train. No time—or cash—for anything fancier. At least the pork and carbs were filling.

On the F train, I withdrew a five-mil spray bottle from my folio: a sample of the batch of Trophy Kill we had decanted today. The first Bright House I'd ever smelled, back in London, in that little shop in South Bank. The thing that hooked me, bound me in chains. Nothing else had smelled like this—nothing else conveyed such disdain for the traditional profile it perfectly fulfilled. Luca Turin and Tania Sanchez had given it a coveted five stars in their seminal guide to perfumes. Jonathan wore that laurel with insouciance, as he did all the praise that came his way.

Trophy Kill was a riff on the classic fougère, the favorite accord of Victorian gentlemen. Fig and violet shifting to a base of oakmoss, musk, and mildewed leather. Dark, toothy, unexpected. Close your eyes and you could be lost at dusk in the kind of fairy-tale forest the Grimms never cleaned up. A fox hunt ending in blood. A strong stirrup cup, and shadows. A riding habit wrenched above the knee.

Other favorite pastimes of the Victorians? Spanking, caning, kink. It seemed appropriate. The conservatism of English tailoring could be sexy: a constraint within which all kinds of perversion contorted itself to fit.

I got glares for applying Trophy Kill on the subway, but at least I wasn't singing or dancing or telling a sob story. Putting on perfume isn't quite as intrusive as showtime.

SoHo was a rugby scrum, as always, and the throng of tourists set my hackles high. It didn't help that these were Jonathan's old stomping grounds. Thankfully, my route didn't take me beneath the gaze of his windows. I didn't know if it would be worse to see a light behind them or to see them dark and wonder if the loft was still vacant, or undergoing a remodel, or held by some absentee owner as a tax shelter. I couldn't stand the idea of anyone but Jonathan in there. Or me.

I had lived there, after a fashion, for about a month. Now I knew that, if I could have stayed longer, I might have gained another precious ounce or two of absolute. But the process was not even in beta then. It was a lucky prototype. Besides, the mortgage came due and there was nobody to pay it.

It had been a very strange month, a sort of half-life of luxury. I slept in his bed, on his Swiss sheets, drank his Scotch, and took sponge baths in his cavernous kitchen sink. The bathtub was otherwise occupied.

It is crass and disingenuous to say that this brief tenure whetted my appetite for the high life; I had begun to salivate long before then. But the solitude, the sanctuarial quiet . . . I could not even hear the downstairs neighbors or the cars in the street below. The soundproofing was expensive. The bed was large and comfortable. There were no roaches; there were no mice.

For the first time in my life I felt at ease in a space. Even in the house where I grew up—*especially* in that house—I had never felt this luxurious uncurling, this freedom to simply *be*. *That* is what wealth can buy. And what I have never been able to afford.

Upsetting, on my way to a party I had hoped would buoy my spirits, to feel the sharp slap of reality on a spot already too sore with its sting.

His spiritual successor I might have been. I had wrested from the lawyers the intellectual property, the lab lease, the tragic corporate bank account. All on the strength of my history with the company and my success as his protégé. Any number of ex-employees could testify to our close creative partnership. But without a mention in Jonathan's will, I was entitled to nothing beyond the business. I wish I could say I've gotten used to the feeling, since I've had plenty of opportunity. But I have a high opinion of myself, and it never fails to surprise me when others don't feel the same.

◆ ◆ ◆

There was a list at the party. I was not on it. Another blow, this one nearly fatal. I clenched my jaw and turned away, debating the merits of heading home. I had come here ready for victory, assured of success. I knew this scene, and knew how to sneer at it. I had not expected it to sneer back.

Since breakfast, I had eaten nothing but the pork bun and was now powered purely by spite and coffee. It had been a long day. I had actually done *work*, for the first time in forever, and my back and feet and headache were reminding me.

That full day of work was all riding on Eisner's deal. I wanted nothing more than to forget about him and the whole ghastly bargain for the evening, but I needed that money, and to get it, I needed Beau on board. So I slouched against the glass storefront and sent a text, conscious of the partygoers mingling on the other side of the window. I must have looked pretty pathetic: turned away, now desperately texting the person who had invited me.

No answer, for minutes on end. I sighed and lifted my eyes up to the lowering sky. Flaky fucking New York artists.

As I thought it, a cab pulled up to the corner and Beau burst out, an explosion of apple-green overcoat and red leather shoes.

"I'm so sorry," he said, opening his arms for a hug and surprising me with an only mildly affected kiss on the cheek. "Why didn't you go in?"

"There's a list," I said, unable to keep the chill out of my voice. "I'm not on it."

He flicked a dismissive hand. Jewelry jangled. "Neither am I. Just say you know Katie."

Of course. Jonathan always had a name to drop as well. In a pinch, he could pull one out of a hat—the odds were good that whoever he knew was already there, or on their way, or the host hoped so badly that they *would* show up that any friend of theirs was welcome.

Standing slightly too close to the woman with the clipboard, Beau gestured at me, pointing inside. Within seconds we were past the red velvet rope in the middle of a crowded corner retail space, windows on two sides, heavy curtains hung in opulent swags along the walls. I smelled gin, sweat, leather, frankincense. Conversation was a rush of sound above shimmering electronic music, and I sank into the noise like a diver into deep water. Hungry Manhattan luxury hunters: my milieu. No matter the party's theme, I knew my way around this kind of social scene. And *this* party's theme was familiar as my own fingerprints pressed into someone else's skin.

The lights were low, with the exception of bright spots fixed on mannequins in smoking jackets, suits, and dressing gowns, their heads wrapped in skintight gimp masks made of patterned silk reminiscent of neckties. On well-lit white plinths, like museum pieces: riding crops embellished with silk tassels, schoolboy paddles in exotic wood, and what the casual observer might have mistaken for equestrian tack. A pleasant departure from black pleather and chrome, these gags and restraints were sewn from cordovan in chestnut, Havana brown, and burgundy. The buckles and bits were brightly polished silver, and gold that glowed with genuine warmth. Drifting closer to a jewelry display, I saw cuff links and cigarette cases with precious inlay in obscene patterns.

Of the guests who had dressed on brief, half had worn conservative suits in the English style, beautifully tailored. The other half were squeezed into latex, locked into chastity belts, or being led on the ends of leashes and wearing very little else. But the majority of the crowd had made only minor concessions to the theme—rhinestone dog collars, handcuffs dangling from one wrist—and had largely decked themselves in unadulterated Fashion. I didn't feel particularly underdressed in my black turtleneck and Chelsea boots. In fact, I felt free from the Best in Show contention engendered by the costume party. With a haze of Trophy Kill hanging in the air around me, I was turned out better than a lot of the people.

"Drinks," said Beau, aiming for the bar, where a brand rep was pouring cocktails. "I'll be back."

In his absence, I tucked myself into a corner by the DJ booth: a protected vantage point with good command of the room and its over-the-top inhabitants. The alien creature at the soundboard rubbed eyes irritated by scleral contacts, then deftly segued from Billie Eilish to the Ink Spots.

As the distorted opening chords of "Do I Worry" made the speakers hum, a draft brought me the barest hint of citrus and vetiver, Proraso and Barbicide. I caught a familiar flash of brilliantine in the crowd, a pale center part dividing dark waves.

"Giovanni?" If the music had been any louder, he might not have heard me. As it was, he turned but didn't immediately mark who had called. I repeated his name, half lifted my hand, and his confusion became surprise.

"Vic? What the hell are you doing here?" There was a jocularity to his tone I had never heard before—maybe he only wore it outside business hours, away from clients. Or maybe it was the free booze. He transferred a sweating plastic cup from his right hand to his left, and we shook.

"I'm here with a friend," I said. "As a matter of fact, you might know—"

"Metzger, you mother*fucker*!" Beau burst into our conversation, lifted a cup of his own, and induced Giovanni to toast. His green overcoat was gone, and I was relieved to discover he wore a suit of Black Watch plaid rather than a leather thong and nipple clamps. His skull-shaped bolo tie was done in scarlet cloisonné. If I were judging the costume contest, I would have given him favorable marks.

"Mr. Singh," said Giovanni, with an ironic twist to his formality. "Nice to see you. How do you know Vic?"

Beau handed me my own cocktail with a bow and a flourish. "My new friend was sent to me by an angel."

"He means Jane," I said, and sipped my drink. The bright berry smell of juniper cleared city stink from my sinuses. "What are *you* doing here?" I didn't want to say it wasn't his scene—what did I know about him, after all? Except the scent of his aftershave, and his ever-moving hands.

"I'm friends with Katie," he said, inclining his head toward a Saint Andrew's cross at the front of the room. The woman hanging upon it wore a pink hunting jacket over a fishnet bodysuit. Flash photography lit her like a strobe light. "It's not really my thing, this stuff"—he made a circle with his finger—"but you know, I came out to support her."

Given Giovanni's receptionists, I should not have been surprised. But in those days, it seemed he was full of surprises. And then, as if dwelling on surprises had invited one, I looked over his shoulder and froze.

Should I have anticipated Eisner's presence? In retrospect, perhaps: it was the sort of party a wealthy gay man with illusions of edgy taste would drop by to say hello. He probably knew the tailor, or the model, or more likely the investors. Perhaps he was one. I never asked.

In the moment, his appearance in the midst of the crowd I had so happily sat back to judge doused my good mood like a bucket of ice water, and froze me just as stiff.

I had been having such a good time. But this was a reminder: while this commission hung over me, Eisner would be everywhere I went, in spirit or in person. My brief ride on the high horse had come to a sudden and painful end, and I wouldn't be getting up again anytime soon. Embarrassing that I had only realized it now.

"Vic?" asked Giovanni, suddenly concerned. "What is it?"

"Nothing," I said. "Just a client. Would you gentlemen excuse me for a moment?"

But before I could slip away to join Eisner, he saw me staring and made straight for us.

◆　◆　◆

The gin, which had landed on my nearly empty stomach, was by now well at work. I tried to remind myself that Eisner had no reason to look askance at my meeting with these two men. So far, my plot existed only in my mind.

What would he do if he found out? Nothing good. He wasn't the kind of man who liked his dirty laundry aired in public. At the time, I tended to agree. I have since learned there is utility in transparency, in more ways than one.

"Vic," said Eisner, extending one thin hand between Beau and Giovanni. I saw it coming like the claw of Nosferatu in a silent film, and like the heroines thereof, I was entranced with terror, unable to escape.

"I didn't expect you at chamber music," he said, smiling as we shook, "but I'll admit, this seems right up your alley."

I disliked that he knew in which alleys I lurked. I hadn't been out to play much in recent years—my amusements had been mostly private since Jonathan died. I didn't remember running into Eisner anywhere, but would I have noticed then? More likely, he had just done his research. No matter that I had never been much online—that didn't stop mouths from running in the analog fashion. Where there were rumors about Jonathan, there were often rumors about me. Though oddly, never the obvious one.

"Are you here alone?" I asked, knowing that he wasn't.

"Oh, my friend Javi's around somewhere." He flicked bony fingers over one shoulder. "Who are your two handsome escorts?"

Standing between them, small and pale and trapped, I introduced first Beau, then Giovanni. Suddenly I was glad of the gin's effects; it made me speak slowly, carefully, and kept my voice from shaking.

Eisner said small pleasant things to each of them, asking the obvious questions: *What do you do? Oh, interesting. And how long have you been in the city?*

Beau had come up after graduating from Northwestern, years ago. Giovanni, I was unsurprised to learn, was a lifelong New Yorker, born in Queens, reluctantly relocated to Jersey. Eisner skillfully elided any information about his childhood, but admitted to a stake in New York real estate and other assets. Stilted conversation and smiles all around.

Beau asked him who made his suits, and he laughed. "Oh, not Jerome, I'm afraid. He's a little too fussy for my taste. Javier's a friend of Katie's. I shot her, you know: last year. She was such a treat to work with."

"You're a photographer?" asked Giovanni.

The false modesty of Eisner's smile was so thick it was spreadable. "I dabble. I've even done a few group shows."

"Cool," said Beau, noncommittal. I clenched my teeth.

Before he took his leave, Eisner turned back to me and asked, "Any progress on our arrangement?" Then, to my companions: "Vic has taken on a very complicated commission for me, and I have to say I'm *salivating* for the results."

Only by dint of fingernails to the base of my thumb did I keep from glancing at either Beau or Giovanni. "I'm making strides," I said.

He smiled that smoker's smile. "I'm pleased to hear it. I'll be in touch."

We shook again. My palms had begun to sweat. Eisner's expression told me that he noticed, and I hated myself and him. Once his back was turned, I wiped both hands on my pant legs and polished off my drink.

"Shit," I said, to no one in particular.

But Beau said, "What?"

And Giovanni, perhaps noticing my pallor, asked, "Vic, are you all right?"

The Ink Spots faded into Roy Batty's *Blade Runner* monologue, stilted speech over the shimmering Vangelis score. I remembered a piece of apocrypha: that Rutger Hauer had ad-libbed the whole thing. If only I could think so quickly on my feet, so well.

"Who was that guy?" asked Beau.

"Nobody," I said. "He's . . ." I swallowed past a dry tongue. How dare Eisner make small talk with my . . . my tools. How dare he ruin my evening. How dare he know Katie too. Was there nothing of mine that was safe from him? The moldy dry down of Trophy Kill caught at the back of my throat and made my breath hitch. "Fuck."

"Hey, really." Giovanni's thick eyebrows made a concerned vee above his nose. "Are you okay?"

"I'll be fine," I said, and willed myself to believe it. "Everything will be . . . fine." My voice came very close to cracking. I willed my statement to be true. It *had* to be. The money I had spent on supplies, the day's long labor, were all Eisner's game. I had been able to forget him, sunk into meditative mixing and dilution, riding high on excitement about the party. But he had not forgotten me. Nor would he.

"Shit," said Beau. "I've had some bad ones in my time, but nobody ever knocked my feet out from under me." With his good eye, he glanced over his shoulder to check for eavesdroppers; for Eisner in particular, I assumed. "You wanna talk about it?"

I almost said I didn't. Except I realized that with these two, I did.

"Not here," I said.

"Right," said Beau. "I know a spot. I'll get my coat."

Giovanni nodded. "Lemme say bye to Katie."

They left me sitting miserably by the window, feeling fragile and absurd. I caught Eisner's reflection in the bank of windows perpendicular to mine: laughing, with his arm around a much younger man in a black harness and a puppy hood. He had never been less worried in his life. Where I was only comfortable looking on, aloof, he had everyone at this party in the palm of his hand. He stood to lose absolutely nothing if this perfume didn't pan out. Or at least, he only stood to lose a few million, and his pride. Both things that, as far as I was concerned, he could afford to lose.

Meanwhile, I'd be absolutely fucked.

7

Notes de Tête: Black Pepper
Notes de Cœur: Jasmine, Ambergris
Notes de Fond: Asphalt, Oak, Vanilla

The bar Beau took us to was walking distance, behind a discreet door and up an elevator that might have led to the loft apartments above. It looked alarmingly like Jonathan's threshold, and I'm afraid I closed my eyes after the chime rang, just before the doors opened. I don't know what I worried I would see: An empty loft? A dark shape sprawled across a mattress on the floor, the curve of my own naked spine as I knelt above him? Or worse: the man alive, and disappointed.

I promise that I'm made of sterner stuff—you'll see what I mean later—but it had been a harrowing evening already. I was somewhat out of sorts.

I recollected myself swiftly at a slight pressure on the small of my back—Beau, I thought. Giovanni wasn't the casually touching type. And the movement inside the confined space of the elevator gave me a breath of the scent he wore: black pepper and the burning, sticky smell of hot asphalt.

Sure enough, I opened my eyes as he propelled me out of the elevator toward Giovanni, who held his coat over one arm and his hat in his hand.

The loft's narrow length extended into dusty darkness, cut with the occasional bare low-wattage bulb. I could make out a few people in banquettes separated by salvaged doors, though not well enough to count how many. Chet Baker sang to himself on low: "The Thrill Is Gone." The mirror behind the bottles of liquor was blooming with black age spots. Like the salvaged doors, it was no doubt a rescue from some venerable townhouse destined for demolition. Ancient pulley-powered fans hung from exposed beams, their blades lazily turning.

"Izzy," said Beau, giving me a push toward the bar. "Let's get this motherfucker a drink."

The bartender, a petite person with a bleached flattop and pierced septum, looked up from their beaker and spoon. "Beau? Haven't seen you in a minute. How's Jane?"

"Prickly as ever, but I like to get poked. You know Giovanni?"

Izzy looked him up and down. "We've probably met. But in case we haven't." They put their hand across the copper bar top and shook. "Who are we getting a drink for?"

"Izzy, this is Vic. Vic, this is Izzy. Used to work with Jane up in the Village."

"Don't remind me. That place was a fucking mess. Nice to meet you, Vic." We shared an assessing look, and I seemed to pass muster. "What do you drink?"

"Islays, usually. But—"

"Shit, one second. These guys have been riding my ass all night." Izzy disappeared down the bar, where one of the other patrons had a hand raised and an unhappy look on her face.

"It's not usually so crowded," said Beau.

Giovanni looked skeptical. "It's half-empty."

"Industry bar. It doesn't really start up until eleven. It's hopping by two, if you're ever in the neighborhood. I used to meet Jane here after work all the time."

"Sorry about that." Izzy came back with a bottle in one hand. "You like Islays? Let me know what you think of this. A rep brought it by earlier, and I can't tell if I like it or it's gross." They dropped three glasses by the bottle, admonished us not to drink it all, and disappeared down the bar again before any of us could reply.

Beau poured. It was some kind of upstate effort to imitate the Old World: heavy handed and still young. But I was hardly in a state to complain.

"All right," said Giovanni, after we'd all toasted. "What's up with that guy from the party?"

I had been thinking, on the walk over, what information I could afford to part with, what would be most likely to inspire empathy without giving away anything too unsavory if either of them should turn to Google.

Eisner's father had died in a nursing home of what seemed like natural causes and had a closed-casket funeral. Pearson's old college rival was assumed to have been a suicide by drowning, body never found. Caroline Yates had been an isolated misanthrope and so far—six months in—nobody seemed to have noticed she was gone. Except whoever had hired Miles. But I couldn't bear to think of that just now.

I could have managed it better, I suppose. I had assumed no one would remark upon her retiring from what little public life she led. I had been assured she interacted even with her own son but rarely. Assumptions, though . . . there was that pesky adage. Given the opportunity I would finesse things more precisely in the future. Or, as I planned to this time: outsource them.

To that end: "His name is Joseph Eisner. And he has me under the gun."

◆ ◆ ◆

No, I didn't ask them outright. Not then. At that point, I wasn't yet so desperate that it made me stupid.

"We've been doing some work together off the books," I said. "He knows a few things about my business I'd rather weren't spread around, and it's in his power to get me in a lot of trouble if he likes."

Giovanni's thick eyebrows went up, and if his hair hadn't been so mercilessly styled back from his forehead, they'd have disappeared.

"I know," I said. "I know, I shouldn't have—"

But he was already shaking his head, and Beau said, "Let he without sin, am I right?"

"I've just been in such a tight spot. And he always pays for his commissions in cash, on time. But now . . ."

"What the fuck is so important to him he's going to put you over a barrel like this?" said Beau.

"I . . ." I looked down in shame. It wasn't counterfeit. But the story I was about to give them, or rather, the intimations I was about to make? Those were. And the conclusions that they drew would, I hoped, be equally false. I had already referenced illegality. If I could get them to believe that my entanglement with Eisner was purely prurient . . . though as I had said to Barry, I wasn't exactly his type. But these two didn't know that. They had never met Eisner before tonight and knew nothing about his tastes; I could construct whatever narrative I needed to. "I'd rather not say. It's . . . complicated. And embarrassing." I had never been a blusher under the best of circumstances, but in the right light I could make a credible effort at conjuring the idea of it.

"What's he threatening you with?" asked Giovanni. "Could you lawyer up?"

I gave him an eloquent look. "This is *blackmail*, Giovanni. The point of it is that I'd rather die than breathe a word."

"Nothing's *that* bad," said Beau, tipping the bottle over his glass. Then mine, and Giovanni's: a somewhat sheepish afterthought. "I mean, come *on*. Celebrity sex tapes get leaked and they keep making movies. How the hell's he going to ruin your career?"

"Totally," I said. And then, to hell with it. I had them both looking at me with bated breath and glittering eyes. They were halfway on the hook, and people like a story they can speculate about. "Prison isn't out of the question."

"Jesus," said Giovanni. "What did you *do?*"

I gave him a tight smile and glanced back down at my bad whiskey.

"Look," said Beau, leaning in. I noticed now that there was jasmine under the asphalt stink of his perfume, and (synthetic) ambergris. The smell of the whiskey was on his breath, but if anything it was an improvement over the nose out of the glass: this gave it something meaty and urgent. "It doesn't matter what you did. This guy's got no right. Unless you fucked him over first." His left eye, his only eye, regarded me with unabashed scrutiny.

"Listen," I said, matching his lean and adding a little hostility. "I'll fuck and get fucked in equal measure, as I please. But nothing about this situation is pleasing to me. Eisner's out of line, and I'm up a goddamned creek."

Anyone else would have retreated from my intensity. But Beau got a little closer, and he grinned. "Damn," he said. "I knew I liked you."

"How are you going to get out of it?" asked Giovanni.

"Fulfill the commission," I said, sitting up straight. "And pray he never comes back for more."

"You know he will." Giovanni pointed at me, lifting a finger from his glass. "That's how shit like this works. As long as he's got something on you, you're working for free."

The ember of pleasure that had begun to smolder at my interaction with Beau crumbled into ash. Giovanni was right, of course. I was deluding myself if I thought Eisner would stop here. "We'll see."

"Yeah, I see enough already. You're screwed unless that old guy bites it."

I shrugged and said, deadpan: "Maybe I should kill him."

Giovanni laughed, because of course it was a joke.

"This was fun," said Beau as the elevator closed on us. "Metzger, I haven't seen you in a dog's age."

"I've been busy. It's not a fucking cakewalk trying to run that place."

"Yeah, yeah. Me too." Beau passed a hand over his beard. He had some kind of oil in it, and I realized the ambergris came from that, rather than whatever he had sprayed or rolled onto his skin.

"Come in and get that thing shaped up some time," said Giovanni, nodding at Beau's beard. "Who's doing it for you now?"

"Jane," said Beau. "So don't say shit."

"I'm kidding, I'm kidding." Giovanni punched the down button again, as the elevator seemed disinclined to move. "I miss seeing you both."

"Come over sometime," said Beau. "We'll cook you dinner. I'll ask Jane when's good."

Tucked beneath Beau's chin with Giovanni talking over my head, I went largely ignored, which was awkward in such a small elevator. But then Beau elbowed me and said, "You come too. Jane likes you."

Giovanni snorted. "She said that?"

"She didn't have to." The elevator finally opened onto the ground floor. "After you."

The temperature had dropped starkly. New York in the colder months always left me faintly disoriented: all the smells died until spring. People complained about the piss and rotting garbage in the heat, but they were just an element in a larger landscape: a dark shadow against the brightness of freshly mulched parks, the bite of gasoline, the smoke from restaurant kitchens. In the summer I could have walked blindfolded from that building and known exactly where I was. Tonight, I made do with my eyes.

"Where are you headed?" Beau asked me.

"Harlem."

"Shit. Guess you won't want to share a cab. I'm in Crown Heights."

"Sorry."

He shrugged. "Never hurts to check. Metzger, don't be a stranger." He stepped into the street and stuck up a hand. Like magic, like a movie, a yellow cab cut out of traffic. I wondered how he could afford it. "I'll text you guys about dinner," he said. And then he was gone.

Giovanni was already shaking his head by the time the driver slipped back into the stream of cars.

"What?" I asked.

"You know he's trying to pick you up, right?"

I always did like to receive confirmation of a theory. "I'd be flattered. But isn't he engaged?"

"When has that ever stopped anybody?" Giovanni checked his watch: plain but well made, the leather strap starting to wear at the lugs. "Jesus, it's late."

"What about Jane?"

"Honestly?" Giovanni shot his cuffs to cover his watch but didn't look back up. When he spoke, he stared across the street, eyes roaming. "If he says she likes you, half the work he's putting in is for her. She's shy; it's why she's got this whole hard-ass thing she does. I've seen them work this act before. Just thought you'd want a heads-up in case it isn't your thing."

"Thank you," I said, and meant it.

"Is it?" he asked, a little sharp. "Your thing?"

I considered the various merits of several possible answers and wondered which, if any, was least liable to get me into trouble. Was Giovanni an erstwhile lover? Did he aspire and feel jealous? Or was he simply forthright, honest, and concerned?

"Would you mind if it was?" I asked.

He gave a deceptive little shrug beneath his chesterfield—a cramped rise of the shoulders that pretended not to care. "Not as long as it doesn't get messy." Seeming to realize that might be construed as innuendo, he went on. "I've just had to mop up after some ugly scenes, sometimes. Emotionally, I mean."

Delicately, I ventured, "But you've never . . ."

He burst out laughing. "God no. I can't even keep up with one houseplant. I don't have the time."

I could not help noticing this was an excuse, and not a denial.

"It's like that thing earlier tonight," he added, like he knew what I was thinking. "Not my scene. But I'll show up for a friend."

"You're too good, Giovanni."

From his expression, he knew it wasn't quite a compliment. "Yeah, I know. At all the wrong things." He tipped his hat. "See you around, Vic."

I touched a fingertip to my brow, in poor imitation of his chivalry. "See you around."

On Saturday, when no one else was in the lab, I bought half a dozen egg-yolk buns at East Broadway and returned to Eisner's impossible project. If only my life and livelihood weren't at the mercy of a petty multimillionaire, I might actually be excited about the prospect of experimenting. I hadn't had the luxury in so long. But with such stakes I could hardly take pleasure in the process.

Earlier in the week, I had attempted to create a memory from whole cloth, using the scents I remembered from the moment, and a dab of my oboist's essence. It had gotten me nowhere, so now I tried a different tack.

Sometimes, adding one element to another can produce an entirely new scent, the illusion of a third element. The phantom I wanted to summon was a moment in time—if I added an element to an existing memory, could I perhaps conjure the ghost of a new one?

Scent helps us recall memories we've already created. But memory is flawed and fickle. It can be changed. Influenced. I wondered if I couldn't slightly alter some memory Eisner already had to suit my purposes. And so I introduced new elements into perfumes I had already created. Could I transform tried-and-true formulations by adding one new aspect?

A bouquet of jasmine on the oboist's bedside table. She is leaning over, naked with the sheets sliding from her waist, nose pressed into the flowers. The meager light from the courtyard shades her skin blue-green and slides over her thick black hair.

I could imagine it so clearly that I almost believed. But I knew what I had added and dismissed the thing as my own fancy. More fool I.

I tried a few more, to see if I could deduce the difference between success and my own imagination: something burning under the broiler in the cramped kitchen of a chef I had seduced and decanted several years ago. An incongruous whiff of orange blossom in the hospital room where Eisner's elderly father had met his end.

Yes, I did make perfumes from other people's elements, if there was absolute left over. Not as trophies, understand, but for quality control. Before assaying a commission I liked to ensure that the absolute functioned as it must.

At any rate, it was my *intent* to introduce these elements into the memories. But as soon as I added an extra note to a fully realized perfume, its uncanny effects became muddled. Not nullified, but not quite what I had hoped for. I couldn't tell if I was on the right track or only ruining perfectly good perfumes with my meddling.

Filled with frustration, I crammed the last half of a cold egg-yolk bun between my teeth and put my face into my hands.

My phone vibrated at my elbow, screen alight. A group text, and not on the thread I kept with Barry and Leila for work-related issues. At first I didn't recognize the numbers. Once I read the string of messages, I realized that one of them was Beau. By default, then, the other must be Giovanni. I had his number, I realized, on the card he had given me last week, but I had yet to enter it into my phone. And I had not yet given Beau's number a name. I did so now, as well as adding Giovanni. When

I clicked back to the thread, their names showed at the top, lending a sudden human intimacy to the series of gray bubbles below.

Brunch tomorrow? read Beau's first text. Our place?

Then, still Beau:

tacky I know but its the only day Jane can do and she needs
to get to bed early
We can shut the curtains and pretend its Friday night
No mimosas
Promise

Giovanni had not answered yet. I set the phone aside, unwilling to seem eager. Let them all think I had better things to do, or could not rearrange my schedule at such short notice.

But upon a moment's reflection, I picked it up again and asked, What time?

We were playing different games, and mine did not require modesty or feigned disinterest. If he and Jane hoped to seduce me, fine; I had much higher hopes for them.

8

Notes de Tête: Green Olives, Citrus, Cappelletti
Notes de Cœur: Browned Butter, Sage
Notes de Fond: Coal Tar and Brandy

I tried to remember the last time I had gone to someone's house on a social call, and failed.

Perhaps it had been Jonathan. I had a hard time framing those afternoons, evenings, and late nights as anything other than exactly what they had been. Which frankly defied framing. Time spent with Jonathan existed in a category of its own.

But I had often arrived with a bottle of wine, bought from the cramped shop on Canal where I came up from the subway. It lent a thin veneer of sociability and style to what otherwise came down to sex and talking shop. We drank so much together: the wine we'd split, sometimes with takeout, sometimes on empty stomachs. And then there was always Scotch after the sex. Jonathan's lessons about whisky were less frustrating to follow than the knowledge he dispensed in the lab. At work, I had to watch and listen closely to catch what he was doing, and he usually only allowed a few questions before irritation overcame him. After half a bottle of wine and an orgasm, presented with his life's second-greatest passion, he could become positively loquacious.

The bottles of wine that I bought were subject to such intense scrutiny that I grew better and better at selecting them, and even at hunting up good bottles for good prices. I eventually outgrew the shop on Canal, after amassing a body of knowledge far greater than that of the staff.

Neither my upbringing nor my formal education had prepared me to choose between Chablis and Spätburgunder. Growing up, my family had drunk Boone's Farm, and that only on special occasions. But Jonathan expected better, when I arrived with my brown-bagged bottles, and so I learned by trial and error to deliver.

Over and above the wine, Jonathan taught me to love Scotch whisky with an intensity that approached my excitement about perfumery, and through our discussion of the first subject, I grew to understand his approach to the second. Ounce for ounce, Scotch is generally a less expensive obsession than perfume—though the margin can shrink or reverse depending on your tastes—but Jonathan never worried about the cost of either. I only learned what a fortune had been sitting on his bar once he was dead and I wanted to continue my education in single malts. Because he had not cared about the money, he had not considered it an important aspect of my education.

I wondered what kind of liquor Beau and Jane kept stocked, and what Giovanni might bring with him. Despite Beau's protestation, I looked up a liquor store after I got off the 4 at Utica and—with some misgivings—procured an overpriced bottle of mediocre prosecco. I just didn't like to arrive empty handed.

Beau and Jane lived on the top floor of a brick row house; the bells weren't marked and I hazarded the top one. A moment later, an elderly woman in a housecoat and satin cap emerged from the basement underneath the exterior stairs, glared at me, and slammed the door as she retreated.

I had better luck on the second try: the vacuum of a door opening above, inside, made the front door shake in its frame. Shortly after, footsteps. And then Beau in a floral apron, ushering me over the threshold. I could smell sautéed garlic, browning butter, sage. A slight accumulation of gas in the stairwell. Beau himself wore simple Bay Rum over a trace of coal-tar shampoo.

"Welcome!" he said, and went for a kiss on my cheek. I was ready this time, and matched him, before presenting the prosecco. He looked at it, raised an eyebrow, and looked back at me. "Don't worry, we'll figure out *something* to do with it. Ah!" He snapped his fingers. "We'll put it in the zabaglione!"

The stairs creaked mightily as we went up, and the smells of cooking grew stronger. The front door had been left ajar in the wake of Beau's descent. On the landing I heard Django Reinhardt and the chattering of a cocktail shaker.

"Shoes off," said Beau. "Take your coat?" I surrendered it. "Go get lubed up. Jane's making negroni sours."

The apartment was a converted railroad, which surprised me at first: Beau and Jane seemed like the kind of couple who wouldn't mind strangers walking through their bedroom. But instead it was tucked away behind a narrow hall, space sacrificed for privacy.

At the end of this hallway was the living room, looking out over the street. Here I found Jane mixing drinks. Bottles crowded the glass-topped table behind the sofa: Old Raj, Old Grand-Dad, Arette. Three elaborate vintage shakers gathered dust among the spirits.

Giovanni waved from the sofa, rosy drink in hand.

"Pink panty droppers," he said, tipping the glass my way. "She's using navy-strength gin." I did not think I had imagined the note of warning in his voice.

Jane struck the intersection of her Boston shaker with professional accuracy and the cheater tin gave way. "What frat party did you ever go to that served amari?"

Flowing through two strainers, the drink came out pale pink at first, then gathered a thick white head of foam. Deftly, Jane rolled the peel of an orange between her fingers. The oils it expressed illuminated the air between us.

"Here," she said, and handed me the drink. "There's some chips and olives on the coffee table, just to take the edge off 'til the pasta's done."

I settled on the sofa opposite Giovanni and drew my feet up. The cocktail felt like custard between my tongue and the roof of my mouth, disguising the proof of the alcohol. The herbal bitterness made me lick my teeth.

Jane mixed two more sours and shouted for Beau as she poured. Her aggression had lost its air of defense and become playful. In fact, it reminded me a little of those elegant floggers on display in SoHo. Pretty and put together, apt to leave a bruise you would touch later with admiration. And she was smiling. It wasn't a particularly sweet smile, but it seemed to have staying power.

Beau came out of the kitchen wiping his hands on his apron and took a glass from Jane. "Everything's all grated. Just waiting for the water to boil. Thanks, babe." He landed a kiss on the top of her head and collapsed between Giovanni and me. The sofa squealed alarmingly beneath his weight.

Jane smacked the back of his head and he relocated without fuss to a leather pouf in front of the nonfunctional fireplace. The hearth was stacked full of vintage *Playboy*s, tits yellowing with age. Above him, a row of crumbling paperback porno books. A set of spurs hung from the decorative newel of the mantel.

Interesting that their bedroom was so private, when clearly someone didn't care who looked.

I thought of the three vintage shakers, elegant but dusty with disuse. Of Jane's expert blow to the base of her bartender's tool. I thought of the difference between aesthetic and function. I thought of Giovanni saying, *Half the work he's putting in is for her. She's shy.* And this was true. But Jane had clearly picked someone who loved to do the work.

She sat in the seat that Beau had vacated. This put her knees very close to mine, but I did not move to give her space.

"Thanks for coming," she said, not looking up. Her fingers barely, briefly, touched my thigh. "It's been way too long since we had anybody over."

Over her shoulder, Giovanni caught my gaze and raised his eyebrows. I did the same with my negroni sour, then tipped the last of it down my throat.

◆ ◆ ◆

Once the water boiled the whole meal came together quickly—sweet squash and sage cooked in browned butter, ladled over trottole tricolore and heaps of finely grated parmesan. The cheese and fat melted together and coated everything in savory silk.

It was very good food, and better conversation. The wine too: a stony, herbal vermentino, redolent of green almonds and lemon zest. A gift from a friend, said Giovanni, a buyer at Astor perpetually buried under bottles bequeathed to him by hopeful sales reps. My prosecco felt even sillier now.

But as the afternoon wore on, Beau brought my contribution out of the refrigerator and expertly popped the cork. "The secret is," he said, "you gotta twist the bottle."

Donning the floral apron again, he covered the front of his salmon-on-pink Oxford. Egg yolks, left over from our cocktails, followed the prosecco out of the fridge. Discarded on the countertop nearby was a stack of nested, jagged eggshells. Beau picked one, rinsed it off, and examined its insides. Satisfied, he filled it with sparkling wine. This he poured into a Pyrex measuring cup, and then repeated the procedure three more times before setting it aside. Sugar was next: four eggshells' worth, mixed with the yolks. This went into a makeshift double boiler of two stacked pots, and he began to whisk it vigorously.

"You're such a show-off," said Giovanni as a ribbon of egg yolk followed the whisk out of the pan.

"You couldn't tell by the wardrobe?" Jane's cheeks were pink, and the edges of her smile had grown soft. She might keep the bedroom door closed when company came by, but she clearly liked to watch him while he put on a show.

Outside, the day was waning into late afternoon, golden-hour light coming just a little earlier than it had last week. Jane tipped the last of the bottle of wine over my glass, then got up to flip the record in the living room. The whisk went on and on.

Then suddenly the idyll broke.

"Fuck, fuck, *fuck!*" said Beau. "The ice! Jane, the ice water!" Realizing she was out of the room, Beau looked at me with wide, appealing eyes.

"I've got it," I said, and opened the freezer. A bag of frozen peas fell on my foot and split open, rolling across the floor like marbles. Giovanni swore and stood, as if he could retroactively avert disaster. Scattering peas, I grabbed the empty bowl that had held our pasta, dumped a tray of ice cubes into it, and filled it at the sink. Flecks of sage floated on the surface amidst beads of oil.

Triumphant, as if he were not squashing peas beneath his slippers, Beau set the top half of the double boiler in the ice. Still whisking, he poured prosecco steadily into the egg yolks. The heat of the custard lifted the sharp aroma of the wine into the air. The egg mixture thickened as it cooled and soon Beau was spooning it over small bowls of quartered figs. Jane came back as he was finishing, took one look at the peas, and burst into peals of helpless laughter.

◆ ◆ ◆

There was grappa on the bar, and Beau poured generously. Giovanni took the bottle from him and read the label, then nodded with approval.

"This is good stuff," he said.

"Cheap too," said Jane. "Right? You wouldn't think." They clinked their glasses.

This time Giovanni took the leather pouf, and I let Beau and Jane think they had been subtle sliding onto the sofa with me. Why put in the work of a seduction when other people were so eager to seduce *you*?

It had worked on Jonathan too. People like to feel they have that kind of power over you. It makes them complacent and apt to indulge your whims. It makes them underestimate *your* power over *them*.

The sky outside was still light, and I wasn't anything approaching hungry, but we were closer to the dinner hour now than lunch. I hardly remembered the time passing. Jane's head rested heavily in one hand and she yawned wide, like a cat, tongue curling in a frame of sharp white teeth.

Despite the sunlight, something of a late-night mood settled as we sipped our grappa. Small talk had grown larger and more raucous as the wine flowed, then petered out through dessert, skirting more serious topics and lapsing into the occasional pensive silence. Brunch had drifted into evening time, stretching the last of the weekend like taffy until the concept of Monday morning and consequences felt unreal. We were like the last guests at a dinner party, deep in a night that felt like it would go on forever. One more drink, a little more cheese, a final heartfelt confession.

"Fuck," said Beau, putting a hand over his stomach. "That was fun. Why don't we do this more often?"

Jane stretched, letting her arms come down along the back of the couch: one behind me, one behind Beau. She didn't touch my shoulder, quite, but the fact of her nearness tingled at the edge of my proprioception. "It's a good excuse to clean the house."

Not so shy on her own territory, it seemed. I leaned back the extra inch. Giovanni noticed, and said nothing.

"Too busy?" I asked.

Beau snorted and toed off his slippers. "How did you guess?"

"Extrapolation from my own circumstances."

"Jesus," he said, and swept a hand through his disordered storm of hair. Gray gleamed in the wake of his fingers. "I need a vacation."

"You need a vacation?" Jane kicked his ankle. "What about me? What about Giovanni? If half his clients dropped dead tomorrow, I bet he'd still be on his feet from nine to seven."

"Try nine to nine."

"Hey," she said, angling her glass in Giovanni's direction. "You're in charge of your own bookings. Nobody's making you stay there past dinnertime."

"Jim," he said, and Jane made a disgusted sound.

"He's this guy who lives in the building," Giovanni explained. "He's been coming since we opened. And he only ever wants a beard trim. I don't do that shit anymore, not without a haircut too. It doesn't pay the bills. But you know, loyal customer, and now he's a pain in my ass. Always comes down at like, quarter after eight. I'm always there cleaning up, and if I forget to lock the door, this motherfucker's coming in like we're old pals. Even if I do lock the door, he knocks. But I don't want to piss him off, you know? I'm not trying to get badmouthed. And he tips really well, sometimes. But if anybody on my list was about to drop dead . . . man, he'd be my top choice."

We all stared at him for a long moment, until Jane started laughing again. I was beginning to grow fond of the sound. "*Jesus*, Giovanni. Should I be worried about this guy?"

"Nah. But you know. There's always one. Or two. Or ten. Sometimes I wish I could just . . ." One of his hands came up, made a vaguely violent claw, then dropped heavily back into his lap. Shot down by futility, perhaps.

I held my tongue.

"You wanna talk about that kind of client," said Beau, "I could give you a run for your money. People are so weird about their suits. Like, no you can't have your money back because you don't look like a supermodel. I *said* that print would look bad on the final product, and now here we are, and you're pissed. I'm the goddamn professional. You *hired* me! I have come so close to strangling so many people."

"At least no one's grabbed your tits," said Jane, too brightly. "It's a miracle more bartenders don't kill people. You could cover it up pretty handily too." Her eyes widened in pantomime, voice rising several pitches and taking on a breathy, innocent tone. "I found him in the bathroom. He must have slipped and hit his head. We cut him off, but I guess not soon enough. I feel *awful*."

"Wow," said Beau. "Not like you've thought about that or anything."

Jane shrugged, smiling: a taut and colorless vee.

"Reg?" I guessed, finally turning the conversation to my own ends.

"Among others."

"It's funny," I said. "Speaking of people you wish would drop dead, I was doing a little digging on Eisner. You know, the man from the party the other night."

Beau and Giovanni nodded.

"The blackmail guy," said Jane. "I bullied Beau into gossiping."

I could imagine that with ease. "It turns out his company owns the building Giovanni's store is in."

"Real estate," said Giovanni, pulling a face into his drink. "Should've known."

"Not quite," I said. "Mixed asset management."

"Who cares." He finished his grappa and poured another glass. "Kill 'em all. Eat the rich." Capping the bottle, he asked, "What's the firm called?"

Now it was my turn to smile. "Eisner, Pearson"—and then, looking at Beau and Jane in turn—"Yates and Yates."

How do you convince someone to commit murder?

There's more than one way, I imagine. Maybe you have some ideas of your own. I can only tell you my tactic, which was to let them all convince themselves.

I thought it was a good one, then. Less chance of pointed fingers, exclamations of shock, phone calls to the police. It makes you a conspirator instead of a puppet master. Trusted, rather than feared. As for how well it worked . . . we'll get to that, eventually.

"Those sons of bitches," said Beau. "How wild is that? If their private fuckin' plane crashed tomorrow, it'd solve us all a bunch of problems."

"Not for me," I said. "I need Eisner. Or, I need his money. Part of our . . . *arrangement* is that he's offered to invest significant capital to help me increase distribution."

"Surely you can get a loan," said Giovanni.

I raised an eloquent eyebrow. "With what credit? I've been pouring borrowed money into this enterprise for years. No banker will touch me. Jonathan never worried about running in the red, but I suppose he didn't have to."

"Jonathan?" asked Jane.

"Jonathan Bright." I should not have brought him up, but all this grousing about the bad habits of the rich had summoned him to the forefront of my mind. "He founded the company: Bright House. He didn't mind paying through the nose to keep it running. It was his vanity project, and he could afford to be vain. I can't."

"You are, though," said Beau. Then, smiling: "No offense. Takes one to know one."

"Guilty as charged."

"So you took the deal," said Giovanni. He looked skeptical, a little annoyed. "I thought he had something on you."

"My vanity is the smallest part of it. I also love my work, like you. And yes, I am afraid of him. I wish I weren't. But he has money, and power, and I don't."

"Fuck that," said Beau, quiet and bitter. "He's a bully. I hate that shit."

I inclined my empty glass toward him. "But bullies like Eisner pay. You know that. You sell to them."

He shrank slightly, abashed, and I realized he still had on his floral apron. "I wish I didn't have to."

Giovanni sighed, staring at nothing. "Wishes, horses."

"God," said Jane. Her smile was gone. "Sometimes I really could kill them."

I didn't jump on it. I waited. Until the grief and silence and exhaustion reached that tipping point—you could only hold it in your heart and mind so long before you had to laugh, to keep from crying. To show you still had hustle. To show it didn't get you down.

I didn't let them get to laughter.

"Could you, though?" I asked. "Kill someone, for that. Or anything."

"Sure," said Jane, without thinking very long.

Beau snorted, but belatedly realized she was serious. "Really?"

She shrugged. "People kill each other all the time. I figure the line's not hard to cross. We're probably all *this* far away." She held her fingers up, a sliver of light showing between them. Her cuticles were ragged.

"Yeah, but like, not about a shitty tip," said Giovanni. He seemed unsure.

"Not *only*. But you know: it builds up. Like with Jim, the beard-trim guy. Who says one day you won't just lose it? Rent keeps going up, you raise your prices, this asshole keeps coming around for his cheap trim, catches you one day when you're tired, says just the wrong thing . . . I don't know. Like I said. People kill each other all the time, for pretty stupid reasons. We're probably not that different."

"I don't know." Giovanni fiddled with his glass where it sat on the edge of the coffee table. The base of it made a sharp, solid sound against the wood, like a joint sliding back into its socket.

"You don't think you could?" I asked. And if it landed like a taunt, a dare, perhaps the others only thought that I was joking.

He sank down on the pouf and laced his fingers between his knees. "I mean, I guess I *could*, but I'd like to think I wouldn't."

"Why?" asked Beau, surprising me. I didn't let it show. "It's not like these guys are saints. If they're fucking us over, they're fucking over other people too."

"Yeah, but . . . murder?"

"It's not like we can sue them for being assholes," said Jane. She slumped against Beau's side, her arm slithering out from behind me. For a moment I thought I had lost ground, but then she picked her bare feet up from the floor and tucked them under my thigh. Her toenails were painted gold. "Even if we could, they'd win. They can afford lawyers. They know how the system works, and the system doesn't give a shit about us. It's like middle school. Teachers aren't going to help you. You have to take care of it yourself. They pull your hair, you punch them in the face."

Beau kissed the top of her head, burying his nose in the feature of interest. I saw him take a deep breath and wondered what she smelled like, up so close. "Sometimes," he said, voice muffled against her scalp, "you scare the shit out of me."

"You wouldn't really kill Reg, though." Giovanni crossed his arms. "Not like . . . you wouldn't *plan* it."

"Is that worse?" she asked. "Planning it?"

"Premeditated murder?" Giovanni's voice rose, incredulous. "I think so, yeah."

"Why?" She turned to stare at him, waiting for an answer.

He didn't have one for a moment, and when it came it wasn't certain. "I don't know. It just feels less defensible somehow."

"Than losing your shit and killing somebody?" Beau shook his head. "You'd just end up killing whoever pissed you off that day. Like Jim, or whatever. Maybe he's an asshole, but it's not like he deserves that."

"And these guys do?"

Beau shrugged. "More than some people."

"Plus," said Jane, "if you just lost it and like, cut Jim's throat some random Tuesday night, you would totally get caught. If I was going to kill somebody, you'd better believe I'd go in with a plan."

"'He must have slipped and hit his head.'" I touched her shin. "It sounds like you already have one."

She looked at my fingertips instead of meeting my eyes, and when she spoke, the words came out unsteadily. "No jury would convict."

I heard Beau shift beneath her weight and felt his movement through the sofa cushions. The record spun to silence, but neither of them rose to change it. The angle of the sun sank another millimeter and cast the room into blue-gray shadow. It was evening, all of a sudden, and the atmosphere had changed.

Giovanni cleared his throat and caught my gaze. "I should get going. Opening early. Long train ride."

Beau looked at his watch. "Jesus, it got kind of late. Sorry."

"No," said Giovanni, standing. "No, this was great. Don't get up!" He leaned down to clasp Beau's hand. "I know where my coat is. And you look pretty comfortable. Jane?"

She tipped her chin up for a kiss on the cheek.

I got a long and crooked glance, a brief shake of the head, and "I'll see you around."

When the door shut behind him, tension grew in the brief silence. Then Jane wiggled her toes beneath my leg and asked, "Do *you* have anywhere to be?"

9

Notes de Tête: Ozone, Milk Sugars
Notes de Cœur: Salt and Cumin
Notes de Fond: Turkish Rose

"I work for myself," I said. "I can open late."

"Ah," said Beau, sliding his arms beneath Jane's, bracelets jangling as he crossed them over her chest. "The wealth of time."

"I wish it spent with a little more liquidity." The pressure of his arms moved her breasts together; pressed them higher in the V-neck of her blouse. She was watching me watch her. Under my thigh, her toes uncurled, then curled. Uncurled again.

"Depends what you're spending it on." Beau gave Jane a squeeze and lifted her, sliding her legs across his lap. I watched with wary interest as he came closer to me, taking her place at the center of the sofa. Over his shoulder I could see Jane still watching, a secret smile tucked into the corner of her mouth.

Outside, a cat screamed in the alley.

"Suggestions?" I asked, opening my body language by a scant few inches, turning my shoulders toward him.

"We're pretty good value for the money," he said. "Two for one."

"Beau!" Jane thwacked his shoulder with her open palm, but he only smiled. His teeth were very white against his beard.

"Give me your sales pitch," I said, folding my arms together and leaning on the back of the couch. God, I did like flirting done well. I liked the darting knife-play of it: the lunge, the parry, the quick riposte.

"I saw the way you looked at those floggers the other night." He moved closer, getting into my personal space. He was very warm—heat came off him like a radiator, and I wondered how the winters were for Jane, sharing a bedroom with him and New York steam heat. "You like that kind of thing. You like it rough. We can do that."

I laughed, wrong-footing him and diving in with blade outstretched. "I like it *interesting*. But I bet *you* like it rough."

His smile faltered. Jane's grew. She reached out to grab the back of his collar and twisted it hard in her fist. "Somebody's onto you," she said.

The crease in the salmon-colored cotton cut into his throat, dimpling the skin. When he swallowed, his Adam's apple slid beneath the knot of his tie.

"That was cute," she said, leaning in to speak into his ear. Briefly, like the flutter of silver ribbons in a sudden breeze, her eyes flashed up to mine. Then down, then up again. I caught the second glance and willed her to let me hold it. A blush rose beneath her freckles, but she didn't look away.

"Really cute," she said, "you acting bossy, when we all know exactly what you are. Exactly what you really want." She was still looking at me. In point of fact, I *didn't* know what he wanted, but from context I thought I could guess.

This wasn't what I had expected. I wasn't sure *what* I had expected, but it wasn't this. And this *was* interesting.

"Beau," I said, putting my chin on a raised set of knuckles. "Did you want me to think you were in charge here? Were you *lying* to me?"

He swallowed again. Looked over his shoulder at Jane. She twisted her fist tighter in his collar, and he whined.

"Bad boy," she said, and it made me laugh again.

Jane's free hand caught Beau's hair, and I heard strands snap in her grip. "Vic is a guest," she said, teeth sliding against the antihelix of his ear. "And that was very rude. I think you should apologize."

"Oh," I said, and flapped a hand, every inch the easygoing friend who didn't want to make a fuss. "Really. I don't mind."

"No, no," said Jane. "I think he needs to learn a lesson." With the hand in his hair, she shook his head for emphasis. "Don't you?"

"Yes," he said, sounding rather more eager than contrite.

"What do you say to Vic?" she asked.

"Sorry," he said, breathless. Sweat had begun to bead at his temples.

"What?" I asked, leaning forward like I hadn't heard.

"I'm sorry that I lied to you," he said, enunciating clearly but speaking slightly too fast. He closed his eyes and, more quietly, he swore. A lush curse, less exclamation than an outlet for desire.

"That's all right," I told him, putting one hand to his cheek. He pressed the weight of his head into my palm. "I'm sure there's a way you can make it up to me."

◆ ◆ ◆

I meant to leave, after. But somehow the sun set, and dinnertime came and went. Beau fell asleep, snoring softly. For a while I thought Jane might have too, but then I felt her shift, and the rush of her breath across my neck.

"You smell good," she said.

"Well, if anyone should . . ." I rolled over in her arms so we were face-to-face.

"Did you make it?"

I nodded. Her bangs brushed my forehead.

"What is it?"

I shrugged. "I don't know. I hate naming them."

She dipped her chin and took another deep breath. "It smells like . . . like Kalustyan's."

"Hmm?"

"There's this grocery store in Murray Hill. They sell spices. Middle Eastern stuff, Indian snacks. A lot of fancy bitters. It smells like this, when you go in. Like . . . rosewater, kind of. And cumin."

I was impressed. Then again, she had a palate: her cocktails were deftly balanced. I had a sudden memory of watching her dip a straw into my drink, the first time we met, and touching it to the tip of her tongue.

"Cumin, yes," I said. "And Turkish rose."

She smiled, satisfied. Then said, "Ugh, I have to pee."

I untangled myself from her and she sat up, not taking too much care about Beau. He didn't wake—only shifted slightly and sighed. A tender sound, unexpected from someone six feet tall and solid.

"He's a heavy sleeper," she said. "He'll be like this all night." Like a mother, or a nurse, she slipped businesslike fingers beneath the black elastic of his eye patch and pulled it from his face. The lid beneath was sunken and slack. I had a strange compulsion to touch it, to feel the give of delicate skin draped over nothing.

"He said the glass eye felt weird." Jane set the patch on the bedside table. "I think he just likes this look better. Drama queen." She stood, the light from the kitchen stretching her shadow diagonally across the foot of the bed. "Are you hungry?"

Brunch had been a long time ago. "I could eat." Then, glancing at the clock behind the curled elastic band of Beau's eye patch, I said, "Didn't you need to get to bed early?"

She shrugged and crossed the hall to the bathroom. I heard porcelain clack as she put the seat down. In his sleep, Beau stretched out to fill the empty space she had left. Tentatively, I traced a whorl of dark hair across the taut skin of his stomach. He didn't wake.

The kitchen was bright gold, the window onto the neighbor's brick wall a dark blue square spangled with reflections of the light inside. Naked,

I sat gingerly on the edge of a chair. Our plates were stacked in the sink, but the table showed small patches of oil, a few stray crumbs and crystals of salt. I pressed my fingertip to one of these and put it to my lips.

The toilet flushed. Jane came out wrapped in a man's flannel robe. Too large, it gapped and showed the pale inner curves of her breasts. She yawned and opened the refrigerator, remerging with a foil-wrapped stick of butter. On tiptoe she pulled a box of matzo from a cupboard, then opened a drawer for a knife. The silverware inside rattled when she hip-checked it shut.

"Cold?" she asked.

I shook my head. She sat down across from me and unwrapped the butter. When she tried to spread it on the matzo, the cracker broke. She swore with more unwarranted vehemence and sat back heavily in her chair. *"Fuck."*

I waited, eyebrows raised.

"I'm just . . . tired. That's all."

I made to stand. "I should go and let you sleep."

"No, no." She gestured at me with the butter knife and I settled down again, tucking one bare foot beneath me. "Sorry. I wasn't . . . you know. Just bitching." She peeled a paper-thin curl of butter from the top of the stick and set it on a new square of matzo, then scraped it flat with the edge of the knife. "Is it true, what Beau said? That Eisner could get you arrested?"

I shrugged, then shivered. It *was* chilly in the kitchen. Jane rolled her eyes, got up, came back with a cardigan. One of Beau's, from the way it hung off my narrow shoulders and past my hips. I took a long time buttoning it while she spread more butter on another cracker. When she had finished, she slid it across the corner of the table. "What did you do?"

I took a bite. The butter was salty, slightly sour. Plugrá, maybe. A little bit cultured. It smelled faintly of refrigerator, which reminded me of Pippin Miles's morning breath. My mouth went dry, and it was hard to swallow.

"Vic," said Jane, voice flat, losing patience.

I couldn't tell her. Not yet. Not like this. And I wouldn't mention Miles, not at first. Something would need to be done about him, and soon. But I wanted her to think that I was good at my job. She should feel safe first, to say yes. Then she could face complications. I would give her that luxury, even if I could not enjoy it myself.

"Have you ever had one of those moments," I asked, "that you wish you could relive?"

She made a face. "What?"

"A moment so perfect you wish you could live it over and over. Your first kiss. An amazing meal. The first time you fell in love. Something like that. You would know better than I do."

She shook her head, less a negation than a reset. "I mean, sure. But . . ." She looked down again, buttering more matzo.

"I can do that," I said. "Preserve memories, perfectly. I make a very particular kind of perfume. For a price."

At "price," her head came up, eyes shrewd.

"Scent and memory are strongly linked," I said. "Imagine if you could capture the essence of a single moment in a bottle and revisit it in minute detail whenever you liked. That's what I do."

"How?"

"In-depth interviews," I said. "To assess each scent present in the memory, how strongly they correlate to the client's emotions. Sourcing the extracts, the raw materials. Some of them are harder to acquire than others. You know what an animalic element is?"

She shook her head.

"They're ingredients harvested from animals—musk glands from deer, the oil off the testicles of civet cats. Ambergris, though that one's up for debate, I think. It's just old shit. And hyrax too—piss, evaporated. They're things that come from the bodies of animals. Physical scents. Frowned upon, now; mostly replaced with synthetics."

"Do you use synthetics?"

"Not for these perfumes. These require very specific animalic elements. For instance, in order to relive your first kiss, you—"

"Oh." Her fingers brushed her lower lip, as though she had meant to halt the sound before it dropped but was too late. "You need the kisser."

My assent was a slight dip of the head, though I was impressed she had caught on so quickly. Impressed and a little bit alarmed. Though it had hit me this way too, the first time, when I realized what I'd done. Surprising but inevitable. I had killed Jonathan out of desire and rage and misguided ambition. Only *then* had I wondered: Could I capture the scent of him, the sweaty skin between his thighs, the damp hair behind his ear? Could I preserve that? What would it take? How could I do with him what he had taught me?

When I blended the first perfume, I was attempting only to leverage scent's inherent nostalgia: its power to refer, to tease, to tug at threads tied to our amygdalae. Instead I created something more. And then I slapped a sticker on it and set up shop, because in this day and age, we monetize whatever we can. Even the things we care about the most. Sometimes, especially those.

I took a small bite of my cracker.

She blinked at me, too slowly. "You make perfumes out of people."

I picked up a crumb and examined it like a jeweler with a loupe. "Eisner's one of my clients. My *best* client."

She stared at her half-eaten matzo without seeing it. "How much does he pay?"

"Quite a lot."

Silently—thoughtfully?—she twisted the blunt tip of the knife on the stick of butter, making a small divot.

"This new commission," I said, "the one he's holding over my head. It's . . . more than one person. It's the rest of the leadership team. Including Reg."

The knife stood still.

"Were you serious?" I asked. "Earlier? When you said—"

"No." She put the knife aside and let her hands fall into her lap, eyes following them. The overhead light cast her face into deep shadow so I could no longer read her expression. Not that it had revealed much before.

"Oh," I said, and similarly looked down. Stupid, stupid, and what would she do now? I had as good as told her I was a killer, and planning to kill again. One drunk threesome did not a conspirator make. I had been sloppy. I had counted on some connection I wanted to imagine: that she and Beau and Giovanni could be partners in this venture. That I wouldn't have to do this all alone. "Sorry," I said, "I shouldn't have asked—"

"But I could be."

I raised my head so sharply that I felt a muscle cramp along my spine. She was already watching me.

"I want a cut," she said.

I hadn't budgeted for that, but as Jane knew from recent experience, I could be very flexible.

"That can be arranged," I said. I held out a hand to shake. She looked at it, looked at me, then grabbed my wrist and pulled me close, kissed me hard.

10

Notes de Tête: Yellow Apple, Yirgacheffe, and Quince
Notes de Cœur: Soy Sauce, Sesame, Woodsmoke
Notes de Fond: Dust

The next morning, Eisner had left me another voice mail on the office machine. Could he not just learn to text?

"Vic," he said, "I'll be in the neighborhood for lunch today and wondered if you'd like to join me." He gave an address and a time. "Just some quick business details to clear up. Call back."

It wasn't a request. I could pretend to ignore it, but to what purpose? He'd only call again later. And I needed his cash.

The rest of the morning was given over to work. I could not afford to be distracted—formulas and measurements are unforgiving in this profession—and so it was only in brief moments of respite that I felt the full magnitude of last night's confession.

Yes, I had help now. Yes, it would mean logistics and payouts and unpleasant conversations. But more than that: Jane knew what I had done, what I would do. And she had kissed me, still. The minutiae were nothing next to that.

But there was also an increasing buzz of anxiety, the knowledge that soon I would have to tell Jane about Pip Miles, a problem that had so far only simmered on the back burner of my to-do list.

Noon crept up on me, and I realized I had never called Eisner back. Well, let him live in suspense awhile longer. Maybe it would teach him a little bit of empathy.

"In the neighborhood" for Eisner meant a very different Lower East Side. I could have taken a cab and been there in five minutes, but the bus was cheaper and satisfied my spiteful streak. Let him sit and wait and drink another spritz while the M15 stop-started up Allen Street.

The address was a private club where there didn't seem to be a written list, but the woman at the door still knew my name. Eisner sat in a corner of the dining room, sunk low in a champagne velvet chair shaped like an abstract clamshell, a half-eaten Peking duck breast on the table in front of him. He had not been drinking a spritz, after all: a bottle of chenin blanc chilled in a bucket at his elbow.

I sat down opposite. There was not a second glass or setting.

"Did you walk?" he asked.

"No," I said. "There was traffic."

"Hm." He sipped his wine, then seemed to notice my empty half of the table. "I'm sorry, would you like some?"

"No, thank you." I leaned back in my own velvet clamshell and crossed my arms. "What is it you wanted to talk about?"

"I thought we could have a little status meeting," he said, slicing a bite from his duck breast and examining its perfect pink muscle fibers. "Just to catch up on your progress."

"Of course." I waited for him to say more, but unfortunately he was waiting for me to do the same. And he had the benefit of his lunch to keep him busy.

"I've been experimenting with a few methods," I said. Thanks to the preceding silence, it came out awkwardly. "And making some progress." Progress in elimination, but he didn't need to know that.

"Do you have an ETA?"

"It's a complicated process."

He raised an eyebrow, fork hanging in the air. I stared back, stone-faced, and he seemed to come to some resolution on his own. In went the duck, and he began to chew.

"You know, Vic . . ." He had a confident man's ability to talk with his mouth full, hand half raised to his lips in a gesture toward better manners. Like he knew what he ought to do, but also knew he didn't have to do it.

"What?" I asked, shoving it into his thoughtful pause.

He swallowed and looked sour. "I *am* operating on a timetable. Corporate machines move slowly, but they *do* move. If we don't execute this soon, we might lose our chance."

I disliked "we."

"Of course," I said. "I'm cognizant of that. I'm operating on a timetable as well." I hadn't meant to tell him this yet, if at all—I had almost hoped to end the issue before bringing it to his attention. But sometimes pettiness is its own reward. "I'm afraid murder investigations move more quickly than boardroom politics."

It was *so* satisfying to see him blanch. To set his wine aside because his hand had suddenly gone weak.

"I'm sorry," I said. "That was a little dramatic. He doesn't know it's murder yet. He's calling it a 'disappearance.'"

"Who?" Eisner's voice was hoarse. I wondered if he'd sucked a little duck down the wrong tube.

"A private investigator named Pippin Miles." If he was going to haunt my waking moments, he could be put to use. Let him haunt Eisner as well.

"Not the police."

"Not yet." I let the emphasis fall heavily on the second syllable. "I'm not even sure who hired him, but he's looking into my last commission."

"Shit." He put his gray face into one bony hand. I caught the waiter's eye and lifted Eisner's glass, pointing to it. When an empty glass arrived, I served myself from the bottle of chenin blanc. It was passable, but paled in comparison to Sunday's vermentino in every way but price. The markup on a mediocre bottle here was probably outrageous.

"You might want to talk to Conrad," I said. "Or even better, talk to Reg. He's the one who couldn't keep his mouth shut when this PI came around."

Eisner's pallor flushed to an angry red. "Of *course* he couldn't."

"I didn't think it was smart," I said, "leaving him out of the loop, but Conrad wouldn't hear it. And the customer is always right. Isn't that what they say?"

Our waiter appeared at my side. "Can I get you anything else?"

"Just the check, I think." I smiled at him, broadly. When he'd gone I finished my wine and stood.

"Joseph," I said, and gave Eisner a nod. "Updates as they come."

He didn't even turn his head.

◆ ◆ ◆

I only felt victorious until Eisner was out of sight. Back on the street, I realized I had won nothing. Miles was still a threat, and I wasn't off the hook for the commission either—in fact, Eisner was going to ride me harder than ever.

And I still didn't have a clue how to make the damn thing. Three deaths were necessary to satisfy the first half of Eisner's commission. But if it was just murder for hire, he wouldn't have come to me. The perfume was the important part. The part that only I could do—we hoped.

It was two o'clock. There was a lot of work to complete in the lab if we wanted to be ready to ship out our first Clairfield & Amos order on time. But I knew as soon as I was back in that clean white basement, surrounded by bottles and jars and beakers and oil, I would only be able to think about Eisner's impossible commission. And Pip Miles. And many other things conspiring to make my life difficult.

It had begun to rain—no, sleet. I slid into a painfully hip coffee place, ordered a single-origin something or other, and settled into an uncomfortable midcentury modern armchair. To Barry and Leila, I texted instructions and productivity targets for the rest of the day, fully expecting they would close up early instead. Barry replied with a middle-finger emoji.

What to do? Head home and tinker? With what? I was out of ideas. If I embarked on any more experiments, I would just be wasting materials, money, and time. I was afraid, also, to find that blue windbreaker lingering on my doorstep again. As if by invoking Miles with Eisner, I might have summoned him. Name the devil, after all, and the devil will appear.

The espresso was very good, which I found obscurely annoying. I drank it quickly and was left with nothing to do except stare at my phone, like everyone else in the place. So much for the NO LAPTOPS sign above the register.

I didn't have my own Instagram account—what on earth would I post?—but we did run one for the company. Listlessly, I nudged my finger past notifications until a comment caught my eye. On an old post, of a bottle that had been new six months ago. Sevilen, it was called. Barry, again; I had completely forgotten the name. Bitter almonds and Aleppo pepper. Cumin. Turkish rose.

I recognize this one.

Just as I recognized the profile picture. Even writ small, I could see the point of Jane's stubborn chin, the shaggy sweep of her hair: her face in shorthand. I clicked through, looked at a few pictures of architecture, the abstract play of light and shadow in unlikely places. She didn't post often, but they were beautiful photos. And not what I would have expected. She was wasted behind a bar, and she would be wasted behind an X-ray machine as well. At least that was a type of photography. Small compensation.

I opened a text, then realized that I didn't have her number. I could ask Beau, but that felt juvenile. An Instagram message, then, though I hated to do it from the company account. So tacky, and Barry would see. Not that I minded his knowing, only his *asking*.

Still . . .

I recognize THIS one, I sent. And then, why not, a winky face. I immediately regretted it. Was I twelve?

I didn't expect a reply—if she wasn't working, surely she was in class or rotations or whatever it was they asked of radiology technicians-to-be. But before I even closed the app my phone buzzed in my hand.

Good eye.

Better nose, I said, and sent my number.

No flirting on the company account? The text preview dropped down above our previous conversation. I swiped over. What are you up to? asked her second text.

The grinder growled into life behind me, rising to a shriek.

Coffee, I said. You?

Library.

Where?

She dropped a pin. To my surprise she was uptown, at City College. Not a ten-minute walk from my apartment.

What are you doing up there?

Studying. Needed a change of scenery.

You're near my place, I said.

Is this a booty call?

   I laughed. The freelancer next to me looked up owlishly from her iPad. It can be. Then, losing my laughter: Actually, I need to talk to you about some things.

   There was a very long pause I could not interpret. Then, Bring me coffee, she said. And after a pause just long enough to turn her manners into mockery: Please.

11

Notes de Tête: Coffee, Dead Leaves, and Wet Pavement
Notes de Cœur: Jasmine, Unwashed Hair
Notes de Fond: Cèpes, Sichuan Pepper

"This is cold," said Jane an hour later, wrinkling her nose. It had an upturned tip: adorably retroussé. Her dishevelment was somehow chic and Continental. Unwashed hair barely held back, pins slipping. Long white throat above a boatneck sweater. Sweat smell.

"Well, I brought it all the way from Houston Street." I sat beside her, leaned in to look at her textbook. Passages highlighted, key words copied out with bullet points in her notes. I understood none of it.

"What? Why?"

"I was getting coffee in the Lower East Side," I said, flipping the page to a blurry gray-and-white image the caption said was a renal cyst. Charming. "That's where my lab is."

"And you came all the way up here? I thought you lived—"

"I do. I left work early."

"Because you need to talk about some things." She shook her head and closed her book. "I fuck you once and you're already getting needy."

"So fuck me again," I said, and the undergrad across the table looked up in interest. I cast them a look of disgusted disdain. They looked down again. Turning back to Jane, I caught the tail end of the glare she had aimed in the same direction.

"Fuck me again," I said once more, "and then we'll talk. I'm not needy. It's important."

I hadn't meant to change my tone of voice, but I heard it lose the lightness of flirtation. Jane watched me from beneath lowered lashes, sultry and skeptical. "All right. You can take me back to your place and ask me up for coffee. *Fresh* coffee."

"I live in a basement," I said.

She threw her textbook into her purse. "So ask me down."

It occurred to me, vaguely, that my apartment was not as nice as hers. But she had Beau's income as well as her own—she would understand. I had done well with what I had, and it was better than some people's places. Clean, for one thing, if a little damp.

The sleet had evanesced into a chill mist, and though it was a cold walk up Convent it was beautiful: the trees holding aloft a gauzy gray canopy of cloud, all the old houses soft at the edges like the world was smeared in Vaseline. It felt as though we weren't in the city at all but in some genteel university town or old European capital.

The illusion was briefly marred by our crossing 145th: traffic honking, hydraulics on a bus, the screams of an ambulance headed to the Bronx. Delivery bikes sped past, electric engines whining. I smelled gasoline and burnt rubber, smoke from the kitchen of the Mexican restaurant down the block. As we waited for the light to change, the backs of our hands brushed. I heard Jane's breath catch. It turned to steam and disappeared into the fog.

In this weather, even Iolanda's shabby brownstone looked romantic. Victorian. Gothic. I carefully went down the steps to the exterior basement door: the servants' entrance, long ago. Dead vines curled over the stone archway below the front stairs. I struggled with the dead bolt for a moment. I didn't usually come in this way—only when I didn't want Iolanda to ask questions. Such as when I had company in tow. Or a corpse.

Once the door opened, I called up to Jane: "Careful of the ice." Still, she nearly slipped on the last step and reached out for my shoulder. Under the dead ivy and the sweating stones, the cold smells of still water and moldering leaves, she was close and warm and she pressed me to the wall and kissed me.

Coffee breath and the powdery smell of dry shampoo. I buried my nose in the fold of skin beneath her ear, displacing bobby pins. Her hair fell against my cheek.

My hands found her waist, pushed her gently past the threshold into the dark of the basement. Into my workshop. She didn't know the shapes of the shadows as intimately as I did. I wondered what she would think if she understood what we stood amongst. She had already surprised me once, twice, more than I expected. And she was surprising me again, right now, suddenly rough and urgent.

"Wait, wait," I said. Without turning on the bare bulb overhead, I found my door and unlocked it. Blue, misty light from the window bathed the whitewashed walls, the hastily made single bed. It still smelled of this morning's scorched moka pot, hovering over ever-present mildew.

"It's small," I said. "I don't usually have company."

She shrugged and pulled the door shut behind her.

◆ ◆ ◆

Without Beau, everything was different. Not better or worse. All right, maybe a little better. Three people, especially the first time around, can make things awkward. Even when you're the focus of all the attention.

Now I had Jane herself, unadulterated. And she had me. It was like an ungrounded current, steel sparking against steel. There was no buffer for our egos, no go-between who could absorb the punishment we meted out and beg for more. This was a tournament of wills; an endurance contest.

Had I not wished for someone to snarl at, who would snarl right back at me? For a stone to whet my edge? I felt scraped by her sharp edges. I would have bruises in the morning. Bite marks. Cuts. So would she.

I wanted to win, but an hour later I came with two of her fingers curled inside of me. I didn't cry out—I had never given Jonathan the satisfaction, so why should I give it to anyone else?

My only consolation was that I felt her surrender shortly after: the helpless grasp of orgasm closing around my hand. Relentless, I made her come again, and then a third and final time. We both stopped fighting and fell back, out of breath.

"Fuck," she said, and burst into laughter. I thought of frozen peas spilled across the floor, prosecco poured into a pan of custard, the repetitive scrape of a whisk against steel. The parts of me that were not already limp relaxed into the sound of her pleasure.

"Coffee?" I asked, and her laughter redoubled. "I promised!"

"Fine," she said, "fine. *God.*" She took my whole ear into her mouth and bit it, gently, then kissed my cheek.

I stood—dizzy, parched—and dumped the morning's grounds into the trash. Lounging naked against the refrigerator while the water heated up, I looked at Jane. Her eyes flicked around the room, lighting on the bathroom door—ajar—and then the high window with its grate. The beaten rococo armchair bought from Housing Works. The bookshelf, and the books: one row, two, then three. She was cataloging my little life, drawing some conclusion from its details and trappings. I turned away, suddenly embarrassed, and busied myself with cleaning spilled coffee grounds off the Formica counter.

When I brought her a cup—spoonful of sugar, but no milk—she sipped and then said, "You wanted to talk."

With a small sigh, I settled onto the bed so our legs lay hip to ankle, knee to knee. She put one of hers over mine, and her stubble pricked my skin. She smelled even better now: warm with the scent of sex like soft green hay, horsey and vegetal.

"Sorry," she said. "I didn't mean to ruin the mood."

I put a hand on her shin and squeezed, the ridge of her tibia pressing into the soft place between my thumb and forefinger. "No," I said. "That's all right. Thank you for bringing me back down to earth."

"You said it was important." She spoke with her lips against the rim of her cup, blowing the words across the coffee to cool it.

"Reg has been talking to a private detective." At the sound of his name I felt her freeze. The ripple of her breath on the surface of her coffee stilled. I had wanted to upset Eisner with the revelation, but I was loath to upset Jane. I almost regretted telling her, but I had only meant to keep this secret until she felt safe. She knew what I was, but she was in my bed, bare skin beneath my hand. I had no excuse.

"Shit," she said at last. "About you?"

I shook my head, then let the negation lapse into a shrug. "Not in the way you're imagining. But it hasn't exactly been helpful either."

"What did he say?"

I drank my coffee, which was too strong and smelled slightly burnt. I was no barista. "He mentioned I had done some work for his father, around the time his mother disappeared."

"You killed her," said Jane.

I nodded.

"Why?" she asked. "I mean, why did he want you to do it? What memory did he want?"

I rolled my eyes. "I've gotten clients like this before, who misunderstand the primary importance of what I offer. Who want a nuisance dead, perfume or not."

My clients generally came to me with an understanding of what my art required. If they didn't already suspect, I rarely worked with them.

You want a special kind of client in a field like mine: one who's quick on the uptake and understands discretion. Few were *troubled* by the deaths their perfumes required—indeed, for people like Eisner they were a perk, or part and parcel.

"I usually turn them away if they're after an assassin," I said. "But . . . well, he could *pay*. Don't tell me you've never gritted your teeth and taken the money."

She was silent.

"She had asked for a divorce, but the alimony payments were going to nearly bankrupt him. The scent I made for him was incidental—just some particularly good sex. Or what he thought was good sex." I ran the tip of my finger down a groove between the phalanges of her foot. "What he *really* wanted was a scent for Reg, to remind him of his mother once she was gone. Sweet, I suppose. Maybe that's the reason I took the commission. He did ask for a memory; it just wasn't his own. Reg never knew where it came from, so he doesn't know what's at stake now, as far as this detective. He just wants to find out what happened to his mother."

"And the detective's onto you?"

"No. He suspects the father. But he knows I spoke to Conrad not long before Caroline went missing, and he wants me to give him a clue."

"Shit," said Jane, again.

"I'm telling you this for two reasons: I want you to understand how things lie, at present. And I'm going to want Reg and Conrad out of commission first. But quietly, if we can."

"And if it comes back to anyone," said Jane, "it can't come back to you."

She'd caught me. No use trying to soften it now. "Right. Which is why—"

"I get it," she said. She sounded tired. All the softness of sex had left her expression.

I looked for somewhere to set my coffee and ended up putting it on the floor so I had both hands free to clasp her ankles, to squeeze the thin skin stretched over the tendons, emphasizing my words when I said, "That's not what *this* was about."

Which was, of course, a blatant lie. Or would have been, before I knew what *this* could be. Now, I wondered if killing Reg was the only thing I wanted Jane for, after all. I wondered if she wasn't more than that, couldn't be what I had missed since Jonathan died.

Since I had murdered Jonathan.

"Sure," she said, and didn't sound like she believed me. But I saw her skeptical squint shift slightly into a smile. It didn't touch her lips, but I knew her mouth could lie. Though it was small and subtle, I trusted this smile all the more.

"It'd make sense to get Beau to do Connie," Jane said later, as we ate. She sat in my single folding chair, and I leaned against the wall. We had ordered takeout, put on our clothes, and walked over to Broadway for a plastic tub of lagman noodles with spicy lamb. The steam made my studio smell warm, savory. It smelled like someone's home, though perhaps not mine. The overhead light turned the whole place yellow, a cozy change from the ethereal afternoon.

"It would?" I asked, as if this had not been my plan all along. I liked that her thoughts ran in similar directions to my own.

"Sure. He's nearly ready to kill the guy himself. And I can get him the rest of the way there." She dug up a lump of noodles with her chopsticks and when she slurped, a delicate spatter of chili oil speckled her chin with orange.

"Really?" I asked. "You think he would kill for you?" He clearly enjoyed flirting on her behalf, but this might be a bridge too far. *Several* bridges.

She pressed her lips together, then rolled them apart. I watched blood bloom under the skin as it escaped the pressure of her teeth. "Yeah," she said, after a heavy breath.

"I suppose I'm not surprised." I reached out with a napkin and dabbed the chili stain away. "He did seem to enjoy following orders."

But she was already shaking her head, batting the napkin away. "No. No. That's . . . different. It's sex, you know? We leave that shit in the bedroom, we don't bring it out into our lives."

I would let her keep this fantasy, despite what I saw later. Maybe her power over the man she loved frightened her. Maybe it filled her with guilt. I, who would have embraced it and swiftly grown bored, failed to understand her ambivalence, her insistence that her two modes of domination were different in any way.

I began, "But you still think—"

And she said, "Yes."

I waited for her to elaborate.

She paused for a sip of water. I had nothing else in the house to drink, except a few swallows of Scotch and half a dusty bottle of Diplomático. I wished I had a six-pack, even a cheap one, to defuse the tension and the mounting burn of Sichuan pepper on my tongue.

"You know his eye?" she asked, picking at a slice of cucumber. It took me a moment to realize what she meant. "It was stupid, the way he lost it. We were trying to get insurance through the exchange, and they do this thing for freelancers where you have to estimate your income and then send proof. So once we had his tax return for the year, we uploaded that and thought we were fine." She put her face into her hand. "Jesus Christ, if we had just *called*. But we didn't. Why would we?"

"And then the eye?"

"And then, the eye." Behind the curve of her palm, the words echoed strangely. She came back up, cheeks dry and voice hoarse. "Anyway, he thought he just had bad allergies, but then it got really swollen and I made him call the doctor. But they called back like two hours before his appointment saying his insurance had lapsed. We never got any mail about it or anything—so we call the insurance, and they said yeah, it's been lapsed for months, they don't know why, call the state. And it turns out they don't want your fucking tax return. They need three months of previous income, or three months of estimated income, just in a spread-sheet or whatever. The guy's even like, if you don't know what you're going to earn you can *literally make up bullshit.* But even if we send it in now his insurance won't kick in for another month."

"Meanwhile . . ."

"Well, he didn't get *better*," she said, and sighed. "A friend gave him some expired antibiotics, but they didn't do shit. In the end we just gave up and went to the ER because his fever got so bad. Jesus, I was scared, I . . ." The long column of her throat moved as she swallowed whatever she had been about to say.

"Anyway, they had to take it out. And kept him for observation. The whole thing cost more money than we would have spent on private insurance. We're still paying it off. Or *not* paying it off, I guess. Even once I start working it's going to take a while."

"Ah," I said. Both of our chopsticks had fallen still. The noodles glistened under the light, suddenly unappetizing. "That's when you went back to school."

"Somebody had to grow the fuck up, fast. And it wasn't going to be him." She took another sip of water. I went and got the rum. "I love him," she said to me, and it sounded defensive. "But he's been fired, or quit, from like five different jobs in the last couple of years. He can't hack it, hates having a boss. He's a nightmare when he's working for somebody else."

"And you can? Hack it?"

"I can put up with anything." She drank her rum in one swallow. "And I will. I'm fucking tired of hand-to-mouth. Fuck my art; I'll sell out for a 401k and good health insurance."

It came together for me neatly then. "He feels guilty."

"God yes. We have the same conversation every six months where he says I don't have to do what I'm doing, he'll get a job. I tell him to shut the fuck up. We fight. Tears. Nothing gets solved because I'm already solving it."

"And you're all right . . . using that?"

She cast a pitying look across the remains of our dinner. "How do you think I get him to wash the dishes?"

"I should go soon," said Jane as I put leftover noodles in the fridge. There was just enough room on the shelf below my jewelry box. I'm not what you would call a cook, and I've never kept much food on hand. "I have some shit to do around the house. And more studying."

"About Reg," I said, "I know I said soon, but . . . don't jump the gun. There's no point in it *just* yet. I haven't figured out how to make the perfume do what Eisner wants."

Jane's hair was just long enough that she could pull the split ends into her mouth. She nibbled on them thoughtfully, unselfconscious or maybe unaware. "You said your perfumes . . . trap memories? How does that even work?"

"To tell you the truth, I'm not quite sure." I wiped up the small spatters of grease our dinner had left on my drop-down table. "I know they only work the way they're supposed to for the person who lived the memory. For instance, if I made a memory perfume for you, and then I wore it, on me it would be like any other scent. Pleasant, perhaps, depending. But without peculiar effects."

"So it's like any smell can trigger a memory. Like . . . fresh-cut grass, or whatever. But more intense."

"Maybe. Probably. I haven't asked any neuroscientists." I poured another ounce of rum for myself, over ice this time.

"How did you even figure out how to do this?" she asked. "Did somebody teach you or you just . . . made it up?"

Ah, the irony. If this had been something Jonathan could teach, I likely would have killed him before he could impart the knowledge. With someone else I might have evaded this question, implied my own genius. But to Jane, who would appreciate the mess, the serendipity . . .

"Trial and error," I said, "incredible as that sounds. I was mostly running on instinct." I picked up the Diplomático and gestured in her direction.

Jane put her hand over the top of her glass. "So what does Eisner want?"

"His colleagues are getting ready to push him out of the company. So he wants them out of the way, naturally."

"Sounds like another Caroline Yates," said Jane, biting her lower lip. The muscles of her jaw tensed and relaxed, tensed and relaxed.

"Ah, but. There was a meeting from which he was excluded. He believes the information exchanged behind those doors is worth killing for."

"Of course." She made a face. "But he wasn't there. How is a perfume supposed to help him remember something he never knew?"

"Now you see my difficulty."

"So what are you going to do?"

"I'm not sure." I wished my studio apartment had more room to pace. I could take four steps to my bed and then had to turn around again. "I've been working on it, trying to build on existing memories, existing scents. I have a theory about synthetics—like you would substitute an invented molecule for civet, there should be a way to create the memory even if it doesn't exist."

Jane looked at me over her shoulder. Her mouth hung slightly open, and I could see her tongue flex against her bottom teeth. She was a woman, I now understood, who thought with her mouth. Who quite literally chewed her ideas. Suddenly I was glad for the scant few feet between us: I was close enough to bend and catch that thoughtful mouth with mine.

For a moment, the kiss was soft and hot. Then, a stinging pain. She was precise in her bite, catching the smallest pinch of tender skin. I lingered a moment and then pulled back. Her eyes were still distracted; the kiss hadn't waylaid her. If anything, it had sunk her further into contemplation.

"But it isn't real," she said.

"What?"

"You said an *invented* molecule. It's not the real thing. It's an illusion." She paused and finally met my eyes. "Why does he want to know what happened in the meeting? Once they're dead, will it matter?"

"Maybe," I said. "But Eisner's also a control freak, and an egomaniac."

"Look who's talking," said Jane, one eyebrow cocked like a pistol.

"Touché." A hot flash of recent memory: my tight grip on her wrist as she tried to touch herself, snatching her hand away and pressing it to the wall. She had red stripes on the back of her arm where the cinder blocks had scratched her.

"He thinks his cronies don't like him," I said. "Honestly, I'm sure they don't. He's probably got some wild fantasy about all the awful things they said when he was out of earshot. All the spiteful, petty plans they made to push his face into the mud."

"Jesus," said Jane.

I shrugged. "They're all monsters. I wouldn't be surprised if it was true."

She was thinking again: the movement of her jaw, the bloodless skin around her compressed lips. "What if it was? I mean, what if he imagined exactly what really went down?"

"That would be . . . impressive. I'm not sure how it helps me."

"No, no." She bit a hangnail, and blood beaded at the cuticle of her thumb. "It means he already has the scene in his head. It's almost real to him. He probably goes over and over it at night, like—"

"A fantasy." I saw the path her thoughts were taking and felt hope uncurl inside me. Pale and thready, but alive nonetheless. Then fury, because I had *seen this work*. My oboist and her bouquet of jasmine. I had been there, watched her put her face into the flowers. I had seen and smelled that moment, which had never happened, and I had dismissed it as imagination. And it *was*, but I could *use* it. Jane had helped me look at this problem like a con artist instead of an engineer. Instead of solving an impossible problem, I could change the problem to suit a possible solution.

I could have kicked myself. I could have kissed her again.

"Something that never happened," I said. "But still a scene that *feels* real to him. And if I could only make him think—"

"Exactly!"

"It isn't what he wanted."

"Do you care?" she asked. "As long as he thinks it's what he wanted, he'll still write a check. Or transfer the funds. Or whatever he's promising to do. And then they'll be dead, and they won't give away the lie."

Less assured, the wrinkle deepening between her brows, Jane asked, "Would you still need . . . ?"

Ah. For a moment she had hoped we were free of the ugly necessities of the job. But I had begun to imagine the mechanics of it and disabused her. "I think so, yes. I would need their scents, in order for Eisner to believe that they were truly present."

"You couldn't use . . . something else? You said there's synthetics, for stuff like civet."

"With millions in research funding, maybe. But three times over, and again every time I had a new commission? Not to mention the difficulty of subjecting someone to gas chromatography without revealing your purpose." Then, remembering to whom I spoke, and why: "Besides: like you said, it's another Caroline Yates. Half of what he wants is these men dead. The perfume is important, but it's not the only point."

"Okay," she said, and I could hear her steeling herself. "Okay."

"He'll need some . . . priming, I think. Psychologically. It's one thing to have that fantasy, but it needs some underscoring. I want him to picture it as vividly as possible. He needs to form a base that I can build on. But I can manage that. Interviews are always a part of my process, with perfumes like these."

"He won't suspect what you're doing?"

I grinned at her and felt air on my teeth as far back as my molars. "How many of your customers could mix the cocktails you turn out? Could Beau's clients cut and sew their own suits? He doesn't have the first idea how any of this works, especially not what he's asked me to do. If *I* didn't know how to do it until now, then he's never even imagined it."

She was nodding, but not in assent—only to herself, as if she could clearly picture a patron struggling with spirits and bar spoon. "If they all go missing around the same time, isn't that going to look weird? How do you know he's not going to hand you over at the first sign of trouble?"

Giovanni had worried Eisner would come back for more and more. Because he had not known the details, he had never posed this question. What if Eisner didn't want to use my skills over and over again? What if he only wanted to use *me*, once, and very finally?

Admitting fear to Jane at this juncture was pointless. "Mutually assured destruction worked well enough in the Cold War," I said, but I was remembering the whisky bar: *It will come down to hearsay in a court, and I have much better lawyers.*

Just another reason to do away with every letter in the acronym, once my funds came through.

"I've dealt with people like Eisner before and come out ahead," I said. And then, like a dare: "Trust me."

She settled back into her chair. "When you say 'dealt with.'"

"Sometimes."

"And with him?"

"If I have to." I would, if he pulled another stunt like this. Or if Jane's suspicions bore out. Though by then, it might be too late. "He is my biggest customer. And he always pays on time."

She snorted: a knowing sound. "Do you want me to talk to Beau about Connie yet?"

"Not quite," I said. "I want to run some tests first to be sure that this will work."

A shadow crossed her eyes: a cloud over clear water. "Say it does. You've got me and Beau for the Yateses, but how're you going to get Pearson?"

"Giovanni," I said, and she laughed at me. This time, I did not picture the scattering of frozen peas. It was a very different kind of laughter.

"Not in a million years," she said. "Have you even *met* him?"

"I have. And I believe I heard him utter the phrases 'eat the rich' and 'kill them all.'"

"Everybody under forty says that like three times a week. Just because he's mad doesn't mean he's ready to kill for it."

"You are."

She blanched and looked down. "Yeah, well. He's different."

I thought of him standing on the cold sidewalk, telling me he was too good at all the wrong things. Too good to make it in a world that required ruthlessness. "Maybe," I said, mulling it over. "But everybody has a price."

It brought her eyes back up. "That's cold."

I said nothing. Only held her gaze until she broke and said, "But true."

12

Notes de Tête: White Flowers, Dusting Powder
Notes de Cœur: Tobacco Smoke, Balsamic Vinegar, Sour Cherries
Notes de Fond: Horse Manure, Leather, Salt

When I told Jane I had to run some tests, I had only the vaguest notion of what they might entail. And in the end, very little time to act on it. With only Barry and Leila, Bright House was running on a hectic schedule to fill our promised quotas for Clairfield & Amos. I had been on the phone to Europe at all odd hours, trying to figure out hundreds of pages of EU and IFRA regulations, frantic that some of our perfumes might contain restricted allergens.

The workweek wore itself out, me with it. On Saturday, I had the promise of an empty lab, but I could hardly get out of bed. My sinuses felt scoured, and the small of my back protested anything other than standing straight or lying down. Too much time bent at forty-five degrees over the counter, squinting at a scale. I was exhausted.

Instead of going into work, I lay with my notebook open on my chest, my handwriting incomprehensible to anyone but me. Thank god. The sheets still smelled faintly of Jane: her sweat and her sex, the talc and white flower scent of her dry shampoo. A rectangle of pale sunlight lay across the kitchen linoleum like a patch of watercolor, swatched to test its saturation. Turning on my side, I watched its progress across the floor and doodled swirls in the margins of my notes.

I had an inkling of an idea, which was a pleasant change from my other recent forays into the experimental. But there were three problems I could foresee with the approach I was considering, each one proceeding from the next.

First, I didn't want to commit any murders at present, owing to the interest of Pip Miles in my business affairs. I would have to use the absolutes I already had at my disposal. Which meant I would need to find someone who had a fantasy about any of the dead people I kept in bottles in my fridge. And then, without explaining what I was about, encourage them to divulge that fantasy to me in great detail.

I owned a selection of scents to choose from, but only a few of them had living associates I knew. Of those, there were even fewer I felt willing to approach. Either because I had harvested an intriguing animalic on my own time and had to conceal my involvement, or because I did not like or trust my clients. After all, they had hired me.

And again, with Miles on the periphery of my operations, I didn't like the idea of renewing anyone's interest in my practice.

There was one option, almost preposterously perfect.

Many people had known Jonathan Bright—and fantasized about him, no doubt. Wealth was enough to engender lust, but he had been handsome as well: a bantam rooster, glossy and well groomed, with the kind of confidence that small men cultivate to make up for some perceived shortcoming. He was a person who took up more space than conservation of mass said he was allowed. He had become, in the time we spent together, a model for my own attempt at masculinity.

Did I want to be him or to fuck him? The honest answer, when anyone asks this question of anyone else, is almost always both.

I felt a deep reluctance when I contemplated interviewing anyone about their imagined trysts with Jonathan, their ideas of how he lived and moved, of what he liked. It would all be wrong, and I would have to build a scent that underscored the wrongness, enhanced and elevated it to the realm of near-reality.

Briefly, I toyed with this initial idea of Eisner's: the ability to give someone the true memory of a moment they had never experienced. Was there anyone with whom I would share my true memories of Jonathan? If I could share him as he truly was, what would it prove? The people who fantasized about him likely didn't want the reality. But who would, besides me?

No, Jonathan was mine, and mine alone. Even at the risk of this commission, I would protect the integrity of his memory. *My* memory of *him*. Perhaps I could create a fantasy of him for myself, but I didn't like that idea much either. It felt, perhaps, a little pathetic.

Of the remaining possibilities, I liked my odds best with someone who'd be dead in the next few months and hopefully wouldn't come back to haunt me.

Eisner would be the easiest, of course. He knew that his project had me opening new avenues of research. But he was clever, and if I asked him to tell me some vividly imagined scenario featuring his father, he might extrapolate and understand that I intended to dupe him.

Gormless Reg, who missed his mother, would have suited my purposes perfectly. No doubt Connie had any number of perverse fantasies featuring his estranged wife. But both Yateses were off limits at the moment—owing, again, to Pip.

Which left me Pearson. As the Yateses' colleague, still dangerous. But discreet, at least. He was sharper than Reg and Connie but not quite equal to Eisner. Exactly as shrewd as he had to be to get whatever it was he wanted, he was so self-absorbed that I found the scope of his desires depressing. But he had paid promptly and, unlike Eisner, left me alone afterward.

How to approach him? The lie was already forming, born easily out of truth. I was working on something new: perfumes that could make fantasies come true. I was approaching trusted (lie), loyal clients (truth, if only because I had no competition) to see if they'd be interested in collaboration, in helping me refine my process. Pro bono, of course! Nobody likes freebies so much as the rich.

I would not say that last to him.

If he happened to mention anything to Eisner, it would be easier to dissemble with a degree of separation, or even frame it as a part of my plan to lure Pearson to an untimely demise. Well. He was pushing seventy and probably not in excellent health, given a penchant for cigars and steak. So perhaps timelier than it might have been.

Extricating myself from the tangle of blankets, I retrieved my laptop from the bookshelf and wrote the email standing at my counter, waiting for the moka pot to perk. When it was done, and the email sent, I took my coffee back to bed and curled up with the smell of Jane, who had given me such a good idea.

◆ ◆ ◆

Gerald Pearson was game for a chat, and insisted I meet him at the Carnegie Club.

I do not dislike tobacco as a rule—it is a delicious ingredient in many perfumes I respect and enjoy, and many I have made myself. But in the form of cigarettes and cigars, I find it noisome and annoying. It deadens taste and smell, and its own sour stench lingers for hours or days in the hair and clothes of anyone unfortunate enough to encounter the smoke in quantity.

But Pearson liked his cigars, and I needed to please Pearson, so I went.

The Carnegie Club is situated, as you might imagine, in the same part of town as the well-known Hall, and it is just as stifling and wealthy. Dark wood, high ceilings, men in boring suits, a hostess in a tight red dress. Exactly what you'd expect for the location and the price. It was almost campy, saved only by the fact that I was actually here to do business and not simply to play at it.

"Fowler," said Pearson when he saw me following behind the hostess. "Have a seat. Yulia, will you bring around a second glass?"

She gave a practiced smile and disappeared.

"What are we drinking?" I asked. The leather squeaked when I sat down. The chair was overstuffed, the upholstery straining.

He shrugged. "Yulia recommended it. Cigar?"

"No, thank you."

He shrugged and puffed on his own: a short and ludicrously fat campana he had smoked almost down to the ring. The bulge of another lurked in his breast pocket. Embers glowing on his current project illuminated a sheen of sweat on his face, casting deep shadows around his jowls.

Yulia returned with a glass and poured, bending low to show her décolletage to Pearson. I tasted the wine. It was not good, but a glance at the menu told me whatever it was, it had been very expensive indeed.

"So," said Pearson, after Yulia had gone. "How can I help you with this . . . experimental work?" The way he said the words gave them subtext I would have appreciated from someone else, because it might actually have been imaginative. For Pearson, no doubt "experimental" was college coeds making out on Easter break, preferably for the camera.

"First of all," I said, crossing my legs and leaning back in my uncomfortable chair, "thank you for taking the meeting. I know you're very busy."

He waved a hand, blithely unconcerned with the ashy cap on his cigar. "Not at all, not at all." Of course. He had other people to be busy for him. "I'm flattered to be thought of. Have to ask you, though, why me?"

"Your case, Mr. Pearson, is perfectly suited for my purposes." I saw him preen a bit, smiling to himself as he fiddled with the band on his cigar. "I already have the . . . materials I require, and I imagine you might be able to supply me with some inspiration." I was very good at laying it on thick when I needed to.

At the mention of "materials," he raised one wild and wiry eyebrow. No tweezers or wax for Pearson; afraid what people might say if he appeared too well groomed. I wondered if Eisner made him nervous.

"I know I outlined what I'm planning in my email," I said, "but let me go over it a bit more thoroughly. I'm pursuing a new line of specialty scents. Similar to what we've worked on before, but if my theory translates, I'll be able to create a scent that lets you experience a fantasy as if you were living it in the flesh."

His first campana had reached the point of no return, and he took great care in removing the second from his pocket. Though he was not looking at me, I could see he had arranged his expression to reflect casual disinterest. But when he did lift his eyes, his pupils were wide. It was dark in the Carnegie Club; I'm sure my eyes were nearly black as well. But the sheen of sweat across his forehead had begun to bead.

"When you say 'fantasy' . . ."

I steepled my fingers and held his fevered gaze. "Anything you can imagine. Provided it includes the subject of your previous commission. For now. If that works, we can discuss different avenues."

He swallowed, hard. Fiddled with his cutter and cigar. "All right," he said, after a moment to compose himself. "I'm interested. What do you need from me?"

◆ ◆ ◆

He kept me there through the rest of his second cigar. My mouth turned fuzzy and sour from the wine, and my stomach started to growl, but I sat and listened and took detailed notes, amazed that he would say such things aloud in public.

Then again, if you were Pearson, the world rearranged itself around your whims. Why would you be concerned about airing your petty grudges and imagined revenge in public?

His college rival was long dead, presumed drowned, and Yulia in her red dress would be discreet, if she bothered to listen at all. Maybe his shit-talking was in bad taste, but given his tastes in other things, I'm sure he didn't care.

Outside, the weather had turned oddly temperate—one of those early December days that remind you winter doesn't actually begin until the solstice. Emerging from the dim interior of the Carnegie Club, I took a breath of cool, damp air and headed north, toward the park.

Smoke lingered on my clothes, and would for weeks until I acqui-esced to the expense of the dry cleaner. It dampened my sense of smell—but I had gotten what I wanted from the meeting. And even handicapped thus, I could still smell the carriage horses of Central Park South.

It's one of the few places in the city where a person can sample the scent of ungulate manure. Not the reek of human excrement and piss, or the moldy-dusty funk of pigeon shit, but the true grassy smell of a barnyard. Like a well-balanced pinot grigio, the air was green and vege-tal, warm with the memory of hay.

I thought of Jane, her sweet smell after sex, and stepped close to one of the great hot beasts to breathe it in.

"Careful," said the man on the driver's seat, not looking up from his phone. "She's a biter."

"I bite back," I told the horse, and put my hand against her flank. She turned a ponderous head to look at me, blew a big sigh, and went back to her water bucket.

Pearson had given me a good starting point, and I already knew some of the specific notes I would need. One of the tricks of my art involved understanding which manifestation of a scent a client carried in their heart. When Pearson said leather, I asked him: Which kind, where? Car seat? Coat? Old armchair in a college common room?

I could follow up as needed, but I was eager to get started. A quick trip uptown from here, to pick up the necessary absolute, and then I could acquire dinner at the steamed-bun shop on my way into the lab.

It was a lot of trekking up and down, but when I got on a tear I had a tendency to cast aside practicality. After all, I was Jonathan's apprentice, and he was renowned for his wild hairs. Woe betide interns, clients, or employees who questioned his practice or interrupted his rhythm once he got started.

It had taken a while to transition from hindrance to help, but eventually he included me in the whirlwind of his inspiration. Instead of looking on helplessly from outside, I was trapped inside with him. We spent three days alone in the lab once, door locked against intrusion, surviving on tap water, Adderall, and a box of granola bars someone else had left behind.

I wondered, then, what he would have eaten if not for those. Now I knew he had never intended to eat at all. Or rather, intent didn't enter into it. Food had simply been beneath his notice.

It was claustrophobic and exhausting. Until it became exhilarating. And then there was no going back. Chasing the passion proved more fulfilling than even other people; see Jonathan, dead now by my hand. I missed him, but when inspiration like this drove me, there was nothing better than succumbing to the urge.

13

Notes de Tête: Charred Meat
Notes de Cœur: Butter, Oak
Notes de Fond: Dry Vermouth

Gerald Pearson's college experience, through junior year, had been made an absolute misery by a boy one year older: Samuel Cordrey. A family friend, in some vague way. Someone important Pearson's father told him to get close to. He had, and suffered for it until senior year.

When Pearson talked about Cordrey, I could sense there was something more to it than he was telling me. He knew better than to lie to me outright. It had been a problem, in the early stages of our first collaboration. I could not create an accurate memory if he was not honest about all aspects of the moment. At least he told me every scent that I required, sans embellishment. But I knew there was something in his memory of Cordrey that he wasn't sharing.

Had I been a gambler—I *am*, in fact, though not with chips or ponies but rather with my business and my credit and my own sorry skin—I would have taken the odds on Pearson having some sad homoerotic obsession with Cordrey. You know, those twisted sexual yearnings that grow out of abuse and denigration and privilege and private school.

Not that I needed to know to create a facsimile of the moment he found Cordrey defeated in the men's room, snotty and weeping.

But I'm getting ahead of myself.

Senior year was Pearson's first taste of freedom from Cordrey's reign of terror. Was it better to be free? Or did he not know what to do with himself, out from under his tormentor's thumb?

I tried to tell him these answers were integral to my process, which was a lie—I was just nosy and could see my pushing made him uncomfortable. I liked to watch him squirm. But though he shifted and hemmed, hawed and twiddled, he kept mum on some specifics.

All I know is this: When Cordrey showed up at the reunion that year, he made a big show of congratulating all the graduating seniors of his acquaintance by inviting them to a strip club, and even extended the invitation to Pearson. Who was, in my opinion, a fool to take him up on it. I imagine that he ended up drunk onstage, stark naked, Cordrey and company pelting him with dollar bills while the strippers laughed.

I imagine that he might even have found it unexpectedly and awfully arousing, and that the state of things grew obvious to all the boys in their tacky black-and-orange jackets.

Remember, in my version of things, he isn't wearing any clothes.

At any rate, whatever really happened, the hallowed tradition of reunions grew to be something Pearson approached with trepidation. But there was no backing out of them; it was important to remain an active alumnus, and even smile and shake hands with Cordrey when fate put them in the same place at the same time. Nepotism doesn't come from nowhere.

Imagine Pearson's dismay when a new job landed him on the same floor as Cordrey, both of them junior associates at a well-known mortgage firm decades before it became infamous for fucking over all America.

And then, imagine his delight when Cordrey was dismissed for repeatedly, blatantly sexually harassing their supervisor, and Pearson walked into the bathroom to find him sobbing over a urinal.

This scene he described to me in vivid detail.

The scent I originally created for Pearson wasn't a pleasant one. You wouldn't wear it in public. Urinal cakes and cleaning products. But there are plenty of people who treasure their perfumes as a private indulgence rather than an exhibition.

Even if that fetid memory was satisfying for Pearson to relive, it was—in his opinion—too little, come too late. It never sat well with him that revenge on his nemesis came from on high rather than his own hands.

So the fantasy Pearson imparted was this:

It is some nebulous reunion weekend—fantasy does not play well with exact dates, in my experience. It's the concept that matters, not the chronology. Pearson knows he will be seeing Cordrey; he just doesn't know where or when.

In this imagined version, it's not in a bar, or in a class tent. It's late at night. So late that, improbably, Nassau Street is nearly empty. Princeton is only forty-five minutes outside Penn by an overpriced express train, so I know the scents of Nassau Street. Pearson paid for me to know them. It was nice to spend an afternoon out of the city on someone else's dime.

Cordrey is drunk, carrying a can of beer in a Princeton Koozie, but Pearson is not. Incredible, in the most literal sense of the word, but remember: this is fantasy. This never happened.

Oh, all right, let's make him just a little tipsy. For verisimilitude, and Dutch courage. Otherwise, why would he dare catch Cordrey by the elbow, chum it up, tell him he's got a flask, steer him into a shadowy patch of landscaped woods in somebody's side yard?

For the sake of this fantasy, let's believe that in his youth Pearson could take a man his size in a fight. He was still an intimidating specimen in his older age—the kind of fat that was at one point football muscle.

He gets Cordrey on the ground and zip-ties him, takes off all his clothes.

The side yard borders the wide green lawn of Maclean House, and soon Cordrey is sitting on the porch of that august institution trussed like a pig for butchery. Or, more accurately, like the victim of a less-than-artful sadist. Zip ties are for amateurs.

The Koozie is placed with some ceremony over a tender part of his anatomy. Pearson shines a flashlight and takes pictures. Lots of pictures. Enough to paper the entire campus as soon as they're developed. Long before the end of the reunion.

In a perfect world, Pearson's fantasy would of course include the more public part of this humiliation. Alas, the creation of such a crowd falls a little bit outside of my abilities. So this fantasy must remain intimate, our two players alone in the night. The scent of satisfaction only just beginning to blow in on the wind.

Warm malt, wet earth, crushed grass. Castoreum and goat's hair, for those musky twentysomethings: masculine and sex-adjacent. This scent, I thought, Pearson could wear in public with pride.

Whether it would work in the manner intended was another issue entirely.

◆　◆　◆

It should not have taken me quite so long to mix Pearson's perfume. But I had a business to run, and doing so had become considerably more time-consuming of late. I found myself embroiled half the week in applying for hazmat approvals in order to send our first wholesaling order overseas. I had assumed the distributors would handle this, but unfortunately there was work on my end I hadn't anticipated, and I didn't catch it until late.

On the night I was finally ready to present my experiment to Pearson, the lab spat me out in a foul humor. All the i's were dotted, all the t's were crossed, and our shipment would be allowed on board its cargo flight, but that didn't mean I was happy or relieved.

The finished perfume hung heavy in a tote bag on my shoulder, banging against my hip with every step. This was exactly why I would rather carry a folio, but I knew a fancy bottle would impart some confidence a plain brown sample vial wouldn't. Even if it wouldn't fit inside my preferred accessory.

At least I would get dinner out of this. I was supposed to meet him at one of those awful steak houses where they would keep bringing dripping slabs of overpriced meat until he told them to stop. A small compensation for my efforts, perhaps, since I was offering the perfume for free.

It was in Midtown, which at least made it easy to get to. And I was absolutely starving by the time I arrived. The scraps of takeout in my fridge had all gone bad, ignored in favor of a swift departure in the morning, a dollar steamed bun for lunch, and whatever junk food Barry and Leila left lying around in the break room. Luckily, I had lots of practice drinking hungry.

Pearson had a table in the center of the dining room, and I followed the maître d' between dozens of Pearson look-alikes with white napkins tucked into their collars, juice dripping down their chins. Like automatons or clones, their eyes all followed me in sync: tracking an intruder, an odd person out. The room was thick with the scent of char and a greasy, protein smell that caught in the back of my throat and made saliva pool behind my teeth and under my tongue.

Unlike my lunch with Eisner, a place was already set for me. I hung my tote on the back of the chair, conscious of its ragged canvas straps, the scuffs that marred the weave. But I was wearing Sevilen, and let that act as my jacket and tie, my leather briefcase. The sticky spice of Turkish rose curled around my wrists and elbows, the hollow of my throat. Sweet peppercorns and sweat-salty cumin, it mixed well with the meat-stink.

I could almost feel the brush of Jane's bangs against my lips, the slip of cotton sheets, the soft ocean swell of Beau's deep breaths, in and out.

At that moment, I would rather have been living in the memory evoked by my perfume. Until I thought about what such an accord would require.

Pearson half rose when I arrived, shook my hand. "Fowler! Have a seat. How have you been?"

"Busy," I said, and laid my napkin across my lap. The waiter poured ice water into an ugly glass goblet and asked if we had gotten a chance to peruse the wine list.

I looked at Pearson, who already had a lowball of Scotch at his right hand, and relished the moment of struggle as his masculinity wrestled with his discomfort. Just before he broke and blurted the biggest, reddest bottle on the menu, I held up a hand and asked, "May I?"

The warm tide of embarrassment receded from his jowls and he smiled. "Well, you are the nose. I bow to your judgment."

My home was single malts, but I could swim these waters well enough—anything so based in subtle scent and flavor was of interest to me. A preponderance of cabernet sauvignon occupied two-thirds of the page. I had little interest in those bottles and read until the silence between Pearson and the waiter grew strained.

Finally, I found it: deep in the syrah section. "We'll have the Cornas," I said, and the waiter blinked at me. I would not point, and so read him the domaine, the vintner, and the vintage, stopping just short of the price. They really should train waitstaff better in places like that—the clientele never knows its ass from a vin jaune.

When the bottle arrived, the waiter poured it out for Pearson first. He sipped, made a thoughtful face, and nodded. Pure theater, but everybody let the lie alone. The waiter filled our glasses—past the widest point of the bell—and disappeared.

"So," said Pearson.

I ignored him and drank my wine. It was an old bottle—you wanted it to be, with these grapes—and had gone nicely dark and intricate in its cellar time. There was oak there, and fruit, but something strange also. Something from the earth.

Pearson cleared his throat.

"Gerald," I said, sweetly condescending. "Let's wait until after we eat. I wouldn't want your first impression of the scent to be muddied by the wine or the meal."

"Of course," he said, chastened. "And I'm sure you don't want to mix business with pleasure."

Which just goes to show: he didn't know me at all.

Pearson did most of the talking, which was fine. I lost myself in a pile of sirloin and emerged an hour later just as he was winding down and asking to see the list of cognacs.

"Don't," I said. "Not yet."

Though he had the menu in hand, he waved our waiter away. When his gaze turned back to me it was expectant, predatory.

"Have some water," I suggested. "Cleanse your palate." This was bullshit: my version of the little act he'd pulled earlier with our wine. But he liked a show, did Pearson.

I took my own advice, if only because I was thirsty. And suddenly very nervous. The meal and the wine and the games had distracted me from the true purpose of my presence: to test Pearson's fantasy perfume.

"I'm ready," said Pearson, lacing his fingers in front of him. It looked less like a thoughtful gesture and more like he was trying not to snatch the bottle from my hands as I set it between us.

It was heavy leaded crystal—not the kind of thing we bottled Bright House in. I had a small collection of vintage atomizers and antique finds

I liked to save for this sort of commission. Well cleaned, of course. There was no ghost of eau de violette or attar of roses to sully this special scent.

I only hoped it mattered. I only hoped it worked.

"Go ahead." I pushed it forward and felt slight friction as it slid over the tablecloth.

He swallowed, and his swollen fingers resisted the first time he tried to pull them apart. Cirrhosis, I assume, had made his knuckles swell. The delicate bottle looked absurd in his puffy, hairy hands.

And yet, he didn't seem to mind. A room full of peers to judge him, but he was laser focused. He pulled out the ground-glass stopper and lifted the neck to his nose.

"You have to put it on your skin," I said, tapping the crook of my elbow, despite my long sleeves. "You want yourself to be in the fantasy, don't you? The only thing it's missing is your smell."

He took out one of his cuff links and let it fall beside his butter knife. Princeton Tiger stripes. I wondered if he had picked them for the occasion. Without the clasp his cuff flapped open, dangerously close to the juices on his plate. He didn't notice.

The perfume shone on his skin for a moment, until the alcohol began to evaporate from the edges, the liquid glimmer receding until it disappeared into the ether. He lifted his wrist to his nose, lips against his forearm, and inhaled.

I didn't realize, until that moment, that I had held an old breath fast in my throat. Exhaling, I was suddenly desperate for air. As I gasped I caught a mouthful of the groiny stink of his perfume. It had a powerful sillage, and this close it was as if I were wearing it myself.

It did nothing for me, except strike the back of my soft palate like a leather glove. I closed my eyes, afraid to look at Pearson. Afraid to face my failure.

But, in the dark behind my eyelids, I heard him make a sound. And so I looked, after all.

His eyes were shut, mouth hanging open, hands slack on the edge of the table. I could hear him breathing, too fast and too hard, and as I watched a smile began to bloom across his face like mold.

I took another breath, less desperate. I savored the rank smell this time, its layers softening into sweat and sex, damp earth and dew.

"Well?" I asked, and he held up one hand, palm out. I bit back any further questions; I didn't need to ask them. It had worked.

As I watched his face flush, jowls reddening past his collar, I noticed flecks of hair on the white cotton, stuck in the pores of his nose. On further reflection, he did look freshly shorn, though somewhat shoddily. I wasn't an expert, but something about the lines of it seemed . . . raw. Giovanni would have given this cut a sidewise glance and known within five seconds how it had been accomplished and how he could accomplish it better. Pearson, I suspected, was obscurely uncomfortable with his hair, self-conscious of its thinning. But he lacked the confidence to confront his barber, because he also lacked any insight into what was wrong. It was the wine all over again, except that in the barber's chair he had no one to correct his course as I had done.

So after Pearson wiped the sweat from his brow and—discreetly— the tears from his eyes, I smiled and said, "Did you get a haircut today?"

If I managed what I was setting out to do, he would never get another.

◆ ◆ ◆

At home, I stepped into the vestibule to find a pile of mail. Rather say, I stepped onto the pile of mail in the vestibule. It slid under my shoes, unstable, and I nearly fell. As I sorted through it, Iolanda appeared in her doorway holding a dish towel and a cigarette.

"Hey, Vicky," she said.

"Good evening, Iolanda." I flipped through the envelopes. A lot of junk for people who'd been gone for months or years. Bills and flyers for the upstairs neighbors.

She *tch*ed and flicked the dish towel at me. "There you go. Always so polite. I knew you couldn't be up to anything."

The envelopes in my hands developed a curious rubbery texture. It took me a moment to realize the blood had drained from my hands. "What makes you say that?"

"This guy came around today. Second time! First time I didn't tell you, 'cause I didn't want you to worry. He said he's some kind of PI. Looked more like collections. Or a meter guy. Old, white, kinda fat. Ugly jacket. He's no Magnum, that's for sure."

I shrugged, like I had no idea. Inside, acid burned my esophagus. I swallowed hard, and the scent of sofrito and onions from Iolanda's apartment stuck at the back of my throat. I felt queasy.

"What's a PI want with you? You murder somebody and hide them in my basement?"

I made myself smile at her, indulgent. "New credit card offers here for you. You want them?"

"I told him you're not here that often. I told him not to come back."

"You didn't have to do that," I said, my shriveled heart giving a painful palpitation of gratitude. Iolanda didn't know what I got up to in her basement, but she didn't like anybody poking into her business and, by extension, that of her tenants. "I'd have talked with him." Not that I'd have said anything of consequence.

She *tch*ed again. "Nobody pays me for gossip. Why should anybody pay him?"

"Thanks anyway," I said.

She waved away my thanks, scattering cigarette ash.

"Got any laundry for me tonight?" The second- and third-floor tenants were barred from the in-building laundry because Iolanda didn't want anyone breaking their neck or setting the place on fire, letting the city know she was illegally subletting to a ragged assortment of drug dealers and Columbia students. I was a spry young thing and an unimpeachable tenant, with many reasons to keep Iolanda happily on the ground floor. I did her washing whenever her basket was full, to save her bad hip and my own privacy.

"Not yet," she said. "Come back in a couple of days. I got a date and I'm going to change the sheets." Cackling, she disappeared into her apartment. I heard a TV laugh track through the briefly opened door.

One deep and steadying breath later—faint asafoetida from the gas ducts, airborne paint dust, Iolanda's dinner on the stove—I returned to sorting through the mail. Nothing had come for me. I set the rest of the flyers and solicitations on the wobbly table by the door and descended. In the mildewed dark, I put my palms over my face and squeegeed down until my fingertips rested on my jaw and I felt cool air on the wet membranes below my eyes.

Fuck.

I wondered if Miles was onto my scent or only after what I might pay out as a lead. I didn't like my odds; I had only escaped discovery this long because no one had ever looked my way. Well, someone was looking now. And Eisner's commission meant three consecutive killings, of people clearly in cahoots. If Miles wasn't already suspicious, he was bound to become so. And if he uncovered anything alarming, I didn't trust him to keep it to himself.

But if I didn't complete the commission, I'd end up in prison anyhow. A conundrum that might have been entertaining if it had someone else in its clutches.

Pouring a double, I emptied the bottle of Longrow at last and sat staring at the cinder blocks of my wall as though attempting some obscure form of augury. No omens manifested, and I fell asleep still holding my glass, a precarious crystal tulip cupped in my sweaty palm.

Jane couldn't get away from school or work for a week, and then she told me she wanted to spend time with Beau. I wasn't jealous. Just impatient. I wanted to tell her the idea had worked. I wanted her to share in my success. I wanted to thank her. I wanted to see her, to fuck her, to smell her scent again . . .

All right, I was a little jealous. But I had my own work to do. Besides, she lived in Crown Heights and I was in Harlem. That was almost as bad as being bicoastal.

When she finally made the trek up, I changed the sheets, cleaned the apartment as rigorously as I had ever done the lab, and bought good vermouth and a bottle of reasonable gin. I couldn't really afford it, but I wouldn't be caught with my pants down about the drinks again. Into the air I sprayed a little bit of Sevilen, as much for me as for her. I had come to think of it as the scent that meant our skins were touching. Now when I wore it, it conjured a phantom olfactory impression of hay to mingle with the spices. A memory of her messy hair. The blue shadows underneath her eyes.

She arrived with a grease-spotted bag that smelled of old butter and yeast. "I was studying in this bakery and they were getting rid of day-old stuff. Croissant?"

I took one. "Martini?"

"Please."

She drank the first half of it professionally, lifting the precise point of her chin as she tipped her head back. The foot of the glass made a tiny noise on the tabletop when she set it down: a soft, decisive snap. For a moment she was still and silent, watching flakes of ice float on the surface of the gin, the slow roll of the lemon twist. Her tongue traced her full lower lip, followed by her teeth. The pink skin there blushed pinker, after.

"Is it time?" she asked, talking to her martini and not to me.

There was something marvelous in the way she said it: the silhouette of a suspension bridge over a chasm of doubt and exhaustion. It should not hold, it should not hold, and yet . . .

I put my drink aside and reached out to her. I surprised myself—I have never been well versed in tenderness—but her bravery moved me. How tired she must be, how at wit's end, to commit to what I asked of her.

One sympathized. Had I not committed to it many times over? And the first time not even out of financial need, or artistic curiosity, but out of spite. Or . . . not exactly. That paints me rather poorly. Out of a different kind of need: a need that Jonathan had no desire to fulfill. The sort of thing it was impossible to explain, which nonetheless felt right, felt like the only thing one could do. A decision that another person would understand only if you could put them in your shoes.

If I could share that moment with her, would it make this easier? Or when the last of the base notes evaporated from her skin would she look at me in horror, uncomprehending?

"Almost," I said, and held her hands in mine. "Not quite."

She let out a breath, and I felt the air move across my knuckles.

"I'm sorry if I had you worried," I said. Only then did it occur to me my frequent texts, my eagerness, might have seemed to her like something more sinister. It made my gut feel heavy, a strange sensation. I had forgotten the symptoms of shame.

I gave her one hand back to drink with but kept the other one in mine, making small circles on the back of it with my thumb. Purple bloomed at the base of her fingernails. She was cold.

"I'm always worried," she said. "How we're going to pay rent, how I'm going to pass my finals, what if I get sick and miss work. I'm used to it."

I kissed her purple fingers. "You shouldn't have to be."

Her laughter was tattered, ragged at the edges. I smelled coffee on her breath. "See, when *you* say that, I believe you."

"As opposed to?"

She shook her head and pulled her hand back, fluffing the mess of her hair back from her face. I thought she wasn't going to answer, but she did. "Beau's just full of . . . righteous indignation, you know? Which is . . . honestly, I wish I had the energy. But when he says I shouldn't have to worry, all I hear is 'I'm not worried,' and then I worry twice as much."

"You know he must be just as scared as you."

"Sure," she said, "but what the fuck is he doing about it?"

"Jane," I said, and then nothing, because she had put her face into her hand and gone rigid: the pose of someone trying and failing not to cry.

"Sorry," she said, after a while. "We had a fight. Not even a fight. I just yelled, and he apologized. He says sorry all the time, about everything. It's like the word doesn't even mean anything anymore. Like as soon as he hears himself grovel, his conscience is clear. He says he's sorry, but he never, *ever* makes it up to me. Not in any way that counts."

He gets off on groveling, I thought, but did not say. *You've seen how he is; you ought to know.*

Instead I said, "He will."

Her eyes were red, the skin beneath them fragile. She didn't ask me how.

Tearing a scrap from my croissant, I said, "I *had* thought Reg would be a good first step."

She took a breath and wiped her eyes with the heel of her palm. "Because of the detective." So quick and collected, even under duress.

I had been trying hard to push Pip Miles from my mind. This reminder made a shudder rise in me, but I didn't let it show.

"Yes," I said. "But after some consideration: Conrad knows more about me and is therefore a little more dangerous to the enterprise."

"Sure," she said. She was relieved; her posture told me that. Maybe this would be easier for her if Beau did it first.

Curiously endearing, this dynamic. Beau was her vanguard, her cavalry: daring, dashing, ready to charge and fail in the attempt. She was a general: strong, steady, cautious. And ruthless, when it came down to the moment of decision.

"If the old men get to talking," I went on, "Eisner might figure out I'm up to something. Besides, Miles thinks Conrad is the main suspect in his wife's disappearance. If he dies first, it might throw Miles for a loop. Reg will be sad if his father disappears, scared at worst, but not suspicious. At least, not of me. Ideally we'd get Pearson next and save Reg for last, because he's least likely to put the pieces together."

She let out an audible breath, and I realized I had placed her in an unenviable position: last in the line of events, with anticipation mounting. But maybe that breath was relief at her brief reprieve. She needn't kill anyone yet.

"I'm sorry," I said, but she shook her head.

"You're right." It came out steady, but pitched too low: she was trying to reassure herself with the sound of her own voice. "Reg is the only one who doesn't know what you're involved in." Then, with a shaky smile: "And if he goes last, I can keep raking in tips whenever he comes by the bar."

"Mercenary," I said, and leaned in to kiss her. Her mouth opened under mine, and she made a sound like a sob. Relief, I thought, and caught that tempting lower lip between my teeth.

I could have gone on kissing her. She was yielding, soft, open to me. The electric current that made her bite and sting had been turned off, temporarily. She was all warmth, all wet. I could have sunk into that feeling and lost hours.

I broke the kiss and leaned my forehead against hers. The thud of her heartbeat passed through her bones into mine.

"If you want," I said, a little breathless, "I'll talk to him with you. We'll drink, have a little dinner." We would fuck too, but I didn't say it. If she didn't want to wield that kind of power in this way, I would let her maintain that illusion. I wanted to keep her happy. At the time, I thought it was only because her happiness would make my work easier. Or perhaps because protecting her happiness was another kind of power.

To my surprise—and disappointment?—she shook her head. "No. You know what? I think it has to be just me and him. No offense. But it's . . . it's between us, whatever he thinks he owes me."

Fair enough. But letting this control slip from my grasp felt dangerous. Trusting Jane was another risk in an already risky endeavor. I did trust her to *try*. I just wasn't sure I trusted her to succeed.

"When does he next see Reg?"

"I think he's doing a fitting on something next week."

"And Conrad will call him . . . ?"

"Two or three days later. Every time."

"When Conrad calls, that's when you push him. As hard as you think you can."

"It won't have to be very." She finished the rest of her drink. "Have you talked to Giovanni yet?"

"I'm working on it," I said, which wasn't true. But it would have to be, and soon.

14

Notes de Tête: Lime and Bergamot
Notes de Cœur: Malt, Bread, Toasted Sesame
Notes de Fond: Dust and Winter Subway Accord

I had a haircut scheduled—I tended to put the next one on my calendar at the end of the last. Every five weeks, which was honestly too long, but I had rent to pay and a business to run and even at a discount a haircut was still cash out of my budget. So cuts didn't come around that often. Usually, I looked forward to them.

This time, not so much.

I kept thinking about what Jane had said—Giovanni? *Not in a million years.* And of Giovanni himself, telling me he was too good for this kind of life, for the machinations it took to get yourself out from under corporate thumbs, investor scrutiny.

There was no way that this was going to work. How could I even begin? *Do you really want to eat the rich? Really want to kill them all? What if we start with one?*

And then in my head, I'd hear his voice: high and nasal, a trace of Queens. He sounded like a man in an old movie. *Stalag 17. Double Indemnity.* He even had the *morals* of a man in an old movie: *Premeditated murder just seems less defensible somehow.*

But he was independent too. Fiercely so, to own his own business in Manhattan. Didn't I know what that took? I didn't imagine his drive was born in the same dark place as my own, but his hunger must be at least equal to mine.

How well did I know Giovanni, really? He was my barber, but what did that amount to? He knew how I liked my hair cut. He tended to be taciturn but posted incongruously quirky selfies to his Instagram. His work playlist was a mix of bossa nova, Miles Davis, rockabilly. In the last month I had learned more about him than I had in years as his client: that he was tired and angry, and friends with Jane. That he and Beau called each other by their surnames like squad mates in a war film. That he lived in Jersey City and commuted to the Village. That he knew the wine buyer at Astor and said things like "eat the rich" but didn't mean them, not to the point of murder.

None of that gave me much to work with, which meant I would have to feel my way.

I called on the day of my appointment and told the assistant a conflict had come up: Could I move my haircut back by a few hours?

"I'm sorry," she said, "but we're booked up."

"Shit," I said. "I'm in sort of a desperate situation. There's no way he could make a little space?"

There was a wavering pause. "Hang on, I'll ask him."

He wouldn't like that. But if he didn't want his assistant bending the rules, he shouldn't be so flexible. This was the eight-fifteen beard trim all over again; he couldn't say no to loyal customers, couldn't not cut them a deal. It was good for building relationships, but it would grind him down to the bone if he wasn't careful.

"Vic?" It was Giovanni who got back on the phone, not the front desk girl. "What's up?"

"I'm so sorry," I said. "Something's come up at work and I can't do six o'clock anymore. Is there any chance you could squeeze me in later tonight?"

"Sure," he said, without any hesitation. "Sure. Come by at eight."

"But you close at—"

"Vic, I'm telling you: come by at eight. I wouldn't do it for just anybody, but . . . I owe you a beer, right?"

"I think I owe *you* a beer," I said.

"Whatever. Come at eight."

And so I did.

He had already closed and locked the door by the time I arrived—closer to eight fifteen, ironically. I had taken a brief detour around Washington Square Park to pick up a six-pack of interesting but not overwhelming beer. Giovanni didn't seem like the kind of man who appreciated a saison brewed with coriander and sea salt.

"Cheaper to buy it in bulk," I said when he took the six-pack from my outstretched hand. "I didn't know your exact preference, but I've yet to meet anyone who will turn down a solid brown ale."

He laughed. His mustache made his smile seem wider. After hours, the shop had a whiff of sandwich bread and vacuum filter. A comfortable smell, not so curated as the lime and eucalyptus that suffused the place when it was open. He and his barbers had eaten dinner here, cleaned up after. It smelled human—a whiff of all the mess and warmth and precarity humanity entailed.

Not to say it didn't still smell like Proraso.

When he locked the door behind me, I saw a weight fall from his shoulders. He was on his turf, on his terms. The music wasn't the usual bossa nova or midcentury jazz but pure nostalgic post-punk. I remembered that he was older than me, by about five years. Maybe more. This was *his* music.

He looked momentarily stymied by the cap on his beer, then grinned and half undid his belt. A moment later, with a hiss of carbonation, the cap tumbled to the floor. He handed me the first bottle and repeated the process, then lifted his drink to touch mine.

"Thanks for the beer," he said, then set it aside and fastened his belt again.

I shrugged. "Thank you for squeezing me in." And then, like the first, subtle move in a game of strategy: "I hope I won't meet the kind of end you're planning for Jim."

"Who?"

And back to me. "The eight-fifteen beard trim."

He snorted into the neck of his beer bottle. "God, I'd forgotten all about that. Those negroni sours are something, huh? Have a seat." He put the sheet over me but left my beer hand free.

"The usual?" he asked.

"What else?"

As he began to comb my hair, cool mist flying from the spray bottle, I considered my next turn. How to recapture that bittersweet, cathartic brunch humor? The mood that would make him feel he could admit to anything?

Well, why not start where we had left off?

"I was a little worried Jane might actually go after Reg." Knight to f3. "Can you imagine?"

"Jane?" He started snipping. "You know, I could. When she gets mad, she's scary. Cold, right? Like, ice-queen rage."

"Oh, I know the type," I said. I was one.

"Not me," said Giovanni. "When I'm pissed, you'll know it."

"I hope I never will."

He laughed. This banter felt to me like the slap of hands on chess timers, the acceleration of play until it moved so quickly onlookers were lost and the two players were moving just to move, respond, keep up the rhythm. Faster and faster until one or the other of them made a fatal mistake: a slip of the tongue, an error in judgment, fingers closing too quickly on the tip of the bishop's miter.

It was just a matter of watching him more closely than he watched himself, then catching him when he slipped up and holding him to the commitment.

"Head down." The tips of his fingers landed on the back of my skull in a precise configuration, channeling pressure. I dipped my chin toward my chest.

"So you wouldn't kill in cold blood," I said, "but if you got mad enough you think you might?"

He shrugged. "I don't know. Like Jane said, probably any of us could."

"A reminder to tip well, I suppose."

The comb scraped my scalp. "Nah, you're good. It's never the people who worry, right? The people who worry about doing right by you, they always do. Service does for service. It's the fucking bankers and tech guys that'll stiff you, every time."

"It's so . . . stopgap," I said. "We're all down here giving each other discounts, legs up, tips and tricks. Living life on each other's generosity."

"I kind of like it," said Giovanni.

Of course he did. I did too. Who didn't like a little special treatment? "But this separate economy isn't sustainable. Discounted haircuts aren't helping me save for retirement. Nobody's going to slip me health insurance along with a free glass of wine."

He opened his mouth—no doubt to say something about Medicaid, the state exchange—and I added, "*Good* health insurance, Giovanni. The kind doctors actually *take*. I don't care about tax penalties if my teeth are falling out of my head. Do you know how many dentists accept Medicaid in this city? Do you know how many of them are any *good*?"

His mouth fell shut and he went back to combing.

After a moment of silence and a sip of beer, I asked, "Do you ever think of getting out of all this? Getting a boss, a nine-to-five, a salary?"

"Like I *could*. I'd just have to find another chair somewhere. What would I even interview for?"

"I don't know. Go back to school, like Jane. Become a consultant for somebody else's small-business incubator. Get off your feet and let somebody else make your money."

He was already shaking his head before he spoke. "No, no way. Not a chance in hell." If this had been a chess game, really, I'd have been losing pieces to him. But that was all right: they were pieces I had meant to lose.

"You're bleeding money," I said. "You told me so. You said you'd be franchising if the rent hadn't gone up every year. I'm in the same boat"—this wasn't quite true, as rent was only one of my myriad problems—"and I can tell you it's a pretty fucking leaky one."

His scissors stopped, and he leaned on the back of my chair. The leather creaked. "Somehow I can't see you going corporate, Vic. Not unless you went straight to the top of the ladder. And they don't really let you do that unless you're somebody's kid."

"Like Reg?" I asked. Back to my knight.

"Like Reg."

"I mentioned, didn't I: his company owns this building. In a roundabout sort of way." Another step across the board.

"You trying to get me to go after him or something?" Giovanni polished off his first beer and cracked a second. "I think Jane has that one under control."

I laughed, like it really was a joke and not part of my endgame. He put a hand on the curve of my skull to keep me still and went back to cutting.

"Reg isn't who you'd want anyhow," I said. "I did some googling. It's one of the other executives who heads up the real-estate investments. Gerald Pearson." With a silent apology to Iolanda, always amenable and incurious, I added, "Fucking New York landlords. Too bad *they* don't come around and find you in just the right bad mood."

"For the landlords," he said, "I'd go out and find them."

I imagined the chess hustlers of Union Square, their swift hands and the hollow thud of flesh on metal as they struck the buttons that would stop their clocks. The pivotal moment, a test of their skills of legerdemain, and suddenly the game was no longer being played by the rules.

"Would you?" I asked. "Really?"

His comb and scissors paused, as if he'd seen my sleight of hand. But when he spoke it was with humor. Still playing the old game, not my new one, but that was fine if I could maneuver around him, herd him where I needed him to go.

"Why?" he asked. "You wanna go out hunting?"

"I'm more of a trapper, myself." This wasn't strictly true. I couldn't catch my prey and come back later. But in a more poetic sense, I was often a moving part in larger mousetraps. Witness the sticky situations I had gotten into with Eisner, Pearson, Yates & Yates. "Don't you think Gerald Pearson would make a pretty nice rug?"

"Jesus," he said. "No wonder Jane likes you." A few more snips, and then: "I honestly can't tell if you're joking." He was starting to catch on.

I met his eyes in the mirror. "What if I wasn't?"

A minute pause. A tiny space of silence, inside of which I had time to hope. And then, incredulous: "I'd call the fucking cops. What do you think?" He pushed my head down again and ran rough hands through my hair.

The rejection hurt more than I thought it would, and I let him hear it. "Come on, Giovanni. I give you a friends and family discount, and you'd call the cops on me?"

Without answering, he retrieved the clippers for a few finishing swipes around the tendons at the nape of my neck. The blades made my skin tingle. "You're kind of giving me the creeps, Vic."

I didn't apologize.

He finished the cut and dusted me off: sweet cornstarch and a quick, toasty blast of the hair dryer. Then the sheet came off and he spun me around so we faced each other without the intermediary of the mirror.

"Really?" I asked.

He took it as lightly as he could, trying to save the situation. "What, giving me the creeps? Yeah."

"No," I said, loading it with ballast. "I mean, would you really call the cops?"

An unsteadiness about the mouth, a tightening at the corners of his eyes. He was wavering, though with fear or doubt I couldn't tell. His beer bottle hovered near his lips, but he did not remember to drink.

"Of course," he said, not sounding quite so sure. But maybe the disbelief was for me: the absurdity that he would need to say *yes*, he *would* turn me in for murder.

"Why?"

"Because that's what you *do*, Vic. That's how it works."

"Says who?" I asked. It came out raw, surprising me. This was not a move I had meant to make. But I was angry, and a little frightened. Surely he wouldn't turn me in for *this*. We were just joking, nothing more. There was deniability.

"Says . . . everyone. I don't know. The rules!"

"Fuck the rules," I said. This was no longer strategy, but intuition. Maybe that was dangerous, but I no longer cared. I was so goddamned tired. I shouldn't have to fight with someone who was already on my side. Especially not about this.

"You know what the rules are? The rules are: they can push your rent up every year. The rules are: if you're born rich you stay rich, and if you're not you spend your whole life trying to get there by kissing ass and making threats."

I had a sudden, vivid image—as vivid as if I had conjured it from scent accords—of Jonathan Bright in a cashmere jacket, scrawling his signature across the bottom of an invoice without bothering to look at what he owed. He had never in his life worked as hard as I had. I wondered if he had ever wanted anything as much.

"I don't want to be rich," said Giovanni. "I just want to make it work."

"You *can't*," I said. "None of us can, without a little help. A lot of help. And by help, I mean luck and money."

"Killing Pearson isn't going to solve my fucking problems," he said.

"*Nothing* is going to solve your problems."

It fell between us so hard that I worried for the clean white tile. My whole body knew what a mistake I had just made, even if my brain hadn't caught up yet. *I* was the one who had made a bad move and now stood to lose the game.

"Wow, Vic," he said at last. "Thanks for your support."

I tried to say something, and failed.

"I've always respected your work," he went on, deadpan. "It means a lot to hear you believe in me and mine."

"I do believe in you." The blood was rushing back to every part of me numbed by shock and shame, and it hurt. "I just don't believe in *them*. And you shouldn't either."

"Thanks for your concern," he said, and gestured stiffly toward the door. "But I can figure out what's worth my faith just fine."

I took out a ten and slipped it underneath his roll of cutthroat razors.

"Vic," he said, voice dangerous, but I didn't take it back.

"I know you need it."

"More than you?"

"Maybe not," I said. "But service does for service."

The bell on the door rang as I exited his doomed little shop: a jaunty contrast to the brittle silence I left behind.

After that I wanted to get very drunk. But I was broke, so I went home.

As the train rattled my teeth on the way uptown, I poked the edges of the wound I had unwittingly torn open in my own psyche.

Where had I lost control of the situation, and why?

I hadn't expected him to fall in line—Jane had told me that he wouldn't. So why had his rejection thrown me so wildly off my game?

He was the one who was supposed to slip, not me. And yet here I was, covered in metaphorical mud.

It was his confidence—his stubborn, stupid belief that if he worked hard enough and long enough and kept renewing that lease, something would eventually fall into place. If he just tugged on his bootstraps hard enough.

He could keep tugging them until they snapped, but he wasn't going to get anywhere. Not in this city. Not today.

How could he possibly cling to those ideas? Hadn't he looked around? If you want to pursue a passion, you need to do what Jonathan did and make a pile of money first.

Of *course* none of Jonathan's fortune was made in perfume—apologies if I've given that impression. In fact it was almost the opposite. In lean months he personally bolstered the budget. Then, I had privately mocked him for it: his vaunted genius couldn't even pay the bills. He was no true artist but merely a wealthy dilettante. Older and wiser now, I understood that most artists throughout history had been backed by some form of unearned wealth—their own or others'—or come to the craft only after earning more than enough elsewhere.

I've never been exactly clear on where his money *did* come from. I don't think it was his family (about whom he never spoke). He didn't seem like a quant, or a techie. I wondered vaguely at the time if it had to do with subprime mortgages. Now I imagine it was the windfall of an IPO. I suspect the stock market was involved in some capacity.

So perhaps he *had* worked for his money, but not in any way I understood. Not in a way most people would. He was one of those lucky few who leave the fast-paced world of insert-some-bullshit-here to pursue their true passion. As though leaving behind all that money they could have made is a noble sacrifice, ignoring all the money they already have, which makes the passion possible at all. Meanwhile their IRAs and nest eggs earn interest that will keep them in rare Scotch and bespoke shoes until the ends of their long and healthy lives. Or until somebody kills them.

No one in my family had ever grasped what it took to earn money from the air like that. And certainly no one in high school or college had taken the time to explain it. Or if they had, I was undoubtedly reading underneath the table or skipping class to pursue more interesting—carnal, violent, or psychotropic—avenues. And still earning straight As, which tells you all you need to know about American education.

They don't exactly elucidate matters of finance in most perfumery certificate courses either. Those were about *art*, and art, I have found, needs the emulsifier of bitter experience before it mixes at all with business.

A pity I never learned any of it from Jonathan.

Yes, I did say that earlier. Perhaps you're sensing some lingering regret on my part. Well, of course. For the impetuousness, the arrogance of youth. I could have been doing better if I had submitted to a mentor's hand—if you can call Jonathan that—but I was still making it work, albeit in an unorthodox fashion. I was emulsified, or mostly.

But when the train dropped me off at 145th, after a long and dark delay somewhere under Harlem, I was feeling distinctly shaken and not particularly balanced.

It wasn't anything Giovanni had said, so much. It was simply his conviction. I almost envied him his faith, the strength of his belief that hard work would see him through the other side. That all he needed was virtue and commitment and good customer service and his little shop would make it, even thrive.

Almost.

Instead, it made me angry. And when I'm angry, as I said: I can be very cold indeed. I wanted him to understand how it really was. You couldn't take the stairs to the top. It was the elevator or try elsewhere. I wanted to prove to him he was being a fool. That he controlled nothing. Certainly not his own destiny.

I wanted to punish him, and show him he was wrong. For his own good, and for mine.

15

Notes de Tête: Metal, Cold Glass, Aldehydes
Notes de Cœur: Ink and Ammonia
Notes de Fond: Mildew, Paper, Snow

Eisner, of course, had been leaving me increasingly piqued messages in the last several weeks, which I had been ignoring. I hadn't had anything to report. At least, nothing I wanted him to know. Now, though, I could call him back with some good news. And ask a little favor.

"Hello, Mr. Eisner. It's Vic Fowler at Bright House. I wanted to let you know that our first shipment has gone out to Clairfield & Amos, and we're very excited to see how we do across the pond." God. "Also, if you have a free spot in your schedule, there are just a few things I'd like to discuss with you. Call me back, at your convenience of course."

I didn't expect "at his convenience" to be so quickly, but I suppose he was excited. He wanted to do lunch, but I needed to get into that conference room, with him, in order to put my newly formed method to work. We settled on his office, after six. Not that we'd have privacy just by virtue of being outside business hours—at Eisner, Pearson, Yates & Yates I felt quite certain even the data-entry drudges stayed well past their dinnertimes.

I was surprised at the quiet on the forty-second floor. Then again, it was mostly executive suites. Not a cubicle in sight. Where the offices weren't dark, the doors were closed. Behind frosted glass, the occasional silhouette stirred, but the secretary's desk was empty. A modernist fountain trickled in one corner, and despite expensive air freshener the space smelled slightly of its chlorinated damp.

Eisner stood in his doorway, leaning on the frame, frowning at his cell phone. When the elevator slid shut, he looked up. "Vic, right on time. Please, come in."

The view over Midtown gave me vertigo. Far below, traffic pulsed on Park Avenue. I could see Grand Central to the south, steeped in winter darkness, its edges picked out in halogen glare. A bank of clouds was gathering momentum over Jersey, growing pendulous with unshed snow. The only illumination was Eisner's desk lamp, which reflected in spangles across the floor-to-ceiling panes of glass. We were shadows in between the lights: our faces indistinct, our edges limned in gold.

"I won't keep you long," I said. "I hear the weather is supposed to take a turn."

He waved me off. "I'll be here late anyway. I have a call with Beijing at nine."

Naturally.

He touched a pile of paper on his desk, as though referring to it, but the movement was too studied, too obviously mime. "I assume all of this means you've made some headway?"

"I have. I've been doing a lot of experimenting, and I think I know how to make what you want. Now I just need to figure out what it smells like."

"I'm glad to hear it. Have a seat." He motioned to a well-concealed cabinet below a wall of mirrors and marble countertop. "There's some sparkling water in the fridge, I think, if you're thirsty."

Given our last interaction, his good manners were infuriating. But I suppose I was one step closer to giving him what he wanted, and merited better treatment because of it.

"No, thank you," I said. "If you don't mind, I'll just jump into it." Because *I* had to get back to Harlem, and it was a long walk to the D from here. Longer in the snow.

"Be my guest," said Eisner.

"May I see the conference room?" I asked. "Where the meeting took place." What I really meant was, May I smell it?

"Of course." He took a key card from his desk drawer. "Come with me."

On our way toward a set of steel-and-glass stairs, we were intercepted by the opening of another office door—the one where I had seen a light and a silhouette. Eisner stopped and I stopped behind him.

"Connie," he said. "Headed home?"

I recognized Conrad Yates without needing to smell him as I had Reg. This was partly due to Eisner's use of his name and partly due to the stiffness that climbed up Eisner's spine like mercury rising in a thermometer. Also because *he* clearly recognized *me*.

The elder Yates was a sagging version of his son. Gravity had gotten to him, pulled Reg's features down like melting wax. Conrad's lantern jaw had jowls hanging off of it. Where Reg had inherited his mother's florid cheeks, her ruddy complexion, Conrad was pale and faintly jaundiced. This unfortunate coloring strengthened his resemblance to a guttering tallow candle.

His eyes were buried deep in the soft flesh of his face, but they lit on me with immediate recognition, mixed with terror and with glee.

"You know Vic Fowler," Eisner said.

We shook hands. Yates nodded, grinned.

"Oh yes," he said. "And may I say again what a great pleasure it was to work with you. Thanks so much for the introduction, Joe."

Eisner's smile was more like a wince.

"The pleasure was all mine," I said. Conrad's palms were grainy and damp with sweat. I stretched my hand wide, hoping to air-dry it. "Please, call me up if there's anything I can do for you in the future."

Once the elevator doors slid shut behind the interloping Yates, Eisner let loose one quiet, potent curse. I loved to see him made so uncomfortable.

"Let's deal with him first," I said. "Shall we?"

◆　◆　◆

The forty-third floor was full of more frosted glass. Meeting rooms, up here, from small to large to truly massive. Eisner unlocked the last, at the end of the hall, and it felt like we were falling into the East River.

I closed my eyes against the dizzying view and took a deep breath. For work, yes, but also to steady myself against that long drop to the water.

The scent of expensive air freshener was weaker up here, but still present: a sort of aldehyde sparkle in the air, like seltzer. Under that, faint traces of toner and white printer paper. The plastic and burnt dust of a projector. As I sifted through the scents, I heard the heat kick on.

"What time of year was this?" I asked. "The meeting you want me to make."

"Autumn," he said, "but early. Mid-September, maybe. I didn't find out about it until later."

"Was the air-conditioning still on? Would it have been hot in here, or cold?" I needed to know, but I wanted him to imagine it.

"Cold, I think. They generally leave the AC on until October."

I added the tang of freon to my conference-room accord. "If you had been here," I said, "where would you have sat?"

He pointed.

"Go sit there, please." Let him think it was for airflow, for distribution of molecules, whatever. For my part, I was playing on instinct, remembering how Pearson had closed his eyes to visualize his fantasy. How the flush had crept past his collar as he sank deeper into his imagined revenge. How to put Eisner in such a state, without arousing his suspicion?

"Can you tell me what's missing?" I asked. "Besides the other three. I have the smells of the conference room, but . . . catering? Coffee? As vividly as you can imagine, please."

"Coffee, yes, but it would have been after lunch. Though Connie would probably be eating—egg salad, from that place around the corner. Foul stuff. He loves it—sends his secretary out for it every day."

Sulfur, mayonnaise, relish. I would have to go smell the egg salad at the place around the corner. "What else?"

"Reg and Pearson both take long lunches. Reg would have come back smelling like whiskey, maybe sex. And Pearson like cigars. Nauseating. It always makes the conference room feel too small."

"Does it drag on?"

"God yes," he said, leaning back in his chair. "We never talk about what we mean to, not until the last five minutes of a meeting. And then it's either decided immediately—in which case why even meet?—or it takes another hour."

"So they talk around things."

"Interminably." He looked down from the ceiling panels to my face, and my belly went cold for a moment, wondering if he knew what I was doing. "It's an old boys' club; everything has to be *friendly*. The whole thing gives me hives. I wasn't born to it like they were, and they know. They can *smell* it, if you will."

"Hence this meeting while you were away."

"They've been trying to get rid of me for years. I know what they talk about when I'm not around."

Well, that was half my job done for me. He already had all their insults cataloged. All he needed to conjure now was the business end of this imagined meeting.

"What would they do without you?" I asked, hitching my hip onto the corner of the spotless glass conference table. Far below, a siren wailed. "I mean, if they were going to get rid of you, what would they do with the company?"

"Something stupid, no doubt." He steepled his fingers and stared over them, beyond me, into the middle distance, where his fantasy was forming. A shiver climbed from my coccyx to the base of my skull. Despite the valiant efforts of the HVAC system, the glass walls and howling storm wind had taken the temperature down several degrees since we'd entered the room.

"Vic," he said. "Can I trust you, absolutely?"

"I should hope so." If he didn't, we were going to have a problem. I, on the other hand, didn't trust him even as far as I could throw him. I have decent upper-body strength for my size—a necessity in my line of work, rather than an aesthetic cultivated in the gym. You'll see why later. Or perhaps you can already imagine.

"My associates," he said, "are not the most scrupulous of men."

Neither was he, but I let that lie. "So I gathered from our previous conversation. Would you like to elaborate?"

"Is it really necessary?" he asked, looking sour and embarrassed.

"It might be," I said. "I've never done something like this before. I'd just like to understand all the details."

He sighed and settled more deeply into the chair—exactly as if preparing for another hour of an insufferable meeting that had already dragged on too long. Perfect.

"If my information is correct, the meeting from which they excluded me was an off-the-record discussion of a tax-fraud scheme—money laundering, to put it plainly—for a collective of questionable investors. There are elegant ways to do these things, you understand. Even semilegal ones, with better profit margins. But these ham-fisted morons only want to do things the way they used to do them in the eighties. Reg wasn't even *born* in the eighties."

And yet his retirement portfolio was almost certainly stuffed to the gills. What a depressing thought.

"They probably got a head start on the whole thing while I was out. As if my exit was a foregone conclusion. Once they're gone, I'm going to be stuck untangling the strings. I need to know what they were getting themselves into, in detail."

Unless I got inordinately lucky, the knot I would help him imagine was probably not the one they would leave him with. But if it came to that—in fact, I hoped it would, as there were many intervening steps that must succeed to get me there—I had my own unique solutions. As Jane and Giovanni had already made me aware, someday they would prove necessary; it was only a matter of time.

"Thank you," I said. "This has been very useful."

"When do you expect to have it done?" he asked, standing from the Aeron chair at the head of the table. Its springs and hydraulics were so well maintained it made no sound but a faint hiss: air being pulled into a vacuum as the seat rose.

"I'm not exactly sure," I said, and when he made a sour face I put up a hand to forestall any complaints. "I have a rough timeline—a month or two, depending on how long it takes to source the more . . . unique ingredients."

His sour face morphed to a more impersonal distaste.

"In fact," I added, delicate, "there's a little hitch in my supply line you might be able to help me with. If you put a word in for me, it would shave a few weeks off delivery."

His distaste took on a faint cast of curiosity. Sweeping open the conference room door, he motioned me ahead of him. "Let's go back down to my office and discuss."

"What about Beijing?" I asked.

"Oh," he said, elevating me in his order of priorities. "They'll keep."

I called Jane that night. Called instead of texting, because although Pip Miles had been quiet since his last appearance on Iolanda's threshold, the thought of him had me nervous about what I put into writing.

And perhaps I wanted to hear her voice. Soft and level, with sardonic wit slipping below the surface of sentences that seemed benign. I was imagining the sound of it so vividly that when she answered it caught me off guard.

"Hey," she said. Too late I realized I could have caught her at work, or in the library. But the background was quiet, and she didn't sound harried. Only hoarse with sleep or sex or maybe a cold.

"Jane," I said, "how are you?" I had meant to say "Has Conrad called? Have you spoken to Beau?" But the throaty warmth of her greeting had wrong-footed me.

She laughed: a low and lovely sound. "Exhausted. You?"

"The same. How's school?" Were we making small talk? Catching up?

"A grind," said Jane. "But the semester's almost over. And then I can start picking up double shifts and sock some money away over break."

"Save a few nights in there for fun."

"I don't have energy for fun," she said, but I could hear that she was pleased.

"I'll do all the heavy lifting, if you like."

"Hmph."

Is it cliché to say that I could hear her smiling? I knew she wouldn't let me, but it was polite to offer. And pleasant to imagine, as an occasional treat. But I wouldn't give up that strike of steel against steel for anything less than autonomy, victory, self-definition. All the things I had taken from Jonathan when I lost everything else he could have given me. All I had asked for was equality—a partnership, even if it remained dynamic with hostility. Unstoppable Force and Immovable Object.

And yet, in the end, he had moved. Or *been* moved.

If I could make the kind of perfume Eisner had asked for—not the sham he would get, but the true memory he desired—there were so many memories of moments with Jonathan that I could use. That I would like to have. That might have saved me from at least some of my troubles along the way. Not all, of course, but some. I had learned a lot more from life than he had ever been willing to teach. But it might have been nice to get the lessons from a school with a different style of hard knock.

"More immediately," I said, speaking past a sudden tightness in my chest—a sudden surge of nerves, and nothing more—"has Conrad called yet?"

She paused, which gave me an attack of acid reflux, then said, "Yes."

"And you've spoken to Beau."

"Yes." This one she drew out, and I couldn't tell if she was delaying bad news or prefacing a complication or only being a tease.

I didn't think the latter—not with such high stakes. "How did he take it?"

"See for yourself."

I heard a swift rush of air, the sound of impact, and then Beau's deep and drawn-out "Hello?"

"It's Vic," I said. "I asked her how you were."

"Hey, Fowler. I'm all right." He said my name with the same lazy affability he had used when calling Giovanni "Metzger." I wondered if I should be jealous, or perhaps insulted. But then he added, "You're all right too. Come around for brunch again." He lost none of his laziness, but his affable tone descended into something more like lechery.

"I'll take a look at my calendar," I said. "You've certainly given me a taste for zabaglione." Surely she couldn't have asked him about Conrad. Not if he was talking to me so easily.

But when his laughter rumbled into silence, he switched to a more serious mien. "Jane told me what you're up to."

I made a noncommittal "mm" rather than admit to whatever she had mentioned. Given free rein, who knew what tactics she had employed? My imagination ran half-wild in the moment before he spoke again.

"I didn't think she was serious at first."

"At first?" I asked. An invitation to continue.

"Yeah, no way. I'm *still* not sure." He wasn't. Or rather, he knew she was serious but he wasn't sure he was committed. Brave face, though. Or, brave voice. Adorable.

"Aren't you?" I asked, in the same tone with which I had asked him after brunch if he was lying, then told him he could make it up to me. Tender, wounded by disbelief. Slightly condescending. The kind of tone that says, *I'm disappointed in you. You must be corrected. It will hurt me more than it hurts you, except . . . not really.*

I learned that tone of voice from Jonathan. When he used it on me, I loathed him and myself. Him for his condescension, myself for the stubborn lust it sparked. But I loved to watch him use it on other people and quickly learned it could be useful in a professional capacity as well as a personal one.

They say everything in life is about sex, except sex, which is about power. By the transitive property, that means everything in life is about power. And that power is all about sex.

"Beau," I said, making the shape of his name in my mouth nearly tangible. "You don't trust Jane? You don't believe her?"

"I . . ." I imagined him then, looking up from the sofa, catching her eye as she carried laundry through the hall or fixed a drink or ran a highlighter across her notes. His mouth dry, hanging half-open. He was helpless, all at sea.

"You don't want to disappoint her," I asked, "do you?"

"No."

"Has she ever let you down?"

"No," he said, this time defensive.

"Of course not," I said, backing off. "She knows what she's doing. She really has her shit together."

"Yeah," said Beau. Some wind had gone out of his sails. "I don't deserve her."

No, he didn't. Uncharitable, it had risen from some place in my subconscious. "Don't you?"

"No. But I guess . . . I gotta try."

That was more like it. I was dying to know what she had said to him, but I expected neither of them would ever tell.

"Clear your calendar," he said, and it wasn't flirtation. "I want to talk. All three of us."

"When?" I asked.

We set a date. "Give me back to Jane," I said. And when he didn't: "Please." He would suffer for that later—he knew he would—but he also knew he would enjoy the suffering.

16

Notes de Tête: Tomatoes and Beets
Notes de Cœur: Toasted Cheese
Notes de Fond: Turmeric, Paprika, Sweet Vermouth

I will never actually know how Jane convinced her fiancé to strangle Conrad Yates. I have imagined it a thousand times. I'm sure what really happened was a tense and tragic conversation in which Jane highlighted Beau's alarming medical debt and framed the murders as a chance to pay it off.

But that's so prosaic. They, and this story, deserve much better. And I have imagined it for them a thousand times. Of the many iterations I've come up with, this one is my favorite. An odd gourmand—more savory than sweet.

Jane comes back from my place, maybe the same night I promised Beau would make things up to her. Conrad hasn't called yet, but she knows Beau well enough to press this point even without that advantage.

She has not showered—it is finally snowing, and she doesn't want to go all the way to Brooklyn with wet hair. You already know what she smells like: that delicious summery scent of dry grass under the sun. Salt and suede and something slightly sour. The smell that lingers on your fingers the next morning.

She opens the door to her apartment smelling like that.

Beau is home—*for once*, Jane would say—reading *The Rake* at the kitchen stove, absently stirring some leftovers. For the sake of a stronger image, let's say . . . lamb stew. But a sour lamb stew, with tomato and beets. Something I used to order at a Persian restaurant downtown. Why? Because the fatty, gamey scent of lamb, the sugary-tart vegetable steam, blend pleasantly with Jane's own smell, that's all. I don't know if he ever cooked it. I created this vignette to suit my fancy, and the lamb stew does that, to a T.

He looks up as Jane closes the door, hangs her keys on a hook. Sheds her coat and unwinds her scarf. As she warms up—the radiators have come on, and it is stifling—the scent of her fills the small vestibule inside the door.

"I thought you'd be home later," he says.

"I'm too old for that." She sits at the kitchen table and he puts a bowl of stew in front of her. He has poured it over couscous (starchy sweetness, pungent with olive oil).

He bends down to put his nose into her hair—just as he did that drunken afternoon I first saw them together. But he doesn't say, *You scare the shit out of me*, though perhaps he should. "You smell nice."

"Like sex," says Jane.

"Mm," he says, and kisses her neck. "How's Vic?"

"Fine."

He pouts and sits at a right angle to her, elbows heavy on the table. "That's all I get, is 'fine'? You used to kiss and tell."

"I used to do a lot of things," she says. And she doesn't say it with regret, but with a little malice. A sprinkling of blame.

He doesn't miss it. He looks pained. "Babe—"

She holds up a hand. "Don't say it."

"Don't say what?"

She puts on a credible impression of his pinched midwestern vowels—this isn't hard, as she shares most of them—and his half-smiling open mouth. The way his eyebrows pucker at the center. "Babe, you don't have to go through with this degree if you don't want to. I can find a job. We'll make it work."

He goes to speak again and she stiffens her hand, presses it more vehemently into the air between them. "Don't say that either."

"Sorry?" he asks. It's a request for clarification, not an offering. She still winces.

"Jane." He puts a hand on her knee, and she goes stiff at the touch. "If you won't even let me say sorry . . . what can I do? You're working your ass off. I want to help. Let me help."

All right, yes, this seems a little on the nose. But you've met Beau. He isn't subtle. Give me some leeway.

Any other night, she might have said, "You can't," and stood, gone angrily to bed. But tonight she's been with me and knows there *is* a way that he can help. The very possibility of an end to this stalemate drains some tension from her posture. Beau can feel it, and begins to smile. She reaches up to touch his face, cup her palm around the curve of his jaw. His beard is soft. I know; you can imagine. It smells like beeswax and ambergris.

"Do you really?" she asks him.

"Yes," he says. Already there's an edge of desire in it. I don't think he's noticed, but she has. He thinks he's in earnest. Maybe she does too. As they say where I grew up, where people pinch their vowels like Beau and Jane: bless their pea-pickin' hearts. But the less said about my childhood, the better. Especially right now.

"Really?" she asks, and now she is *that* Jane. Not a different version of herself so much as a self she carries within her. She drops her brusque practicality like a satin negligee. Nothing underneath was ever exactly concealed, only veiled as a nod to convention. Maybe she thinks she leaves this in the bedroom, behind a demure closed door. But we're always naked, underneath our clothes.

"Please," he says, and now—of course—he's on his knees. Too eager.

She sneers at him and sits back in her chair, spreading her thighs. "Prove it."

And he tries.

It isn't really what she means, though. That comes later, on the kitchen floor, when she has her fingers curled against a slick, soft place inside him, and he's helpless.

I know how this feels too. Well, not the helplessness.

She squeezes his most vulnerable parts like a woman testing the ripeness of an apricot. Not hard, but with intent. He whines, high in his throat, says please again. Says sorry. Jane pinches one of his nipples, but it only brings on another apology. She slaps where she pinched. "You said you wanted to help."

"Yes."

"You'd do whatever I asked?"

"Yes."

"Anything?"

"Yes."

"I want to hear you say it."

He can't quite manage words. She flexes her fingers inside him and he cries out, "Yes, I swear to god, I'll do anything, please. Just let me—ah!"

She does.

◆ ◆ ◆

Forgive me that interlude. I know, it doesn't even explain how she brought him around. But extrapolate. You know how people get just after orgasm—sleepy, weepy, apt to think their lives could change. Especially after something like that. The cottony come-down, the after-care. If someone trusts you to push them that far and bring them back, what else will they trust you with? If you tell them they're good, they're sweet, they did just what you wanted . . . I imagine it's intoxicating.

I've never really gone in for that part of the proceedings. The point of the whole exercise for me is the power. But poor Beau lived for it: the aesthetic, the ritual, the performance. He knew just how angry Jane was; perhaps he felt her slipping away. He might have agreed to anything to make it last.

"Business first?" I asked, after I had doffed my coat and sat down at the kitchen table where my vivid fantasy took place. "Or pleasure?"

"Business," said Jane. "Dinner won't be done for a minute anyway."

"Fifteen minutes and thirty-nine seconds," said Beau, checking the kitchen timer. "None of this 'ten minutes at four fifty' shit. I cook 'em low and slow. Which means there's time for a sundowner."

Nothing fancy, this time. Carpano Antica on the rocks. I wondered what he had in the oven. The kitchen smelled like cheese.

"You want soda?" asked Jane, who was drinking her own aperitif without. The reddish-black vermouth slipped around the ice like blood.

"No, thanks." As I lifted my own glass, the vanilla and fruit hit me first. Then the bitterness of orange pith and wormwood caught in the back of my throat. I smiled with the ice against my lips before I drank.

Beau settled, elbows on the table—I'm very good, aren't I? You know just what that looks like now—and held my eyes for about two seconds before he glanced back down and started fidgeting with a stack of mail. Committed, yes, but not a convert to the cause. I could work with that.

"Business," said Jane again.

"Of course." I set my vermouth aside and cleared my throat. "Am I right in assuming you're both new to this sort of thing?"

Jane raised her eyebrows impatiently. "Vic, for real?"

It was warranted. I was being facetious. Better to jump in.

"Right," I said. "Here's what I need from you. No blood, no broken skin. Catch them on an empty stomach if you can. If you can't, don't worry too much."

Beau grimaced. "Do I want to know?"

"You really don't." I had been lucky with Jonathan, who had to be reminded half the time to eat. There had been a few messy incidents in the interim, but by now I had developed a—rather undignified—system for flushing out most of the waste and microorganisms that might cause bloating, bursting, and subsequent contamination. It worked better if the subject's alimentary canal was unobstructed. I already knew Pearson would be a nightmare.

"Strangulation has historically been my method of choice. A garrote is generally best, but not too thin. Clothesline is good, or nylon twine. Thinner than that and you can cut through the skin. If you opt for another method, I'd prefer if you don't use anything they need to ingest, as it can sometimes subtly alter their scent. Though if it induces vomiting it will solve the empty-stomach issue." I looked back and forth between them: Beau wide-eyed, Jane looking grim and practical. "I'm sorry, I thought I'd try to do this more like pulling off a Band-Aid rather than going the delicate route."

"I'm not sure there *is* a delicate route," said Beau. "Jesus, Vic, you've really done this?"

Jane turned to him, incredulous. "What does it sound like?"

"Sorry," he said. "I just never knew a murderer before!" Then, to me: "You seem so . . . normal, I guess."

Jane snorted. "Are you kidding?"

"I don't know if I should be flattered or insulted," I said. "By one or the other of you."

"How about you just keep telling us what we need to do?"

"Of course." I suppose Jane wasn't subtle either. Not when it came down to it. "The most difficult thing, I think, will be moving the bodies to my workshop once the deed is done." I carefully avoided the word "killed," and this went over a little better than the line about vomiting. "Obviously you're going to need to get them alone, but you'll also need an alibi for after they're dead. Something plausible that explains why you were alone with them and how they might have gone missing afterward."

"Easy," said Jane, cold and clear as a martini. "Reg stuck around after his buddies went home. Stayed on 'til close, made a pass. I cut him off and told him to clear out. He was *real* drunk when he left. That's the last I saw of him."

"And if his buddies say you led him on?"

"So what if I did? I gotta make good tips."

"But you never led him on before, not like this."

"I'm fucking desperate, all right?" she snapped at me, and it was real. The cops would be convinced. "I've got Beau's medical bills to pay, and I won't be out of school for another year. If rich assholes are going to hit on me and pay for the privilege, I'm not going to tell them no."

Ice shifted in Beau's glass, though he didn't appear to have picked it up; perhaps he had only tightened his grip on it.

"Fair," I said. "Beau?"

"I'll have to think about it."

"Also fair. But you don't have much time. I can help you if you need it."

"We'll figure something out," said Jane.

"I'm happy to workshop it, once you do." I polished off my vermouth. "After you drop off the bodies, I'll do what I need to and dispose of them. Without the corpses, they'll have a hell of a time proving any connection to either of you."

"Well then why can't *you* do it?" Beau asked.

"I have done," I said. "Many times. Which is why I know this is true. The issue here is not evidence but probable cause. Because of our history, I'm the more obvious suspect. And I doubt I'd stand up to intense scrutiny."

"And we will?"

"If all goes well," I said, "you won't have to."

There was a pregnant pause, loaded with anxiety. And then the timer rang, rattling against the fridge, where it was affixed by a magnet. Beau jumped up but looked momentarily lost until Jane said, "By the sink," and his eyes fixed on a pair of oven mitts. He put them on, but they didn't seem to solve whatever problem had him so distracted.

He pulled a soufflé out of the oven. The top was perfect, crisp and brown and flecked with pepper.

"Fuck," he said. "I was gonna make a salad. It'll fall now."

"Shut up," said Jane. "Just get some spoons."

The soufflé was excellent: colored orange and lent smoky flavor by pimentón, it was bitter and milky with some kind of swiss cheese and crisped on the bottom with parmesan. It smelled like salt and skillet and the musk of lactic fermentation.

I want to take a moment here to step back from discussions of murder and mention Beau's cooking. I know it interrupts narrative flow, but bear with me. It's poignant and important.

I appreciate good food; with senses so finely tuned, how could I not? But the time it takes to shop and chop I have always found better spent elsewhere. And—this is embarrassing—I don't have the patience to perfect it, nor the fortitude it would take to eat my failures. I've more than mastered one sensory skill. Don't begrudge me outsourcing the other four to their respective experts. Aside from perfume storage, my refrigerator at the time was a classic New York wasteland, my diet composed largely of takeout.

Beau, meanwhile, was a jack-of-all-trades when it came to living luxe on a shoestring. An absolute whiz at making something out of, if not nothing, then at least very little. Think back on that brunch I described. Squash and pasta are cheap. Butter a little less so, but you're likely to have it around. Same with eggs. Well-made domestic parmesan is almost as good as something stamped *DOC*. The wine with brunch came free. Jane probably knew where she could get good vermouth cheap, or at least from someone who would cut her a deal when the boss wasn't looking. Still, it wasn't the kind of thing I thought she'd do for herself—Beau injected indulgence into her life, where she would have pressed on in broke asceticism.

But it was luxury conjured up from staples, cheap ingredients, and other people's generosity. The innovation must have taken so much effort. I always wonder if it tired him, this bricolage. How exhausting it must have been: a constant struggle to create the life he craved, MacGyver-like, out of thumbtacks and a twist of string.

Maybe it was much easier to sway him to our scheme than I imagined.

◆　◆　◆

Perhaps it seems like a strange transition, from this conversation to coitus. But think of the way people laugh at funerals, or at the grisliest parts of horror films: a need for release that manifests—often inappropriately—in the face of mortality. Or maybe simply at the abject.

I suppose death *does* drive us to affirm life. But I find the latter set of psychological call-and-response much more interesting. The spike in fascination that accompanies a foul but intriguing smell. The morbid curiosity some people feel for gruesome or scatological acts. The focus of the news cycle on unimaginable sadism. Collectors of medical curiosities. Serial killer podcasts and their fan clubs. I had Beau cracking jokes by the end of the meal, and it wasn't a big jump from humor to hedonism. Jane let him lead—it was interesting to watch how he drew her along, how his surrender gave her permission. I knew she did not *need* it, but she yielded to her own desires very differently when placed in a position of responsibility. I couldn't help but think of how we'd fucked alone. I wanted *that* Jane back again.

Much later, she asked, "What about Giovanni?"

Beau lifted his head from her shoulder. "What about him?"

I sat up, parched by the radiator and the sex and stiff from clinging to the edge of a full bed never meant for three people. "I talked to him."

"And?"

"Shit, is he in on this too?" Beau was up at that, and suddenly the whole thing had a sort of absurd slumber-party air. All we needed was some popcorn.

"There are three men I need dead and only two of you," I said. Four I needed, really, but Eisner was a personal project.

"I kind of figured *you'd* get the third."

Clearly Jane hadn't told him everything. "If I could, I wouldn't need your help. I had hoped Giovanni would pitch in, but——"

"What did I tell you?" asked Jane. She was still lying at her ease down the center of the bed. I noticed scraps of the gold polish on her toenails, remnants of the glossy coat she had applied for that fateful brunch.

God, it was almost Christmas.

Yes, and all my paperwork had cleared. My first shipment to Clairfield & Amos had gone across the Atlantic already, with more to follow soon. I would be stocked in Paris and Milan. Maybe even at that little shop in South Bank where I had smelled my first Bright House and started my career.

Online orders too had been ticking steadily up in the last month. If I had had more time or money for advertising, numbers might have been higher, but as it was, Leila and Barry kept up moderately active social media accounts and updated the website as often as necessary.

Maybe if the holidays went well for us I could give them a bit of a budget for sponsored content. Or even act on the idea of an intern I had briefly toyed with. Toyed with the idea. Not the intern.

"Vic."

"Sorry," I said, putting a hand on her foot. "Just woolgathering."

"Who *says* that?" asked Beau.

Jane smirked. "Not normal people."

"Fine, all right, I'm an idiot." He slouched against the headboard. "Metzger didn't bite? I always knew he was smarter than me. I bet you told him the empty-stomach thing and he backed the fuck out."

"Things didn't proceed to quite that point."

"Does he *know*?" asked Jane. "What you're up to?"

"Hard to say."

"Jesus." She pressed the back of her head into the pillow and looked hard at the ceiling. "Great, so now what?"

"I have the matter in hand," I said. "Don't worry."

Jane cut her eyes at me, full of the same dubiety she had so recently aimed at the crown molding. "Careful. You're starting to sound like him." This with a wave of her hand toward Beau. He retaliated by flicking her nipple. A brief tussle ensued, and for a moment I thought we had passed through this sticky situation and might move on to something more interesting.

But once Jane had subdued Beau, she tossed her hair out of her eyes and asked, "Can you give me a timeline?"

"On Giovanni?"

A curt nod, to which I could only reply in negation: "But I'll be able to soon."

"Are you fucking kidding me?" Jane sat up now too, and if there had been popcorn, she would have thrown it. "You keep being like 'wait, not yet,' and then when you come down here to tell us 'yes, do it now,' you're like 'oh, but the third guy hasn't committed yet.' Fuck you, Vic! If I'm going to do this, it better actually come together for you. It's a lot to put on the fucking line, for you to be like 'it might not actually pan out.'"

"I have a plan," I said. "I'll get him." I tried to touch her, but she slapped my hand away.

"The fuck you will," she said. "I'm not moving on this shit until you tell me he's locked down."

She caught me looking over her shoulder at Beau and moved into my line of sight. "And neither is he."

I took a deep breath and stilled my anger. They needed time to get their strategies together at any rate. I was sure I could land Giovanni, given another week or so. I had set those wheels into motion, and Eisner had promised to work fast. He wasn't as desperate as me, but he was impatient and had the power to solve the problem. Or at least put pressure on the man who could.

"It's being taken care of," I said, as evenly as I could manage.

"Fine." Jane snatched up a blanket and wrapped it around her chest, refusing to meet my eyes. "Let us know when he's on board. But if you don't get him, you don't get us either."

17

Notes de Tête: Cinnamon, Juniper, Gingerbread Spice
Notes de Cœur: Burnt Sugar and Scorched Almonds
Notes de Fond: Fry Oil, Charcoal Smoke

"I need it done by next week," I told Eisner. No preamble. "A lot of my plans are riding on this."

"I'm working as fast as I can." I could hear him typing in the background, though I doubted he was working on this particular project. "Real estate moves fast, once it moves. The ball's just been a little slow to get rolling on this one."

"So shove it harder."

"It's the holidays," he said. "*I* don't care, but it's the time of year when the secretaries start bringing in rum balls and nobody wants to talk business."

"I'm glad you have such a festive company culture," I said, with acidity. True, thanks to pre-Christmas purchasing across the pond, we had actually hit a sales target for the first time in what felt like a thousand years. But beyond that the holidays meant shoppers on the train and street closures for parades and pop-up markets. Both of which I could do without.

"Forgive me for asking," said Eisner. "I wouldn't normally intrude on your creative process but . . . I just don't see what our divesting of this building has to do with perfume."

"Well, Joseph . . ." Alone in my office, I leaned back in the dusty swivel chair. It squeaked. I thought of the perfectly calibrated Aeron in the conference room at EPY&Y. "What you're asking me to do is unprecedented. You should have expected a few surprises along the way. Do you at least have some prospective buyers?"

"A few. It's a great location. The problem is, nobody wants to go up against the city as far as demolition and permitting for new construction."

"So make it worth their while. Lowball the property. You can afford it."

"Vic—"

"If you want what you asked me for, I can't negotiate on this."

"Fine," he said, his composure breaking at last. I could hear it in the word, and in the echo after he slammed down the phone.

I hoped he meant it. I hoped he could do it. I hoped that, once he did it, Giovanni's morals would prove a little more flexible. Because anything will bend, once you break it in half.

It was a shame. Giovanni's shop was in a lovely prewar building. Sculptural keystones, decorative brickwork, deco tile . . . all the works. The stuff they were putting up nowadays, whenever they tore down something old and elegant, wasn't a patch on anything built before nineteen forty-five.

I had asked Eisner if his company could just raze the place, but he said he'd have a hard time pushing that through. Let him frame the property to Pearson as an inconvenience, he said, and he could have it sold to a developer ready with a wrecking ball in just a couple of weeks.

I didn't have quite that kind of time. Or rather, *he* didn't. And if I couldn't meet his deadline, because he couldn't get Pearson to punt this building to some megalomaniacal real-estate tycoon who wanted to build a mirrored excrescence amidst the Federal row houses of the West

Village, because the secretaries were bringing in *rum balls*, it would not be his fault, but mine.

Funny old world, isn't it?

◆　◆　◆

Somehow, incredibly, we sold through what we had in stock at the lab, and two weeks before Christmas I found myself frantically decanting the newest batches of our staples.

Barry knew a woman who ran some kind of artist-collective booth at the Bryant Park holiday market who had been asking for weeks if she could stock our perfumes. We hadn't had spare inventory while everything was going out to Europe, but Barry had been after me to plan for it in the next batch so here I was, a box of samples and full-size bottles on my knees, riding the F up to Forty-Second.

I had asked Barry to do it, and Leila. I had too much on my mind, and anyway, we had just found out the concentrations of musk ketone in one of our exports might trigger a review. But Leila was a dab hand at sweet-talking paper pushers, and Barry was out with a violent stomach flu I strongly suspected was a hangover in disguise.

I fucking hated holiday markets.

Guarding my precious cargo against errant shopping bags and elbows, I struggled to the surface and exited the subway into a soggy wind that hadn't yet decided on rain or snow. Dirty piles of the latter were slopped over the curbs, remnants of last week's plowing. Smoke from candied-nut carts made my nose burn and clung to my soft palate. It wasn't exactly picturesque.

At the edges, the market seemed almost festive. Farther in, it became a mixture of quicksand and mosh pit. All to pick over mass-produced paisley pashmina scarves and eat some quickly cooling frites. Fry oil and fake cinnamon hung over the clouded breath of the crowd in a cloying fug. But I couldn't deny there were a lot of people opening their wallets.

It wouldn't be a bad place to move merchandise. I just had to find the damn booth.

They all looked the same. I had texted Barry and emailed his contact, and I had a meeting time but not a precise location. I supposed the former was too ill and the latter simply assumed I would find her by the light of her unique and beautiful inventory. But everything was technicolor and brightly lit, and the Christmas carols played at maximum volume precluded calling out anyone's name. If I could even remember this woman's name.

In despair, I set my box on a miraculously empty table—only after checking that it didn't wobble—and pulled out my phone. My service was essentially nonexistent. With growing irritation, I attempted to refresh my inbox over and over again, wincing as the shrieks of ice-skating children sheared through the stinking miasma of smoke and mist.

Everything finally updated, and I had at least the woman's name, if not a good idea of where to look for her. I stowed the phone and picked the box back up, and then promptly almost dropped it when I looked up and saw Pippin Miles not ten feet away, staring straight at me.

Our eyes met. His mouth popped open. He looked like one of those ugly bearded fish you see wallowing in the mud on nature documentaries. I kept my jaw resolutely clenched and managed to smile at him. Even gave him a little finger wave around the corner of my box.

Of course, he started walking toward me.

"Mr. Miles," I said. "What a surprise." For me. Because for this to be coincidence seemed like too much. How long had he been tailing me?

"Of all the gin joints in all the world," he said, offering one red and ungloved hand. "Merry Christmas."

I had to put the box down again. He put his other hand over my knuckles in one of those shakes that feels condescending and a little too intimate. I was grateful again for my gloves.

"What brings you to this . . ." I wanted to say "mess" and couldn't find a suitable substitution that encompassed all the awfulness of the market.

Miles apparently thought I had trailed off rather than stumbled. "My grandson wanted to go ice-skating," he said. "And I have some last-minute shopping to do." If it was a cover story, it came out with admirable ease. Of course it did. He was a professional. "How about you? What's in the box?"

"Merchandise," I said. "I'm here to sell rather than to buy. I just got a bit turned around looking for the person I'm supposed to meet. I can't find her booth."

"I've been around this place a million times in the last two hours. What's she sell?"

"Oh, things by local artists. I don't really know. She gave me a booth number, but hell if I can figure out what it means."

"What's the number?" asked Miles. "Come on. You help me, I'll help you."

I froze at that. "I'm afraid I'm awful at shopping for other people, Mr. Miles."

He waved a hand. "No, no. Listen, I'm still on the Yates case, and I'm not making much headway. My buddy Jeff—retired NYPD detective, but he's still got a couple of friends on the force—I was talking about it with him, just over a couple of beers, and he said, 'What about that perfume kid, Fowler? You checked up on that lead again?'"

Everything after "NYPD" was diverted to a small white room in my brain, soundproofed against the klaxons that had started ringing insistently everywhere else. As within all soundproofed spaces, I could hear the words perfectly well, but something about them was dampened and they did not quite register as speech.

"I've been trying to get in touch with you," he said, "but you're hard to track down. You trying to avoid me? Don't worry, I'm used to it."

"I'm sorry," I said. My own voice fell as flat on my ears as his had. The police had my *name*. "But the holidays have me absolutely swamped. You know how retail gets. It's really the worst timing."

"Sure, sure. Of course. No problem." He put his hand on my shoulder, gave it a gentle pat, and started to steer me away from the table where I'd put down my box. I'm ashamed to say I let him. At least I had the presence of mind to snatch my samples and my merchandise back up. Glass rattled inside, and I could faintly smell a little juniper, a little spice. If you *had* to smell seasonal, it was better than fake cinnamon and fry oil.

"Come on," said Miles, pushing me back into the press of manic wassailers. "Let's go find your arts and crafts lady. We don't have to talk shop today, but maybe give me a call when business slows down? Start the new year right. Maybe we can get some pork and sauerkraut."

I smiled and smiled and held my tongue. I hate the smell of sauerkraut.

◆ ◆ ◆

According to Barry, things went well at the holiday market. I had no time to keep tabs on it, as most of my days were spent on the phone with the lab that had tested our musk ketone, trying to figure out if we should pull it from European shelves.

My nights were spent losing sleep over Pippin Miles. Maybe he hadn't been following me. But maybe he had. And if he had, was it because I was a suspect? Or a valuable source? Why had his friend Jeff told him to follow up with me? Standard procedure? A hunch? Why had Miles mentioned him? He wasn't on the force. *But he still had friends.* That was calculated, surely. It must be a threat.

I tried to soothe myself: old men, gossiping. One friend to another, advice to tie up loose ends. I was winding myself up over an offhand remark.

Unless I wasn't.

All of this, and Jane hadn't texted. Beau had, once, but only to send me an article about a perfumer who had spent years of his life perfecting the smell of one woman's genitalia. No other context except a string of emojis all followed by question marks. The tulip, the kiss, the conch, the taco.

I answered with a kiwi, a honey pot, a racehorse, a bursting champagne bottle, and a mug of beer. Less visually evocative, but then, where do my strengths lie?

He sent me back an emoji of a dark-haired woman with pale skin, and a question mark, which could have meant, Was I describing Jane? Or could have meant, Would I make something that smelled like her?

I didn't answer, though I felt bad about it. I suspected he was texting me without her knowledge. Maybe he felt guilty about Jane's ultimatum. I didn't have the mental fortitude to navigate those waters just now—too many other, nastier squalls to sail through.

I got some good news on Friday—musk ketone didn't have to be listed as an ingredient on our labeling at all. Relief made my spine go limp. When my head fell back against the office chair, I could feel crumbs of yellow foam padding come loose against the nape of my neck.

First order of business, once the balance of Eisner's commission came in: replace the office furniture. Hell, upgrade to a nicer lab. Sales in Europe wouldn't stay so high after the holidays, but we were doing well enough I thought the new year might bring some pleasant surprises.

Still in debt to my eyeballs, of course, so maybe before we moved to Midtown—god forbid—I should use Eisner's money to pay that down. Then, new office. Or at least new chairs.

I was still in the midst of my daydreams when my cell phone buzzed in my folio. I almost didn't answer it, so delirious with potential was I, but then I remembered I was waiting on news from Eisner that could pull the plug on all my upwardly mobile dreams.

I caught the call just before it went to voice mail.

"Mr. Eisner," I said, because familiarity hadn't won me much the last time we spoke. "I hope you have something nice to tell me. I'm in a good mood and I don't want cold water poured on it."

"Lucky you," said Eisner. "Crack the champagne."

That got me sitting straight. "You sold it?"

"*Pearson* sold it, yes, after some relentless prodding. Not finalized yet, but that's just a matter of inspections and paperwork. The important thing is, he's got a buyer. He's suspicious, though, so I hope you work fast."

"Suspicious how?"

"Not of you. He just knows I'm up to something. But they *always* think I'm up to something, even when I'm not." It came out bitter, before a long pause. So long I wondered if he had set his phone down. Just before I asked if he was still on the line, he added brightly, "How nice it will be when none of them are breathing down my neck anymore."

How nice for me too, when he stopped breathing down mine. "When will they notify the tenants?"

"When the sale is final. Not before the new year, I don't think."

Damn. "Can you spread some rumors for me?"

"I could send an email or two, I suppose. *If* you'll tell me why."

"Certainly not. Bcc me, though. And enjoy your rum balls, Mr. Eisner." I hung up and clutched my phone, staring in delight and disbelief at my vague reflection in its dark screen. The penultimate piece of this puzzle was in place. And I had the last one in my hands, ready to complete the picture.

18

Notes de Tête: Wet Dirt, Melting Snow
Notes de Cœur: Pine Sap
Notes de Fond: Grilled Meat and Diesel

I texted Giovanni on the night before Christmas Eve. Just after official business hours, which meant the shop was still open and he was working for a little while yet. And which also meant, if he wanted to call some-body—the landlord, the management company, another tenant—he would have little recourse and no chance to make a fuss. Except with me.

We need to talk, I said. I'll be there at eight.

I whistled while I cleaned up the lab. Barry watched me from the sides of his eyes, expression increasingly dubious. Upstairs, Leila yelled, "Barry, you're driving me *nuts*; quit *whistling*!"

He didn't correct her. Just gave me a silent look that read *what the fuck*, as if the words had been written across his face.

"Happy holidays," I said. "Lock up when you go home."

"Where are you going?" he asked. "You got a date or something?"

"Just going to see a friend."

"That friend you were messaging on the company IG? If me or Leila pulled that shit you'd be all over us."

"I'm the boss," I said.

"Right." He shook his head. "Okay, head-bitch-in-charge, do we get tomorrow off?"

"If I'm in a good mood."

"When will you know if you're in a good mood? If I'm gonna go out tonight, I need to find somebody to pay for my drinks, you know? I need a little lead time to work things out."

I looked at the clock hung over the Metro shelves, which ran ten minutes slow. "Mm, eight fifteen?"

"I'm gonna text you and ask," he said.

I swung my scarf around my neck with a flourish. "Be my guest."

"Will you answer?"

I patted his cheek on my way out the door. "I promise nothing."

The temperature outside had jumped up to a disconcerting mid-fifties, melting the snow further and bringing out a hint of piss smell from the alleys. At West Fourth, halal cart generators belched out diesel fumes and traffic kicked up oily water from the gutters. Sweaty boys in unseasonal shirtsleeves screamed obscenities on the basketball courts. At the corner, waiting for the light to change, I closed my eyes and took a deep breath. It smelled like spring.

Then a bicycle deliveryman sped by blasting Darlene Love's "Christmas" on a Bluetooth speaker, and I was rudely reminded of the holiday season.

Giovanni had strung fairy lights along the inside edges of his windows and hung a wreath on the door. A tasteful wreath of real pine, still fresh enough its resinous odor hung in the vestibule. The bell rang when I entered, and the scent of sap gave it the air of a sleigh decoration.

"Hi," said the girl at the counter, eyes smudgy with last night's liner. "Can I help you?"

"I'm here for Giovanni," I said. Over her shoulder, he was already watching me. His hands had paused on the head of his client, who clearly didn't know him well enough to feel alarmed. The other barbers had all gone home; he was the last man standing.

"Sorry," she said, checking her schedule. "We're about to close up. I can schedule you for the twenty-sixth, though."

"No thanks," I said. "We just need to talk."

She opened her mouth to say something, though it didn't look like she knew what.

"Babs," said Giovanni. "It's all right. This is my last." He didn't say anything to me.

He didn't rush the rest of his cut. If anything, he took more time than he might have, clipping carefully around the man's ears. I poured myself a glass of water from the carafe on the end table and sat down with an issue of *Harper's Bazaar*, flipping idly through glossy advertisements for bad perfumes that sold ten times better than mine.

When Giovanni finished up, he shook the client's hand and sent him on his way. Babs took his credit card while Giovanni swept, and then she too was ushered out, with a kiss on the cheek and a "Merry Christmas." Too close to the date proper for a noncommittal "happy holidays."

She looked over her shoulder as she went, her Louise Brooks eyebrows puckered with worry. I smiled at her, but it only spooked her further. Giovanni locked the door after she left.

He went to his station, put a hand on the counter, considered his razors. His clippers. His own reflection. Still without looking up at me, he fell into the chair.

Leather creaked. He let his head fall back against the neck rest, and his eyes were closed. Beneath the neatly shaved skin of his vulnerable throat, his Adam's apple moved in a hard swallow. I almost spoke. And then, he began to cry.

No heaving sobs. No single tear. It was silent weeping, incredibly contained. Like everything else about him, his tears were neat and tidy, colored completely inside the lines. They spread in shining threads along his crow's-feet, eventually dampening the close-clipped sideburns that bracketed his ears. The only sounds he made were sharp inhalations, released in staccato beats that felt like counted measures.

It was very efficient grief.

Eventually he reached some bargain with himself, took a deep breath, and squeezed the heels of his hands into the hollows beneath his brows. He sniffed, took a handkerchief from the pocket of his white coat, and touched it to his nose.

"You said we needed to talk," he said.

I set aside *Bazaar*. "I did."

"So talk."

◆ ◆ ◆

"They're going to sell," I said. "This building."

He nodded. I hadn't surprised him. The tears told me as much.

"I heard they're going to make it a food hall or some shit," he said. "Like Chelsea Market. Little shops, and coworking. Offices on top."

This was what I had inferred from Eisner's emails. It made sense. This was a historic district, but if they kept the exterior, I had no doubt they could completely reconfigure the inside. Midcentury lamps, velvet sofas, the smells of crisp venture capital and desperation. Believe me, it *does* have a smell. If I had distilled the sweat that regularly gathered under my arms during this period of my life, I would have an excellent example for you now.

In with the cold-pressed juice and kombucha on tap, out with the cornstarch and Proraso. Out with Giovanni and his humble three chairs. Unless . . .

"Little shops like yours?" I asked.

He lifted his head, looked at me like I was hopeless. "Of course not. They'll replace me with fucking Fellow Barber or something."

"Ah, but you're better than Fellow Barber. Why shouldn't they keep you?"

"Exactly," he spat. "That's *exactly* why they won't keep me. I'm not a goddamned *brand*. I'm not the Blue Bottle Coffee of barbers, so nobody gives a shit."

"I do," I said.

"Yeah," he said, "and I'm sure you can stop this right in its fucking tracks."

I smiled. "Maybe."

The pause that followed had a curious dynamic quality. It began as one thing: hope, surprise, disbelief. But I felt the moment it became something else. The moment Giovanni realized the gist of what I'd done.

"You piece of shit." He radiated a taut and quivering put-together-ness, and I was afraid to approach lest it shock me or snap. Instead I put my back to the wall behind his chair and watched us both in the mirror.

He was small, hunched, white coat rumpled and eyes red. Over his shoulder, reflected against a backdrop of bright white tile, I was a silhouette. A cutout. My wardrobe of all black, my dark hair, made me look like a hole punched through the pristine wall into the vacuum of space. Cold and hungry. Irresistible.

"Maybe I can stop it," I repeated. "More likely, I can simply ensure your continuity. And who knows? Maybe the advent of your success."

"What did you do?" he asked.

"Nothing that couldn't be undone," I said. "Or mitigated. But service does for service, Giovanni. You told me that yourself."

"What the fuck can I give you?" Then, backpedaling: "Vic, *how*? Why me?"

"You remember Eisner," I said. "His firm owns this building. And he had me over a barrel."

"So what, you switched?"

"I've been known to." My levity landed on an unappreciative audience. "Not quite. But it was in our mutual interest to . . . *motivate* you."

"Motivate me to *what*?"

I waited to see if he would work it out. But he was stubborn, and believed in people. Or in something. "I wasn't joking," I told him, by way of a hint. "Though we won't actually turn him into a rug."

A beat, and then it landed. "No," he said, the shake of his head like an echo. But he couldn't look away from the reflection of my face.

Our brains interact curiously with mirrors—put one straight down the center of your body and you can feel the flex of your reflected hand even if you haven't moved the hidden half. Maybe he felt safer looking in the mirror than at me. But it meant exactly the same thing.

"I knew it," he said, contradicting himself. He sounded shocked, disgusted, as though he had only just discovered some truth that had lain hidden inside him like a teratoma, or a bezoar.

"But you didn't want to believe it." I thought of Beau. *You've really done this? You seem so . . . normal.* "Why didn't you call the cops, then? If you thought I was serious."

"I *like* you," said Giovanni. A surprise to me, just like hearing him call me "friend," and running into him at Katie's pop-up. Did *I* like *him*? There's that word again. I appreciated what he did and how he looked. I admired the care he took with things. Our business arrangements furthered my interests. I needed what he could offer me. What other metrics were there? What was I to him?

"I thought you were up to something, sure, and I just wouldn't get involved. But murder . . ." He collapsed against the back of the chair again and swore. Then, despondently: "What do you want him for, anyway?"

"I'm going to turn him into perfume."

"Jesus fucking Christ." What little blood was left in his cheeks drained fast.

"A special kind of perfume. One that only I can make. Eisner hired me to do it."

"The one who's blackmailing you."

"Yes. I wasn't lying about prison. If I don't succeed, he'll turn me in."

"Will you? Succeed?"

"Yes."

Silence for a moment. "Why can't you do it yourself?"

"Circumstances have conspired against me." I would keep Pip Miles to myself for now.

"Great, so you redirected them my way?"

"Circumstances have been conspiring against *you* for a while," I said. "If anything, you should view this as an opportunity. I'm sure the marketing budget for this new development will put your shop on the map."

"Fuck you," he said, and not the friendly version. This had real venom in it. Then, defeated: "Is it just this guy? Pearson?"

"And the Yateses."

He shook his head. "I can't—"

"Oh no. Don't worry. They're taken care of."

His eyes widened, then narrowed, then closed altogether. "Beau and Jane." For a moment I thought he would start weeping again. But he breathed in and looked up.

I nodded. He shook his head. Outside, a drunk girl laughed.

"You've been planning this," he said. "Since brunch, you've been planning this."

"Since a while," I said. "But it isn't as though I have any choice."

Glaring into the silvered glass, he said, "And how am I supposed to get at him? Break into his house? Follow him down a dark alley?"

"Don't worry. He'll come to you."

"Right," he said. "Because you've already handled all of it, except the dirty work." He closed his eyes and gave me a brief respite. "God, it isn't fair."

Hadn't I said those very words to him weeks ago? And I had hated myself for saying something so obvious, so pathetic. Of course it wasn't fair.

But when he said it, he sounded truly betrayed. Like the bottom had gone out of something he believed.

"No," I said. "It isn't."

19

Notes de Tête: Gin and Peppermint
Notes de Cœur: Coconut, Coffee
Notes de Fond: Mildew and Concrete

I did give Barry and Leila Christmas Eve. At that late date, anything that needed to be shipped would never make it to the buyer in time for the big day. Not if you weren't Amazon. I resigned myself to a few angry emails, which I didn't mind answering. Maybe I'd send a couple of conciliatory sample packs. Or not.

After a festive breakfast of cornflakes and bad coffee, I marshaled my wits and called Jane. She had not been happy with me when I left her house. I doubted she was happy with me now, having been left in uncertainty for more than a week. Had she been hoping to get out of it? Surely not. She needed the money as badly as I did, and hated Reg even more than I hated Eisner.

Still, it was a long time to wait in suspense.

The call went to voice mail, which probably meant she was busy—though the semester was over and the bar wasn't open yet. Studying? Or she had seen the number and thumbed the ringer off. Maybe she just had her phone on Do Not Disturb and was taking the rare opportunity to sleep in.

I called back. Voice mail again. If it was on Do Not Disturb and I called a third time, her phone would let me through. I bit the inside of my cheek, put my dirty bowl in the sink, and wished for a slug of Scotch to add to my burnt coffee.

Everything was closed, or would be closing soon. I had bread and eggs and milk and could survive the next two days, but I was already chafing with boredom. And now there was no distraction as I waited for Jane's call, if it would even come.

I could tinker, I supposed. Not on Eisner's scent directly—I had none of the ingredients. Though I had already proved that what needed to be done could be, Eisner's original idea still held some temptation. Jane had solved the problem of my commission. She had not solved the challenge it initially presented. With time on my hands now, I could pick up that thread and begin to untangle it. If it could be untangled. But where would I even begin?

Lost in thought, I came to staring at the clump of damp cornflakes in the drain when my phone went off.

"Jane," I said, breathless, without bothering to check the number.

"And what am I?" asked Beau. "Chopped liver? I just heard her phone go off twice and checked it, saw your number. Who calls twice in a row? Slow your roll."

"It's important."

"She's in the shower. But you can chat with me until she's out. Did you see that article I sent you? Crazy, right?"

Was he yanking my chain, happy to chat, or covering for nerves? I honestly couldn't tell, and wondered if his expression kept pace. If so, he'd be a terror at the poker table.

"What do your next couple of days look like?" I asked.

"Pretty chill. I'm going to run a sample sale on the second, I think. Like, kick off the new year with new looks, you know? But until then, not a lot going on. Why?"

There was the first inflection of doubt, the first wavering in the smooth surface of his calm.

"Because I have a lot to do before I come check out your sample sale," I said. "And I'm going to need your help with it."

"Right," he said. Then, after a steadying breath: "Right. Yeah."

"How soon can you bring in Conrad Yates?"

"Jesus," he said. "Not today. Not tomorrow either. Maybe like . . . *maybe* the twenty-sixth? Like, *late*, though. It will depend."

"On what?"

"His schedule. My charm. Fucking Mercury in retrograde. I don't *know*." His tone got sharp. Then: "Sorry. I really don't know. I can find out, though."

"Do that," I said. "Please."

We sat in awkward silence for a moment before he said, with palpable relief, "Oh, here's Jane."

"Thanks." And like a chump I added, "Merry Christmas."

"You too," he replied. He sounded like he meant it. Muffled, I heard him say my name, and the bumps and static of the cell phone changing hands.

"What?" asked Jane, and even scent-blind I could still picture her: wet hair wrapped in a towel, wearing Beau's flannel robe. The way it gapped at the chest. I filled in blanks: coconut lotion, peppermint soap. Beau frying eggs and flipping toast in a cast-iron skillet.

Maybe these were little lies I told myself, but I could see and smell it all so clearly. If I shut my eyes I could nearly put myself in that scene instead of in my chilly studio, which only smelled like mold.

I imagined a perfume that would preserve this imagined moment. But that would mean sacrificing Jane and Beau. Unlike my oboist, whose appeal had been somewhat limited in scope, I preferred these two living and breathing and making more moments like this one.

"Hi," I said. "I—"

"Is Giovanni in?" she asked, and I realized she had moved to cut off an apology I had not known I was about to offer.

"Yes." The last cold dregs of my coffee tasted like penance, and I hoped the caffeine would sharpen my edges a little. She didn't want to hear me say I was sorry. She wanted me on my game. So I would be. "Yes, he is."

"Okay," she said. "Fine. Then we are too."

◆ ◆ ◆

If you ever have to kill someone, I recommend the six days between Christmas and the New Year. Quite seriously. No one is following up on business deals or faults you for not answering your phone. Half the nine-to-five workforce is on vacation. The service industry is so slammed that none of the waiters or delivery guys or baristas have half a moment to spare worrying over a regular who hasn't come in. Or things are so slow, it isn't a surprise if they don't see a familiar face.

Perhaps the object of your designs promised to come to a New Year's Eve outing. Or two. But once the champagne pops and people start kissing, who will remember the no-shows?

In short, it will take at least a week for anyone to realize your victim has gone missing, and longer still for any authorities to take notice. Think of the backlog that must build over the holidays. Think of the gray, miserable game of catch-up the homicide detectives and the missing persons squad must start to play on January second.

It gives you a lot of room to maneuver.

Not that I was doing a lot of maneuvering. I felt like a field general must, anxiously awaiting each movement of my troops: wary of the outcomes, hoping for victory but bracing for defeat.

It felt strange. Almost as if I had delegated a part of my creative process. I know I said I didn't enjoy the killing, but it was certainly an unavoidable part of making these perfumes. I had never outsourced it before.

I tried not to nag. I didn't want to distract my deputies. Besides, the less we all knew about what the others were doing at any given time, the better. Especially for me, who had the most to lose.

So I spent my Christmas Eve rereading *The Diary of a Nose* and *The Debt to Pleasure*, and my Christmas Day drinking the bottle of passable gin I had bought for Jane. In between books and bad cocktails, I started to arrange my workspace. Iolanda had gone to spend the holidays with family in Santo Domingo, which gave me an extra measure of safety. It had been some time since I'd received a special commission, and everything needed scrubbing down. The mildew got everywhere, and so did the dust and dead spiders.

I cleared a path from the basement's front door to the very back of the room, near the cellar doors that let out into the backyard. There was an old claw-foot tub there, which I had owned for years. I don't think Iolanda knew I had ever moved it in—the delivery had been scheduled for a weekend she was out of town.

Likewise the claw-foot tub's two new fellows, which I had bought from my favorite salvage shop and paid for in cash I imagined would never be reported to the IRS. The delivery happened the day after Iolanda left, so once again, she was none the wiser.

All three tubs had been bears to bring down, but with some spit and soap and prayers I had taken possession and set them up in a dusty corner near the sump pump. The new tubs were just inserts rudely pried from their bathrooms—you paid a premium for cast iron and claw-feet. But I needed height, so I had put them up on cinder blocks, in the shadows behind their fancier fellow.

By the time the gin was gone, my tools and tubs were sparkling clean. Hidden underneath a tarp, they joined me in my interminable wait. I fell asleep listening to a podcast about the importance of the customer life cycle, which, like many things to which I should have paid more attention, failed to hold my interest for very long. I woke in the middle of the night with a mouth like a dirty sponge. A quick swish with some mouthwash and I fell back into bed. The podcast was still playing, by now having passed into a new season.

The host laughed at some jargon-filled piece of advice from the guest and said this had helped her increase customer conversion from social media engagement by forty-five percent.

"Wow," said the guest. "You're going to put me out of business!"

I fell asleep before I heard the host's reply.

All in all, it was no worse than most of my Christmases, and certainly better than some.

20

Notes de Tête: Tennessee Whiskey
Notes de Cœur: Asphalt and Ambergris
Notes de Fond: Shit and Fear Accord

At three thirty in the morning on December twenty-eighth, Beau double-parked outside my door in a car he had borrowed from a friend, which he had driven down the block with its lights off.

"Hey," he said when I came up. A painfully loud stage whisper. I held a finger to my lips, but his "Sorry!" wasn't much quieter. He bounced on the balls of his feet, shifted his weight from one side to another, rubbed his upper arms with restless hands.

First reiterating my symbol for silence, I aimed a thumb at the trunk of his borrowed car.

"Sorry," he said again, this time truly under his breath. With some effort, he stilled his jitters. Nervous energy, barely contained, still sang in every movement that he made, and he fumbled the key fob more than once. His breath gave him away as well, coming in shallow, panicked puffs of white.

He looked over his shoulder, down the silent stretch of trees and blacktop, then paused. His deep, preparatory breath went in silent but clouded on the exhale. A streetlight lit the plume of steam from behind so it briefly obscured his expression. Before the air cleared, Beau stepped up and popped the trunk.

He had hidden Yates inside a garment bag. It did nothing to disguise the fact of the corpse, but it certainly added an ironic savor to the proceedings.

The load was awkward and stiff with rigor mortis, but we wrestled him from the trunk in less time than it took me to do such things on my own. Once he was on the pavement, Beau shut the trunk slowly, quiet as he could. The clouds of his breath were still coming fast.

Deadweights are always heavier than you expect, just accounting for their size. I had a trolley I used when I was on my own, but it was quicker and quieter for the two of us simply to lift him and stagger over the curb.

I kept a weathered two-by-eight just inside the basement door, and we used it to guide him down the icy steps. Beau giggled when I set it up and said, "It's like a slide." I shushed him again, conscious of all the apartments looking out onto the street, of New Yorkers' habit of cracking their windows even in winter to relieve the sweltering steam heat.

Beau managed to bang into just about everything in the basement, cursing all the while. I'm sure he thought he was being quiet, but every thump or rattle or scrape of metal on concrete made my heart contract painfully behind my ribs. With Iolanda out of town, I didn't trust the other tenants not to come downstairs investigating strange noises.

And, of course, he kept apologizing. Bless his pea-pickin' heart.

Yates fit into one of the tubs, just, with his knees bent against his chest. We had talked about this and, despite his initial squeamishness over the empty-stomach dictate, Beau had followed my further instructions well. Because you tend to get cadaveric spasm with violent death, I've found that some judicious restraints applied antemortem will lock up the body in the preferred position for tincturing. Conveniently, it also makes the corpse compact for transportation.

After I pulled a tarp over the tub, and over Yates, Beau wiped his forehead. Despite the cold, he was sweating. "Jesus. Can I get a drink?"

"No," I said. He looked crestfallen, but I said, "You're double-parked in a strange car in front of my house at four o'clock in the morning." It had taken us some time to move Yates from the bottom of the stairs to the tub. "Besides, you don't want to get pulled over on the way home."

"Vic," he said, almost a whine.

"How about I owe you one?"

We shook on that. To my surprise—I should not have been surprised by this anymore, but the circumstances seemed like they might have precluded it—he pulled me forward for an accustomed kiss on the cheek. This one was less effusive or affectionate than it was . . . freaked out. Duct tape slapped across a sudden failure of social convention. After, he laid his heavy head on top of mine and let out a long sigh. I could feel it come in and go out as his chest expanded against mine. My mouth was pressed into the folds of his scarf, and I smelled his beard oil and his asphalt perfume.

"Shit," he said. Then, with the faint rattle of chattering teeth and the instability of laughter: "*Holy* shit." A shuddering breath made him shake, and stiffness climbed his limbs after it, spreading like the rigor mortis that had locked up Yates's corpse.

I stepped back and reached up, took his face between my hands. It was dark in the basement, except for a little light from my studio, where I had left the bedside lamp on. I could not see his expression well, except the gleam of his wide eyes. But I could hear his breathing—fast—and feel the pump of his heartbeat beneath my hands. Layers of winter clothes kept his scent close to his body, but I caught a faint and musty stink of fear.

"Beau," I said and, when he didn't look at me, repeated it. His gaze skittered across my face, searching the dark corners behind me. He wouldn't like what he saw there, if he could make it out. If he understood it.

He had begun to curse, over and over, barely audible. Not the manic, performative profanity of stubbed toes and an awkward bundle, but a reflexive chant not unlike the recitation of a rosary. This would never do.

Imitating Jane, I grabbed a fistful of his wild hair on each side. He stopped cursing, at least, to draw a sharp breath in. I pulled him down for a real kiss, to ground him like a current. To pull all his nervous energy out and through myself, who could handle it.

How did Jane do this? I was at the limit of my patience. Perhaps I should have felt admiration for her, but I felt pity. Maybe condescension. I wanted to tell him: *get your shit together*. But I knew he would only apologize.

His mouth was dry and sour. When I pulled away he was finally looking straight at me, lips still parted slightly, eyes glassy but focused. Feet back on the earth, or almost.

"You did a good job," I told him, letting my grip on his scalp go loose. He sagged, as if I had been holding him up. "Now it's time to go home."

◆ ◆ ◆

Of course, I wasn't present for the actual murder. I can't tell you exactly how its particulars played out. But I know what I told Beau to do, and I think I have enough of a grasp on his character, and Conrad Yates's, to make a good guess at what might have happened.

Yates had been enough of a thorn in Beau's side, and Reg's suits such an irritant to Conrad, that it only made sense for Beau to be the bigger man, to invite Conrad for a face-to-face before the relationships soured irretrievably.

Beau called up Conrad, offered to meet for drinks, chat it out. One thing led to another and it just became convenient for Yates to drop by the atelier one evening. Late, of course, though not too late. Union Square was still crowded and well lit, but people tend to look away from strange things faster after the sun goes down.

There were no security cameras in Beau's building. There was a service elevator, and a parking lot. I was reasonably familiar with the neighborhood and helped him see it with my more experienced eyes. Who would question a man rolling a rack of garment bags, its bottom heavy with a plastic storage container? Or a canvas laundry bin, piled high with linens? Who would second-guess him as he loaded these things into the back of a car or a van?

As you can see, I have a clear conception of his journey from atelier to parking lot, and from the parking lot uptown. I helped to plan them. As for what happened in the atelier proper . . .

You've been there. You've seen it. It's not a large space, but it's cozy. If you're the kind of person who appreciates fine clothes, interesting films, good liquor, and excellent music, it will put you at ease immediately.

Yates Sr. probably appreciated only one of these things. Luckily, Beau knew to be liberal with it. So let's imagine Yates drunk. Red-faced, sloppy. Full of noblesse oblige.

"We both know my son's a little headstrong," he says. "His mother didn't think he ought to rise so high in the company so young: too cocksure. But I thought, no better way to teach him responsibility, make him a man."

Beau smiles, nods, pours another drink. What's playing on the turntable? Something twangy? No, Otis Spann. That's better. Masculine and melancholy.

"Sometimes I wonder." Yates stares into his whiskey—let's say Beau is serving him Johnnie Walker. Burnt caramel, heavy on the vanillin. "I wonder if . . . but he'll learn. I think he's learning." He blinks moistly up at Beau. "These things he's asking for—they're *fashionable*, aren't they? I've told him over and over, keep it classic. We're not in the razzle-dazzle business. Our clients need to trust us."

Beau nods and nods, knowing "classic" can be as wild as a Prince of Wales plaid. He putters around his worktable, picking up pins and chalk pencils, looping his tape measure casually around one wrist. Yates natters on, apologizing sincerely for any trouble he's caused, but he's just trying to teach his boy a lesson, and Beau can understand that, can't he?

Of course, of course he can. His dad always wanted the best for him.

"Exactly," says Yates. "You understand. A father wants his son to succeed! You're a hardworking, self-made entrepreneur. A real American success story, right? Wouldn't you want that for your son?"

Beau smiles, and Yates smiles back, blissfully ignorant. But you know Beau by now. His true smiles are wide and full of teeth. A little dangerous, like he's about to bite into a bloody porterhouse steak. He even smiles when he's nervous, and those make him look like he's waiting for a blow to fall and hoping to forestall it with an obsequious grin.

This smile isn't dangerous or pathetic. It doesn't sit well on his face, because it's so much more like mine. The expression I offer to people who have displeased me, when for various reasons I cannot offer them the flat of my hand or a few choice words.

Yes, you know the one. I don't know where he picked it up.

"I don't think Jane wants kids," he says. That isn't what he's angry about.

"That's a shame." Yates polishes off his second glass of whiskey. He hasn't eaten dinner yet—good job, Beau—and it's working fast. "Don't you?"

Beau shrugs, that awful smile getting tighter and tighter until the pressure of his teeth against each other turns painful.

"Doesn't matter," he says, and something about his tone finally alerts Yates to the gravity of the situation. "Can't afford 'em."

Beau's skill and speed with his tape measure are those of a consummate professional. He has measured many necks in his career and can judge their size at this point without equipment. Yates's neck, he estimates, is somewhere around seventeen and a half, eighteen inches, though an ill-advised English spread makes it look larger.

He pulls the tape measure much tighter than that.

Yates is startled, drops his glass. It bounces on the turquoise love seat, strikes the floor, and rolls. Beau gets one foot on the love seat for leverage and pulls up. He's a big man, and Yates is drunk, and there's no room between tape measure and skin for scrabbling fingers.

In cases of strict asphyxiation, it takes two minutes without air to lose consciousness. Four minutes for permanent brain damage. Six or seven to die. But the tape measure makes a good garrote, and those work much more quickly—they cut off blood to the brain. In about fifteen seconds Yates has gone slack. At this point Beau ties the tape measure in place and slides Yates to the floor for the trussing up, so he'll fit in the trunk, and then in the tub. He's still alive at this point, though unconscious. Per my instructions Beau will leave the tape measure tied in place for five minutes, counted by the hands of his watch.

Remember? In amongst all that jewelry, he has a very nice one. A gift from family in India when Beau's father defended his dissertation, passed on at Beau's own matriculation from Northwestern. An HMT Aishwarya: not easy to find, unless you're up for a deep dive on Facebook Marketplace or eBay. Yellow gold, showing brass where the plating is worn away. Rectangular face, a piscine curve to the metal band. Yes, rather like mine. The style doesn't exactly work on me, and the whole thing is slightly too large. But when you can't buy new . . .

At any rate, Yates finally shuffles off his mortal coil. It's a bit messy, but Beau was expecting this because I mentioned it, and bought a tarp at Home Depot on his way into work. In cash, of course. It's always nice to have a mentor for tasks you've never undertaken. So the turquoise love seat is spared everything except bad memories. And while the floor will need some spot cleaning, there's no need for a bucket, a mop, or ammonia.

Once Yates is finally down for good, wrapped up in the tarp, he goes into a garment bag. The garment bag goes in a laundry bin, and the laundry bin into the service elevator, which lets out on a dingy courtyard with a driveway to the street. Running on adrenaline, sweating the fear-stink I will catch on him later, Beau loads lumps of dirty sheets into the back of his borrowed car until finally, he heaves Yates in after them and shuts the trunk. Locks it. Rolls the laundry bin back into the service entrance of his unsurveilled building. And then drives uptown, to me.

◆ ◆ ◆

But again, that's all conjecture. I can only speak with certainty about things that have happened to me.

Once Beau was gone, I got to work. The smaller the span between time of death and beginning of tincture, the better. But first: the particularly unpleasant bits.

I donned a respirator—Home Depot, again, an excellent supplier for unsavory projects—and a pair of rubber gloves. Yates I stripped, neatly cutting his clothes away with bandage scissors to avoid any unseemly wrangling with his rigor-stiffened corpse. Awkward echoes of a particular kind of intimacy as the blunt blades skimmed his breastbone, slipped between his thighs.

I set the pile of rags aside to be disposed of later; Beau's garment bag came in handy there. Then I hosed him down with the sprayer from the basement sink.

Apologies for the next part. I only include it so you aren't left with awkward questions jangling around in your head later. I don't want you to doubt my expertise.

In an ideal situation, I'd treat my animalic components like oysters: fasting for a day or two before they died. Really, the way to do it would have been fasting, then death by alcohol poisoning. Specifically, a large volume of extremely high-proof alcohol, administered at both ends. But that's impractical in terms of setup and, I'll admit, a little gruesome for my tastes. I'm not *that* kind of sadist.

The fact remains that intestinal flora presents a problem in this line of work, so I did the best I could and let it drain out the sump pump. Then as much alcohol as I could get into the corpse with a funnel and a hose, and a little bit of glue in the relevant areas to keep everything sealed inside.

Once he was stripped, scoured, and sealed, I started to fill the tub. I used a siphon, because I kept my alcohol in fifty-five-gallon drums, which were delivered to the lab but . . . found their way uptown, every once in a while. A fire hazard, but so was everything else in Iolanda's basement.

Once Yates was covered in booze, I took the restaurant-size roll of plastic wrap from the workbench and sealed the top of the tub. Over this, the tarp again. In a few days, I would drain off all the alcohol—the tub's disconnected plughole worked for this, as did a series of plastic storage containers that slid neatly under the tub to catch what came out.

The human body is so aqueous it only renders a little of its scent at a time; when water and ethanol reach balanced amounts inside and outside the cell membranes, the process stops. You have to renew the alcohol bath again and again until the cells are saturated, no water left to give. Each tincture is weaker than the last, but it leaves you with a body that will burn nicely.

Distillation might have served my purposes better than tincturing—faster, for one thing, with less chance of an untoward intestinal incident—but that kind of setup for a sample this size? On her few trips down the basement steps, Iolanda hadn't noticed the old tub or the plastic bins. I think she might notice a still large enough to hold a full-grown man. I would use my small stills later to render the large volume of tincture into a much smaller volume of distillate.

Anyway, tincturing an animalic can capture some of the darker, subtler, meatier aspects of its composition. And those aspects are the entire point and purpose of using natural animalics.

Earlier, I mentioned the use of synthetic ingredients in perfume. Most perfumers these days employ a mix of natural and synthetic ingredients, and the synthetics tend to be cheaper, easier, and more consistent. Ethyl maltol, phenylethyl alcohol, Kephalis, cis-3-Hexenol. In a way, I have been lying to you about what you smell when you spray my perfumes. When I say Aleppo pepper, cumin, fig, leather, charcoal, iris, rust, what I mean more than half the time is olfactory illusions of those scents: careful mixes of chemicals called accords that evoke the idea of a single element.

These molecules occur quite naturally in the world around us; modern perfumery merely isolates them and makes them available for a mad scientist's mixing and matching. When we say "a pear accord," we're really talking about fructone and hexyl acetate, and maybe some essence of rose.

But convenient and versatile as synthetics are, many of us mad scientists still have an affection for, a fascination with, the extracts and absolutes rendered from blossoms, rinds, and resins. From the flesh or intestines of living creatures.

There are plenty of serviceable, and indeed sexy, synthetic animalics available. Jonathan had a soft spot in his shriveled heart for the carcinogenic nitro musks that have been banned since the seventies. But there is nothing like true civet.

Naturals you want for depth, for power, for that ineffable note that gives a perfume personality. Galbanum: the scent of broken stems, of medicinal herbs and recently pulled weeds. Seaweed, for its umami ocean funk, still crisp somehow, and clean. The incomparable bergamots of Calabria's giardini.

Or Yates, in all his sweaty, middle-aged man stink.

Peeling off my rubber gloves and respirator, I took a deep breath of boozy air and got a little whiff of shit and fear. Then I stowed my equipment, took a scalding shower, and caught a few hours of sleep.

21

Notes de Tête: Coconut and Champagne Yeast
Notes de Cœur: Scorched Steel, Smoke, Brown Sugar
Notes de Fond: Beef Fat and Jerk Spice

At work the next morning I was bleary and irritable, but my irritability had a different tenor than it had before the holidays. I was no longer worried about setting up my dominoes but rather preoccupied with watching them fall. Hoping none of them stalled or wobbled or were placed too far apart.

I was also operating on three hours of sleep and far too much coffee, which had me jittery and sour-mouthed.

"Did you have a good Christmas, Vic?" Barry wore a sly and pitying smile, like he already knew the answer. "You look like shit. There's some cookies in the break room."

Indeed, there were. Mounds of bonbon amidon and candied coconut, mixed with peanut butter kisses and some smashed-up petits fours. I recognized this particular plastic tub from last Easter; it was still stained pink with the memory of Holy Week salad. He always did this after holidays: brought leftovers in his mother's Tupperware. And he was always exactly as pointed about steering me toward them. On multiple occasions I had made clear my disregard for holiday celebrations of any season, but Barry persisted in importing day-old festivity and shoving it down my throat.

Without any particular subtlety, he watched through the break room door as I poked through the sweets on offer, and didn't leave until I had put a few things on a paper plate. The plate had reindeer on it.

I didn't realize, until I put the first cookie in my mouth, that I was starving. I hadn't eaten since . . . sometime before yesterday. What was it now? Still the twenty-eighth. Time felt mutable, like a polymer. Fluid, until you slammed against a deadline and found it unforgiving.

I polished off the first plate and had to sneak back into the break room while Barry was downstairs. He would have been unbearably smug if he had seen me go back for seconds. As I was picking through to find the best of the unbroken cookies, a phone call came through on the landline. I could have yelled for Barry or Leila, but I was right there. And at this point, who knew what was waiting on the other end of the line?

"Bright House, Vic Fowler speaking."

"Ah, Vic. Hi. It's Pip Miles."

Shit. "Mr. Miles." I scrubbed my itchy eyes and sat down in the desk chair. It squealed. "To what do I owe the pleasure?" It wasn't one, strictly, but I'd be damned if I asked how his holidays had been. I thought I'd be free of him until the new year. Assuming our last conversation had been in good faith and not a front.

"Strangest thing," he said. "I can't get ahold of Yates Senior. I don't suppose you've heard from him?"

I stifled a yawn, which had sneaked up on me but at least gave me the illusion of nonchalance. "No. I . . . were you expecting to? It's just after Christmas. Maybe he's out of town."

Of course he wasn't. No wife or little kids, no family gatherings. Just Reg, who had probably spent his Christmas getting drunk in a Santa costume with a couple of well-paid escorts. Cheers to them; let's hope they took him for all he had.

Besides, Yates had a business to run, and assets don't take Christmas off. Almost like retail or the service industry, in that way, except the pay is probably worth it.

"I have it on my calendar," said Miles. "Today, ten a.m. I was supposed to come by the office."

Which meant Eisner had seen him. More ruffled feathers to smooth. "And?"

"He's not here. Receptionist won't tell me anything."

"So why did you call me?"

"You promised to help me out," he said, and I couldn't tell if I believed him. Goddamn it, I *hated* talking on the phone. Was he sweating? Breathing rankly from his mouth? Or was he calm and collected, giving off only the scent of cheap clothes and cheaper aftershave? That grayish old-man smell: part spray deodorant, part oily skin. Comfortable and reassuring for the person who inhabited and exuded it, off-putting for everyone else. I would much rather he be drenched in sour nervous perspiration.

"I'm not sure I can," I said. "I haven't heard boo from Yates since . . . when did we last meet?"

"April," he said, and there was an edge to it I couldn't parse. Knowing humor? Had he caught on that I was acting? Or was it simply impatience with people who didn't pore over the same case files every day?

"That was ages ago. I haven't been keeping tabs on him. I thought that was your job."

"Huh," said Miles. "Funny. From what I hear, you ran into him just a couple of weeks ago."

"What?" For a moment I was genuinely confused. And then I remembered: Eisner's office, the darkened corridors, the frosted glass. Yates appearing like a shambling, melting, monstrous apparition to slyly grin at us and make assumptions.

Had Eisner said something to Miles? Of course not. Yates Sr. had been talking to the detective. Reg was in the dark about the whole thing—his father wouldn't have told him about meeting me at the office.

If Yates Sr. thought Miles was onto him, wouldn't he have wanted to shift the blame? And who better than the person actually guilty of the murder? Or maybe Jane was right, and Eisner was beginning to set up his *own* dominoes so that the whole thing came crashing down on *me* at the end.

"Oh," I said. "Yes. Sorry. We did speak to each other. But only in passing." What had Yates told Miles? Surely not the whole truth, or I'd be in jail by now.

"You were with Joseph Eisner at the time?"

"Yes," I said. "Another client."

"Referral from Yates?"

"No, actually. Eisner referred him." If the pastor at my childhood church had been correct, I was going to go to hell when I died. And it would be eternity on this phone call.

"Interesting. How long have you known Eisner? When did he refer Yates?"

At that blessed moment, Barry starting shrieking downstairs. The sort of shriek that meant something had broken or someone had been hurt. Then he started calling my name.

"I'm so sorry," I said. "I have to run. My assistant is having some trouble in the lab."

"Of course," said Miles, too genial. He knew he had caught me in something. And now I was going to have to slip free or chew off my own leg.

◆　◆　◆

Barry's emergency was merely an exciting email about our December sales figures. He insisted on running out for a bottle of cheap sparkling wine. Landing on a thin layer of cookies, it got me quite drunk and would get me more hungover. Too much sugar. Where Barry turned even giddier with the wine, I grew more and more morose.

Are you working tonight? I texted Jane.

She sent back a thumbs-up but didn't elaborate.

I called her while Barry was out taking a smoke break. I had told him that cigarettes would make him useless to me as a nose (not to mention the weekend coke and party drugs), but sometimes even I could see the appeal. A quick rush of feel-good chemicals without any accompanying impairment. Something to do with your hands. A ritual to calm your nerves.

If there was ever a time I needed a cigarette, it was now. I settled for the rest of the wine, which I drank from the bottle. I could feel the place in my head that would hurt tomorrow. Or—I checked the clock above the Metro shelves—later tonight.

"I only have a minute," said Jane. No preamble, no affection. But what had I expected? I had played a rude trick on her, with Giovanni, though I had not meant to do so. Of course she would treat me briskly, even harshly. The way you treat someone with whom you have been intimate, when intimacy is no longer on the table but some form of communication is required. "I'm going in early. Staff meeting."

I should have felt chastened by her tone. Instead, I felt a rush of unbearable tenderness. Because I had pitied her, this anger made me ache. "Do you think he'll show tonight?" I did not say who I meant.

"If not tonight, tomorrow. Or the night after."

"Is there any way you can find out?" I knew the answer would be no, but I asked anyway.

A small pause. When she spoke again, the tone of her voice had changed. It was no longer to the point, but hovered in the dim halfway between suspicion and concern. "Vic, what's going on?"

I set down the bottle of wine and pinched the bridge of my nose. "Nothing." But I owed her, after the last time we had seen each other, and that answer wasn't what she deserved. Apparently, pity made me magnanimous as well. "The detective. He's onto me, and I'm going to take care of it, but I can't risk anyone else talking to him in the meantime. Nobody who knows what I do."

"Yeah, but Reg doesn't know. That was the whole point of doing him last."

"Miles has twigged I've worked with the whole C-suite. Order doesn't matter anymore." I had two options: I could pull back, delay, hope he lost interest. But I didn't believe it would happen. Which left me with option two: acceleration. It was risky, because once things started rolling downhill I would lose some measure of control. But momentum could usually be relied on—the laws of physics would be on my side. It would just be a matter of dealing with whatever happened at the bottom of the slope.

"Miles will start asking Pearson and Eisner questions soon. Pearson might talk, which would be bad, but I'm hoping Giovanni will work fast and he won't get a chance. Eisner isn't going to talk if he can help it, but I wouldn't discount the possibility. At the very least he won't like it, and might get cold feet as far as this project is concerned. And Reg's ignorance is going to make him dangerous now: he's the only Yates left to pump. If he comes to the bar tonight, bring him in. I need to wrap everything up, and fast."

I was panicking; the words were pouring out unconsidered. I could feel speed and force gathering behind the plans, pushing everything past the point at which anyone had a hope of stopping it. At least saying it all out loud made it feel real, and therefore manageable.

"What about the detective?"

"Don't worry about him."

"You know how I feel about 'don't worry.'" Grave, but familiar. Better than the brusqueness she'd been using earlier. Was she coming around? If so, I had to be better than Beau on this score.

"I'm worried enough for both of us. But I'm planning to do something about it." I heard the door upstairs squeal. "Call me later. Let me know if he shows up or not."

"Okay," she said, sounding uncharacteristically unsure.

"It's all going to come off without a hitch," I said. "I promise. You'll do great."

She made a noncommittal noise. There was an awkward moment of silence, a void where some other pair of people might have inserted an endearment.

"Um," I said, and was immediately embarrassed.

"Bye, Vic," she said, slightly strangled. Then she hung up.

"Bye," I said, into the silence.

"Who was that?" asked Barry, and I nearly pissed myself. The cheap wine had made its way into my bladder, and the pressure was exacerbated by my nerves. How long had he been standing there? I had heard the door open and shut after we got through unpleasant necessities, which meant he only could have caught the end of the conversation.

"A friend," I said, and immediately realized I had made a mistake.

I should have said a client. A creditor. The bank. Anything else. When had I ever spoken to a friend on the phone? When had I ever mentioned having one?

Barry's eyebrows hit his hairline, and he tucked his chin in campy disbelief. "Same one?"

Oh. The Instagram messages. Goddamn it.

"I like this for you, Vic. You need something besides the hustle. Some*body*." His eyebrows came down and he started smiling and nodding, full of himself and his opinions. "I worry about you."

I laughed abruptly. "Really? Why?"

"All you do is work!" he said. "The juice is all you care about."

"You care about it too," I said. "Or you wouldn't be working for me."

229

"Sure," he said. "But I have *friends*. I party. I do dinner with my mom. I volunteer at the community fridge! What do you do? Nothing. It's fucked up; you shouldn't be so lonely."

Barry had only come on board after Jonathan's death. He had never seen me willingly spend time with another human who wasn't on my payroll, paying me, attempting to extract money I refused to give, or vice versa.

Barry would have called Jonathan a fuck buddy. A friend with benefits. A bad idea. I don't know what *I* would have called him. Probably not a friend. Yes, we spent hours together outside of work. There were certainly benefits, over and above the sex (though that was not to be discounted). I didn't trust him, but . . . do you need to trust a friend?

I trusted Jane. Instead of unpacking that thought, I said, "I'm going home early. You can too, if you want. I'll see you tomorrow."

Barry was still looking at me funny. "Tomorrow's Saturday."

"Oh." That was convenient. I could sleep in after a busy night.

Maybe Jane would stay with me. We could go for breakfast after.

I had to call Giovanni.

For this, I waited until I got home. And before I got home, I stopped at the overpriced but surprisingly well-stocked liquor store at 145th and St. Nicholas to replace the Longrow that had been missing from my bar since November. Medicinal, for me. And if Jane stayed over . . .

But I was getting ahead of myself.

Black bag in hand, I climbed up Sugar Hill into the beginnings of a slush storm. Icy pellets stung the back of my neck and whispered against the windshields of parked cars. Bad weather for driving. But wasn't Jane from somewhere in the Midwest? She'd know how to handle it. Though that was no guarantee of safety, if everyone else was sliding and spinning out around you.

Giovanni's cell phone rang and rang and eventually went to voice mail. I hung up rather than leave one and sat on my hands waiting for him to call me back. I didn't want to leave a suspicious call log. Just in case.

After sixteen and a half minutes—reheating leftover curry in a pot at the stove made staring at the clock unavoidable—my phone rattled against the countertop and displayed Giovanni's name.

"Hello," I said.

"What do you want?" he asked, and his voice had the shape of a cleaver: flat with resignation, honed at the edge by hostility and resentment.

"Has Pearson made an appointment yet?" I asked.

Silence, as if he dearly wanted to tell me no. Then, buckling: "He's on the schedule for next week."

Damn. "Not soon enough."

"Sorry," he said, not sounding it. "That's when he's coming in."

"Call him," I said. "Tell him it's tomorrow."

"What?"

"You do reminders," I said, putting the plan together as I talked. "Every time I have a cut, your receptionist calls me the day before to confirm. So have her call him tonight. Tell him his cut is tomorrow. You think he pays attention to his calendar?"

"Yes," said Giovanni.

"No," I said. "He pays someone for that. And the blame will fall on his assistant for getting his schedule wrong. Call him. I need it done."

"Oh, you do?"

"As I established, yes. And *you* need to do it. Sooner rather than later. Tomorrow, ideally. Tonight would have been even better, but I'm trying to be realistic."

A taut pause, in which our mingled breath made the connection crackle with static. And then he started laughing.

"Jesus fucking Christ," he said, and kept on going.

"Tomorrow?" I said. "Like we talked about?" I had given him an abbreviated version of the spiel I'd laid on Beau and Jane: no dinner, no poison, no bloodshed.

The laughter spun down slowly, reluctantly. I was taking this seriously, and soon he would have to take it seriously as well.

"I'm never cutting your fucking hair again," he said.

"I hope you'll reconsider." A thin thread of spicy smoke smell rose from my pan of oxtails, and I yanked them from the orange electric burner.

"Fuck you," he said, and hung up.

Lashing out like this was childish and unattractive, and I was faintly embarrassed for him. But I pitied him too. The man loved what he did, found purpose in it. If I could empathize with anything, it was that kind of passion and commitment. Yet I had pulled it all out from under him so he would fall into place as it pleased me. I might stand to gain from this deal with Eisner, and save myself from losing much, much more. But I *would* lose a barber, even if I came out on top in every other way. And a good barber who would cut my hair the way I wanted was no small thing to lose.

22

Notes de Tête: Coffee
Notes de Cœur: Camphor, Menthol
Notes de Fond: Mildew and More Shit

The early part of the evening passed like hot tar, slow and acrid. The Scotch had been a sound investment. Not only did its profile match the tenor of the evening perfectly, but it kept me from wearing through the linoleum with my pacing. After two helpings of two fingers each, I would much rather sit in the armchair and clench my teeth. Besides, it kept my sparkling wine hangover at bay.

Would Reg show up tonight? Would I have to wait two nights? Three? What if Jane and Giovanni showed up on the same night? Could I handle two corpses at a time? Could I handle both of them at once? They were both angry at me; what would happen if we all ended up in the same room?

The Scotch meant these anxious suppositions took on the languor of inevitable despair. While this was preferable to heart-pounding terror, it was still deeply unpleasant. I was about to turn to my tried-and-true soporific of entrepreneurial podcasts when my phone buzzed on the bedside table. I sat up to grab it so fast I put a crick in my neck.

Jane. What are you doing later?

A fantastic pressure built and burst in my chest. Elation and panic and relief. Despite a deep breath, my fingers were still numb and shaky as I replied.

Nothing. Come over?

A long pause, a test of faith. And then, ten minutes later:
Another thumbs-up.

I went limp all over and lay heavily on my bed, podcasts forgotten. For two hours I slept the sleep of the just, or at least the dead, and didn't wake up until Jane called to say she was upstairs.

She didn't show up in the same vehicle as Beau—she had rented a Zipcar after signing up for a free trial with a coupon code. Her idea. "You don't want the same car showing up both times," she had said, and I agreed.

When I came up to street level, she was still sitting in the driver's seat, tight-lipped and pale. Her ragged bangs swept across her forehead, pressed over her eyebrows by the brim of a knit cap. Somehow, she had found a proper parking space, on the curb, at a legal distance from the hydrant. Her breath clouded the inside of the windshield.

I knocked on her window and she jumped before she realized it was me. I tilted my head toward the trunk, and she nodded.

The sleet had become small snowflakes: dense chips of ice that fell fast and didn't glitter in the streetlights. Her car door opened loudly in the late-night quiet, and she slipped on the asphalt. I felt the impact of her elbow in my palm before I realized I had moved to help her.

I saw her inhale, as if she would speak, and braced myself to scold her as I had Beau. But all she released was a sigh. It curled up into the cold air, so slowly I could have cupped it in my hands and caught her exhalation against my gloves as it condensed into water droplets.

Of course she understood she could not speak. Against whatever better instincts I might have had, I leaned forward and pressed my lips against hers. The skin was chapped and tasted like blood and Carmex.

She did not kiss me back. All of my earlier excitement withered. In its absence, I felt like a used balloon: stretched out and wrinkled, my skin left cold after rapid contraction.

She was still angry with me. What had I expected?

Reg was trussed up like his father before him, covered by a cheap fleece blanket we ended up using as a sling. Even with Jane helping, the sleet made things difficult. I nearly bought it on the icy stairs. The Scotch had dulled my reflexes, though I didn't feel drunk. Maybe it was Jane's unmoving lips driving me to distraction. Their apathetic yielding underneath my own.

"Okay?" she asked. I thought of the first time she had come home with me, how she slipped down the stairs, and I caught her, and we kissed in the portico.

I nodded and shut us into the darkness of the basement. Again, a little light from my apartment showed the path from front door to back. With heavy breathing and the odd curse, we got Reg into one of the newer tubs. The cinder blocks beneath it made ominous grinding sounds, but ultimately held. Sweating, I leaned back against the crowded workbench, dared myself to meet her eyes and gamble.

"Want a drink?" It was hard to sound nonchalant while whispering.

She made a face and looked back at Reg. "What about him?"

It was true I should deal with him first. But I wanted her to stay. I wanted her to kiss me back. "He's going to take a few hours. I don't want to keep you." But I did. Oh, I did.

"What do you do to them?" she asked. The tarp-covered tub that held his father was conspicuous if you knew what to look for, which by now she would.

It was a bad idea to offer. What was this supposed to prove? But still off-balance, still wanting, I asked her back: "Would you like to help?"

It is a testament to some aspect of Jane's character that she said yes, and that, once she understood what helping would entail, she didn't back down. I don't think it was tenderness toward me. If anything, the opposite. Some drive to prove that she could do anything I could. That she was capable and cold and not on the verge of cracking. The affection that had bloomed from my pity evolved into admiration. Perhaps into pride, which was as patronizing as pity in its own way. Embarrassing, in retrospect. She deserved better.

In her snow boots, with her sleeves rolled past her elbows and her watch cap pulled low over her shag, Jane was grim and tidy and suddenly butch. I could picture her twenty years ago: a middle-school tomboy. Volleyball, fistfights, hopelessly in love with an oblivious best friend and trying desperately to impress her.

She was trying to impress me now, and I was not oblivious: I was more than willing to be impressed.

There was a force and economy in Jane's motions that reminded me of her bartending. I would have thought she felt no more for Reg than she did for an old-fashioned served up, except that whenever her gaze strayed across his face, or her hands had reason to touch his skin, the small muscles of her face gave her away.

She *hated* this man, and she was glad that he was dead.

Still, the grimness lingered. And by its lingering, I identified its most likely cause as guilt. Or if not guilt, then fear. The longer we worked on Reg—cleaning him out, sealing him up, dousing him in alcohol, and finally mopping up the mess his body had made—the deeper Jane descended into her dour mood. I became obsessed with her frown, and the way it made her lower lip plump and pouty.

We worked mostly in silence, but I knew I should speak beyond orders, advice, instructions. She wanted . . . what? Reassurance? No. That was Beau. Jane only needed an opening.

After the last gallon of alcohol went into the tub and the final length of plastic wrap was pulled into place, I peeled off my gloves and threw them into the battered paint bucket that served as my garbage can. Jane stood at the side of the tub and looked down through the layers of cling film. The liquid and the overlapping plastic turned Reg into an abstract painting: flesh tones and reflected light.

I didn't know how to provide a gentle entrée. What did she want me to say? She was the one who had shut the door in my face. She had scorned me and was waiting for me to make amends. I should be piqued. Instead I wanted to appease her. And that wanting piqued me in its turn. When had I lost the advantage of condescension? Probably around the time I began to focus on her frown. Had Jonathan ever felt this way about me? An upsetting thought.

Finally, confounded by subtlety and fearing the consequences of further silence, I asked, "Do you feel guilty that you're glad he's dead?" She flinched, but I pressed on. "Or are you just worried you'll be caught?"

Rubbing her gloved hands together as if she could clean them—*Out, damned spot! Out, I say!*—she was silent a long time. And even when she drew a breath, her answer was its release. In the delicate pause between, her gloves squeaked against each other.

"Jane?" I asked. Alcohol fumes made it painful to breathe, and I felt light-headed. "Which is it?"

Before she spoke I saw her reconstruct herself, reassemble her armature, buckle on her pads and armor. She didn't even want to impress me anymore. She just wanted to take the hits and stay standing.

"I don't know, Vic. Why not both?"

What could I say to that?

"You said you figured out how to do all this by *accident?*" She wiped her forehead with her forearm—a gesture I had first seen her use behind the bar, to keep her hands clean for work. Now she was trying to keep her face safe from her hands. "What the *fuck* kind of accident taught you this?"

She watched me struggle to dredge something up. When nothing came, she finally took pity on me and said, "I guess I'll have that drink."

"If you don't mind," I said, stopping at my threshold. "Just . . . I'd rather clean up first."

Jane looked down at herself, made a face.

I opened the washing machine that backed up against my exterior wall. But she didn't move and instead looked at me. So that was how it was going to be. Fair enough.

I stripped efficiently, having worn clothes that were quick and easy to get out of: old black jeans and a black T-shirt that wouldn't show stains. No undergarments. I hadn't wanted to get my fingers so close to my skin, no matter that my hands had been in gloves the whole time. Tarquin Winot's comments on the hand that has touched the abject surfaced briefly in my mind. I thought of Jane wiping one yellow rubber palm against the other, then one after another across the opposite knuckles.

Naked, I shivered in the basement chill.

Satisfied that I was vulnerable and she had the upper hand, Jane peeled off her flannel shirt and the black V-neck beneath it. White crusts of simple syrup flaked off the cotton as it stretched over her head. She kicked off her snow boots and peeled black leggings away from her skin. The seams had left red indents behind. Goose bumps came to life along her arms and thighs.

I plucked the delicates bag from my hamper just inside the door and held it open for her lingerie. Surprisingly fine stuff, worn under her work clothes. But then, don't we all draw confidence from secret luxuries like that? It's a sense of superiority worn close to the skin, hidden from all but our intimates. The band of her bra had been taken in, close to the hooks and eyes—she had owned it long enough to stretch out the elastic.

She hesitated before removing this final layer, fingertips poised but held in check.

"You can use my shower," I said. A moment more of hesitation, and then she slipped her hands between lace and skin.

The pipes banged when the washer started. I shut us away from the sound, away from the scene of our handiwork, into the cold and humid quiet of my studio. Careful not to touch the rug, the walls, the shelves, I led her to the bathroom and shut us into a smaller, colder, damper room.

The tile bounced our own stink back to us: ethanol and sweat, Jane's coconut body lotion, the remnants of Reg's shit. Despite my dousing it regularly in store-brand bleach, the grout still exhaled a faint scent of mildew. I found it almost comforting in this context: it was the smell of my space, and Jane was in it.

The floor was cold. I cranked the water as hot as it would go and waited for steam to start rising before I pulled the shower curtain back and gestured Jane in first. Her shivering had spread and intensified, and now her teeth began to chatter. She had held it together much longer than Beau, but under the hot water she started to come apart.

With Beau, I had known what to do. With Jane, I was at a loss. She wouldn't—couldn't—gracefully accept any form of thanks or comfort.

I stepped into the shower with her, blinking water from my eyes, and put the pad of my thumb to that captivating lower lip.

"Now?" I asked her. "Can I?"

Her mouth fell open and she inhaled. I felt cold air pass over my wet skin and leaned forward. But her teeth clicked shut and she turned her head: one sharp movement of her chin.

"Jane," I said, and reached into the void for words. I didn't know what I was going to say until I said it. "I'm sorry."

That got her to look at me again. "No," she said, and for one paralyzing moment, I saw that she was desperately afraid. Then disdain slammed down over it, bulletproof. She was sneering. Disgusted. Disbelieving. "No, you're not."

"No," I said, awash in relief. I hadn't meant it anyway, but something else. "You're right. I'm not."

Now she was the one who looked relieved. I could see it behind the sneer, in the softening curl of her lips, the slackening line of her shoulders.

"Good," she said, and I let her push me to my knees beneath the spray.

◆ ◆ ◆

She stayed. By the time she was done with me it was nearly sunrise. We fell asleep naked and still damp and didn't wake until lunchtime. Rather, *I* woke, and realized I had not seen her asleep before.

Sleep makes some people look younger. Not Jane. Drained of cynical animation and of focus, her features gave in to gravity. Deeply asleep, she looked more exhausted than I had ever seen her awake. How old was she, after all? Not too many years more than me, but maybe some.

What would Jonathan have looked like, sleeping? I never found out. We didn't trust each other that far. Would I have wanted to know? I thought of my weakness over Jane last night, slipping from the advantageous high ground to a much more dangerous position of indulgence. Jonathan had never indulged anyone except himself. Had he?

But I was fairly certain I enjoyed indulging her. When I kissed the shadowed hollows below her eyes her lashes fluttered against my lips, and I continued to enjoy it. "I'm taking you out for coffee," I said.

"Shit." Her gravelly morning profanity was impossibly sexy. "The laundry."

I had never put the clothes in the dryer, which meant they would smell foul now. As if they hadn't before. "I'll just run them through another load," I said. A good excuse for it, in case the first load hadn't washed away the evidence of our crimes. "You can borrow some of mine."

I was smaller, slighter, but Jane fit into a T-shirt and a sweater. They stretched tight across her breasts, and since her bra was still tangled up in the delicates bag, the borrowed clothes left little to the imagination.

"I'm afraid it will have to be sweatpants," I said. "Or . . ." Digging into a deep corner of my bottom drawer, I produced a pair of black leggings lined in fleece. "From my very brief tenure as a jogger."

She raised a critical eyebrow, and suddenly I heard myself saying, "I had . . . an ex. Very fit." Not a lie: Jonathan's body was subject to the same high standards as his employees and perfumes. As well as the same micromanagement and obsession. "For a while I thought I would . . . well." I faltered, and she noticed. "Anyway. They'll stretch."

"Sounds like it didn't end well."

"He was my boss," I said.

Her face pinched up. In distaste or pain or empathy, I couldn't tell.

"It isn't exactly what you think." Which was probably quid pro quo, something along those lines. Or tawdry workplace romance.

"So what was it?" she asked.

Instead of answering, I said, "He died."

At first, she had the shocked and guilty expression of someone who has blithely uncovered a scar, exposed a negative to the sun. And then she remembered who I was, and the expression became hard, suspicious.

"Did he?" she asked. And: "How?" Although I'm sure she already knew.

When I didn't answer, she took the leggings and wriggled into them, fleece against bare skin. "At least I won't get panty lines."

The skies had cleared at some point in the night, and the temperature had dropped. A keen wind off the Hudson made my eyes water and turned the tips of Jane's ears red. We didn't speak on the walk down to Broadway, though I sneaked glances at her and wondered what she was thinking. There was no disdain left in her, but the grate was still down, and I was on the outside trying to look in. I hated how this made me itch with need.

She gave me an opening just before we turned the corner. "Will it be okay?" she asked, and at first I thought she meant an all-encompassing "it" and had no answer. *It* what? Everything? My life? Hers and Beau's? Then she added, "Leaving them like that, just . . . in the basement."

"Oh yes," I said, waving away her concern. "Iolanda never comes down. She has her own entrance to the backyard. Anyway, she's out of town until . . . next week? I've never had a problem."

"Yet," said Jane.

"And I won't this time either." I sincerely hoped.

She didn't look convinced. "What about the detective?"

"He's shortly to go the same way as Reg and Connie." I said it with confidence that I willed myself to feel but didn't, quite. Her mood had undermined my self-assurance.

Jane was quiet for a moment, chewing on her lip. Remembering the fear in her eyes the night before, her guilt and relief and grim purpose, I began to worry what she might say next.

What came out at last was just, "You've only got three tubs."

It made me laugh. But I still wondered about all the things she hadn't said.

The coffee shop was also in a basement. I gestured for her to take the steps ahead of me, and as she picked her way down I glanced over my shoulder and quickly scanned the street. No blue windbreaker. No white beard. No Pippin Miles to catch me at breakfast with Jane.

Well. At brunch.

When we had settled on a sunken sofa near the window with our coffee and our scones, Jane met my eyes and said with no preamble, "Your ex. Your boss. Tell me about him."

I had just taken a bite, and in my surprise I nearly choked. However, the scone gave me some time to stall. Jane's tone told me she would not brook evasion, and I needed a moment to figure out what I should say.

What did she want to hear? She thought I owed her something, that was clear. My mercenary streak spitefully reminded me that she was going to get a cut of Eisner's money. What else did she want?

But this transaction had gone somewhere beyond business, and perhaps those rules no longer applied. She wanted a story about Jonathan, and by extension, she wanted to know something about me.

I had lost any feeling of superiority; I could no longer *deign* to tell her something. Only trade it, or offer it as a gift.

Jane was watching me with interest now. With hunger. The longer this silence stretched, the hungrier she would get.

"Do you work today?" I asked.

She blinked several times in rapid succession, as if trying to focus her eyes. "What?"

"Do you work today?" I just couldn't do it, not yet. Jonathan was mine. He always had been, since he stopped belonging to himself. I had gone to the odious Gerald Pearson in order to preserve my memories of Jonathan. I didn't want to share him, or even attempt to explain what he had meant to me. If I understood it myself.

"Don't change the subject."

"It will take your laundry about an hour to dry," I said. "If you like, you can wear my clothes home, and I'll bring yours the next time we see one another." The last sentence came out so crisply formal that I sounded like a secretary. An assistant principal. Softening a bit, I added, "Or you can come back with me and wait." Provided she stopped asking questions. Despite myself, I wanted her to pick the second option. But of course, she picked the first.

"Thanks for the coffee," she said, and now that she had realized what game I was playing she had gone brittle and cold. "I should go home before work. See Beau. Get some dinner."

I bit back an offer of takeout. She could eat while her work clothes dried. I was supposed to be angry with her. I *was*. "Tell him I said hello. And thank you. I know it was all a bit . . . intense, for him."

She stared at me across her scone and coffee, eyes blank. I counted one blink, two, and then she snorted and shook her head. "Yeah, 'cause for me it was a walk in the fucking park." She kept shaking her head, laughing without mirth. "Jesus Christ, Vic." Then, looking at her phone: "I have to go."

"Jane," I said, and it felt like the thousandth time that I had said her name with no idea what should come after it. Her name had begun to take the place of "please" or "wait," two words I rarely said and therefore did not know how to use. I disliked being at a disadvantage.

"I'll see you," she said, and left me sitting there wondering when.

23

Notes de Tête: Anise, Lemon, and Green Grape
Notes de Cœur: Menthol and Warm Cotton
Notes de Fond: Excrement, Meat Sweats

Back at home I stuffed the wet clothes in the dryer and went back to sleep. I didn't need to, really. In the past I had successfully pushed past the forty-eight-hour mark, and I had gotten a few winks here and there over the last couple of days. But last night had drained something out of me that I hadn't been prepared to lose.

The pillowcase beneath my cheek still smelled like Jane.

The end-cycle buzzer on the dryer woke me up late in the afternoon. I made a pot of bad coffee and unloaded the clothes while it perked. Jane's flannel shirt crackled with static. When I held the warm cotton to my face, I breathed in only hot lint and detergent. I thought about putting it on, but didn't.

Giovanni was due tonight. Checking the final empty tub, I wiped out a little bit of dust and chased a daddy longlegs through the drain hole. Briefly I entertained a fancy that the arachnid might be some kind of omen. I had known what to expect from Beau, and been pathetically excited and confused about Jane. With Giovanni, I had no idea what would happen. Though I suspected—strongly—that it would be bad.

I rummaged in the drawers of my dusty worktable until I found a plastic wheel of vinyl clothesline, bright green and translucent. With pliers I clipped a length about five feet long. Wrapping the ends around my hands a couple of times, I pulled the slack tight between them. Plastic squeaked where it overlapped across my knuckles.

Just in case everything went irretrievably south. Better safe than sorry.

Coiled up, the clothesline fit neatly in my back pocket. I settled in with my terrible coffee to wait. This time, I didn't listen to any podcasts.

I tried to picture how Giovanni would do the deed. I hadn't bothered to attempt it with Jane. She had already told me exactly how she would manage. As far as getting Reg out of the bar and into her trunk: she was an ingenious woman. Very resourceful. I can imagine it perfectly. Can't you?

But Giovanni, who thought premeditated murder was more reprehensible than the kind you committed in a passion . . . how would he have planned this? What provisions would he have made?

Surely he sent his desk girl home. Maybe after she signed Pearson in. Maybe mid-cut. Maybe she took Pearson's card, and when he stepped back to the station to give Giovanni his tip—I hope it was a good one—Giovanni asked him to stay for a drink.

However it happened, let's set them up alone together in the shop. But the front of the place is all windows, looking out on a street swarming with nightlife. How does he manage that?

The office, of course. The barbers disappear into it for lunch, for breaks, for coffee. You pass it on your way to the tiny bathroom in the rear of the shop. On occasion I had glanced through the half-open door and seen fluorescent lights, an ancient printer, a corkboard fluttering with schedules in the breeze of a rotating fan. A windowless, depressing cave.

Perhaps Pearson finds it quaint. Maybe he thinks that's where Giovanni keeps his good liquor—not the midshelf stuff the desk girl offers to less elevated clients.

He's in for a rude surprise.

Or maybe not. Let's say Giovanni does have a good bottle back there. Ouzo, maybe, or sambuca. He just doesn't seem like a whiskey man to me. And I enjoy the notion of Pearson in his last moments putting back shots of something that tastes like black jelly beans. I bet he doesn't even enjoy it—he's just doing this for the novelty of drinking with a workingman, drinking a workingman's drink.

Giovanni leaves the bottle open in between pours, and the smell of anise gathers in the corners of the tiny room, thickening the air. Giovanni: citrus and vetiver, Proraso and a hint of Barbicide, perspiration intensifying the natural smell of his body beneath all the tonsorial product that has clung to him over the course of the day. Pearson: the lemon, green grape, sweet-tart pink pomade Giovanni uses on customers. Bad breath from bits of meat still stuck in his teeth after a late lunch. Stale tobacco smoke and smugness.

There is poor airflow in the office. It grows hot and pungent almost as quickly as Pearson gets drunk.

"I really admire what you've done here," he says. "It's a terrible shame about the building. I wish I'd heard about your shop sooner—if I'd known you were here I'd have thought twice about the sale."

This is a blatant lie, but for a brief moment I'm sure it sparks remorse and hope in Giovanni's heart. He is wishing that he had ever cut Pearson's hair before this, that he had given Pearson trims at eight fifteen at night. That Pearson was a regular customer, and not someone coming in for his inaugural cut. Giovanni does not realize, or doesn't want to, that even in this reality—*especially* in this reality—I would have asked him to do the same thing I am asking now.

Then Pearson says something like, "I'm sure you'll find another spot, though. Maybe even nicer than this one!"

The remorse gutters. The hope goes out.

"There's nowhere nicer than this," he says.

"Listen, son." Pearson burps. "This is my bread and butter. I know you can find something great. Maybe out in Astoria. Long Island City! There are a lot of places nicer than this that will come cheaper too."

But Giovanni is the man who handpicked the backsplashes; who sweeps up after his barbers have already swept; who sits in a folding chair outside the shop during breaks and knows all of his neighbors' names. He is not talking in terms a real-estate agent would understand.

"Honestly, son," Pearson goes on. "The West Village? Pretty big balls on you to open up here. What is the rent on this place?"

"It didn't used to be that bad. I got really lucky with the lease." His luck hasn't held, because I made sure that it wouldn't. But even if I hadn't come along and clipped his wings, someone else would have done it.

Right about now, he is starting to see that I was right, and he is hating me for it. But he is hating himself more. And hating Pearson most of all.

It turns out, you can still murder someone in a passion, even if you've been planning on it.

Giovanni uses his hands. Either because he didn't like the idea of setting aside some tool for the job or because it seems fairer to him somehow. He didn't count on being able to feel the moment Pearson's throat collapsed.

If you've broken your nose—or someone else's—you may have some idea what this feels like. The sickening crunch of cartilage that doesn't quite snap like bone but doesn't give like flesh either. A sort of jelloid collapse; an implosion. If you've never broken your nose—or someone else's—how can I describe it? Have you ever cleaned a fish? The fragile plasticity of a salmon skull is similar. Or, if you're one of those people who takes the paper off their garlic by cracking the clove with the heel of your hand . . . like that. Something whole, suddenly splitting under pressure. Satisfying, in some contexts. In others? Unsettling.

This is the latter.

He finishes the job, and I'm sure he is crying by the end of it. Not efficient tears of contained grief, but that violent, masculine weeping that is the exorcism of emotion rather than its expression. He didn't buy a tarp, because he was trying very hard not to listen to what I was telling him, and so he has to mop up after everything is over and lay Pearson on several layers of trash bags so he stops leaking onto the floor.

Then, he has to wait. And wait. And wait. For Christopher Street to quiet down, for the traffic cops to pass. For the ten minutes of opportunity that will give him a chance to move Pearson—now swaddled in a barber's cape—from back room to borrowed car. Borrowed car with a ticket stuck beneath the wiper, because as Giovanni knows: life isn't fair.

◆ ◆ ◆

He arrived much later than Beau or Jane. It was nearly dawn, and I had nodded off with Jo Stafford playing low on my laptop. I woke to the insistent sound of a phone call patched through to my computer.

I clicked the pop-up and said a rusty hello.

"I'm outside," said Giovanni, and hung up.

By now you're familiar with the process: down the icy steps, front of basement to the back. Notably, Giovanni was silent the whole time. Not once did he curse or try to make small talk. He looked haggard, on the verge of illness. Even more so than you might expect at half past four. This was not mere sleep deprivation. It was the expression of a man who has lost someone, something, and knows there is no way back to what he used to have.

"Into the tub," I said, and he helped me heave and lift.

When Pearson lay in the belly of my last bathtub, Giovanni wiped his hands down the front of his coat—a beautiful double-breasted herringbone tweed. Midcentury vintage, I thought. With those buttons, it couldn't be repro.

"You should have that dry-cleaned," I said. "As soon as possible. The rest of it too, if you can't wash it at home."

He looked down at his coat, his knife-creased trousers, and his shoes.

"Ah, maybe brush the bottoms of the shoes as well. And polish them."

None of it would stand out as odd, if it came to investigation. Giovanni kept his clothing impeccably clean and well cared for.

"You gonna foot the bill?" he asked, openly hostile.

"Sure." I pulled a tarp over Pearson. "Venmo me."

"I'd prefer cash."

I ran a hand through my hair, conscious that I had just been clutching Pearson's soiled pant leg. Oh well. It would all get worse before it got better. "I'll bring it to my next cut."

One of the load-bearing beams in Giovanni's perfect posture snapped. "God*damn* it, Vic. I'm not going to have a shop in a couple of months."

"You will," I said. "I promised. The question is: Will you still cut my hair?"

He made a sound like something going wrong beneath the hood of a classic car.

"Right," I said. "Well, I can always drop it off with Jane and Beau. If you'll still speak to them, when this is over."

"When will it be?" he asked.

"For you? It can be over tomorrow, if you like. You never need to see me again."

"What if something goes wrong?" he asked. "What if the fucking cops turn up on my doorstep tomorrow?" Something about the tone of his voice reminded me of Beau, the way he could make anything sound like *please*.

"They won't," I said, briskly but firmly, the way you let someone down when you aren't going to give them what you know they want. "Nothing will go wrong, and your shop will stay open."

"And we can all move on like this never happened, and I'll give you discount cuts again?" Unable to stop fidgeting, he jammed his hands into his pockets. "Sounds great. Why didn't I think of that?"

"You're under a lot of stress."

He yanked one hand out of its pocket, fast. I wish I could say I didn't flinch, but now I knew he was capable of violence when pushed. And I had pushed him.

"You know what?" He let his hand fall away, shoving the dusty air aside like a delicacy offered up on a platter that nonetheless did not appeal. "I don't care what happens. Fuck this. Fuck you."

Ineloquent, but expressive. As I watched his back retreating toward the basement door I said, "Remember, dry-clean that coat."

By the light of my bedroom lamp, I could see him flip me the bird.

He said he did not care what happened. I would choose to believe, for now, this meant he would not act to influence the fallout one way or another. The important thing was that I had all three of the bodies I required. Now I could tackle Eisner's perfume. After that, I would have time and energy to . . . deal with Giovanni. I wanted to assuage him. I did not want to think about what would happen if I failed.

But first I had to patch things up with Jane. After all, you can only eat an elephant one bite at a time. And I'm a hopeless sybarite—I wanted to eat the best cuts of the elephant first, avoiding the gristle where I could. A critical error, but you can sympathize. I hope.

24

Notes de Tête: Dryer Lint
Notes de Cœur: Jerk Spice
Notes de Fond: Smoke and Frozen Earth Accord

It takes some time to tincture. More than I had, really, but you can't rush an art like this. I reached out to Eisner with an updated timeline and told him not to contact me unless there was an emergency.

The old year rolled over and died. The new one arrived already squalling. Iolanda and the college kids came back from vacation. The house filled up with noise and cooking smells and thumping bass, but nobody came into the basement. Much as I had expected. I didn't hear from Jane, and didn't reach out to reassure her.

Things slowed down at work. Sales dipped, but that was to be expected. They might bump up again in February, when men bought women perfume that they never wore, or didn't like, or gave them allergic reactions. We had done well enough over the holidays to hold us comfortably through the gray stretch until equinox.

"Do we want to do a V-Day launch?" asked Barry. "Or like . . . something for spring? Have you been working on anything new?"

If he had any idea! "Maybe," I said.

"Can you let me know sooner rather than later? I want to do some kind of campaign. I can get a deal on boosted posts if I go for it now."

"Sure," I told him. I could gin something up between now and then. Barry was canny about marketing, more so than I; whatever I made, I was fairly certain he could sell it.

Three weeks went by, blissfully devoid of Eisner or of Pippin Miles, though without communiqués from Jane or Beau or Giovanni—and why should that bother me, I wondered. I had skated along smoothly enough before they came into my life. Still, my silent phone became a constant itch at the edge of my consciousness. It made me irritable.

Late one night, at the icy end of January, I drained the tubs and replaced the old alcohol with fresh. The old stuff was translucent dilute brown, with small bits of particulate extant throughout. First each tincture went through a sieve lined with clean cheesecloth, and then into my tabletop stills. Clustered together, the three of them just fit onto the fold-down table in my studio, which kept them safe from potential prying eyes. Their mad-scientist silhouettes were harder to shroud in a tarp and hide in a corner.

The consequence, of course, was that my home smelled like middle-aged man for some time. Despite Reg's age his scent was much the same as his father's. A little ranker, a little less musty, but overall when he was stripped of his big floral beast mode perfume, or the special recipe of mine, he was the olfactory equivalent of his elders.

The stink of them clung in my hair and clothes and fouled up whatever I cooked or ate at home. I bought a lot of two-dollar patties and coco bread from the cash-only place a couple of blocks south on Amsterdam, then lingered as long as I could over a happy hour drink at the bistro down the street. Got a lot of reading done. Drafted formulas for something Barry could talk up on Instagram come spring. Poked at the idea of something bigger, something stranger: this idea that what Eisner had asked might not be impossible after all. And what memory would I make, if I thought it could be made? A thought experiment, at least, which kept me occupied through my lonely glasses of wine.

Eventually I had evaporated all my tincture into syrupy brown distillates, strong smelling and certainly not pleasant. These I put into my mini fridge. Technically, I could start mixing now. But if I gave it three more weeks the bodies in the tubs would render up another batch of tincture, less intense, that would give me half again as much distillate to add to this.

Unfortunately, in the first week of February, Eisner called. I let it go to voice mail, both wary and annoyed. When I worked up the courage to play it back, all he said was "Vic, call me back. It's an emergency."

◆　◆　◆

"When you say emergency—" I started, but Eisner cut me off.

"That detective. I thought you said you had it covered."

"When did I give that impression? I told you to talk to the Yateses. Did you?"

Silence.

"Goddamn it." Blaming me for things that were his fault, of course. But when has a customer ever admitted their own failings? I could handle this. It was just another iteration of retail. "Listen, it doesn't matter now. Too late to talk to either of them, and Miles has gone and done whatever he has. Which is?"

Eisner made an indistinct grumble—the tail end of getting over whatever grudge he felt he held against me for failing to do a job that was his by rights as well as by request. "He was in the office again. Hasn't been able to get ahold of any of the other leadership team. He's going to file missing persons reports."

"Jesus," I said, "you couldn't put him off of that?"

"I told him we hadn't expected them back for a while after Christmas anyway. And then I spun some bullshit about a business trip that won't hold up if he starts cross-checking it with their assistants."

"Relax," I said, so sharply I'm sure it didn't do him any good. "Miles is a two-bit private eye with a suspicious mind. If we're lucky the police won't pay him too much heed." I tried to put the specter of *my buddy Jeff* out of my head. "None of them were minors, and none of them had dementia. The cops won't treat this as high priority." It's possible I had done some research on the subject.

"What if he ties it back to Caroline?" The pitch of Eisner's voice rose, though his volume dropped. "That looks pretty bad."

This wasn't the time to tell him I agreed. "No," I said. "It looks like conspiracy. Calm down. Did he say who hired him?"

"Not outright. I think it was Caroline's mother."

"She's still alive?"

"Apparently. Unfortunately. She lives out in the Bay Area, didn't talk to her daughter much."

"Did she find out through Reg?"

"I didn't ask," he said. "I'm not supposed to know about any of it in the first place."

"Take a couple of breaths," I said, and began to pace the confines of my apartment. "Miles was dogging me the last few nights before we kicked things off. I was already planning on removing him from the picture. I just haven't had space to deal with him." I should have said to hell with it and thrown him into the river, but my usual method was tried and true. Bodies burned much faster after a stint in the tub, and none of the scraps of bone I buried in the windbreak near the barrel had yet been discovered. Besides, I was loath to waste an opportunity. There were no memories of Miles I particularly cherished, but he might be useful to have around for experimental purposes. For instance, he would have saved me the trouble of cigars with Pearson. And if I wanted to work on this idea that had been nagging at me like an itch just out of scratching reach, I would need raw materials.

"Do you have space now?" asked Eisner.

"I could make some." It would give me less distillate for Eisner's perfume, but it would probably save me a whole lot of trouble in the end.

"Do you know where to find him?"

"I have his number and his email. I can set something up." It would be touchy—normally I preferred to do extensive recon before the big event. I didn't know if Miles would give me the chance. Maybe I could get him to come to me?

"When you say he was dogging you, what exactly do you mean?"

I wanted this conversation to be over so I could move forward with my plans. "He may have been following me."

"May have?"

"Hell of a coincidence, otherwise. And he's been poking holes in every story I give him. But only after I offer it up. Cat-and-mouse style; he just wants me to know he knows I'm bullshitting. He thinks he's onto something. And the worst part is, he's right."

"So why hasn't he gone to the cops yet?" Eisner asked.

"I didn't ask," I said, mimicking his intonation. "He probably wants some solid proof. Like I said: two-bit detective. He worries he won't be taken seriously unless he's got something incontrovertible."

"Death," said Eisner, "is incontrovertible. Let's give him that, shall we?"

◆ ◆ ◆

A small part of me was relieved at Eisner's panic: it pretty much put paid to Jane's worries that he would use me as a scapegoat in the endgame. Unless he was worried about Miles as an unpredictable element in some plan he had already cooked up.

One step at a time. The endgame was at the *end*, and I was still mucking around in the middle.

Pippin Miles agreed to meet at the end of the week, uptown. Near enough to my place I thought I could reasonably convince him to come back and take a look at . . . something. I had a couple of days for that. In the meantime, I had to make some space for him.

I chose Conrad to dispose of first, for symmetry. Picked up my usual Zipcar after I got home from work. On disposal runs I had to load up earlier than I was really comfortable with—the drive upstate, and then the actual fire, would take a long time. I needed to make sure I had enough night to spare.

By the time I got Conrad into the trunk I was in a full sweat. After I buckled myself in, I started to shiver—the sweat had gone cold, and it would take a while for the engine to warm up. Even then I would want to crack a window for the fumes. Already, I could smell the boozy reek making its way between the seat cushions from the trunk.

Traffic on the parkway was sparse, which was always a little surreal. There were a few other cars, of course, mostly headed out of town. It was late on a weeknight, and the weather had taken a turn for brutally cold. Nobody wanted to be out, which meant fewer ride shares on the road, and fewer cabs. I headed north through the blackness of Inwood Hill Park, the self-satisfied opulence of Riverdale, more blackness as I cut through the corner of Van Cortlandt.

Traffic picked up a bit through the suburbs, where more people drove by necessity. So it wasn't until I hit the deserted Taconic that I started to wonder about the pair of headlights that kept pace about fifty yards behind.

I first noticed them by chance, winking in my rearview. When I looked up to double-check, the other car had disappeared around one of the parkway's picturesque turns. It was a pretty drive in the daytime. At night it could be a little treacherous.

We played this game for mile after mile. Sometimes I convinced myself the other driver was simply another late-night traveler. After all, the Taconic was long and narrow, lined with trees. Not many exits, and if this other car was headed as far upstate as I was, it might be behind me for many miles yet.

If we both obeyed the speed limit.

I tend to, on these errands, because I can't afford to be pulled over. Why was this other car staying at a polite fifty-five?

Maybe the driver was elderly, or had bad eyes. Perhaps they were cautious about driving in the dark. I told myself all this. Do you think I believed it?

The farther we got from the city, the bolder my pursuer became. Finally showing some initiative with the accelerator, they arrived at an assured clear distance off my rear bumper and remained there. Having begun to steadily curse some miles back, I now resorted to chewing fiercely at my lip. Soon my teeth tasted like blood.

I couldn't see through their windshield in my rearview, but I knew who it was. You know who it was too. And in my trunk, I had exactly the incontrovertibility he was looking for.

So what to do?

I couldn't waste time on a detour to throw him off the scent. I had promised to take care of him, and he was giving me an opportunity. There was some small risk that he had a GPS logger on his car; it wouldn't be out of line with his profession or suspicious nature. I couldn't drive two vehicles. Wherever I killed him, his car would stay there. If I took him to my burn spot and dispatched him, it would lead trouble straight to the evidence.

Luckily, the Taconic is riddled with twisting little side roads that plunge into the forest and obscurity. The next time I saw the flash of a green road sign in the trees, I slammed on my brakes and took a hard right. Miles missed the turn, which gave me an extra fifteen seconds to speed down the access road, veer right up a gravel drive, and cut the lights when I hit a dead end.

Just in time. Miles crept around the bend, and I saw him hesitate at the fork, then take the left. My engine ticked-ticked-ticked and cooled. Maybe if he thought he'd lost me down the side road he would give up, go home. But I knew better than that. I understand obsession; *I* wouldn't have given up.

In the distance I heard his engine quiet and then climb again, this time as an insistent whine. He was reversing up the road. I saw his brake lights first, and then his headlights, and then, sure enough, he came up the right side of the fork.

By this point, I had gotten out of the car and hidden in the scrub. It was freezing cold, and I held my breath as best I could to keep from giving myself away in clouds of steam. With the key fob, I popped the trunk of my rented car remotely. I would trick Miles into standing exactly where I needed him.

He parked, but left his engine running and his lights on. The halogen glow cast the shadow of the open trunk into sharp relief. To his credit he didn't go straight to it but cased the interior of the car first, and then the clearing.

He carried a matte-black handgun. Unsurprising, but unpleasant. With any luck, he wouldn't need to use it. Or rather, wouldn't have the time.

Finally, he approached my trap. Gun half raised in his right hand, he slipped the fingers of his left into the dark and lifted the trunk lid high.

"Holy shit," I heard him say. His last words weren't any for the ages.

There was no way they would both fit in the trunk, so I trusted my sober driving and the loneliness of night to cover for Pippin Miles's lifeless body in the back seat. I sweated nearly through my coat during the last fifty miles of my drive, though I kept the heat turned off for fear of accelerating Miles's decomposition.

It would be hours yet until I had him safely stowed in the basement and could get to work. I'd be cutting it close, so the colder he stayed, the better.

After a thorough reconnaissance of the surrounding fields, I got started. Conrad went up as quickly as his wife. I would have liked to stand near the fire to keep warm, but as you no doubt remember from our first foray, charnel smoke has a very particular smell. Very difficult to get out of clothes. I sat inside the car with the windows rolled up against the greasy reek of barbecue and burning hair. Pippin Miles grew slowly stiffer in the back seat, where I had tied him into a fetal position with his own shoelaces and that awful blue windbreaker and wrapped him in Conrad's tarp. On balance I thought alcohol in the trunk was less likely to raise eyebrows at the Zipcar garage than shit smeared on the seats. The alcohol would evaporate. The shit would not.

Then again, they don't pay the people at those garages enough to really care *what* you do with the car, as long as it comes back in one piece.

It took Conrad a long time and a lot of added brush to really crumble down. When his soft parts had gone sufficiently ashy, I used a stick to sift through the barrel for bones and put them in a paper grocery sack, breaking what wouldn't fit beneath my heel until it would. In warmer weather I would have buried them, but the ground was frozen solid. They would have to go into some random trash can on a corner. Maybe if I stopped for gas on the way home. Pippin Miles, meanwhile, went into the recently vacated trunk.

What would Jane think of this part of the process? The thought came unbidden—perhaps summoned by the faint smell of excrement, and its associations with our last night together. She had been focused and efficient at breaking down Reg. She had killed him and brought me his corpse, for god's sake. Surely she could handle this as well. Perhaps the wait would not have felt so long. Perhaps if we shared a seat we could have kept each other warm. Hands slipped inside each other's coats, her cold fingers in my armpit.

Pretty sappy thoughts, for an illicit cremation.

By the time I got back to the city I had lost any sense of my extremities. I could see my hands on the wheel but couldn't feel them. I regulated my speed solely by watching the dial, because I certainly couldn't tell how much weight I had put on the accelerator. I will admit to pushing sixty here and there in my eagerness to be home.

Once I arrived, the awful rigamarole of wrestling another corpse into the basement, struggling with the frozen deadweight. Once or twice I dropped him, and it's a miracle I didn't crack his skull.

I felt like hell. Blood came back to my fingers and toes, and soon I was in agony. I worried about frostbite. The basement was cold, so even as I thawed I didn't warm. I worried about hypothermia. I took a break for a hot shower—not to clean up, for there was still dirty work ahead—and the water felt like acid at first. Then, I didn't want to get out. My body finally remembered to shiver, and I couldn't stop.

I thought of Beau, and Jane. I wondered if Giovanni had broken down, before or after he came to me. I clenched my jaw against my chattering teeth and waited to feel warm on the inside. There was nobody to kiss me, to go down on their knees.

Then it was back to the grind. By the time I finished up, the sun had risen and I could hear Iolanda moving around upstairs. Risky timing, but I hadn't exactly had a choice.

I had just started a load of laundry when I heard the basement door swing open. Irrational with exhaustion, I froze. Standing naked by the washer.

"Vicky?" she called. "Vicky, you down here?"

My jaw felt strapped closed, teeth aching against one another. I couldn't answer.

"Vicky! You all right? I can hear the washer." Then, god help me, she started to come down. Slowly and gingerly, favoring the bad hip. I was frozen to the spot.

When her head cleared the ceiling she gasped and said, "Madre de dios!" Then, collecting herself enough to stare frankly at my nakedness: "Aren't you cold?"

"Sorry," I said. My voice was hoarse, my throat sore. I made no effort to cover myself. I was too tired for modesty.

"Put some clothes on," she said. "You're gonna freeze."

"They're all in the wash."

"Damn," she said. "I was going to ask you to do a load for me. How long on this one?"

"Half an hour," I said. "I just put them in." A wave of goose bumps rippled up my skin. I was pretty sure I was coming down with something.

"Okay, well. Let me know when you're done." She turned and took a step up, then said, "Does it smell like shit down here to you?"

I sniffed ostentatiously. "A little? I don't know. Could just be the sump pump. Or the pipes."

She took a deep breath and wrinkled her nose. "Maybe. God, somebody should clean this place out. It's a fire trap, you know?"

I felt cold straight through, and this time it had nothing to do with the weather or the damp concrete.

"Just tell me when your laundry's done," she said. "And eat a big breakfast. I can see your damn ribs."

I nodded weakly, and waited until the basement door shut to completely lose my head.

◆　◆　◆

For the next week I lay prostrate on my bed, sick as the proverbial dog. I ordered soup and curry and picked despondently at it, appetite destroyed.

I hate sinus issues for the same reasons anybody does—the pressure, the pain, the uneven distribution of snot that makes deep sleep impossible. But the absolute blockage of my nasal passages is worse for me than it might be for you or anyone else. Beethoven, robbed of the sound of his symphonies.

But like Beethoven, I could still draft formulae, and so I did. Pushing molecules around, I imagined the colors and textures they would make when mixed together. Somewhere in the middle I caught odd hours of sleep. Whenever my snot switched sides.

I was too tired and too miserable to imagine a solution to the impossible project that continued to haunt me. But I could work on something . . . I hesitate to call it "more mundane." It was not—I have never made a scent for which that epithet would be appropriate. Instead, let us call it less esoteric.

Barry wanted something in time for Valentine's Day, I knew. I didn't think I could make that deadline, not with Eisner's commission over my head. I had been building that formula for the last month or so and was eager to get started on actually mixing once my ingredients matured.

But I could craft a new Bright House in time for spring. For Easter. Commonly believed to be an ancient ritual of sex and birth, fecundity and sacrifice, the truth is that Ostara is a more modern festival, a neo-pagan reclamation of the Catholic tradition spun from tenuous branch tips of the Indo-European language tree, based on theory and guesswork of folklorists and scholars.

A tempting idea, though. It *feels* so right. And feeling always sells better than fact. So, a spring perfume. Something about the green, the wet, the mud, the earth. People had such high hopes for the spring, but the season was a tease. Snow in April. Forty and gray. Downpours for days on end.

Somehow, it made me think of Jane. And in my fevered, isolated state, the whole project became a gift for her. What I might mix to capture the idea of her. Or the idea of her absence, as I lay alone in the damp and cold.

I imagined what her absence smelled like. Something that skimmed the skin like fine cloth: a sheer drapery of icy linen. A scent that let light through, but muted it. A sheet that would not keep you warm.

Lilac, I thought, picturing those blue-gray eyes. Lilac and violet leaf. The scent of a springtime garden under cloudy skies and incessant rain. The kind of rain that never lets up, that drives you half-mad listening to its footsteps on the roof. A cold smell. A smell on the verge of decay. Earth so soaked the worms come up to die, sprawled across the pavement.

This would not smell like sex or birth. It would smell like spring where there was yet no hope of summer.

This was a gift I could give without losing ground. A piece of myself I *wanted* her to have. When my fever broke, I wrote the formula in an hour, and knew that it would be a stunner. And then, like it had been waiting in the wings for the stage to clear, the next idea came to me:

If I could reinforce someone's fantasy of an event that never happened, could I also somehow . . . build memories from scratch? It couldn't be far off from what had worked on Pearson, and what—god willing—would work on Eisner. It would only require some skill with narrative, and some groundwork to familiarize the wearer with the base notes of the scent.

The process I envisioned would require at least one party—me—to know the details of the event, to relate them in enough detail to create for the subject a vivid sense of how things *had* been. Which also meant I could never access memories of Jonathan I did not have, only share the ones I had already. An idea that did not, initially, appeal. I was much more jealous of him in death than I think I had been in life. Or perhaps it was merely that I could exercise my jealousy to better effect.

I had been so wrapped up in the idea of Jane as I drafted my lilac perfume. Evoking her presence, or her absence, must have got me thinking about her role in my current project, and how that project could be adapted, transformed, built upon. She had not only solved the issue of Eisner's commission, she had cracked open the seed of this new idea. And now, it wanted to unfurl.

But first I had to get Eisner off my back and launch this new thing. When all of that was done, then I could play around.

25

Notes de Tête: Rain and Lilacs
Notes de Cœur: Sea Salt, Clay, and Scallions
Notes de Fond: Freshly Baked Bread

For about a week, I was certain that Iolanda would follow through on her threat to clean out the basement. As she failed and failed, that fear ebbed away. By then I was slightly less sick and back in the office, snuffling my way through unpaid invoices and Barry's last-minute Valentine's Day marketing plans. His knack for that end of the business meant I would lose him soon unless I started paying more.

On the big chocolate heart bonanza day, I slogged home with a headache and a crick in my neck and realized it was time to drain the tubs again. I could probably stand to dispose of Pippin Miles too, at this point. After tonight, all three of them would be out of the basement and ease the stress on my poor cardiac muscles every time I heard Iolanda pass by the basement door.

I wasn't looking forward to another trip upstate in this weather, but at least I could leave the heat on when I came home.

Unusually paranoid, I lugged the plastic tubs full of undistilled tincture into my apartment and locked them in, and then called up the U-Haul place down on Broadway. They had awful reviews and pretty regularly scammed their customers, but in this case that was an asset. If I didn't ask questions, neither would they.

I paid cash, and used a fake ID. A Zipcar record is one thing—I'm in the right demographic for a trip up to Hudson or Catskill or Beacon a couple of times a year. Maybe I enjoy vintage shops or installation art—both, as it happens. But a U-Haul on my credit card and no antiques to show for it? Questionable. The guys at the rental place gave me a discount too.

The whole situation went much more smoothly this time, even with three bodies to dispose of. I dropped the cargo van off in the Bronx early in the morning, took the 2 down to Ninety-Sixth, and wandered up Broadway to arrive at Absolute Bagels just after they opened. It was deliciously warm inside, the moist air thick with the smell of yeast and toasted bread. I took a deep breath, marveling at the ability to do so. My sinuses were finally clear.

Settling at a corner table with my coffee and a plush salt bagel oozing scallion shmear, I considered the merits of home versus work. At home, I could sleep. Or try to. I would likely end up working, if only to get those tubs out of my studio. And then I would be stuck smelling whoever I decided to distill first. The day—dawning bright and clear—seemed too full of promise to fill with fusty steam.

Work it was, then. I ordered a second coffee and headed downtown.

◆ ◆ ◆

The lilac perfume came together like . . . I don't want to say a dream. First, because it's cliché. And second, it felt more logical than that. Maybe it makes better sense to describe it growing. Like a snowflake, or a crystal. Particles of matter neatly accreting around an idea, growing in orderly matrices whose end product was a delicate, translucent beauty.

When I brought it to Barry for beta testing, he held the test strip to his nose without much fanfare. I waited, unconcerned, until he made a face and handed it back.

"What the fuck is that?"

From Barry, this was not necessarily a negative reaction. Sometimes his cruelty was affectionate.

"It smells like wet concrete," he said. "Or like . . . clay. Like moldy clay in a pottery studio."

I nodded, waiting. He had a good nose. Not as good as mine, but better than most.

Another sniff. "Mmm. Rainy. And . . . hydrangea? No, lilac. Those little ones, Miss Kim."

"You're full of surprises."

He grinned at me. "So are you."

I did not give the grin back.

"I did summer camp at the Botanical Garden when I was a kid," he said by way of explanation. "Anyway. Not what I was expecting, but we can work with it, yeah? What do you want to call it? Maybe just Kim? Or . . . I'm trying to think how we can strategize here. What kind of words do people google when they really want to smell like . . ." He screwed his face up and stared at the test strip. "Cold sludge?"

"None of that," I said, leery of the trap of search-engine optimization.

"Sorry," he said. "I just know you hate to name them."

"I know what we'll call this one," I said.

"Yeah?"

"Yeah. We'll call it 'This One.'"

"Don't tell me you're serious."

I nodded.

"Why—" Then, glee bloomed across his expression like a time-lapse clip of some particularly over-the-top flower. *Passiflora platyloba*, perhaps, or night-blooming cereus. Given his revelation about the Botanical Garden, he would have known better than I did. "Oh my god." He somehow made the phrase sound like its popular text message abbreviation. "This is that girl from Instagram. The one you were messaging on the company account. Are you talking to her? Like, *talking* to her?"

"We talk," I said. "Sometimes."

"I fucking *knew* it," he said. "You've been acting so weird. I thought like, the mob was gonna break your knees or something."

"You have an active imagination."

"Jesus, though, you couldn't have made her something that smells a little nicer?"

"I don't care about nice things," I said. "Neither does she." Not in the sense he meant it, anyway. "Nice" was such a watery word. As far as I could tell, Jane cared about *fine* things, just like Beau and Giovanni. Sophisticated things, things made well. And while this perfume wasn't *nice*, it was sophisticated and then some.

"Well," he said, watching me with unwarranted fondness. "I'm glad you finally found somebody on your level."

Found, and now possibly lost. But I could deal with sewing up that rent in my social life once Eisner's commission was turned in. I didn't have time for anything but work until then.

"I was kind of starting to worry about you," Barry went on. I rolled my eyes. "No really. The thing about you, Vic—"

"The *one* thing?"

Unperturbed, he continued. "The thing about you is, you want everyone to think you don't need anybody, but you can't really live that way. Nobody can."

"I don't need her," I said. "Not like air, or water. She isn't *essential*."

He flapped the test strip in my direction, and I tasted lilac on the tip of my tongue as I inhaled. "Neither is what we do. This shit ain't oxygen. But bread and roses, Vic. Bread and roses." Then, reconsidering, he added, "Sometimes, I think maybe you just live on roses."

"I live on those egg buns from the shop down the street." I dug in my jacket pocket for my billfold. "You want some? I'm buying."

"Fine," he said, "I get it. I'll back off. I'm just . . . I'm really happy for you, okay? That's all. I won't make it weird."

If only he knew how weird it was already. "Don't get too excited," I told him. "We're sort of on the outs."

"Goddamn it, Vic! What did you do?"

That was one to steer well clear of. "I . . . she wanted to know about an ex. I didn't want to tell her. I think it kind of scared her off."

He clucked his tongue against his teeth. "This is what I'm saying! You gotta open up with her if you want her to stick around, y'know? Honesty and openness equals emotional intimacy." He mimed some kind of math equation with his hands. "What are you, an Aquarius? I have dated an Aquarius and let me tell you, you will get dumped unless you give a little."

I glared at him.

"Bread," he said, cupping the equation into the bowl of his palms and offering it to me. "Bread, Vic. You gotta feed her."

"Fuck off, Barry." I finally found the necessary cash. "I'm going to go feed *me*. And you can forget about me feeding you."

◆　◆　◆

But Barry's New Age bullshit stuck with me like excrement in the treads of my shoes. A whiff of it seemed to follow me wherever I went.

Jane had wanted to know about Jonathan, and after a night like that—and after everything she had already done for me before—I owed her some kind of truth. Instead, I had stiffed her.

In between sessions on Eisner's perfume, I poked at the problem like a sore tooth. But when I was working, I didn't have time or attention to ponder anything.

When mixing a perfume, you can't slip up, you can't fudge numbers, and you have to write things down. The proportions of a test batch have to be replicable at scale, and if you don't perfectly note what you've put in, you're going to be fucked when you try to re-create it later.

I had taken an afternoon to sample the egg salad from the place around the corner. More importantly, I had a strong scent memory and could conjure the atmosphere of that conference room as if producing it from a filing cabinet and spreading it across my kitchen table.

Freon, dust, hot plastic, paper. Corporate office accord. The egg salad, sulfurous with a sharp note of sweet vinegar for the emerald studs of relish. The barest hint of stale tobacco. Whisky breath, which was peat, fermented sugars, rotten meat. The smallest trace of orris root and musky jasmine for the whisper of sex Eisner swore would cling to Reg. Why and how it got there I didn't like to imagine.

And, of course, the pièce de résistance: the scents of our three star players. Reg like a steamy locker room, a spermy sock. Conrad fusty—the sourness of a humidifier filter left too long in the dark. Pearson was the meat sweats and not much else.

Drip, drip, drip, and swirl. Write it down. Sniff to check. Sometimes I got it right on the first try, the promises of my formula bearing out. Other times it required adjustments, which meant the balance fell off in other quarters. All of it assiduously noted, referenced, replicated.

The strangest thing began to happen, as I mixed—as I smelled each sample, I could almost see it. The closer it hewed to my vision, the more perfectly the formula fell out, the clearer the picture that coalesced in my mind's eye. A ghost of what I was used to with my memory perfumes, but present nonetheless. It was not my fantasy, but I knew the men. I knew the room in which it had supposedly happened. The scents were all familiar to me, and their context. Eisner's fantasy had become such a focus of mine that I wondered if I was deluding myself, or if some of his fanaticism had rubbed off. Was this an effect, or only wishful thinking?

Even if it was working on me, that didn't mean it would work on Eisner. His fantasy was strongly drawn, specific. I could extrapolate on anything. He needed an exact accord.

Still, this was promising evidence that my theory about implanting memories via scent and suggestion was viable—that with a story to tie the elements together, a perfume could create something stronger than mere association.

No time to look into it, though; I had a commission to earn.

Eventually, I created three formulations I was willing to risk on a trial. I capped all of my brown glass bottles, stowed everything in the mini fridge—which was near to overflowing—and poured myself a double. I had a crick in my neck and my nose was tired. Stuffing it into the crook of my elbow, I breathed my own scent deep to clear my head. The whisky did the opposite, but in a nicer way.

It was one o'clock in the morning, but I still called Eisner. It went to voice mail; I didn't leave one.

He retaliated by returning my call at seven in the morning, when I was barely awake and mildly hungover, on account of not eating much besides whisky the night before.

"Good morning," he said when I greeted him with an interrogative grunt. "I saw I had a missed call."

"I have some testers," I told him, voice rasping. "When can you meet?"

"Oh, excellent." He actually sounded pleased. Giddy, even. "Today is absolutely manic. Actually, the rest of this week is bad. You know, things are really up in the air with three of our executives missing."

Something about the blithe tone of it froze my blood. Under the ringing in my ears, Jane's words replaying: *How do you know he's not going to hand you over at the first sign of trouble?*

"No shit," I said, airless. "How's it working out for you?"

"Oh, don't you worry about me." I didn't, really; I had more important skins to save. Like my own. "I'm up to the task," he said. "It just means I might not be able to meet until . . . could you do the weekend, actually? Come over. I'll make brunch."

At this point I pulled my phone away from my face and checked the time; you're not supposed to be able to read clocks if you're dreaming. Seven oh three. This was real life, and I was going to have to deal with it.

"Brunch?"

"I'm not a bad cook," he said. I thought of Beau's pasta con zucca and wondered if Eisner measured up. Then I wondered if I would ever get to eat Beau's cooking again.

Later. Later. First, wrap up this business.

"Fine," I said. "But no mimosas."

26

Notes de Tête: Clorox, Orange Oil
Notes de Cœur: Brown Butter and Coffee
Notes de Fond: Cooked Egg, Hudson River Accord

Eisner lived in the West Village, in exactly the place you might imagine he would live if you didn't imagine him living in a high-rise at the south end of Central Park, or sunbathing on a balcony above the High Line.

He owned a townhouse on Perry Street—owned it, the entire house—in a neighborhood so full of beautiful things it inspired first lust and then rage. Sleepy Federal brick buildings, gnarled old trees. Tiny boutiques purveying raw chocolate and pink sea salt. Coffee shops where they inexplicably sold high-end Scandinavian hand cream. Sidewalks populated by an aesthetic sprinkling of impeccably groomed dogs and people.

After the smeared chewing gum and general stink of the rest of the city—its incessant, insistent noise—stepping into the tangled, tree-lined streets of this old and monied part of the island felt like a magic trick. Or like crossing the border into a fairyland full of cruel creatures you would never understand, amongst whom you did not belong.

I marveled at Eisner's willingness to give me his address. He knew what I did. What I had done, for him. Maybe he trusted his money to keep him safe. Or my continued reliance on his money. But he had *blackmailed* me. His arrogance, or ignorance, in this regard was astonishing. Or perhaps it was neither arrogance nor ignorance; perhaps he truly had cooked up some further plan that he believed would tie me up and keep him safe.

If he had, I should act soon. Our holiday sales had been damn strong. Valentine's orders were excellent. I was looking forward to what would happen with this springtime launch Barry was planning. I wasn't going to need Eisner's money again, not after this. Not if it worked.

Jane and Giovanni were both right: I couldn't afford to let him stick around, knowing what he knew and acting like he did. But I did need Eisner's money *now*, even if I wouldn't later. And so:

There was only one doorbell, centered in a decorative brass plate. Above it, awkward in the centuries-old doorframe, a glossy black dome obscuring the lens of a camera. I rang, and shortly I saw a shadow beyond the leaded glass.

The door opened to the sounds of *This American Life*. Ira Glass, and Eisner in athleisure, were both unpleasant surprises, but I suppose it was a Saturday.

"Come in," he said, sweeping me across the threshold. "I'm running a little behind schedule, sorry. Got caught chatting after yoga."

There was an image I didn't like to contemplate. "I don't mind." I had not brought a bottle of prosecco this time, and there was an awkward moment where I would have otherwise presented a host gift. He hurried us through it by ushering me down the hall—dark wood banister curving tightly to the second floor, black-and-white photographs in minimalist frames. They were not his. I had seen his photos, and these were better.

The kitchen was full French country: high ceiling, white tile with a decorative backsplash. A butcher's block, a breakfast bar, a bare wood table with an enameled tin bowl overflowing with citrus fruits. It looked like a magazine shoot, except for Eisner's AirPods and closed laptop sitting on one hooked-rag place mat. He swept these up and deposited them on the breakfast bar before asking, "Orange juice?"

The citrus in the enamel bowl turned out to be more than ornamental. The juice was very good. This made me angry in the same way that very good espresso in the Lower East Side had, long ago. I recognized it now as the idea that I appreciated something in a way other people couldn't possibly. Namely because they lacked a certain set of aesthetic skills, or because they didn't have to worry about how much it cost. It was a feeling worse than simple fury, because it was *covetous*. It felt like reading an issue of *Monocle*: a magazine I could only page through at newsstands because it cost too much to buy.

I set the juice aside and put my ragged tote bag on the table, which made it look less like a magazine shoot. "Would you like to try these now? Or after brunch?"

He cracked an egg into a cast-iron skillet and let it sizzle. "Anticipation is the greater part of pleasure, don't you think?"

◆ ◆ ◆

Eisner made a good fried egg. I'll give him that. His brunch was serviceable if uninspired. There was no booze involved, which was probably for the best. I had no desire to get drunk with him.

Conversation was stilted. What did we have to talk about, besides the commission?

"Are things at EPY&Y as chaotic as I imagine?" I asked.

He shrugged. "The business is actually running better than ever. Rumors like wildfire, of course. And a couple of police detectives in and out."

"The real police," I said. "Not just Pip Miles?"

"Speaking of," said Eisner.

I felt cold like a ghost in my bones. Felt my lungs ache with the memory of alcohol fumes and a hacking cough. "Taken care of."

Indulging in a self-satisfied smile, Eisner scraped a bit of quinoa salad off his knife and onto his fork. "Excellent."

"The NYPD is another story," I said. "What's your plan for them? I don't think I can tackle every single officer they send your way." How much could I convince him to give up?

"Easy," said Eisner. "You know the deal they were doing wasn't on the up-and-up. So do I. It was bald-faced money laundering. The police haven't figured it out yet, but I can ensure they do. Then it's a foregone conclusion: something went wrong and somebody—powerful—got angry."

"And you had nothing to do with it."

Eisner shrugged, all innocence. "I wasn't in the meeting, was I? Sometimes it pays to be the black sheep."

This came as a relief—if it was true. It seemed like it could be. It had elegance, which went a long way in my book. I didn't trust *Eisner*, but I trusted his dedication to what he perceived as aesthetic. He liked this solution because it had clean lines and a nice color palette.

"Well," I said. "If you have all that in hand, then the only thing outstanding is this." I put one hand on my tote bag, covering the shape of a box of samples. I pressed hard to stop a tremor that wanted to climb past my wrist.

Whatever I had in that box, it worked for me, at least theoretically. All the components necessary to capture my idea of the moment were present, and even conjured an image, a moment, when they should have given me nothing but a smell. Would they all come together for Eisner?

"Shall we?" I asked, almost hoping he would say no. But where would that leave me?

Unlike Pearson, his breath did not catch. I watched his face for the telltale flush, or the anxious, anticipatory drain of color. He gave me nothing, and I, in turn, felt a grudging respect.

"Sure," he said. "Let's do it."

From my tote, I withdrew a small cardboard box I had swiped from the office. The same kind we used to ship our discovery sets, or bigger orders of samples. Inside, though, was no perfume our house had ever sold.

Neither was it exactly the perfume I had mixed. These I had diluted, doctored with perfumer's alcohol until the scent was minimal and the evaporation swift. Remember, I said the memory only lasts as long as the scent remains. Eisner wanted the memory, and I didn't trust him not to cut and run once he had it. He would get a taste of the goods and no more, not until he paid for them.

"Here." I popped the box's top and slid it across the table, showing him three unlabeled sample sprayers nestled in shredded paper. They were all nearly clear, each tinted pale amber by the unique natural components at their base.

"Which one first?" he asked.

I shrugged. Normally I would have an opinion—much in the way of tasting wine or whisky, perfume was best smelled light to heavy. But in this case, the three perfumes were almost equally balanced. They differed only in the emphasis they placed: on people, on office environment, on egg salad. None was stronger than the other, none had a more intense sillage. I had simply held their various parts like threads to ply and adjusted the tension, varying the texture of the finished product.

"Just make sure to clear your nose between," I said.

He lifted his coffee and I shook my head. Coffee—a strong scent in itself—would merely overwhelm whatever he had been sniffing before. I mimed smelling the crook of my elbow, where my own scent had caught in the weave of my shirt, the knit of my sweater. The familiar molecules of his own body, his unwashed clothes, would bring him back to neutral territory.

"Huh," he said, and mimicked me. "All right."

Now, the moment of truth. Suddenly, I wished he had given me weeks to sit in that conference room, to parse the currents of air, the vicissitudes of scent. I had been so confident in my own recollection, but this man sat in that conference room at least once a week. Maybe every day. What hubris to think I understood its scents more intimately than he.

I took a breath, and held it. The orange and Clorox dissipated quickly. The egg fat followed, dragging its heels. Soon all that was left was the bitterness of coffee at the back of my throat, and the burn of air turning stale in my lungs.

Eisner sprayed the first perfume. The mist settled across his collar-bone, in between the lapels of his zip-collared workout shirt. I gasped, starved for oxygen, and he looked up sharply. His eyes were clear. No joy.

"Smells right," he said. "You nailed the eggs." Sniffing again he said, "Doesn't last very long."

"Try the next one," I said. It was a battle not to sound grateful for my breath. One down. Two more chances. Then it was back to the drawing board, back to the mixing palette. Back to rationing my raw materials as I experimented, hoping for success.

I couldn't read his mind. All I could do was throw spaghetti at the wall and hope it stuck.

Looking down at the two vials left, I panicked. Which one? If the next one failed him, so much would ride upon the third. But if the second worked, the third would languish unappreciated. Did that matter, really? If the second perfume worked, I was home free. Except which of these two would work, if either?

I didn't know which I would pick up until I had closed my fingers on the slender tube, felt its glass slide between my fingers and the cotton pad upon which it rested. Air bubbles inside shifted as I lifted the tester. Uncharacteristically, I couldn't remember the formula for the sample I had chosen—which was this? Was this number two or number three? Did it land more heavily on its base, or sublimate those notes beneath the orris root and freon?

I could not care. If I cared I would pause, and if I paused I would dither. And dithering was both unprofessional and unproductive. So, clenching my teeth hard enough to approximate a smile, I handed him the second vial.

He lifted his left wrist and sprayed.

◆　◆　◆

I felt physically lighter, leaving Eisner's. And more expansive. As if helium had been pumped into the space behind my ribs. The late-winter sun sparkled between the bare tree branches. No, not bare—I could see the small swellings of buds stippling each stem. Equinox was approaching swiftly. The days were growing longer, and soon it would be spring.

You can see where the neo-pagans came up with the whole idea of Ostara, of estrus and sex and rebirth. The smell of it hangs in the air, charges each inhalation until just breathing is a party drug and you're desperate to move, to touch, peel off your clothes and feel the fresh movement of mild air on your skin.

I bought an exorbitantly priced coffee from the place that sold Scandinavian skin products and sat on a bench out front, watching dogs. I even smiled at a few, and petted one particularly effusive specimen. Nothing could put me out of my good humor. The money was mine. All outstanding threats had been successfully dispatched. No Pip Miles, no blackmail, no ghost of time behind bars. Eventually I would need to do something about Eisner, to keep myself out of similar soups in the future. But I deserved a moment of respite to celebrate my success.

Once more, I let myself relive the moment:

Eisner's face, blank but for a haughty crook in one thinning eyebrow. The ostentatious widening of his nostrils as he sniffed. The heart-pounding pause. The reward of his surprise. It hit him like a splash of paint, a clown's thrown pie; he jerked back, head bobbing at the end of his skinny neck. And then that haughty crook was gone and the muscles of his face went slack. He was lost reliving a moment that had never been.

And just as quickly, it was gone.

"That's it?" he said. "That's what you expect me to pay for? I could hardly—it was nothing. It was gone in half a second!"

Months of hard work and personal peril, and those were the first words out of his mouth? I felt not one iota of sympathy.

"It was a proof of concept," I said. "A dilution."

"Why?" he asked, sounding almost wounded. But like any fearsome animal, it would only serve to make him vicious.

"Joseph." I swept the sample bottles into a tidy pile on my place mat and resettled them one by one in their box. "Please don't take this the wrong way, but I don't really trust you very much." The winning vial I set in between the other two, as if it were an Olympian on the gold-medal podium. "When I've been paid, you can have the perfume at its full strength, in a full-sized bottle."

He licked his teeth and regarded me with narrowed eyes. I regarded him right back. Let him posture. For once, I had power over him.

"I've got to move some money around," he said at last, leaning back in his chair. "But I'll have the payment to you sometime late next week. Does that work?"

"Splendidly," I said. When I set the lid back on the box, he watched me with hungry eyes. My relieved sigh—silent—smelled of egg salad on the inhale.

Now, breathing the free spring air outside, I didn't try to analyze the components of its many scents. I only stretched my lungs, expanded my diaphragm, and felt the spasming muscles between my hips and spine relax. The first time I had breathed easily since this all began.

I thought I had won.

27

Notes de Tête: Butterfly Pea
Notes de Cœur: Coffee
Notes de Fond: Scalded Milk and Paper Money

"Surprise," I said to Barry, first thing on Monday morning. For once I had beaten him to the office. Or, for once I had let him know he was beaten.

The shock stopped him on the threshold, and he flinched so hard he nearly spilled his fancy coffee. What was the seasonal beverage of late February?

"You gave me a freaking heart attack!" He set his coffee on the desk and put his hand against his chest: fingers spread, cocked at the wrist, like a Hollywood ingenue's *who, me?*

"I'm about to give you another one. I'm bumping up your advertising budget for the springtime launch."

"By how much?"

I handed him the spreadsheet I had just printed. The paper was still warm. His mouth fell open before he had even finished closing his fingers on it. "Vic, where did this money come from?"

"Are you my accountant now?"

"No, but I'm not trying to be involved when they come to arrest you for . . . whatever it is you're doing."

"I'm doing business," I told him.

"As long as it's not the kind of business that gets you sent to prison. *Somebody's* gotta watch my cousins on the weekend." He looked at the spreadsheet again. "This is really all for me?"

"I want that juice popping up every other Instagram post. Slather it across Facebook. Is Snapchat still a thing? Do that. Come up with something twice as clever as that stupid self-effacing Etat Libre d'Orange campaign, and beam it straight into people's brains. I want this one to stick. I want it to be big. Bigger than Santal 33."

"This isn't Santal 33," he said. "That smells like teddy bears. This smells like worms."

"Rain and lilacs," I corrected. "Make it happen."

He flounced off to the break room to set up his laptop, leaving his coffee behind. I picked it up for a sip. It tasted like flowery dirt and stained the plastic top blue. Butterfly pea. And he was giving me shit for this perfume. Hypocrite.

"Gross," he said, catching me in the act. "Weren't you just sick?"

With great ostentation, I selected a tissue from the box by the computer and wiped the lid. The paper came away purply-gray. "Get to work."

What did I want with this marketing blitz? Simple. I wanted Jane to text me back. If she wouldn't answer my calls or texts, I would have to try something different. This perfume was my text message. It was my late-night phone call. It was . . . a love letter, I suppose. Or the closest thing to a love letter that I could bear to write, and thought she would accept.

It was nice having money again. Or . . . having money at all. Our budget was neatly balanced for the first time in my memory. We paid up all our accounts, made nice to vendors we had screwed, and generally picked ourselves up and dusted ourselves off until we looked like a respectable business again.

I was pleasantly surprised by the number of orders that came in when This One launched. But though I combed the exported CSVs each day, I didn't see her name. Maybe I had been foolish—she had told me, to my face, that she didn't wear perfume. But surely she would have seen the advertisements. She had posted a single photo to Instagram since we started the campaign and added to her story on four separate days, which meant she had been scrolling.

The equinox came and went in the midst of an interminable cold drizzle. Easter was on the horizon, but the weather for the parade didn't look favorable. It gave me a certain schadenfreude to imagine all the pastel dandies wilting in the rain. Waiting for any word from Jane frayed my nerves, and this in turn made me mean-spirited.

When she finally texted me, I was scrubbing my hands in the cavernous laboratory sink. In my pocket, the phone buzzed once, twice, three times. People didn't text me that often. Barry was the usual culprit, but he was standing behind me packing boxes. Beau might have, I supposed; he was exactly the kind of person who would send three messages in quick succession when one longer message might have served. Hell, it could have been a mailing list, a campaign text, a notification from the city.

But I was not waiting on text messages from Beau, or from the city. And because I wanted them to be texts from Jane, I believed that they were. In that moment, I happily subscribed to the quack quantum-physics theory that my believing made the uncertainty certain, in my favor. These messages could be from no other sender but Jane. So I was unsurprised, when I dried my hands and retrieved my phone, to see her name on the screen.

I tapped through the unlock sequence, equal parts eager and anxious: Was she angry? Had she smelled it? What did she think? But in the end, she answered none of the questions I wanted to ask.

Three messages:

jjbetjeman@gmail.com
my paypal
you owe me

I blinked at the screen, thrown off my stride. The money. *Fuck.*

"You okay, Vic?" asked Barry. "You look like you just woke up short a kidney."

Of course she didn't give a shit about the perfume. I owed her a significant sum of money. I had gotten so caught up in the spring launch, in crafting something that reminded me of her, something that would show her what I was capable of, I had completely forgotten she had accounts of her own she couldn't balance without my help.

God, this was embarrassing. How would I explain? Would she even let me? My cheeks turned hot. Treacherous circulatory system.

"Are you blushing?" asked Barry. He looked at my phone and though he was several feet away and not at the right angle, I still blanked the screen and let it fall to my side. The gesture did not go unnoticed.

"Is it back on, then?" he asked. "She's sending you dirty texts? Did you tell her about the perfume? Did she like it?"

"I need to run some errands," I said. "I probably won't be back before the end of the day. Lock up?"

"Did you talk to her about your ex?" he asked. "Have a heart-to-heart?"

"Barry," I said, "did I not make it clear? I want you to have *my* conversation rather than me having yours."

Frustratingly, he grinned. "I told you! Emotional intimacy." He struck the first syllable of each word like a kick drum. "Shit like that, you just gotta open up."

Had I been emotionally intimate with him in that moment, things might have gotten violent. But as I stomped to the first of several banks to make the first of several withdrawals, Barry's unsolicited advice stuck with me just like it had the first time. I had ignored it then and gone about this all wrong.

I saw now that the gift of This One was no gift at all. It was arrogance. It had felt easy to give because it required me to *give* her nothing. It only demanded that she appreciate what I was already offering. And what I was offering was clearly not enough. I had not been ready at Christmas—it had not seemed worth it. More fool I. What might we have shared in the intervening months, if I had given her what she asked? What would she have given me in return?

Maybe under all the New Age claptrap there was something worth examining. Only after I got home, though—I didn't want to be walking around the seedy part of the Lower East Side with my head up my ass, carrying thousands of dollars in cash.

At home, I set the stacks of hundreds side by side between my stills, which wanted cleaning. Fastidious as I was in the lab, at home I tended toward laxity where it wouldn't influence the quality of my product. All the absolutes were put away. The only thing that would induce me to clean was eventual frustration with the lingering stench of middle-aged man. Or a houseguest.

I scoured my stills until the only smell that lingered in the studio was the eye-watering evanescence of perfumer's alcohol. Disassembled to dry, the glass bulbs and tubing covered every flat surface in the apartment except the meager square footage allotted to Jane's money.

The laughable thing was how small this sum looked in comparison to what Eisner had paid me. It cost a lot to bail out a company. And to him, it wasn't even a hardship. He could have made Beau's medical debt disappear, taken care of Jane's student loans. Eisner could have made all their credit card balances go up in smoke.

Instead he'd paid me to kill three other men as rich as he was so he could take their shares. And I, like a broker, had paid Jane even less.

If I was as bad as Eisner, at least I was stingy out of necessity. What reason had he to pinch pennies? What reason had anyone with pockets so deep?

Unbidden, a memory of Jonathan surfaced. One of those memories that goes unexamined for a long time. So long you may have forgotten that you have it. Consequently it's as crisp and fresh as the day it happened: all its colors bright, the emotions startling and potent. It lends context to every other worn-out memory you've tumbled smooth with touching.

The night before I started work at Bright House, Jonathan took me out to dinner. Some chic New American bistro, back when that was fashionable, in a neighborhood where rents had gone up so rapidly you could feel the vacuum from the vacant brownstones. I didn't know about wine then, not like I knew about perfume, but I knew the bottle he ordered was good. Then, I thought it was a special occasion. I didn't realize this was how he lived his life, and would continue to live his life even if his passion project faltered, folded, fell.

When the waiter brought the check, he uncapped his pen and signed with such force that the nib left a divot in the paper. He hardly glanced at the receipt. If it had been me, that skittish look would have been an attempt to spare myself the pain. It was not an affordable meal, and even then I knew small businesses ran on even smaller margins.

I *didn't* know then what I know now: that he had means beyond what Bright House brought him. I believed he was as leery of an overdraft as I was, and so I thought I understood when he didn't leave a tip.

The intensity of this newly remembered moment caught me unawares, and I came to sitting on my bed, staring at my disassembled stills. When I blinked, the patterns of light reflected by the glass blazed in purple afterimages in the dark. It was as if I had dosed myself with one of my own concoctions, except I couldn't smell any of it—not Jonathan, not the wine, not the stink of the river on the Brooklyn breeze.

Tell me about your ex, Jane had asked. How could I? Anecdotes like that made me look foolish, made him seem like a boor. I was, and so was he. And yet, the alchemy that existed between us, the chemical ignition bright as magnesium . . . it was real. Some things you can't explain in words.

But I didn't need words, did I?

28

Notes de Tête: Lime Juice, Lime Zest, Cherry Soap
Notes de Cœur: Rain and Juniper
Notes de Fond: Wet Hair, Damp Cotton, Paper Money

Most people have a catalog of scents in their heads: coffee, rainstorms, that awful cherry-scented mopping soap they always seem to use in hospitals and apartment buildings. All of these scents are attached to the memory of sensations: emotional, physical, existential. And everyone's associations are different. Maybe when I say "cherry-scented mopping soap," you think of the odd cul-de-sac of a hallway outside your high school cafeteria, where the popular girls gathered to make your life miserable each afternoon.

Eisner's associations had already been set; I had merely needed to re-create the scents that would trigger them. But now I wanted to create something wholesale. With a convincing enough narrative, I thought I could at least temporarily usurp someone's scent associations.

If they thought of daddy's nightly gin and tonic when they smelled juniper and lime, let me tell them the story of an icy gimlet in a Nick and Nora glass, cradled in the manicured hand of a gorgeous woman. Let me tell it in such vivid detail, the imagery so strong, that through the dry down *that* is what they picture, more clearly than they remember their own father.

I could do that. Working on Eisner's project, seeing ghosts of a fantasy that wasn't mine, had proved the concept was viable. Certainly. Except.

What about the scent of the woman?

We all know the scent of a lime. We're familiar with it in many guises. No matter what perfume I put limes in, you will recognize them. You'll know whether I've used juice or zest. The rest of the perfume's story lends the limes context. Paired with black pepper and white flowers, limes are summery, a cocktail and dinner on the patio. With leather and violets and darker smells, they become refined: a barber's tonic. Limes I can manipulate to many ends, because you have met them many times.

Only *you* smell like yourself. And if I put you at the heart of a perfume and gave it to someone who had never met you, it would be like reading a sentence in which the object noun is written in a language you do not speak. Almost legible, but not quite.

Similarly, no scent can be substituted for that unique note.

I knew the smells of Pearson, Conrad, Reg. I had grown familiar with their funk and sweat and mix of molecules over any number of occasions. The other absolutes, snug in my thrifted jewelry box and chilled to thirty-eight degrees, each held some meaning for me. Like the chef and the oboist. If I diluted any of those elements and touched them to my wrist, I would smell the same scent my lover had left in the armpit of an unwashed shirt. I would recall the last gasp of a client's loved one, nemesis, father, wife. Each of those mixtures was the concentrated essence of a human being *I* remembered. I had touched the flesh, breathed the breath. And so, on smelling, I relived the moment.

Could I impart that memory, that fluency and familiarity with the scent? Could I make the language of my remembrance legible to new readers, if they had never met the subject of the memory?

I had to let go of the hope that I could ever communicate an exact replica. All I could do was draw a direct connection between a certain smell and the idea of a person, which was just a type of storytelling. Let them sniff the unadulterated odor, build a connection in their mind, and then move on to the more complicated constructed memory once the association had been forged.

Perfume has always been a way of telling stories. Just look at what people name the stuff, at what the copy marketing departments write:

Sixteen92, Youth Gone Wild: new vinyl records, warm night air, polished arcade wood, burned rubber.

Nasomatto, Nudiflorum: a result of a quest to find a vanishing point in nature, the translucence of our senses, nude desire.

CB I Hate Perfume, Eternal Return: the scent of sailing toward the shore.

All we noses ever try to do is encapsulate a moment, a feeling, a story. The things we otherwise have no way of expressing. We are not writers or singers or actors. We cannot dance these things, or speak them. But, as with all other arts, we are hindered—or developed, elevated, evolved—by the interpretation of our audience. We can provide the content, the experience, the *thing*. What it means to others, how it lands? All we can do is hope.

Jane wanted to know about Jonathan. Fine. If I tried to explain it all to her in person, talk it out and fit it into the confines of mundane conversation, I would bungle it. No virtuoso violinist ever succeeded in packing the same punch through poetry or video installation. I would stay in my lane, use the skills I trusted. I could build a story for her to explain my relationship with him. I had refused to experiment on people who knew him, to trot out their tawdry fantasies and realize those in scent; now I wondered if I could spin some semblance of my own memories into a perfume that would help Jane understand something about him, and something about me.

A soliflore—a perfume dedicated to the pure essence of a single flower. That was what I needed. A soliflore to help my subject understand what they should be smelling in the context of a more complex perfume. I could make that handily. Everything that came after? Like so many other things, I would figure it out as I went along.

◆ ◆ ◆

"Thank you for coming all the way up here."

She crossed the threshold warily, as though the door would snap shut behind her and the basement swallow her down. It was raining—the kind of rain I had imagined, drafting the formula for her perfume—and in the stark light of the bare bulb overhead, fine droplets shimmered on her hair.

Well lit, the basement only looked like what it was: dusty cement floor, cobwebs, old tools hung on a pegboard. Moldy cardboard boxes full of junk. A couple of bathtubs jumbled in one corner beside a scarred workbench and some rusty Metro shelves.

Her gaze lingered on the corner with the tubs. She shivered. But then again, it was cold outside. And in.

We paused awkwardly at the entrance to my small studio. I stood just beneath the lintel and stared at her, as though watching through a pane of glass. Which of us was inside the cage, and which the voyeur?

"I have it," I said.

She held out her hand. The light shifted on her skin as she moved her arm from the yellowish glare of the basement proper to the thin blue half-light of my apartment. I had not turned my own lamp on. The watery subterranean gloom suited my temper.

"Come in," I said. "Sit down. Have a drink."

Her hand remained extended for a moment, palm open. When I didn't move she flipped it and let it fall, chapped knuckles disappearing up her sleeve.

"Please," I said, though her motion was tacit assent.

The mood grew no easier once I had shut the door. She looked over her shoulder surreptitiously as the latch clicked. I could imagine the creep of gooseflesh up her spine—locked in with a murderer. Well if she was, so was I.

"Sit," I said. She didn't. The money lay on the table in front of us. Neither of us reached for it.

"It's all there?" asked Jane.

I nodded. We stared for a minute longer. It became almost comical, the silence, clinched when Jane made a small sound like laughter. "I've never seen that much cash before. It looks fake."

I, who *had* seen that much cash before, still tended to agree. It looked like a prop from a movie.

"I'm sorry I don't have a briefcase with handcuffs," I said. "I *could* have PayPal-ed you, but I don't think the transaction would have gone through."

She shook her head. "No, I get it." More awkward silence. Then: "How do I . . . I mean, I can't just walk up to a bank."

"Small increments," I said. "Over time. Report it as tips on your taxes. Keep the tips you do get and don't report them."

"And just . . . keep the rest of it in my mattress? Jesus Christ." Now she did sit, suddenly. She stared at the pile of cash like it was a cryptid: something she had heard of, but never expected to see.

"Not the mattress. Somewhere you can get at it faster if there's a fire. Preferably something that locks."

"Yeah." She reached out, hesitated, and picked up the top stack of bills. "It's heavy."

I hefted the banded bundle that had lain opposite and weighed it in my hand. I thought about the weight of a corpse, the weight of debt, the weight of despair. "Really? I don't think it's much more than a couple of pounds."

Jane had a backpack on her—a canvas thing, trendy but stuffed too full of books and thermoses and scarves to look good hanging on one shoulder. She set it on the table and began to rearrange the contents to make room for her money.

I watched as she packed things into place, efficient as an IKEA designer. With each stack of bills that disappeared, I lost another moment. But I didn't know how to say what needed to be said. She was zipping up before I gathered my wits.

"Last time we spoke . . ." She looked up. I looked away. "I was rude."

A lesser woman, a woman better trained to accept what the world expected of her, would have apologized for pressing me too hard. Jane just nodded.

"Jonathan is . . . difficult," I said.

She laughed. "Difficult? *Difficult?* Fuck you, Vic. I *know* difficult."

And she did. A woman only comfortable when she dictated her own terms, even to her detriment. Photography wouldn't pay the bills? Fine, she dropped it, and not because anyone told her to. Big tipper was a creep? She would put up with him as long as she could. No offers of help accepted. I thought of my hand on Giovanni's arm, restraining him when he rose to her defense. I thought I had understood.

But I had put her in an intolerable position. She had reached the end of her rope and had not known what to do; I had swooped in, seen all her problems, provided a fix and the means to enact it. I had encouraged—entrapped?—her into murder for my sake. And now that she had the money, she still had to ask my advice on how to use it safely.

She had been drawn fully into my territory and had no frame of reference, no firm place to stand. I held all the power here.

It was what I had wanted, I thought, when I killed Jonathan. It was what nearly crushed me once he was gone. Unstoppable forces and immovable objects are uninteresting on their own. And now I had stopped Jane. We were no longer equals.

"I want to fix this," I said.

In the blue dusk-light her gray eyes were almost clear, like empty glasses. I thought of the scent I had made for her, also clear, an evocation of absence. I didn't want to lose her, but I had come so close to making her disappear.

"I'll tell you anything," I said. "I'll even tell you about him."

Her pupils bloomed, pooling in the translucence of her eyes like ink poured into a well. "Fine," she said. "How did he die?"

Naked. Smelling of sex. Streetlights through the rain-streaked windows, projecting rivulets onto the floor. "Is that what you want to know about him?"

"No," she said. "It's what I want to know about you."

What did she hope to learn about me, from this moment in my past? She asked how Jonathan had died, but what she really meant was, Why had I killed him? She didn't care about the method. She cared about the motive, about the antecedent.

And I, as the storyteller, controlled what she would hear, what she would see. So what did I want her to know? It would not be fair to lie. To her, or to me. If I was going to share this with her, I would share it all. But . . . what did I hope she would take away from this?

What had *I* taken away from it?

Nothing useful, at the time. Only short-lived triumph and a lingering, complicated regret I regularly quashed with flimsy self-affirmation. I did not want Jane to wake from this reverie with the feeling that I had made a colossal mistake. I did not want her to know how badly I had failed to live up to the idea of myself that I had back then. Instead, I wanted her to see how much I had grown. I had become, in some ways, like her: I had made ugly compromises and learned to live with them.

But now I was tired of compromising. And it looked like I might have the means to set my own terms. At least for a while.

None of my Jonathan perfumes preserved the moment she had asked me to re-create. I had never needed to remind myself: every moment of that night was burned as cleanly into my memory as if my mind had been coated in silver nitrate and the whole scene bathed in blazing light.

Though I have become adept at premeditation in the intervening years, this incident was impulsive, born out of a storm of sadness and anger, passion and thwarted ambition. The act of it passed quickly, though not as quickly as you might think, and not as quickly as I expected. It was surprisingly intimate. Not sexually, but physically, and in other ways less easy to qualify. It was the closest I had ever been to Jonathan Bright, if only because I finally had some power over him.

It was easy to remember what notes the story contained but difficult to imagine how Jane would interpret them, how she would take them and run. I would have to tell her such a version of the story that there was no bending it, no flights of fancy. The details would be crisp, precise, specific. I would be objective. She could interpret the undercurrents however she wanted, but the idea she would see anything other than the stark silent film that played in my head when I thought back to that night . . .

It would need a wet cement accord: rain in the city, running in the gutters of SoHo. Scotch, of course—specifically a particular independent bottling of Ardbeg, impossible to find now. Black pepper, vanilla, the rum-raisin sweetness of sherry, all of it wreathed in the oily peat smoke of an Islay. Wet wool. We had not had umbrellas, and the rain caught us between taxi and apartment building. The smell of his deodorant—vetiver, chemicals—and his perfume. It was an unnamed blend, nothing he had ever released for sale. It had taken me a long time to copy it, and once I had I didn't release it either. I didn't want to risk catching a hint of it on the person in front of me at the coffee shop, the commuter swaying at my side.

The mushroomy, metallic scent of spit on skin. Tide pool pear tree semen-scent. The warmer, sharper smell of my own arousal. The faintest soapy trace of detergent on his sheets—he used unscented, but even that leaves a footprint, toasted in the heat of the dryer until it sets between the threads. The radiators had a smell too: hot iron and burning dust.

This would be a good scent. An art-house horror movie, a Shirley Jackson novel. The top notes were sophisticated, the middle cozy. The base bodily, sexual and abject, but also stark. The shock of seeing someone nude and debauched in an abandoned house.

I could make it. It was, in some ways, what I had been working toward since I started smelling samples in that little shop on the South Bank. The aesthetic was mine. The memory was mine. The blood was on my hands.

And now, it would be on Jane's.

29

Notes de Tête: Grapefruit and Geraniums
Notes de Cœur: Lilacs, Cantaloupe, and Grappa
Notes de Fond: The Sea

You know how jealously I hoard my memories of Jonathan. You likely didn't realize what a privilege it was, early in this process, to be allowed a glimpse of him in an unguarded moment. Or . . . a moment alone. I'm not convinced he ever let his guard down. Perhaps he had no guard at all; perhaps he showed the world his petrified core, stripped of all softness that might require protection.

Sometimes it's hard to tell the difference. I couldn't tell the difference with Jane either.

"Is this . . . this is *him*?" She pinched the slender glass sampler I gave her between thumb and forefinger. Cap still in place—I did not want her to smell it until I was ready. Until *she* was.

I nodded. "It doesn't smell good."

"Is that why you killed him?" she asked archly. "He smelled bad?"

"Jonathan Bright," I said, "was not a very nice man."

"I'm not very nice either," said Jane. "Maybe you have a type."

I did.

"Why did you like him?" she asked. The unspoken question: *Why do you like me?* Or maybe, *Will you kill me too?*

I could have said, *Oh, he was handsome. Haughty. A force to be reckoned with. He lit a fire in me to do better, and moved the benchmark every time I hoped to succeed. He was a challenge. He surprised me.* I was drawn to him for every reason I was drawn to her.

Or I could have said: *I didn't like him at all. But I understood him, or wanted to. The way I want to understand you. Like I hope you'll understand me.*

Instead, I took the sample delicately from her grasp and popped its tiny plastic cap. No spritzer, this, but something to be tipped and smeared against your skin. A trace of it touched my fingers as I worked the plastic free. That small streak of his scent was enough to strand me in my past for a moment. I curled my hand into the open collar of my shirt and lifted it to breathe through the fabric, where it smelled of soap and my own skin. Jonathan's ghost lay back down.

"Imagine you have spent years of your life hounded by a half memory." I spoke into my lifted collar, eyes downcast. This was already more than I wanted to part with—the idea that I had *had* a life before. But I had chosen this. To explain Jonathan to Jane, I would have to explain myself.

"Imagine it has made the hairs on the back of your neck stand on end, kept you awake into the wee hours, driven you half-mad with almost remembering. And then along comes someone who raises the veil, who clarifies the thing that lurks in the mist at the edge of your awareness. How could that person not make an impression? Liking has nothing to do with it. Do you understand what I mean?"

She bit her lip: a thought welling up like blood in a wound. "Like . . . when you can't remember the next line in a song. And you just loop the same verse over and over again."

I wanted to kiss the pale depression left by her teeth, but even as I watched, it blushed pink and disappeared.

"Cantaloupes did this to me, for years. I knew the smell reminded me of something, but I couldn't have told you what."

I half expected her to say "honeydew," like every idiot who thought one melon smelled like another. But Jane remained silent, listening. She recognized the gravity of what I was saying. Or maybe she was just being polite.

"Not long after I met Jonathan," I said, "I mentioned this fixation. And then, like it was nothing—and it was, to him—he said: 'Of course. The sea.'"

I watched the flick of her eyes as she searched a mental catalog, the comparison of one scent impression to the other. The parting of her lips in surprise, the faint gleam of her tongue between her teeth.

"I had only been once, when I was very young. But he was right." Jonathan had delivered revelations like a king casting coins in front of a beggar. As I told Jane this story, I knew the worth of everything I parted with, to the penny. I hoped she did too. "Though he didn't mean to, he taught me something about his art. I had to learn everything from him like that."

"What?" she asked.

"People love aquatics because they're clean, and fruit because it's sweet. But that thing they share? That ghost of salt and musk? That isn't sweet or clean at all. It's vital, *bodily*. The sea is full of life and death. Fruit is a womb, and its seeds grow as it rots." My next sentiment was an echo of Jonathan, as Jane would come to know if her experimental perfume panned out. But it was a lesson I had learned long before I met him. "People think they know what they want; they're usually wrong."

"What, and he was right?"

"Most of the time," I said. "Yes." I capped the sampler and gave it back to her.

She turned it in her hands, watching the dark liquid inside. "But I never met him."

"You will."

She shook her head. Her hair had grown, and swished across her face like grass whipped in the wind. It made the same dry sound. I wanted to lie down in it and stare up at the sky. "But you told me. You said that isn't how it works."

"I said I didn't *know* how it works. You gave me the idea. I made a perfume that fulfilled Eisner's fantasy. Took the scents he *might* have smelled and built a moment he imagined. Now I want to know if I can use the smells you *would* have smelled, if you had been there, and show you a moment that I *lived*."

"So I'm a guinea pig."

"No," I said, sharp as a slap. It startled her, and she closed her fist on the tiny vial. There was the answer I wanted, even if she hadn't meant to give it. "You're not a guinea pig."

"Yes," she said. "I am."

I caught the conviction in it that time. She had not asked a question. She was telling me exactly what she had decided to be.

◆ ◆ ◆

The problem with storytelling is that someone has to tell the story. And as I've said already, copy has never been my strong suit. I've gotten better with experience, but that night I stumbled over my sentences, doubled back, used words that weren't quite right until I found, too late, the ones that were.

In the end, I could never be sure I did the job credibly. But Jonathan was incredible, in the strictest sense of the word, if you weren't willing to suspend your expectations, your understanding of the way things usually worked.

Small and fastidious, Bright was under forty but grave and disdainful in the manner of a much older man. He loathed to be labeled "precocious," going so far as to punch an older colleague for employing the epithet. He had strategically fucked his way through an influential minority of stockists and perfumers, as well as half the board of the Fragrance Foundation, in affairs ostensibly involving ball gags, role play, and rigorous documentation.

Well, I say "ostensibly." I've seen the videos.

But nobody else had—to them it was merely delicious gossip. People who claimed to have been his paramours—under condition of anonymity—admitted that the quality of the sex had distracted them from the imprudence of allowing Bright to collect photographic evidence of their indiscretions.

Similarly, it was not blackmail that kept Bright in booming business and acclaim. Instead, it was one single, irrefutable fact: he was damn good at what he did. Bright was the only American who could rival—some claimed surpass—the venerable houses of Europe. Because he, unlike most Americans, wasn't afraid to get dirty.

He was making the most interesting scents in the industry. The kind of things you would catch a whiff of on someone walking by and obsess about all day. Dank and mineral oceanics, moldy chypres, sticky gourmands. The kind of florals that reminded you their sources were sex organs. Animalics that wouldn't let you forget.

Sometimes there were suggestions—usually half-hearted, already admitting defeat—that Bright ought to be censured, or sanctioned in some way, or perhaps reported to the police. But no such reports were made. This, despite Bright's rude remarks, misanthropy, and general bad attitude. He had the charisma of an enfant terrible: mad, bad, and dangerous to know. I never quite matched him, there—not enough flowers to make up for my thorns. And you needed the charm, I had learned, if you wanted to behave that badly.

Did I say all of this to Jane? Maybe. What matters is I'm saying it to you, right now. And that I said enough to her that she thought she understood.

I told her the story in which he hadn't left a tip.

"What an asshole," she said.

I told her how he had blindfolded me and lifted Glencairn glasses to my lips, describing in exquisite detail the tasting notes, the noses, of his favorite whiskies. How I had learned the craft of perfumery from him in his moments of weakness, and had sometimes wondered if the only way he could talk about and teach the art he truly loved was in surrender. And whether that meant he thought I was his equal, or close enough that he was willing to let himself slip that vital half an inch. Maybe the only way you *could* learn, from someone who never knew how to explain himself and wasn't used to trying.

After that, she was silent for a long time.

"He was good-looking," I said. Not as an excuse, this time. Just another piece of data.

"Show me," she said, and I realized that I had no photos of him on my phone. I had to google him.

Opting for a profile in *Nez* rather than his obituary, I turned my laptop so she could see his face. The photograph was monochrome and showed him standing in profile against a white background, dressed in black.

"There's nothing for scale," I said. "He was short, for a man. Your height, maybe. Five seven?"

She nodded, staring hard at the photograph. Jonathan's arms were crossed over his chest and his chin was up, at an angle. His nose was large but straight, over a wide mouth given to cynical crookedness. When his lips moved, to eat or speak or sneer, they were expressive, eloquent. His hands, like the rest of him, were small and neat but so fluid in their gestures they seemed bigger. Every three weeks, he had his thick, dark hair cut in the same short back and sides. He kept clean-shaven, though when he was on a tear in the lab and forgot to go home, his stubble came in reddish.

The picture did not show these things. There was too much to tell.

But she didn't want to know about him, did she? She wanted to know about me, and he was a means to an end. This should be enough.

She knew his face, and from what I had told her she could imagine the rest.

"All right," I said. "Go ahead."

She uncapped the vial, and Jonathan filled the room.

◆　◆　◆

"Was something supposed to happen?" she asked when she had smelled her fill.

"Not yet," I said, though I was clutching the edge of the table. It felt like he was standing at my back, breathing into the hollow just behind my ear.

"*Will* something happen?" Alarm poorly disguised as skepticism.

"I just need you to know what he smelled like. A face to the name, as it were." Her eyes flicked down to his photograph, still open on the screen. I wished, suddenly, that I had ever snapped the kind of photographs I knew he had taken of me. In the memory she wanted me to make for her, Bright was not wearing a black turtleneck.

"Take it home with you," I said. "Keep smelling it. Look at the picture. Think about what I said, and keep thinking until you can almost see him. Almost feel him standing in the room."

She put the vial into the front pocket of her backpack with a care that belied her attitude.

"The next step is the perfume," I said. "The one that will show you the moment. I hope."

"How long will that take?"

I shrugged. "It depends. I have my work at the office. And it's never a sure thing, how long any scent takes to come together."

She scowled; this meant she was reliant on me again. "Fine. Text me, I guess."

"Jane," I said as she was zipping up her jacket. It was her name, but it was also *please*. It might have been *stay*. She had an alarming ability to wrong-foot me, to catch me by surprise; I didn't know what I wanted to say to her until she looked up with those clear eyes and I remembered: "I have something for you."

Before she could protest—for once I was thankful for the small span of my studio—I retrieved a white box from my bookshelf. No more than three by five, less than two inches deep. I set it on the table between us and withdrew.

Dusk turned the matte-white cardboard blue, and the oblique angle of the light showed glossy embossed letters, also white: BRIGHT HOUSE. Jane read it, touched the text. I said nothing—why mar the presentation with useless babble?

"This isn't . . . *that* kind of perfume, is it?" she asked.

I shook my head, just once. Who would I have given her? Not Reg. She'd had enough of him while he was alive.

She lifted the lid, revealing glass with beveled edges, a bright metallic spray-top capped in white ceramic. This wasn't in some cut-crystal flea-market find, like the heavy leaded and ground-glass piece I had given Pearson. This was a Bright House bottle, proper. It was sleeker, more architectural, more Jane.

She stared at it in its neatly folded cardboard nest. Touched the glass. I bit my tongue against an exhortation: *try it on*. My gift of Jonathan had ironically imbued this one with more meaning. I truly cared now what she thought of the perfume, not just of me. In speaking of Jonathan I had revealed enough of myself that she could make inferences about my art, and judgments too. She would smell this and she would know that I had *tried*. That my genius was not effortless. And that was terrifying.

The label, set slightly off center, a little more toward the lower right-hand side, told her what she was looking at. Her fingers came to rest beneath the perfume's name where it was printed in black against silver, the typeface an imitation of imperfect letterpress.

"Vic," she said, rereading it. "What is this?"

Now I let the words free, as though exhaling air from which I had sucked every atom of nourishing oxygen. "Just try it, Jane. Please, just try it on."

Finally, she smiled. A small one, and not very nice, but a smile that I knew. I realized I had asked her, begged her, and had not even thought about it first. I had given way without strategy, without cunning. She had won a point. I was happy to let her have it.

For a moment she surveyed the box, and then inverted it over an open palm. I approved. Much more elegant than prying it awkwardly from its resting place, created by industrial designers to cradle the bottle so tightly that it prohibited almost any movement besides this one that Jane had chosen.

I heard it come free. The release of suction, the slap of heavy glass into her hand. The sharp sound of the ceramic cap releasing. Abortive clicks on the first two pumps, a satisfying spritz on the third.

The air filled with the scent of lilacs. Mud. Icy linen. The sound of Jane's indrawn breath. I felt a ghost of moving air across my lips—my imagination, most likely. I followed the feeling with my tongue and tasted what I smelled.

The molecules drifted between us like a transparent curtain, scent combinations shifting with each minute movement of the air. I watched her through it, as though through sheer muslin rippling in the breeze.

The opening notes of the scent began to fade, and she said nothing. It became clear that she expected me to break the silence and explain myself.

"What do you think?" I asked, because it was less naked than asking if she liked it. Besides, what does "like" mean? "Like" is as watery as "nice." Jane had asked me, did I *like* Jonathan? But the verb is meaningless to me. I do not *like* people, and I have never wanted to make scents that people like. I want to make scents that fascinate, that captivate, that stop people in their tracks.

She had certainly frozen on the spot. Surprise? Or something more esoteric?

Lifting a hand, she threaded her fingers through the air as if pushing aside my imagined curtain. "It's . . . cold." Then, rubbing the pad of her forefinger against her thumb: "It's supposed to be me?"

There was sorrow in the words that I had not expected. It made me blush, made my heart beat fast in a panic to correct her.

"No," I said. "No, no, Jane. It's . . . it was *for* you. It's . . ." I traced a void in the space between us—a slender shape with rounded contours, finishing with a cupped hand six inches from her chin. "It's the space you left behind."

She considered this a moment, then sprayed another small burst of the perfume against her wrist. She inhaled, and stared at the skin over her veins as if she were watching herself disappear. "I never thought a smell could be so sad."

"This one is," I said, catching the pun on its name too late.

She frowned. "I wish it weren't."

"*You* don't smell sad. Not at all."

Looking up from the map of vulnerable blue-green descending from her palm, she asked, "What *do* I smell like?"

I closed the distance between us cautiously, alert to any hesitance on her part. There was none. She stood as still as if she had a venomous snake twining round her shoulders, a tarantula on her arm. Frightened, yes, but fascinated too.

I leaned in so that my cheek very nearly brushed hers. "Let me tell you," I said, and breathed her in.

◆ ◆ ◆

"Have you heard from Giovanni recently?" I asked, sometime after night had fallen. She was lying beside me, not touching: a feat in that small bed. And strange, given how close we had been recently. But I let her have the inch of space. Hopelessly, I realized there were many things that I would give her, if I could. If she would take them from me.

"Not really," she said. "He replied to a couple of my Instagram stories. Just emojis. Why?"

I sighed. "I think things ended . . . badly, between us."

"No shit. I'm surprised you managed to wrangle him in the first place." She turned her head. "How did you?"

Useless to pretend I hadn't heard her, hadn't understood: her mouth was four inches from my ear and my skin knew it. Still, I stalled with a long breath. In the quiet moment that it bought me, I contemplated the curve of her hip bone. Its silhouette softened where the streetlight caught in the fine down of her body hair, silver and diffuse.

"It was a less elegant agreement than ours," I said.

"No convenient medical debt?"

"And no serial harasser." I put my fingertip between her breasts, to remind her of Reg's spit-slick cherry. "It's harder to feel justified in murderous anger against an abstraction."

"Is it?" she asked. "Abstractions don't have a face. Or families."

"You feel guilty?"

"Yes."

"So did he. But you're still speaking with me."

"Only because you owed me money."

"It's in your backpack," I said. "You can leave anytime. You could have left hours ago." I tried to look into her eyes, but she kept her face turned obstinately away. "Why did you stay? Why didn't you take the money and leave?"

She shifted and lifted her hand, quickly nipping a hangnail from the rough cuticle of her thumb. Blood welled up like a red seed bead until she swiped it away with a pass of her middle-finger pad.

"Well," she said, staring at the streak of dilute rusty brown across her first knuckle. "You had your little science experiment. I was curious."

"And after Jonathan? You could have left then. You could even have taken the new perfume and left. But you're still here." I stroked her skin for emphasis, along the ridge of her hip that had held my gaze.

She tucked her bloody hand away. In the taut silence I heard mouth sounds, the movement of her tongue in the wet tightness between her cheeks.

"It . . . God, this is going to sound stupid." She sucked air between her two front teeth. "But that perfume . . . it was *clean*, Vic."

"That's the lilacs," I said. "They can smell a little soapy if you aren't careful."

"No. I mean, yeah, it was like water, and cold rocks. Sauvignon blanc. That kind of clean. But . . . ugh." She turned her face so it was hidden by the pillow and her hair. "This sounds so dumb."

"No," I said. "It doesn't."

She let out a noisy breath. "It was . . . pure. Like you want art to be. Before you realize it's about money, and what *other people* like. Before you figure out it isn't just talent; it's who you know, and kissing ass, and taking commissions."

"You're good at kissing ass," I said. "I know."

She rolled her eyes. "Yeah, but I kissed all the wrong ones, and now look where I am. That stuff"—she jabbed a finger across the room, to where the bottle of perfume sat by her backpack—"that's like, when you still think you're going to make it, even if other people don't, because your shit is *real*. You didn't *owe* it to me. I never *asked* for it. It wasn't what I *wanted*. You're right, you know? I didn't *know* I . . ." She bit down on a smile. "It was just this clean expression of an idea. Just itself, doing exactly what it needed to."

I thought of her Instagram account: the lines and planes and plays of light. The black-and-white prints on the walls of Giovanni's shop. The photographs she didn't take anymore, because people paid for X-rays, not for art.

"I miss that," she said. "Just making a thing because it spoke to me." The mattress flexed slightly, and I realized she had finally relaxed, just a moment before her skin touched mine. At last she looked up at me. "What are you going to do now that you've got Eisner's money?"

She meant, Would I make art instead of trying to make a living? She also meant, Was I going to kill anyone else? Soon? Ever?

Would I? What reason had I, once I put Eisner in the ground? Which I would do, at my earliest convenience.

Jane didn't need to know that what I did wasn't always out of necessity. At least, not necessity of the financial sort. If my experimental scent worked on her, she would find that out soon enough. And after all, it had always been just what she described: making a thing because it spoke to me.

"I don't know," I said. "I suppose I'll try not to worry. For a while."

Late that night, before Jane left, I said, "Tell me if you hear from Giovanni."

She scowled—fondly?—and said, "I'm not doing your dirty work. If you want to talk to him, *you* have to talk to him."

Rich, coming from someone who'd made her fiancé pick me up. But that was pleasure. This was business.

I paid a visit to Astor the next day and prowled among the eaux-de-vie until I found the bottle of grappa Beau and Jane had served at brunch. It was, as promised, pretty cheap. A staff pick too.

It wasn't a long walk across town to Giovanni's, and the weather had turned. I crossed Washington Square Park with my jacket open, dodging skateboarders, tourists, and the man with the bubble wand. In my tote bag, the bottle of grappa banged against my hip.

There was a new receptionist—I sometimes wondered if they quit or if he fired them—in the same old Bettie Page makeup. "I'm here for Giovanni," I said.

"Um . . . I'm not sure . . ."

He was already staring at me from his station, holding a towel wrapped around his current client's face. But he didn't intercede.

"I don't have an appointment," I said.

"He's not available for walk-ins," she said. "I'm sorry. But Jovan or Richie could take you in about a half an hour. They're really great."

"I know," I said. "They wouldn't work here if they weren't. But I don't have a bottle of grappa for either of them. I *do* have a bottle of grappa for Giovanni."

He lowered the towel and tossed it into the laundry bin. Pink cheeked, the man in the chair stepped down and shook his hand. The receptionist took his credit card, all the while looking nervously over her shoulder at me.

Giovanni wiped his hands on a blue bandanna from his coat pocket and came across the room slowly. It was a small space, but he made the distance last.

"Vic," he said, "do you like scaring my girls?"

"Certainly not," I said. "But you don't seem to be hiring for nerves."

The receptionist blanched and turned her attention more fully to the man checking out.

"What are you doing here?" he asked.

"Social call."

"I'm working."

I looked at the man on the bench, who was reading *The Cut* and pretending not to listen in.

"Five minutes, Giovanni," I said, brandishing the Astor bag. "For old times' sake."

He realized I was not going to go away, and rather than wilt him, the resignation stiffened his spine.

"Sorry, Kyle," he said to his next client. "I need to take this. Do you have five minutes?"

The man nodded and flapped the covers of his magazine. Giovanni jerked his head toward the back room.

It was exactly as I had imagined it. Someone's sandwich sat half-eaten, abandoned in a rush. An old metal fan churned the stale air. Schedules fluttered in the artificial breeze.

Giovanni shut the door. "What do you want?"

"I hadn't heard from you," I said.

"That was on purpose."

I set the grappa down on the desk. "I just wanted to check on you. I was concerned." A low blow, but: "I've heard from Beau and Jane."

"I'm happy for you."

"Have you talked to them?" Surely he had done more than just like a few of Jane's photos? But his lips didn't move from their tight line.

"Has Eisner's company gotten in touch?" I asked. "Or the new owners?"

His nostrils flared, and I thought he wouldn't answer. Then, after a little bit too long, a sharp incline of his chin.

"It's all settled?" I asked. "You'll keep the space?"

"They want to knock a doorway through the back wall," he said. "Where the bathroom is."

"So you won't have to clean it anymore," I said, and he glared daggers.

"Vic," he said. "If you don't have some reason—"

"Just to say hello," I said. "To check that everything's all right."

"Bullshit."

It wasn't. "Giovanni, no one cuts my hair like you. I . . . I can't go back to Astor Place. I know I joked about it but . . . not really." No one else had ever understood what I wanted. They were too pushy. They were less skilled. They had a strange, overwrought aesthetic. They were playing at something they didn't truly understand. They had an idea about how I should look, based on how other people thought they should look. They didn't listen—they imposed.

At my first appointment, I tried to show Giovanni a picture of my ideal cut, which had sometimes helped confused stylists understand my requests. He waved it away and said, "No, just tell me." It was the only place I had ever felt comfortable in the chair.

Giovanni was genuine. Just as Jane had said, Giovanni made a thing, a space, an atmosphere, because it spoke to him. He was driven not by marketing or fashion, but by a pristine vision. I wondered if Jane felt about him and his shop the way she felt about This One, if she thought he was clean and pure. What would she think of the deal I had cut? Nothing good. But she would, I thought, understand its utility. Jane and I had both looked down the barrel of artistic freedom in this economy and decided we would rather not be shot.

I wasn't proud of it. There was something special in that kind of conviction, even if it was chronically undervalued.

"Giovanni." It sounded more bereft than I had intended, too raw. "I . . . I don't *want* to go anywhere else."

He had never taken his hand off the doorknob, and now he jerked it open. "You can get out now," he said. And when I didn't move: "Get the fuck out. Right now." All delivered in a high, tight tone of voice that wouldn't carry. "Do you think I'm joking?"

I didn't.

"You fucked me over, Vic," he said. "You don't get to come back from that."

"Fucked you over?" I stood in the fluorescent brightness of the office, not quite able to believe what I was hearing. "I saved this place. You were going to go under. Now your rent's going down and you'll get more customers than you can take." It wasn't that pristine vision from which his shop had been born, but this iteration would at least pay the bills.

"Did I *ask* for that?" Now his volume jumped, and the words rang back from the white tile walls of the shop. All ambient noise dropped to zero. "I never asked you for anything. You did all the asking, and when that didn't pan out, you dictated terms. So I did your dirty work." That tripped him up: his voice came perilously close to breaking. He seemed to realize he had drawn the attention of his clients and staff and lowered his voice again. "Now we're done, all right? We're finished. You never come here again."

When I finally took a step toward the door, he said, "And take your fucking grappa too."

In that moment, I should have known what would come next. But I wanted to believe what he said: That we were done. That I would never come back. That this was a clean break for both of us.

I doubled back, picked up the bag, and passed him as I went out the door. He smelled like geranium and grapefruit, a hint of blade oil and Barbicide. Underneath that, his own smell: essence of angry barber. He watched me all the way out the door.

30

Notes de Tête: Cilantro, Naranja Agria
Notes de Cœur: Ambergris
Notes de Fond: Stale Cigarette, Fresh Mulch, Nighttime Leaves

Later that week I stood in the center of Beau's atelier with my legs spread, staring down at the top of his head as he worked. The window was open again, though this time the breeze that came in was warm, and carried the sounds of the Union Square green market.

I had not told Jane I was commissioning a suit. But I loathed the revealing clothing of warmer weather, which left me feeling vulnerable as a frog's exposed belly. Too pale, too soft, slender in all the wrong places. Beau could make me something suitably austere that would breathe well in the New York summer.

Besides, I was a little curious to see how the flow of information might have changed—what did Beau tell her these days, about me or anything? And what did she tell him? What would eventually make its way to me?

A petty game of small powers, but perhaps not inconsequential; it was always good to know who would tell you what, and what they would tell others.

I wondered what she had told him about her last visit with me.

The tape measure traced the inside of my thigh, kissed my knee, and ended just inside the arch of my foot, where his thumb pressed its metal tip to the floor. He stood and made a mark in the little notebook pressed flat on his worktable. "Arms up."

I lifted them, and he stepped in slightly too close—I couldn't tell if it was an average Beau mannerism, a necessity of the trade, or something he would only try with his intimates.

"So . . . you and Jane worked things out?" He threaded his arms beneath mine and drew the tape measure around my chest so it crossed from nipple to nipple, kissing the tip of each shoulder blade behind.

"Did she tell you that, or are you just inferring from the commission?" I enjoyed when people played my games.

"Gotta do your neck," he said, and his hands didn't even shake, though I saw him swallow and lick his lips. Trauma, of course, but maybe arousal too. I have a very beautiful neck, five inches long and narrow as a stem: tempting to people who go in for that kind of thing. Though as far as I knew, he far preferred to *be* strangled. I wondered if that had changed.

"You need a haircut," said Beau, unwinding the measuring tape from my neck. "It's getting a little shaggy in the back."

Not the turn I had expected this would take. "Where do you go?"

He grinned, rakish. "Jane cuts my hair." Then, more soberly: "Giovanni won't see you?"

"Not until I die and we meet in hell. And maybe not even then."

"That blows." Beau marked the final measurement in his notebook, not quite meeting my eyes when he looked up. "What happened with his building? Didn't it get bought?"

"He'll be fine," I said. "I heard they're going to let him keep the space."

Pausing with his pen raised above the page of numbers that described my form, Beau gathered himself. Unlike Jane, there was no guile in him. Did she find that sweet or tiresome? I could see as he prepared himself to broach an uncomfortable topic, and I settled back onto my heels to receive it. This was not the intelligence I had hoped for, but it would perhaps prove of more practical use.

"Man," said Beau, and shook his head. Tried to start again. Set the uncapped pen flat against the page. A fine spray of ink from the nib left a spatter of lilac over my measurements. "This is . . . I don't even know how to ask this. But Giovanni said *you* got the building sold. Like, to . . . what, to bribe him? Blackmail? To hold it over him, he said."

"I'd call it leverage," I said. "More accurate, less loaded."

"But like . . ." He did a quick recalculation—he had not been expecting me to admit it. "How?"

I was trying to figure out where he was taking this. Whether it was something Jane knew or cared about. When Giovanni had told him, and why. "I told my client I needed his company to sell the building. He did."

"Like that?"

"He really, *really* wanted this perfume." I shrugged, a little flirty. "Rich people are weird."

But he was already shaking his head. "I mean, isn't that kind of fucked up, though? I thought we were all in this together."

Did Jane think we had been in this together? She had always been in it for herself. But she and Beau already differed on so many things, somehow this misinterpretation did not surprise me.

"So did I." Earnest, tragic. Even off balance, I knew what tone to strike with Beau. "But I guess Giovanni didn't think so."

He wavered. I saw him waver. But then he said, "I mean. It was kind of a big deal." Dropping his voice, he added, "Murder isn't like . . . easy."

"No," I said, thinking of that frozen night with Pippin Miles in the back of my car, the bone-deep exhaustion of hauling corpses in the cold. "It isn't. But if you and Jane were steeled to it, why not him?"

Something had shut across his face, though: like Jane's steel grate but softer, sadder. A curtain furling across a stage. The sway of a sign just turned from **Open** to **Closed**.

"When did he tell you all of this?" Then playfully: "Beau, did you have brunch without me?"

It struck the wrong note; he winced. "No. We just grabbed drinks a couple of nights ago."

"What night?" I was done cajoling. This was a demand.

"Earlier this week. Tuesday."

After I left Giovanni and took his grappa, that bastard had texted Beau and talked shit about me, tried to drive a wedge in. What did he hope to accomplish? Did he think that because Beau did all of Jane's flirting for her, he could handle her breakups as well? That wasn't how this kind of thing worked.

Beau was still talking. "He's really upset, Vic. I'm kind of worried about him." He considered his tangled tape measure for a moment. "I mean, I'm fucked up about it, I won't lie, but he's . . . Giovanni follows the *rules*, Vic. When shit goes down, he calls the cops."

My bowels turned to liquid. "Did he say he was going to call the cops? Beau?"

"He wouldn't," said Beau. "No way. What about me? What about Jane?"

"Did he say *anything*?"

"No," said Beau. "No. He didn't. He just said—"

Fuck. *"What?"*

"He just said he thought it wasn't fair. Getting away with it. That it wasn't right."

"You shouldn't go bankrupt running a successful business either," I said. I was *livid*. And not only at the state of American socioeconomics.

Giovanni had *lied* to me. He had cared very much what happened after he left my basement. I was a chump for taking him at his word. But I had wanted so badly to believe in his apathy, because anything else would necessitate action on my part. I didn't want to hurt him any more than I already had. This realization caught me almost by surprise: I didn't want to hurt any of them. But it was far too late for that.

"Your goddamned life shouldn't be ruined by medical debt," I said, a paltry expression of this sudden, wrenching sentiment. "You shouldn't have to give up everything you love just to pay your rent. That isn't fair either." Like Barry said: bread and roses.

"I know," he said. "I know. But—"

"But fucking *nothing*."

"But," he insisted, "your friends shouldn't fuck you over. There's nothing fair about that."

Service does for service. I wondered if Giovanni had told him about that too.

"How much do I owe you?" I asked. "For the deposit?"

He gave me a number. It wasn't small, and he didn't offer the friends and family discount. Jane would have approved.

As I came out of the elevator on the ground floor of Beau's building, my phone chirped. My first instinct was to reach for it—a newish habit. I hadn't had any reason to check my texts so fast, before all this. It would have been Barry, who was paid to wait, or a client, who could afford to. But these days—or the days that had preceded them, before murder made everything so difficult—there were people I wanted to talk to.

But murder *had* made everything difficult—an outcome I had not foreseen or cared about at the outset of this project. This text might be Beau, with some brittle logistical follow-up. A sad contrast to his salacious missives of mere months ago. It might be Giovanni's last words before flinging himself into the crushing arms of Justice. Or it might be Jane. She hadn't texted me since she left my apartment, and I didn't know if I wanted her to or not.

So I paused with my hand hovering over my back pocket. If it was Barry, I would lecture him about independent decision-making and ownership of his projects, which would make me sound very supervisory. If it was a client, I was free to refuse any pleas, offers, or persuasions that came my way. Except from Eisner, who still lurked in my peripheral as a problem that needed to be dealt with. I had given myself a vacation of some months, but eventually that loose end would need to be knotted, ends snipped neatly flush.

As I hesitated, my phone buzzed again. A second text, or the automatic reminder? If I knew, it might help me decipher the sender.

I should just look at it. Instead, I stepped into the street. As I walked to the subway I waited. Would it buzz again? Three in a row would mean Barry, maybe Beau. But I only got silence. It wasn't until I was safely out of signal, deep under Union Square and waiting for the L rendered unreliable by construction, that I finally pulled out my phone to check.

I'm not sure who I expected, or who I wanted it to be. All right, that's a lie: I did want a text from Jane. I wanted two texts in a row. But it was Eisner, one text, the second vibration a nagging reminder that he refused to be ignored.

Call me, it said. That was it.

On the one hand, he was a self-centered sack of shit who firmly believed that his desires were sacred. This could be one of those *I need yous* that ended in sinister inanity, like *Sunset Boulevard.* On the other hand, Gillis did end up dead, and Eisner had enough leverage to see me, if not a corpse, then at least pretty thoroughly fucked.

I would have to wait twenty minutes to swipe in again, the downside of my new unlimited MetroCard. Still, I trekked back aboveground and collapsed on a bench to call him.

"Vic," he said when he picked up, and I knew immediately that something was very, very wrong.

"You texted me. I called."

"Ye-es." I heard a phone begin to vibrate in the background of the call. Faint voices. He was in the office, maybe. But then I thought of the quiet C-suite, the trickling fountain and soundproof glass. Not his office, but someone else's.

"Why?"

"Well," he said. "I've just left the lawyer's office. The corporate lawyer."

That didn't bode well.

"It's just . . . well, it seems there are some discrepancies between the version of events you and I agree on and the legal realities of my current position."

"Interesting," I said, and wished I were still midwestern enough to imbue the word with as many shades of ire as I felt. Jane could have, I was sure. Jane could have handled Eisner so deftly he wouldn't realize she had done it, and left him with a faint whiff of shame he didn't exactly understand.

"Perhaps you'd care to explain?" he asked.

I would *not*. But I couldn't hang up. What did Eisner *want* to hear? Catering to his fantasies had gotten me this far—maybe it would get me a little farther. Just far enough.

"You trust your GC?" I asked. "You didn't trust Pearson or the Yateses."

Silence on the other end of the line. Encouraging.

"All I'm saying is: I made you a single meeting. How much do you think you really know about this deal your colleagues were doing? About who else might be in on it?"

"Well, I thought I knew *enough*," he said. And then his frustration began to seep outward: sibilant, slow, corrosive. "But after all, I suppose this was an *experiment*, this perfume. If you've fucked up . . . Do you realize what this will cost me? Do you know what kind of shit I'm in right now?"

Not nearly the kind of shit I was about to be in, if he was this angry. This man knew everything bad there was to know about me. Or, almost. And that was plenty.

"Everything I have worked for was riding on this," he said. "On stopping this. And now I'm months too late, and on top of *this* investigation, there's . . . the other issue. I can't afford any scrutiny right now, and if you're wrong, and the lawyer's right? It's going to hit me like a fucking searchlight."

My heart bled. "Take a few deep breaths. You can afford good counsel. You told me so yourself."

"What the fuck do *you* know about it?" In that, I heard a familiar kind of despair. The same kind that I felt whenever I was faced with someone—like Eisner—who simply couldn't comprehend what it was like to live so close to the edge. Who wondered why I didn't just budget better, eat out less, cancel my gym membership. (What gym membership?) It was too vast a gulf to bridge.

Lucky for him, he would never have to try.

◆　◆　◆

My order of priorities had just been reshuffled. Tonight was no longer a quiet night in. I resented that Eisner had called while I was already downtown—now I was faced with a trip up to Harlem for supplies and a change of clothes, and another trip down later. Then again, even well supplied I would have had several hours of lurking until full dark, and more after that, waiting for the neighbors to fall asleep. New York is a wonderful city for many reasons; ease and speed of travel is not one of them. To prepare yourself for an entire day in the city took foresight and planning and an enormous tote bag. Never mind preparing for the perfect murder.

Iolanda caught me on the way in. "How's business?" she asked, and I smiled and told her the truth, two things that hadn't gone hand in hand until recently.

"How's that friend of yours?" she asked. "That pretty girl I've seen coming and going?"

So she had noticed Jane. For a moment, I felt warm: not embarrassed, but suffused with a sort of ridiculous pride. I thought that they might get along; I wanted, absurdly, to introduce them.

Then I paused to wonder if Iolanda heard more through her floor than I had previously believed. Alarming, if so. Not so much because it afforded the chance to eavesdrop on my sex life; rather because there were other things I wanted to keep quiet. But she didn't place any particular emphasis on "pretty" or "coming"—it was a statement of fact, not an innuendo. I wondered if she was much more conservative than I had expected and didn't realize what was going on, or far more open-minded than I gave her credit for.

Whichever, it made me uneasy that she paid such close attention. She hadn't struck me as a mother hen, or a gossip. Maybe it was all that laundry; there was such a thing as too much good will. How could I put her off? Just enough to chill this burgeoning interest.

At any rate, I would have to go out the basement door later, to avoid any more small talk. Maybe if she didn't see me again, she would even think I had been home all night. Though if she had seen Jane out the windows, there was no telling how long she sat watching in a given day, and what she noticed. An unnerving thought. But she had left me alone so far; I would have to rely on her a little longer at least.

Downstairs, I gathered a new length of clothesline from the roll on the workbench and curled it into a loop that fit in the back pocket of a pair of tight black jeans. Less for aesthetics—though I can lean into heroin chic when I want—and more to keep track of where my clothes were at any given time. Loose fabric was asking for an untoward spatter or stain.

As dusk moved ponderously across the sky, I ate dinner. Over a bowl of reheated barbacoa I asked myself how I was feeling. Ready to jump back in? The sense of panic and overwhelming exhaustion that had dogged my footsteps throughout January and February was absent. I wasn't exactly looking forward to the task—I was more looking forward to its completion. But I felt rested, refreshed, and prepared to tackle it head-on. Or from the side. Or whatever angle I could get, as quickly as I could get it.

He never should have given me his address.

◆　◆　◆

At night, Eisner's windows were lit gold, and looking into them felt like peering into the period rooms at the Met—much better illuminated than the dingy, dark little alcoves at the Brooklyn Museum, with bad glare on the glass and children's greasy handprints blurring the view.

If anyone ever reconstructs my apartment from that time, I'm sure that's how it will measure up to Eisner's place.

The indoors was unobscured by window treatments. After dark in this neighborhood, you left your shades up and your curtains open so that less fortunate people could look in on your splendor like the Little Match Girl and appreciate your comfort and good taste.

The less fortunate do not appreciate the view, nor your having offered it. They feel acquisitive, angry, at the very best merely aspirational.

The night was mild, so as I stood looking into Eisner's windows I didn't feel the insult of cold as well as that of exclusivity. If I hadn't known whose house it was, and hadn't been on a particular type of errand that didn't allow for conspicuous loitering, I might have stopped on the sidewalk to assess the crown molding, evaluate the choice of light fixture hanging from an original medallion. But I was, so I did not.

Despite the difference in architectural styles, his elegant old Federal-style row house had the same convenient service entrance under the front steps as Iolanda's brownstone. The servants' entrance, a hundred years ago. I hoped this one led to Eisner's basement and not a converted apartment on which he made a little extra each month. What the hell would he need it for? No, far more likely it was where he kept his Peloton.

I had circled the block a few times trying to find parking for my Zipcar and settled for something a few blocks away. I could always double-park when it came to the pivotal moment. There was little traffic here to disrupt.

I had already put a few dozen miles on the odometer, running interference all over Manhattan and even taking a trip into the Bronx over the Willis Avenue Bridge. It wasn't the cleanest alibi, but it might confuse the situation somewhat if anyone started looking.

They wouldn't. I was good at my job.

I climbed the steps, flexing my hands inside gloves that were almost unseasonable now. But better sweaty palms than stray fingerprints. I wore a beanie as well, to keep any loose hairs in check.

The street was so quiet that I could hear his doorbell—resonant, a proper ring. Iolanda's bell was an awful buzzer, and my apartment didn't even have one. Not that anyone ever stopped by uninvited or unchaperoned.

Briefly, I recalled the cluster of bells at the front of Beau and Jane's building, the shudder of the front door as the door at the top of the stairs was opened. The anticipation in the proceeding interim.

I wished that I were standing on those steps right now; I wondered if my welcome would differ, depending on who opened the door. Would Beau let me in? Would Jane? He would do what she told him; that had become abundantly clear. But what would she tell him to do? Did I want to know?

Not important. And dangerous to get distracted. I moved down one step on Eisner's stoop, out of the range of the security camera above the button. Better not to advertise my presence before he saw me in person. Did he have cameras inside? I couldn't remember. Too late now.

Footsteps preceded a shadow on the frosted glass. I took a deep breath. I just had to get inside, and then behind the overhead sconce in the hallway—otherwise what happened would be projected like a shadow-puppet play for anyone who walked by. It was a distance of . . . eight feet? I could cover that in no time. If I slipped past Eisner, I thought he would pursue me rather than move into the street. Thought, but wasn't sure. So as I heard the latch click, I took the final step again and then some, pressing my way inside before Eisner realized who I was or what was happening.

It wasn't an inconspicuous way to enter someone's house, but it was better than loitering on the stoop, or a confrontation in the doorway. I trusted the late hour, the overcast night, the helpful ambivalence of most New Yorkers to apparent conflict. The security camera would only have caught a blur.

Staggering back, he tripped on the corner of his rug. It gave me time to shut the door. By then, he had seen my face.

"Vic?"

"Hello." It was far too late for *good evening*. And to promise one would be a patent lie.

"What are you—"

But I took him down before he could get it out.

"What am I doing here?" I asked, knee in the center of his chest. He scrabbled uselessly at my jacket—leather, slippery, unyielding to an old man's brittle fingernails—reached for my face and fell short, tried to find anything to use as a weapon. His frightened gasping smelled of mouthwash, the guilty specter of a bedtime cigarette. His hand closed on the leg of the hall table, but it was heavy American oak and didn't budge. I looped the clothesline around his neck. "*This* is what I'm doing here. What else?"

He tried to draw breath. It didn't work. I pretended not to notice.

"What did you expect? I can't afford to be blackmailed. Literally cannot afford it. This is just business."

His struggling weakened and died. I wished I had a wristwatch—I didn't wear one then. I had never come across one that appealed, within my budget. Instead I counted Mississippis under my breath and made sure he was lying on the rug when he at last expired. It wasn't an antique—that would have hurt—but a minimalist white cotton hall runner, probably ordered from Denmark or West Elm. It had those little irregular nubbins in the weave. Who owns a *white* rug? It had always been destined to be soiled.

31

Notes de Tête: Grappa, Semen
Notes de Cœur: Scotch
Notes de Fond: Wet Wool and Mothballs

Why tincture and distill him anyway?

The same reason I had lugged Pip Miles home that frigid night. I wasn't eager to tamper with a method that had so far succeeded, at least where it concerned detection and discovery. Boozy bodies burned fast. And it was always good to have a little extra distillate with which to experiment. I still tended to be precious with my supplies—there were some notes I could barely face the prospect of polishing off.

Jonathan was my most precious. Tincturing him had not been so utilitarian; in the aftermath of the act, faced with what I had done, I had breathed deep and the scent of him filled my head for what I realized might be the final time. And then, I had an idea.

Working gave me purpose, so I worked. Not as well as I would come to, later, but well enough to end up with a small supply of sticky brown distillate and a gruesome side hustle.

I have often used my work to avoid harsh truths, to put off dealing with the inevitable. This time, while I worked on the perfume I had promised Jane, I forgot to worry about Giovanni. Dwelling in the past, conjuring one moment of irrevocable change, I would not have to face a new one, the consequences of which remained opaque and threatening.

If this perfume functioned technically, I would know I could accomplish what I had set out to do. How I hoped it might function otherwise, in other ways . . . The past was my area of expertise. I was learning to deal in fantasy, but I could not tell the future, and I refused to allow myself the empty luxury of daydreaming—I didn't want to get my hopes up. Jane's reaction remained an ominous blank: one I could not fill until I had completed the perfume.

I worked very hard to create a scent that conjured the moment for me, exactly. I relived that rainy night over and over again, diving into each olfactory detail. It would mean nothing to Jane—it would only be an illustration, an embellishment, relying on my retelling for substance. But like a tailor carefully pressing French seams nobody would see, I perfected the scent inside and out. I strangled Jonathan a hundred times, each time realer than the last, until I could not tell the moment from reality when I was within it.

The full effect of this perfume blooms outward. At first it's only the booziness of Scotch, the chill of wet cement. As it opens up, Jonathan's apartment unfolds like a puzzle box, pieces sliding out to reveal the depth and breadth of space that previously appeared much smaller.

Jonathan unfolds as well: at first his own perfume, and then his hair, and then his skin and clothes fill in like pigment touched to wet paper. The commercial note that they call "cashmere" smells nothing like the wool, which in truth smells more of the soap it has been washed in and the sweat of the person wearing it. The rain that night had coaxed a faint trace of mothballs from the yarn, and a hint of goat.

At its fullest, this perfume is deep, complex, physical. As it dries down, the scene dissipates like mist in a breeze: in some places tearing into patches, in others merely thinning so slowly that you don't realize it is going until it's gone.

Jonathan, though: he hangs on. He always does, no matter what I mix him with. Which here gives him the uncanny ability to linger after death. His shit and ragged breath and fear slowly decay until all that remains is the sweaty, bitter scent he carried secretly beneath his arms, between his legs. And then he is alive again, almost, a ghost rising with every breath, every current of the air.

The perfume is not a scrubber, but I found myself scrubbing more often than not: rubbing my skin raw to remove any last traces that might linger. Still, sometimes I missed a spot and woke with my heart pounding in the night, convinced a man long dead was lying beside me. The empty sheets were both a disappointment and a relief.

Perhaps my obsession with perfecting this moment, reliving it over and over, was an effort to perfect my own ability to retell it. To convince myself that it was real, and that I remembered it correctly. The whole thing felt, sometimes, like a particularly vivid dream. The scene was crisp in my memory, but memory was unreliable—it was feelings, impressions, moods. Now that I had captured Jonathan's murder in a scent, it was immutable. I had it fixed in alcohol as though in amber.

All that remained was to show it to Jane. Or, at least, to try.

◆　◆　◆

"Iolanda thinks you're pretty," I said as I closed the door behind her.

"Your landlady? How does she know?"

"Apparently she's more of a busybody than I thought. Can I get you a drink?" I had stocked my bar with essentials over the weekend and hoped she would say yes so I had an excuse to pour one for myself. I was electric with nerves, and not in a pleasant pre-thunderstorm sort of way. More like someone had attached a car battery to my fillings.

"No," said Jane. "Thanks." She set her tote bag on my armchair and looked around, as if seeing the place for the first time, unsure how she'd ended up here. Dorothy in Oz, except slightly disappointed. I clenched my jaw and the voltage of my anxiety jumped several ergs.

"Well do you mind . . . ?" I gestured vaguely to the bar cart, feeling about fourteen and deeply unsuave.

She shrugged.

I poured myself some grappa, neat, and shot it with my back to her.

"Nervous?" she asked when I turned around.

If I had been less so, I might have given her a flippant answer. Instead, I set a small bottle down between us and said, "This is it."

"Not very pretty." It was just a brown dropper bottle, the kind she would keep bitters in at work.

"Well." I swallowed past the lingering burn of brandy. "Iolanda never made any such claims about it. Be nice."

She picked up the bottle and rolled it across her palm. "Beau told me about Giovanni."

My stomach sank, cold and heavy as a rock through thin ice. "And?"

The bottle rolled back and forth. I stared, wondering if it would fall, if it would break, if the perfume would be set free all at once, overpowering.

"I tried to call him," she said. "No answer. And he won't text me back. Beau either." Back and forth, the liquid casting an indistinct shadow on the glass. "He wouldn't turn us in. I've known him since college. He wouldn't."

There was one possibility, not pleasant but certainly less dangerous. "He's not . . ."

"The shop's been posting," she said. "And he reposts. Nothing of his own, but he's not . . . he isn't dead." Gathering some attitude, she managed a scoff. "He wouldn't kill himself. Too selfish. He needs to suffer for his fuckups. Ask me how I know."

"You've known him since college," I said. "I'm sure you've seen him fuck up any number of times."

"Just a few." She finally closed her fingers around the bottle and turned it right side up. "And every time, he took it hard. But he always did the right thing. What *he* thought was right, anyway."

I had been stalling and stalling, waiting for someone to absolve me of the awful responsibility I could see looming on the horizon. Instead, Jane had affirmed it. I didn't *want* to kill Giovanni. But I also didn't want to go to prison. I didn't want Jane to go to prison either, or Beau. I didn't want to lose the things that I had finally gathered together, the fragile bubble I had blown around myself to push back the crushing pressure of the world. But it seemed doomed to pop, no matter what I did.

"I'm sorry he's taking this out on you," I said. "I'll . . . I'll talk to him again. Or try." I was not confident of the outcome.

She shook her head. "He's not taking it out on anyone except himself. We'd only get in the way. That's why he won't text back; he needs some space to beat himself up." Lifting the brown bottle to the light, she scrutinized it in a stagy sort of way, a calculated effort to turn the conversation away from our precarious reality.

I focused on the brown glass bottle, on Jane's bitten fingernails, on the potential trapped inside their grip. This did nothing to ease my racing heart, my uneven breath, but it reminded me of a more immediate reason for the high-voltage current simmering the blood beneath my skin. I could even, if I concentrated, convince myself that part of it was anticipation.

"I'm not sure it will work," I said.

"One way to find out. Do I open it now? Or wait?"

"Wait," I said. "I have to tell you first. How it happened. And then you smell it, and tell me what you see."

She put the bottle in between us, on a table bare of anything else. It stood there like a monolith, a silent audience of one, and I told my story toward it rather than watch her eyes to see how her opinion of me changed.

337

We have been at dinner with a client, someone who talks about a collaboration to bolster each of our brands. Someone who thinks they understand our job as well as we do.

Jonathan is not very interested—this is a commission in disguise, and he does not work on commission. But I have pushed for this one, because I think I understand his job as well as he does. In fact, I do not understand his job at all, because he doesn't have one. Bright House is not his job: it is his playground.

Our guest—our host? It is unclear as of yet who will pay for dinner—is unsure to which of us he should defer. Obviously Jonathan is my superior, but this man can't keep his hands or his eyes where they belong, and during dinner his gaze keeps straying to me, to the low vee of my unbuttoned shirt. Jonathan leans into it, sending all the technical inquiries my way, deflecting questions, acceding to my opinion. And then finally, when he has directed the man's attention fully to me, he sulks and interrupts. He enjoys putting me in an uncomfortable spot, perhaps even enjoys the echoes of voyeurism, but he prefers the limelight. Maybe he's even jealous. We fight bitterly in the cab back from Brooklyn. It has begun to rain.

The steam heat in Jonathan's loft does little to combat the high ceilings, the excess of glass. The room is almost empty, scrubbed antiseptically clean. It smells faintly of brick dust, traces of coffee caught in the corners, but mostly it smells like the high-proof spirits we use to clean equipment in the lab. He is a fastidious man. After sex, he will only lie for a few minutes before he needs to shower. He does not take the train.

Jonathan locks up behind us, hangs his coat on the single hook, kicks off his expensive boots. The anger in him changes as he moves through his routine. The wrath is replaced by purpose, each movement less erratic. By the time he pours two tumblers of Scotch—burnt rubber, peaty smoke, faint fishy stink of salt; in that ascetic space all scents stand out in sharp detail—he's smiling. It is not a pleasant smile, and I want to bite it off his face.

"Come here." He taps two fingers on the kitchen counter by the bottle.

I don't move.

His hand curls into a fist. "Come here." This time in the voice you'd use to call a dog. Catlike, I stare at him and stand my ground until he opens his mouth to speak again. Before he can, I step up and take my drink.

"You were certainly on your best behavior tonight," he says. Sourly.

I turn the glass, falsely contemplative. "Anyone would think, Jonathan, that you don't want to work on this collaboration."

"I don't do work for hire," he says. "People are stupid; they never know what they really want. Half the time, they're afraid to find out."

"Jonathan Bright doesn't take orders from anyone," I say, mocking.

"No," he says. "I don't."

"Not even for money? I hear some people will pay through the nose for that."

He snatches a handful of my hair and pulls. "There's not enough money in the world." He is talking against my temple now, too loud and mostly growling. "No one pays me to grovel. And nobody pays you to do it either. Not while you work for me." He licks my ear.

"That means you pay me not to grovel," I say. "And I won't." Dipping my head, I sink my teeth into his neck, tasting the bitter sheen of scent left on his skin. If I pressed a little harder against the corded tendons of his throat, I could draw blood. I almost want to.

With my mouth, I clean the last traces of perfume from him until all he wears is sweat and saliva. The delicate stretch of blue-white skin beneath his jaw bruises purple-black.

When I'm finished, I turn away and tell his kitchen cabinets: "Take the commission. You can elevate it, turn it into something good."

There is a knife block by the sink. Jonathan draws a Japanese blade of silk-sharp steel and presses its tip to the small of my back.

"If you want to do what I do," he says, "you make what you want, when you want to." Expert as a butcher, he draws the point swiftly through the stitches of my slacks. Cold metal passes between my buttocks and kisses the insides of my thighs. "You don't give people what they ask for. When you feel like it, then you give them what they don't know they need."

"Oh, and you know what I need?" I ask, because it's too easy.

He flips the blade and slams it back into the block, then boxes me in against the counter's edge with both his arms. I feel a rush of air as he inhales, hear the teeth of his zipper parting.

"Don't get smart," he says.

"Too late." I look down at our hands on the counter and cover his with mine, alternating our fingers like the closing teeth of a trap.

That's foreshadowing, but it won't pay off for a while.

We fuck all over his apartment, even pressed against the cold, curtainless windows looking down on SoHo. Shadow rivulets slink across the unfinished floor, limned in sodium yellow. The lights of occasional passing cars sweep across the bare boards, red and white.

We have never trusted each other enough to sleep in the same bed, so we lie together and fight it. A sheen of cooling sweat sticks our interlocking legs together. I press my face into the blush of broken capillaries on his neck. Taking a breath in time with his, I smell him without perfume: unadulterated Jonathan Bright.

After sex, still unshowered, slick with spit and sweat and come, he does not smell good. Without his expensive shower gel, his hair products, his moisturizers, the finishing sprays of whatever unlabeled experiment or impossible-to-find vintage bottle, he smells just like anybody else.

He smells like me, maybe. Like any hungry, desperate kid who wants to make it in the big city. Who needs to make it, because there are no other options. And he *has*.

More fool I, for thinking he had done it on his own. But in this memory, I hadn't put those pieces together yet. In this memory, the thing inside me that *wants* is wakening, and suddenly the disparity between us is unconscionable, when we are alike in so many other ways. I imagine, impossibly, that by destroying him perhaps I can finally take his place.

Crushed against Bright's body and bruises and softening cock, the fragile stem of his delicate throat, I inhale him and imagine what I might do without the bludgeon of his condescension, the jerk on my chain at every change of his whims. I imagine what I might make of Bright House, without his ego foiling every chance of success. What I might do if *I* were Jonathan Bright, but better, because I am me.

He has told me to make what I want, when I want it. And I *want* it, right now.

◆　◆　◆

"Vic?" Jane's voice shook. "Vic . . . you're crying."

I put my fingers to my face, which felt numb, and found my cheeks were wet. I licked my lips. "Oh. Strange." How many times had it happened as I tested this, with no one watching to tell me?

"Jesus Christ," she said, more to herself than me.

"It worked, then. Was it good for you?" A feeble attempt at humor, dead on arrival, belied by my stupid tears. I knuckled them away.

She lifted her hands—they were shaking—and ran them through her hair. Scraps of scent eddied in the air: Jonathan, whisky, semen, rain. "And after that, you . . . you just hosed him out? Or what? You said it was an *accident*."

"It was," I said. "The whole process was . . . I didn't know what I was doing."

"But how could you, after that? I've seen you, I've seen the way you work. You're cold as *fuck*, Vic. You're like those guys who clean the fish at Chelsea Market. How did you *look* at him, and touch him like that, and then do *that*?"

"I had to," I said, helpless. It hadn't been easy. I remembered watching my own hands in disbelief; how his wet hair clung to my forearms as I wrestled him into the tub. "I had to try, because I wanted . . . I wanted to . . ."

"Keep him," she said.

"No." Maybe, but not quite. I floundered until I found the words, and when I did, I would not have spoken them to anyone but Jane. "I wanted to *become* him. And I didn't know how else to do it."

"That's fucked up," she said.

"I know."

I waited for her pity. But she only asked me, "Why?"

"I could see all the ways I could do it better than he could. And I have. I *am* better. But it doesn't matter. I'll never have the ease of it, the fearlessness. He just . . . didn't have to care. He didn't have to *try*. And I always will." My eyes were stinging—this time I felt the tears building, and I shut my eyes against them so hard that my forehead ached.

"I thought I could make people pay for what I wanted to give them. But you can't be what he was without what he had; it's too fucking expensive. It turns out there is no purity in this game; you know that. You can't sell the 'clean expression' of your own ideas; people just want their own inane shit hurled back at them. You bankroll your pet project, or you smile and take orders for money."

In the quiet after my tirade, her pity finally came. For this naïveté, I deserved it. I pitied myself for ever having believed it.

"At least you make them pay through the nose," she said at last. It punctured the tension as neatly as a pin and we both laughed, bitter and unsteady.

Once she caught her breath, she asked, "So, what about Eisner?" Not a non sequitur. After all, he had paid a hefty sum.

I said nothing, but the silence was very evocative.

"So that's it." Her words fell into an awkward pause—she had waited slightly too long for me to speak. "It's over. Now nobody asks you for shit. You're free."

She sounded . . . almost hopeful, like it might be true.

"From one particular onus, yes. I still have to make money." I was resigned to the impure fact of it these days.

"Boo fucking hoo," she said. "So does everybody. How's that lilac stuff selling?"

"All right, so far." I'd seen good reviews on Fragrantica too. "You're famous."

She shook her head. "No. It's the space I left behind, remember? That's what people like."

"Not me," I said.

She laughed, less shaky. "You're so fucking smooth." Then her gaze skittered back down to the bottle. "Did you get that from him?"

I closed my hand over hers, where she still held the scent. "He would never have hired me if I wasn't already myself. I've just gotten more so."

"You were always like this?" she asked, cocking an eyebrow like she couldn't believe it.

"Why do you think I came to New York? I certainly didn't fit in at home."

"Where *are* you from?" she asked.

Now that I knew it was possible, I imagined the scent I could make to explain. Tar bubbles cooking in the sun. Corn ripening in August. Cherry-flavored disinfectant mixed with mop water. Bubblegum lip gloss. Bath and Body Works Cucumber Melon. The air-conditioning in a shopping mall—off-brand Estée Lauder. Weed smoke underneath the bleachers. The smoke of fentanyl in the cab of a truck. Spilled beer at parties I wasn't invited to but went to anyway, sometimes. The smell of sweat. The smell of shame. Metallic, raw meat blood-stink, the way it smells coming down the back of your throat when your nose is broken and you've tilted back your head to stop it from staining your new

Abercrombie shirt. The smell of a pretty girl's hair. The smell of the football captain's crotch. The smell of wanting everything you know that you don't know to want yet. The smell of cantaloupe, which grows all around your town in the summer in flat brown fields that stretch to the yellow horizon, until you feel marooned in the middle of all that dusty monochrome. Cantaloupe, which is the smell of the sea: a metaphor you won't understand until someone who knows all the things you want to tells you why you have felt like a castaway all your life.

They never know what they really want, Jonathan had warned me. *Half the time, they're afraid to find out.* I never had been. And I didn't think Jane would be either.

"The Midwest," I said. "Outside Indianapolis, about an hour. West."

"Oh," she said. "I'm from Sandusky. Neighbors."

"Now do you want a drink?" I asked.

"God yes," she said. "I do."

32

*Notes de Tête: **Proraso, Citrus, Barbicide***
Notes de Cœur: Blade Oil
Notes de Fond: Blood, Sweat, and Fear Accord

And then my pigeons came home to roost.

I had been putting off the inevitable since my fitting with Beau, since he told me about Giovanni's wavering resolve. My conversation with Jane should have galvanized me. It did the opposite. Memories of Jonathan meant memories of my own thwarted ambition. Meant empathizing just a little too much with someone who had poured everything they had into an enterprise that couldn't give enough back, who stuck to principle even in the face of immolation.

I had put him off too long. I had put myself at risk, and Jane and Beau, to prolong the tenuous sense that we had succeeded. That despite the dangers and our bruised and strained bonds of friendship, we had pulled off what we set out to do.

If I had waited any longer, I would not even have been able to snatch my own small victory from the jaws of defeat. But I still believe that it was a worthy goal, and a worthwhile delay. It bought us all a little time, at least. The only time I have been able to treat my friends to anything.

I wasn't *sure* he would turn himself in. It only seemed *likely*, and that from secondhand accounts and intuition. He had never actually *said* he would, to me or anyone. Then again, would he? He didn't seem like a grandstander. But if so, why weren't there cops at my door right now? Why had he hesitated? What was he waiting for? Perhaps whatever had held him back could be bent to my advantage. Perhaps it could be used to maintain the fragile state of things as they currently stood.

This is the little loop of positive self-talk that I played for myself as I prepared to go downtown.

I armed myself this time not with grappa but a stack of cash. He probably wouldn't take a bribe, but greater men than he had weakened at the sight of green. I prepped negotiation tactics—Beau and Jane as collateral damage, and what would happen to the business he had worked so hard to build?

It was not lost on me that the success of my own business was built on his sacrifice, and that its continuance relied on his willingness to live with his guilt. Was Bright House worth more to me than Giovanni? I had thought so, not that long ago. I had to keep thinking so, or else I would not make it through this night.

Because it always pays to be prepared, I coiled a new length of clothesline in my back pocket. I didn't want to do it. It should never have—and I hoped still wouldn't—come to this. We were on the same side. His only problem was that he believed in the system. And if I had gamed the system to crush that belief, it was only to save him from the impact of a more permanent blow. I had done him a goddamned favor. If he made me kill him now . . .

The coiled clothesline pressed into my buttock on the long ride downtown. But at least I had been lucky enough to get a seat.

It was risky to have this confrontation in Giovanni's shop, especially if it came to . . . the conclusion I hoped to avoid. But I didn't know where he lived—except that it was in Jersey—and even if I had, it seemed like he was always at the shop. After hours, some nights, I had walked past on some other errand in the Village and seen him sweeping, polishing, fiddling with the register. Sometimes he was nothing more than the movement of a shadow cast by the office light across the white tile. That shop was his life.

Maybe it was fitting, if his life was going to end tonight, that it would end here, where he had poured out so much of it already.

I waited around the corner, first eating an expensive ice cream cone and then lurking in a cramped bookstore reading the first ten pages of a history of Stonewall over and over again. None of it stuck. At eight fifteen, I went back out to lurk in the mulch-scented shadows of Christopher Park until his receptionist left. And then I crossed the street and knocked on the door, which I had seen him lock behind her.

He was sweeping up, and the sound startled him. The broom jerked, scattering dark hair across the tile. He squinted, and I wondered how well he could see me, with all the lights and mirrors inside. As usual, I was all in black. If he saw anything, he saw the pale thumbprint of my face in the gloom. But he came to the door, and by that alone I knew he hadn't recognized me. It wasn't until he had his nose nearly to the glass that he realized who I was, and balked.

I knocked again, my knuckles rapping the space between his eyes.

"Hello," I said, and imagined the submarine echo of it on the other side of the door. "Can I come in?"

He looked over his shoulder at the empty shop. No witnesses, no one to come to his aid. But no one to overhear anything we said either. Was he more worried about me, or about anyone else? The devil he knew, or the myriad devils he didn't?

"Giovanni," I said.

He bit his lip, hardened his expression, and shook his head. Only after he had turned his back did I recover from my surprise and redouble my pounding on the door. The **CLOSED** sign rattled against the glass with each impact.

"I will *break down this door*," I hissed, unwilling to shout and draw that much more attention from any passersby. The threat would have been inaudible, but Giovanni seemed to get the message from my insistent fist. Stiff with anger, he turned on his heel and came back. The dead bolt snapped and he jerked the door open.

"Fine," he said, already retreating.

I closed the door behind me. As I went to lock it, he snapped, "Leave it." So I did. Was he already sensing he might need a quick exit? I stepped to the side, leaving him a clear path to the door. A measure of tension left his shoulders, but only a measure. He kept plenty back.

"What do you want?" he asked, all semblance of civility gone now that there were no clients here to see him. Had he wanted to speak so forcefully when I came by the other day?

I sat down on the leather bench where I had waited, a hundred times, for his smile and his hand, open for a shake. Where I had drunk espresso and eyed the stack of magazines I didn't have time to read, because in five minutes Giovanni's chair would open up and I would settle in to sit under his swiftly moving hands and emerge exactly how I had always imagined myself looking.

"I want a haircut," I said, surprising myself. "Please."

He shook his head, more taken aback than anything. Then his knuckles went white on the broom. "If I cut your fucking hair," he said, "this once, will you leave me alone? I mean it. If I do it tonight, you'll never come back here again."

I would need another haircut next month. Who would I see then? But that was a problem for the future. And if he was offering . . .

"One more for the road," I said, and stood from the bench, almost expecting him to shake my hand.

As I sat in front of him, I realized too late how vulnerable I was: you couldn't ask for a more perfect position for a victim of the garrote. Or, perhaps more likely, a slashed throat and a fountain of blood. But Giovanni only set his broom aside in favor of a spray bottle. As ever, he worked silently. Conversation would be up to me.

I let him get very close to finishing before I broke the increasingly tense silence. He had set his clippers aside and begun to neaten the top, sectioning too fast and too hard so the teeth of the comb scraped my scalp. As he paused to spray me down again I said, "Beau's making me a suit."

Spritz, spritz.

"He measured me the other day. A black silk-linen blend. A warm black, almost brown. Good for summer."

A smattering of hair fell into my shrouded lap.

"He said you two got a drink together. Did some catching up."

The comb slowed, sliding up a section of hair toward Giovanni's bloodless fingers. I said nothing else, waited for him to keep cutting. Instead, he let the comb continue into the air. My forelock fell into my face. By the time I had flipped it back, he was against the wall. I watched him in the mirror, and he watched me.

"He's worried about you," I said. "Jane too."

"I'm fine."

"They're worried about what you might do." I ran my hand through my hair—a little uneven on top, but otherwise mostly done. He hadn't buzzed my neck, but that grew out so fast it hardly signified. If this was as far as we got, I could live with it. "If you turn yourself in, Giovanni, you turn them in too."

"Yeah, and you. I know."

"Would you do it, to hurt me, knowing you would hurt them too?"

"Jesus," he said. "It's all about you, isn't it? It's always all about you. And your problems. What *you* want. Did you ever stop for one second and wonder, hey, maybe I'm not the center of the fucking universe?"

"Oh," I said, "I *know* I'm not the center of the universe. Things would be very different if I were."

Giovanni put his scissor hand to his face, so the blades stuck out from his forehead like a silver horn. A unicorn: virtuous, pure, utterly unsuited to survive the guile of hunters.

I spent a lot of time in the library as a child. These images stick with you.

"It isn't about them," he said. "Beau and Jane. If I could do it without hurting them, I would."

"But you will," I said. "Hurt them. Worse than that. You'll betray them, and someone *else* will hurt them, and their lives will be absolutely over, just like yours. And not because *they* decided they needed to be punished. Because *you* decided *you* did, and dragged them along for the ride."

"Maybe they should have thought of that before they went all in with you!"

The cape rustled around my shoulders as I stood. Stray pieces of hair slid to the floor. "Maybe you should have thought of it too."

"I'm thinking of it now," he said. "I've been thinking about it every fucking night since . . . that one. My mind's made up."

"Why now?" I asked. "Why have you waited so long?"

"It isn't *easy*." His voice cracked. "I *love* Jane. She and Beau are my *friends*, Vic. I don't want to hurt them. But what we did—what we all did—I can't live with that. I have to tell somebody."

"And you call me selfish."

He flushed red. "Fuck you."

There was no getting out of this. The escalation had happened almost without my noticing. Each step up had been the only logical next move, and now we were standing at the edge of the cliff without ever having looked to the left or the right for some other path to take.

It had been too easy to reach this point. Fleetingly, I wondered whether, if I had worked a little harder, things might have turned out differently.

Ponderous, as though in deep thought, I took a few steps to the right, so I was in between him and the unlocked door. The receptionist's table and the coatrack made a screen. If I maneuvered him correctly, and brought him down fast, my exposure to the street through the windows would be minimal.

"Why did you let me in tonight?" I asked. "You could have kept that door locked. You told me never to come back, but you opened that door when I knocked."

He said nothing. A muscle in his jaw jumped.

"If you wanted to suffer for your crimes, Giovanni . . ." Two long, slow steps toward him, a backward shift of my weight so he wouldn't feel threatened: a cover as I reached into my pocket. "You only ever had to ask."

He sneered, mostly bravado. "I'm not into that shit," he said. "I'm not like Beau and Jane."

"Oh," I said, and underneath the barber's cape, I wrapped the clothesline around each hand like a boxer wrapping tape. "That's a different kind of punishment. You want the kind that sticks."

Too late, he looked over my shoulder at the only exit from the shop. If they had started construction, he could have left through the back. An exit he had never asked for that might have saved him now. As it was, there was only me, and the tight green line between my hands.

The cape swirled between us, distracting him. He threw his arms up, but I unbalanced him and he fell back. His head hit the tile floor with a resonant crack that rang off the mirrors.

For half a second his face went slack, and he looked as relaxed as a man asleep. Or already dead. I caught my breath, arrested by this premonition, and didn't twist the clothesline into place as quickly as I should have. And in that moment, Giovanni struck.

He had never dropped his scissors.

The tips of the two blades caught against my ribs and skittered upward, puncturing the barber's cape and the fabric of my T-shirt as they gouged two ragged parallels from my waist to my armpit. The butcher-shop tang of blood bloomed between us. Before he hit my axillary artery, I got his wrist in my grip. Because both my hands were joined by the clothesline, the defensive maneuver threw me off balance. Giovanni bucked his hips and sent me sprawling.

He could have run then. He should have. Instead he kicked me in the stomach and came at me with the scissors, and I knew that no matter his regret, no matter his intent to seek justice, this had always been something of which he was capable. Briefly, it filled me with fellow feeling, perhaps with pride. I sure knew how to pick 'em. Then I jammed my heel into his crotch.

He fell as if hamstrung, red in the face and wheezing for each breath. The scissors spun out of his loosened grip and slid underneath the coatrack.

I didn't move immediately to finish the job. A film of yellow had flooded my vision, the precursor to a blackout, and my ribs stung like I'd been flayed. For each of my painful breaths I heard him take two, almost sobbing. Lying there and looking up, I saw the row of black-and-white photos hanging on the wall: chiaroscuro studies of West Village architecture. The scrawled signature in the white margin: *J.J. Betjeman.*

I closed my eyes and inhaled, smelled Barbicide and citrus, vetiver and oil. I saw Giovanni on the sofa, holding a negroni sour, smiling up at Jane as she shook another at the bar. I saw the smile turn to me, saw his eyes crinkle at the edges as he laughed and said, *Pink panty droppers. She's using navy-strength gin.*

She would never forgive me for this. Would she?

"You don't have to," I said, the words weak with a lack of air. "Giovanni, you don't have to tell."

He groaned, forearms pressed between his thighs. Through clenched teeth he said, "Fuck you."

Rolling to my side, leaving blood smears on the tile, I got up on all fours. Nausea made me gag. I swallowed sour spit and sat back on my heels. The clothesline was still wrapped around my knuckles, biting into my skin. Slowly, aching all the way, I walked on my knees across the tile floor to where Giovanni lay.

He was watching me, panting, not even attempting escape. We both knew what was coming. It was too late for anything else. Maybe it had always been too late for anything else.

I looked at the clothesline between my hands and suddenly loathed it. When I started to unwind it from my knuckles, Giovanni's eyes widened with confusion at first, and then with a fetal kind of hope. I cast the line away, but before he could ask any questions, I put my hands to his throat. His well-barbered skin was soft, in the arc between my thumb and forefinger, marred by a faint scratch of stubble that had begun to emerge toward the end of the day.

I felt him swallow, once, and draw a single breath, and then I put all of my weight into the vulnerable place below his jaw. His windpipe gave—a palpable crunch—but it wasn't his breath I hoped to stop. It was the blood that fed his brain.

Why my hands, and not the clothesline I had brought? I owed it to him to feel this fully. The clothesline was impersonal, and this murder was the opposite.

Giovanni wanted to suffer for his crimes? Well, so did I.

33

Notes de Tête: Alcohol Fumes
Notes de Cœur: Dust, Mildew, Damp Concrete
Notes de Fond: Old Paper, Old Piss, Used-Car Accord

I called in sick the next morning. I wanted to call Jane. Or Beau. Or both of them. Nauseatingly, I wanted to text Giovanni. I wanted to sit in a room with human beings and make small, snide jokes and laugh and drink and eat and be surrounded by things and people and conversation that made me remember why I bothered.

If all of that was impossible—and it was—I only wanted Jane's cold eyes, her skeptical mouth, her conviction that the ends would justify the means. I came so close to texting her, to asking her to come uptown. If not to comfort me, then at least to offer reassurance I had made the correct decision.

Of course, I couldn't. There was no one I could turn to, not with this.

I hurt all over from the exertion of wrestling Giovanni into the car, out of it, into the basement and the tub. My knuckles were split from the alcohol. I had run out of gauze and Band-Aids, patching up my ribs. When the adrenaline drained away, I felt shaky and hollow. Food made me queasy, and so did coffee, but I braved the latter to stave off a brutal headache.

I did laundry, but when the end-of-cycle buzzer rang, I was loath to leave my studio for the basement. Morbidly, I entertained the idea that I would hear sloshing in the tub, fingernails peeling at the underside of the plastic wrap.

It was just difficult to believe that he was dead. I couldn't have killed him. Could I?

Iolanda heard the dryer when it finished and called down the stairs, asking if I would do a load for her. I had to swallow twice before I could answer, and she called down again in the silence, sounding worried.

"You okay, Vicky?"

"Yeah!" It rang brightly off the damp concrete. "Sorry. Just had the door shut. You need laundry?"

"Just some sheets and towels, no big rush."

"I'll be up in a minute. You can just leave it by the door."

"Besos, baby. You're the best."

Debatable.

How was I supposed to live with Giovanni's corpse in my basement for a month? But I would have to. I needed him to be as flammable as possible before I carted him out to the country and burned him to a crisp.

My coffee, which had lain quiescent for the last hour, threatened to turn on me. Maybe tomorrow, when Barry inevitably inquired about my welfare, I could tell him I had been struck with a twenty-four-hour stomach flu.

Except the next day, he ran late—probably with tummy troubles of his own, no doubt brought on by too much fun the night before—and by the time he arrived I had bigger problems than a nosy assistant.

Have patience with this next part. Think of it as further proof of concept. I have already explained, in a manner of speaking, why it is that I still need a person's body to create this kind of perfume, even if the client has never met the subject. I can give you the plastic and ink and dusty carpet of my office. But now I will show you what happens when I attempt to create a perfume without that key ingredient.

Let us call my problems Detective Virgilio and Officer Ryan—those were their names, after all. *I'm* not liable to forget. And they were very concerned because they thought I might have some information on a recent disappearance they had been assigned to investigate.

There were any number of recent disappearances over which I *could* have panicked. But there was only one to which I jumped: the one for which I deserved to suffer. Because this was another way to do so.

"Of course," I said, overdone as an actor in a low-budget daytime drama. My face felt motion-smoothed and artificial. I comforted myself with the thought that anyone in this situation would feel the same way, whether they had killed the man in question or not. "If there's anything I can do to help . . ."

Detective Virgilio smiled at me like she could tell I wasn't being sincere. I wish I could show her to you—Virgilio, I mean. She isn't what you would imagine, I don't think. And Officer Ryan . . . loomed.

She told me, "Normally we don't jump on cases when the person isn't a vulnerable adult, but—"

But I could fill in the rest. Giovanni wouldn't miss a day of work unless he was flat on his back. And even then, he'd call someone. The concerned receptionist would text her friends, his coworkers, asking what she should do. Someone would stop by his apartment but nobody would answer, no matter how long they leaned on the buzzer.

The receptionist would tell the police there had been someone in the shop a few days ago, raised voices, an altercation. She would give a description. Someone at the shop would know I was a client, would mention that I was a friend. They would find me, and ask me when I had last seen him, and if he had been acting odd. I knew the answers to give—he had been angry and depressed, about to lose everything he had worked so hard for. I could twist this so they suspected a suicide, and I felt sick at the thought. But it was the best option I had, and it was believable. It might even keep them from really digging for clues.

Not that there should be many. I had been very careful cleaning up the shop. Once I had him wrapped in the barber's cape and removed to the trunk of my Zipcar, I had wiped down the scissors and stowed them in the Barbicide at his station. I had swept up all the hair and bagged it to take away with me and burn. I had mopped the floor to a sparkling white that would have satisfied Giovanni, if he had been around to see it. There was no evidence that I had been there on the night of his disappearance. As far as the NYPD was concerned, the last person to see Giovanni alive was his receptionist. The last in a long line of them—he would never fire her for failing to meet his exacting standards.

But I digress. The police in my office! And my poor sweating carcass abject before them, my brain overclocked trying to play the whole conversation out before we could have it.

But then Virgilio asked: Pippin Miles. When was the last time I had seen him?

The frantic hamster wheel of my thoughts stopped so fast that it threw me off completely. "The detective?"

Virgilio was very clear that Miles was a private investigator, not a detective, but yes. He had some kind of ongoing case about a string of disappearances connected to a big investment company. My name was in his notes, and they were speaking to everyone involved.

The way she talked about the case made it sound like a Hollywood blockbuster: the C-suite of a shady financial firm all mysteriously vanished, and then the lone wolf looking into the crime. It sounded like it should be turned over to the feds, solved on primetime TV.

And yet I could not summon fear. Nor could I conjure a shred of misdirection, of defensive charm. I could not climb back on the hamster wheel and sprint in the opposite direction.

There was a ringing in my ears that slowly resolved into a shout: *Pip Miles?* That two-bit detective was who they wanted to find? What for?

What about an incomparable barber, an artist, a well-dressed man, an ornament to the streets of this vicious city? Why weren't they looking for *my friend*?

Detective Virgilio seemed both intrigued and disappointed when I described meeting Miles at the holiday market. Nothing after that? she asked. He hadn't called, or sent an email? I did not mention Eisner's irate relation of Miles's visit to the office. I simply reiterated details of the smoky air, the slushy snow. I told her Miles wasn't wearing gloves; his hands were red, and chapped across the knuckles. Little things. She left unsatisfied, taciturn Officer Ryan in tow, and told me that she'd be in touch. She left her card, extension circled in ballpoint pen.

I thought of Giovanni's hands—manicured and clean, always in motion. The wave his hatband left in his oiled hair. The smell of his pomade, his cologne. The kiss he'd placed on Jane's left cheek, where I had kissed her later that same night. Little things.

I almost wanted to call Virgilio back. Almost.

When I got home, Iolanda caught me at the door.

"Vicky," she said, looking grave. "The cops came by and asked for you."

It only knocked me off kilter for a moment. "Yeah," I said, and if I sounded shaky, what came next would explain it. "A, um . . . a friend of mine is missing." Not that the police cared much.

"Not that pretty girl?" Her face fell.

"No," I said. "Not her."

"You got a lot of friends you never invite over?"

"Some."

"Well, I hope this friend's okay," said Iolanda. "Only, the cops asked could they come in and have a look around."

"Did they have a warrant?" It came out more sharply than I intended. But I had used up all my suavity some hours ago.

"Jesus, no. What for? I told them fuck off, so they did. I don't want no cops in my house." She leaned against the doorframe and cocked her head at me. "You sure you're okay, Vicky? Not in any kind of trouble?"

"Only the usual kinds."

"Yeah, I bet you're *made* of the usual kinds of trouble. Hey, thanks for folding those sheets, but you gotta get better at the fitted one, okay?"

"I'll google it next time," I said. I was incalculably tired and hoped next time wouldn't be tonight.

"Get some rest," she said. "You look like shit."

"Thanks," I said, and staggered down the stairs.

Via text, I told Barry I needed a mental-health break of unspecified duration. It wasn't far from the truth, and he would take it seriously because he was that kind of person. I should be safe from any office-related prying for a week at least.

Hopefully, that would buy me enough time.

When you're in my line of business—the murder-for-hire business, not perfume—you spend a lot of time thinking about what you'll do if things take a sudden turn. I had a plan for this scenario. Or . . . if not this *exact* scenario, something enough like it that my contingencies could still be put into place.

First I bought a beater, for cash. The seller didn't have the title; that wasn't a problem for me. I parked it about ten blocks uptown, accessible in a pinch but not obviously associated with my immediate surroundings.

Next, I spent a couple of afternoons at the library—dried piss, vanillin of aging books—using their boxy old computers to trawl Craigslist. Each day, once I had a long list of phone numbers next to brief descriptions of shady-sounding properties, I went back home and used a prepaid phone to call increasingly odd and unorthodox people until I had zeroed in on what seemed like the best bolt-hole of a bad lot: the most space for the least money, with an absentee landlord on some kind of artistic sabbatical in Berlin. Sight unseen, of course; it was probably a shithole. But I lived in a basement right now, so I could make the best of it. I put cash into the owner's account at a strange little credit union, claiming a distrust of money orders and PayPal skins that he seemed to share. The teller didn't even ask for my ID.

If I didn't end up needing any of these options, I would happily eat the cost of the car and the deposit on the rental. It was all Eisner's money, anyway.

Speaking of Eisner: successfully distilled, burned, and dumped.

I packed necessities and a few professional appliances. Two of my stills, for instance, each delicate piece wrapped in paper towels. I kept the third out and assembled for the unpleasant eventuality of distilling Giovanni. Morbid? Maybe. But I wouldn't let him go to waste.

I made all of these preparations hoping they would be unnecessary. But it was always better to be prepared for the worst.

The week went by. I heard nothing from the cops. Nor did I hear anything from Jane.

Had she guessed what I had done? Had she tried to text Giovanni, tried to call him? Worrying that the strength of their long acquaintance would not, in fact, give him pause, had she wanted to reason with him, to plead, to threaten? When all her overtures came to nothing, did her clever mind turn to me?

If so, I expected we might never speak again.

I imagined her cradling Beau's head on her breast, stroking his hair, staring sharply into space. Impatient, and in pain. She would not share her grief with him. She wouldn't trust him to receive it. As if she would trust me, its author.

While packing up, I tried not to think about the fact that leaving New York meant leaving Jane. Even if she cut me out of her life forever after this, leaving the city meant losing the possibility of encountering her on a street corner, of catching her scent in the air after she had left a room.

Perhaps I would not have to leave. Or perhaps . . . but I should not even entertain the hope. She had a whole life here.

Yes, and it was *crushing* her. There was a part of her that *wanted*, I thought. In the same way that *I* wanted. While the greater piece of her heart would never forgive Giovanni's murder, that dark yearning might enjoin her to push past it in search of *something*. I only had to figure out what.

I did get texts, and on Monday started getting calls, from Barry. I ignored them—he could manage on his own. Loath as I was to admit it, he was capable in his way. Not a hero among noses, but he had a better head for business than I did. Given a little bit of budget, he had made good on his marketing promises. And he was the opposite of a misanthrope, which went over well with a lot of our suppliers.

Maybe if I vanished in a puff of smoke, Bright House would stick around. Barry could make it work on his own, at least for a while. It hurt to think of relinquishing my hold on something I had striven so hard to maintain. Barry would make changes I would not have approved. But he would sell perfume, and Jonathan's name would be on the labels. Mine would go unwritten, haunting Bright House, remembered by industry insiders. Barry wasn't even the worst nose in the business—if he ever quit smoking he might get somewhere.

Two weeks. Barry was leaving voice mails. I deleted them. Sent a couple of texts telling him to fuck off, in language only slightly more elegant than that. If I made it three weeks, and got rid of Giovanni, I could go back to work. I had always told myself—told Jane and Beau, even—that the lack of a corpse made things confusing. Once my basement was empty of everything but ghosts, I could go back to normal life.

I made it seventeen days.

For full potency, for the highest ratio of volatiles, I should have stuck it out a little longer. For better volume, and better flammability, I should have cycled out the old alcohol for fresh. But I *hated* having him down there with me.

I told myself it was because of the cops—I was nervous they might come around again, this time with a warrant. But I had hated it from the first moment I stepped back and stared down at Giovanni under his cocoon of Saran Wrap.

On day seventeen, I woke up late and fast, sweating from a nightmare I couldn't remember. I skipped breakfast—or rather, lunch—and went straight to the messy business of removing my friend's mortal remains from my home.

I debated a rental versus the new-to-me '93 Corolla parked on 159th. I didn't think the police would yet have a warrant to check my rental history, but if they did . . . On the other hand, we were several weeks out from Giovanni's disappearance, and I wanted the beater fresh for any potential escape I had to make. Leaving it idling in front of my house at two a.m. wasn't ideal for its so-far spotless reputation. So I made a Zipcar reservation for the evening. Then it was time to start draining the tub.

It was risky, working at this hour. But I had to get him out of here. I couldn't focus, couldn't sleep. None of the others had ever . . . *haunted* me like this. I could *feel* him in the other room: under the tarp, behind the plastic wrap, his face just beneath the surface of the liquid. In death, Giovanni was as skeptical, as swift to make a harsh judgment, as he had been in life.

So I was draining his tub in daylight, hoping to get him out of the house as soon as darkness fell.

The basement was quiet except for the purling of liquid against plastic, and then eventually against itself. Outside the dirty windows that peered onto the back garden, a cardinal made a series of shrill descending calls. The sound pierced the glass as sharply as the single shaft of sunlight that had made it through the grime.

In this dusty stillness, the nasty buzz of Iolanda's doorbell was like an emergency klaxon. Involuntarily, I gasped. Alcohol fumes burned the back of my throat, the inside of my nose. My eyes began to water.

Up above, I heard Iolanda's feet on the boards. Felt the shudder in the ceiling as she opened and shut the door to her apartment. And another as she opened the front door to whoever was standing on the stoop.

I realized I had frozen, and that the extract was coming dangerously close to the top of the plastic bin. Scrambling up, I plunged my hand into the alcohol bath to plug the drain. Giovanni's hair stuck wetly to my arm. Like a record scratch, my thoughts skidded to a halt as the weight of memory fell on me—Jonathan in the tub, Jonathan's hair on my arm. The same squeamish disbelief at what I had done. But I had no time to feel it now.

The lid was propped up against my workbench. Even under duress, I got down on my knees to affix it to the bin rather than pull the full thing out uncovered and risk a splash. I was tugging the heavy bin out from under the bathtub when I heard a knock on the basement door.

And then another knock, more insistent, because several seconds had gone by and I had not answered. Or even moved. Crouched like a gargoyle over my bin of tincture, I stared over my shoulder and forgot to breathe.

"Vicky?" Iolanda's voice was muffled by the door. "Vicky, are you down there?"

If I didn't answer, she would go away. Surely she would go away. She never wanted to try the stairs. But someone else was with her—someone looking for me.

I had a horrible vision of Pip Miles, swollen tongue poking from between his lips, standing at the top of the basement steps in the blue windbreaker I had shoved into a trash can at the gas station just outside of Philmont.

Or it could be the NYPD.

All was quiet upstairs for a long moment. I took a shaky breath and dared to take my hands from the bin of extract. No sooner had I done so than I heard the latch on the basement door click and the creak of hinges as it swung inward.

"Vic?"

It was Barry. Barry Baptiste had come to my goddamned house. What for? I had answered his texts, or at least some of them. I had trusted him to run the office in my absence—why look that gift horse in the mouth? Yet here were his feet in their spotless white sneakers, worn sockless so his skinny brown ankles showed below the carefully folded cuffs of acid-washed jeans. And they were coming down the stairs.

In a hurry, I shoved the bin of extract back beneath the tub. I pulled the tarp and soggy plastic wrap into place. It made a racket. I didn't care. My arm was wet and stank of alcohol, which made my ragged cuticles sting.

"Vic?" said Barry. He jogged down the last couple of steps. I heard his feet hit the concrete; I wasn't looking at him but standing at the workbench, fiddling with my still and trying to make it look like I was busy with something innocuous.

"Vic," he said, and I finally turned. In the dim and dingy basement, his bright print shirt and gleaming sneakers looked out of place. They were. *He* was. A sunflower blooming in February. A parrot perched in a morgue.

"Barry," I said. "You shouldn't have come."

He took a step forward, and then another, and I would have moved back but the workbench was in my way. Instead I stepped sideways, toward the tub, and regretted it.

"You're okay?"

"I'm fine, Barry. What the hell are you doing here?"

"I wanted to make sure you were okay." He paused, looked around, seemed to realize where he was for the first time. "You . . . your landlady said you live down here."

I jerked my head toward my studio. The door was open so I could hear the radio streaming on my laptop. I was listening to WQXR. Debussy: *Prelude to the Afternoon of a Faun.*

He didn't look convinced by that small glimpse of refrigerator and area rug. My face grew hot. Shame made me furious: What did he expect? He knew what we made in a year. And he knew nothing of my circumstances. This place was perfect for me. Yes, I wished for more, but I had my work, and this place made that easy.

Without thinking—fear and anger made me sloppy; when had I ever not stopped to think?—I put a hand out to the lip of the old bathtub. The blue tarp crackled under my grip.

"What's that?" he asked. And then, he sniffed the air. "You working on something down here? Smells like alcohol. And . . . musk?"

"I dabble in my free time," I told him. "I'm tincturing." More than he needed to know. "How did you get my address?"

"You left some bills at the office," he said. "I was going through the mail. And I hadn't heard from you in so long, I was worried. I mean, with the cops coming by the office, and your friend gone, and you wouldn't answer my calls."

"You're too kind," I said.

"Vic," he said, "are you okay? Really?" Then, following the tense line of my arm toward the tub: "What's in there?"

"Nothing that concerns you." Please, I thought, just let him leave. I knew that I could do this, but I didn't want to. What was the point? It was Giovanni all over again, but worse because Barry wouldn't see it coming. There was no symmetry here, no understanding, no irony, no art.

This was cold-blooded murder.

You think it's silly of me to draw a distinction at this point? Maybe. But my commissions, and my independent pursuits, those were in service of my profession. Pip Miles was merely an unpleasant part of that profession, like paying bills. Eisner too a loose end to tie up. Jonathan was born of some deeper urge, some profound desire that transcended what was about to happen here.

Giovanni had hurt. He had not needed to die, but he had insisted on it in the end. And if Barry took another step, if he lifted the edge of that blue tarp . . .

I was on him before he could. Not with my hands around his throat, but grabbing at his arm. This close, I could smell him: warm, woody copaiba oil. Bay Rum and shea butter. Sweat and pollen, toasted by sunlight. "No," I said. "Barry, please—"

He looked at me with wild eyes, and I saw it was too late. He knew what was under that tarp, even if he didn't understand it yet. He was going to pull it back whether I struggled with him or not. And so, I let go of his arm and stepped back to a spot just behind his left shoulder. Watched as he flipped back the tarp like a bedsheet and looked down at Giovanni's swollen face. I hadn't finished draining all the tincture—there was probably another two bins' worth. But it was shallow enough now that Giovanni's nose and chest broke the surface. He was unmistakably dead.

There was an awful moment of silence. I saw the muscles in the back of Barry's neck engage, saw the beginning of movement in his spine. He was going to turn around, or at least look back at me. Before he got any farther than an open mouth, before the indrawn breath, I hit his back with all my weight and drove him forward over the lip of the tub.

I'm not large, and I've only ever been as strong as I needed to be. Barry was shorter than me and weighed nothing at all, and I had the element of surprise. Getting his head under the surface wasn't the hard part. Keeping it there was. I had experience with the garrote, with strangulation. Drowning made me feel like an amateur: terrified and awkward, expecting every moment to be the one in which I failed.

He kicked, scuffing his clean white sneakers on the dirty concrete. Great gouts of bubbles came up around his ears. His locs twisted in my grip, loose strands snapping. I could feel his muscles spasm frantically, feel the moment he finally gave up and inhaled.

I wanted to let go then. It was worse than the crunch of cartilage I had grown used to, crushing windpipes. This wasn't violence; this was surrender. He had done this to himself; I had merely facilitated it. I felt sleazy, like I had tricked him.

Just like asphyxiation, drowning takes longer than you think. It isn't like the movies. So I held his head under. Kept holding until he went limp and hung over the edge of the tub on his own, head still submerged. Even then, I kept a hand between his shoulder blades. More to steady myself than him.

This was it—the end of Bright House. Even if the cops didn't finger me for Pip Miles or Giovanni, this was too close to home. And now there was no more Barry to keep things afloat after I was gone—no one to schedule Instagram posts, to network with influencers, to push popular products and demand scents that would actually sell.

Bright House was dead, and I had killed it. If Jonathan had been alive to see me now, he would have laughed. Even without the rank scent of his soliflore, I could hear the sound. Not the hot exhalation against my ear, the laughter he saved for mocking me in private. This was a laugh like the light in an interrogation chamber: the one he aimed at the victims of his humor. It used to be that I had stood behind the light with him and laughed along in darkness. Not so, now. No shadows left to hide in. I had been examined by circumstances and found insufficient. I had failed to live up to my own grand expectations.

When I finally caught my breath and started to wonder what I would do next, the basement door creaked on its hinges again, and I realized I had never heard it close.

One footstep, followed by a cautious second. The tread of someone with a bad limp, careful on the stairs. Someone who wouldn't be coming down at all if they weren't determined to see things for themselves.

"Vicky?" said Iolanda. "What the hell is going on?"

34

Notes de Tête: Pear Blossom
Notes de Cœur: Smoke, Hot Metal, Ambergris
Notes de Fond: Asafoetida and Sulfur

I was really in the shit now. It didn't matter if I got rid of Giovanni: if the cops came around with a warrant I was done. And sooner or later, they would. So I dumped another couple of gallons into the tub with him and canceled my Zipcar reservation.

Iolanda and Barry? I still had two tubs empty and I filled them on autopilot, rationalizing it ex post facto. Easier to burn, just like Pip and Eisner. Besides, it helped get rid of the drums of alcohol I didn't plan to take with me. The weather was getting warmer too—the booze would keep the bodies from smelling. I didn't expect to have the time to tincture them properly, but maybe New York City's finest would surprise me.

No one would report Iolanda, I didn't think—she lived alone, and her visitors and adventures were infrequent. Rent had just come due, so nobody upstairs would be searching for her yet. That gave me a little less than a month.

Barry was another story. He talked to his mother on the phone in the office. I thought of the bonbon amidon in Tupperware, the Christmas plates, the cousins he babysat on the weekends. My stomach clenched.

How long would she wait before she called him in? Barry had grown up in East Flatbush and—quite rightly—distrusted cops. But a mother whose son had disappeared? Even if she shared his misgivings, wouldn't she try everything? Whether the cops would do the same . . .

Filthy and soaked in alcohol, sadly none of it inside me, I sat on the concrete floor and listened to the quiet. No creak and shuffle as Iolanda moved around upstairs. The other tenants were either out or still asleep—college students and party kids and drug dealers, they all kept odd hours. Just me and WQXR. I was alone with my work—as I had always wanted to be.

Except the work meant nothing now. Leila didn't even have a key to the office. Bright House had become a memory. Ironic. With Barry's tincture I could summon up its ghost, relive a moment in the lab. But the enterprise itself? Finis.

Someone braver—or stupider—might have tried to keep up their regular patterns. Been spotted at their favorite bars. Might have gone downtown, unlocked the lab, pretended diligently to work. I stayed in. For a few days, I was on high alert. Hypervigilant. But maintaining that level of anxiety was so draining that it left me nearly catatonic. After eighteen hours of sleep, I woke in a sustainable state of disassociation. I'm not entirely sure how many days went by before I got the call.

At first, I wondered what the sound was. A buzz deeper than the refrigerator compressor, and less regular. I so little expected anyone to call me—I had been waiting for boots on the pavement, a fist bashing on the door.

By the time I realized what was happening, I had nearly missed the call.

It was from Beau. Once I saw the name, I almost didn't answer. An involuntary freeze. But of course, I overcame it. Curiosity, and compulsion.

"Hello?" my voice croaked, stiff with disuse.

"Hey." All was not well. I could almost envision him—eyes downcast, angled to the side. A look of shame, with heavy weight across his shoulders. "What's up?"

He was not actually asking. It was reflexive. As traditional a greeting as good morrow, or peace be upon you.

"Nothing," I said. Technically true, and simultaneously a lie. I was flat on my back in bed, staring at the ceiling, and had been for days. Also, my entire life was falling apart.

"So . . ." He took a deep breath. "Jane didn't want me to call. She . . . she didn't. But. Your suit is ready for a fitting, and I'm trying to get paid, you know?"

I blinked at my bubbly ceiling paint and asked, eloquently, "What?" His words echoed in my head like it was the deep end of an empty swimming pool. *Jane didn't want me to call.* Did she suspect? She must suspect. And now he did as well.

"Your suit. I need you to come in and try it on." He sounded miserable. "I could do today, but honestly later in the week is better for me."

Because he wanted to put it off. Because Jane was mad at me, and he probably knew why but was trying to maintain some thin veneer of plausible deniability. Or maybe he didn't believe her but didn't want to piss her off. Or maybe she didn't know what I had done, but both of them were gutted that Giovanni had gone missing, and even if I hadn't murdered him it was still my fault.

I had shit where I ate, and eaten where I shit, and then shit there again.

"Sure," I said. "Sure. Any time that works for you."

◆ ◆ ◆

When the day came, it was excruciating.

For one, I hadn't been off my block in some time. My only excursions had been to empty my trash and accept delivery. The subway was overwhelming: the smells too strong and varied, the people too many and too much. Piss and garbage, hot metal, drainage from the gutters overhead. There was a police station at 145th. I plunged past it as fast as decorum allowed.

For two, Beau clearly did not want me in his atelier. But he wanted the second half of his commission more than he wanted peace and quiet, because once you've been broke you never forget what it feels like. Money, to both of us, was worth pretty much whatever it took to acquire.

For three, he was not Jane. I was ashamed of that. He had been my entrée to her affections, yes, but surely more than that. I enjoyed his company—didn't I? But there was being at ease with someone and then there was . . . whatever I felt for her. And what she felt—I hoped—for me. To have him here, and only him, was intolerable.

Stepping into his atelier I found my suit set up on a hanger, first in line on the rolling garment rack against the far wall. The color, I realized now, was the same as dried blood: a black silk-linen so bleached and warm that it looked rusty red in the light. Two buttons, single vent, notched lapels. I had sketched it for him roughly, what felt like a thousand years ago, and he had made my crude lines flesh. Or fabric, as it were.

The man himself appeared from his small back room already rubbing his neck. He looked at the suit instead of at me. Fair—I had looked at it first as well. But now I surveyed Beau, from the bags beneath his eyes to his unpolished shoes. His beard was dry and I caught no whiff of ambergris. He looked like shit.

"So, yeah," he said. "I think it turned out okay."

I walked forward and touched it, felt the rubbery flex of the fabric against my palm, the crunch where it folded. It would crease easily, aesthetically. The air would pass through it to my skin. To wear it would be to have his hands on me. Would that be as painful as this? Because they were not her hands?

"It's beautiful," I said. Then, masochistically: "Have you heard from Giovanni?"

"What?" he asked, with a desperate edge. Then, leery: "Why, have you?"

"No." The gambit had neither confirmed nor put paid to my fears.

"Oh." It seemed like more than disappointment. Had he been counting on me to tell him something new, maybe something he could take back to Jane and say *you're wrong*? Or was I just reading into things?

"Me neither," he added, belatedly. "He never . . . the last time we heard from him was . . . what I told you about." He finally met my eyes. "Vic, I swear to god, if—"

"I know." I interrupted him before he could finish; whether it was suicide or murder, or some nebulous other supposition, I did not want to hear it. "Believe me, I know." The surreality of this conversation made the whole scene feel too bright, too saturated. What were we even talking about? I had no idea what he knew, what he had guessed, what Jane had told him. I didn't even understand my own reassurance—what *did* I know? He swore to god about *what*? It felt like we had the scripts of two different Stoppard plays. Or perhaps we were merely missing the third actor, whose part made sense of ours.

A long moment of sun-drenched silence in which we waited to see who had the next line. Then he sighed and said, "All right, try it on."

I could have stripped and changed right there—he had seen me in the nude. But our new, uncomfortable formality made him gesture toward the back room and close the door on me. I maneuvered around his desk and sewing machine, breathing the close hot air with its traces of Beau-sweat and mechanical lubricant, and shed my clothes.

The suit fit like . . . well, like it had been made for me. None of the pouches and wrinkles and odd tight spots I found in off-the-rack menswear. I usually had things taken in and let out by a competent tailor–cum–dry cleaner at 125th, who had hit on me once and lived to regret it. But this suit was another story entirely. I had been making do. Now I was made myself.

The trousers were cropped just a little short. The jacket too, and the sleeves. A sort of Thom Browne schoolboy look. Something snarky in it, though the lines were clean and the cut otherwise impeccable.

Beau had seen my ragged sketch, taken in my posture and my pos-tur*ing*, and made this thing that made me *more* of myself. I smoothed it across my front and felt the slight curves of my body beneath the cloth: familiar to my touch, but elevated. The interpretation of the audience changing the artist's creation. It was perfect. It was, like Giovanni's hair-cuts, something that made me feel utterly at home in my own skin.

I felt like I had been kicked in the stomach.

"Well?" asked Beau through the door.

I stepped out for inspection. He sucked his lower lip, flipped a piece of chalk into his hand, and knelt in front of me, all business.

"It's perfect," I said. I felt remorse. Five minutes ago I had almost written him off, consigned our relationship to some sad and secondary category. But the suit said he knew me in a way not many people did. And unlike Jane, I had not *told* him; he had discovered it for himself. She would not have told him, not that special secret; he could not have learned this secondhand. Or perhaps she *had* said something: maybe I wanted to imagine them that way, speaking me into existence, caring enough about what I hoped they would see to convince themselves they saw it.

Jane loved him, and so it made some sense that feeling as I did for her I felt . . . *something* for him, and he *something* for me. A transitive property of understanding and, if not affection, then at least affinity. Two separate links in a chain, occasionally touching within the embrace of the link that bound them.

I wondered how it made him feel, to know me like that and also know what I had done.

I just never knew a murderer before. Well, he did now. Intimately.

"I need to do the buttonholes, at least." He tugged at the right cuff. "And this could be a little longer, I think. Shows too much white."

I said nothing. He was the professional.

"I'll have it done in a week," he said. "I have some other important stuff I have to get through first."

That stung like a whip: immediate and sharp, but bearable. The true pain of it came later, as the implications started to sink in and the ache spread outward like a swollen red welt.

No matter what bound us to one another, I was not friends and family anymore.

◆　◆　◆

It became a challenge to myself, every time I wanted to load up the car and run: wait for the buttonholes. I could hold my ground another hour, another day, another two. When I heard footsteps upstairs and thought of bolting, I imagined the crunch of linen in my fist. When a shadow crossed the barred basement window, I shut my eyes and saw bloody blackish red.

I would wear A City on Fire, with that suit. I would wear Cuir de Gardenia. Leather, smoke, indoles, musk. Scents I normally reserved for colder months. I would drag dark winter in my wake, trickles of sweat streaking the fleshy scents against my skin.

That color and that cut would pair well with Sevilen: its earthy spice and voluptuous rose. But these days, I couldn't bring myself to wear it.

Where had I gone wrong? Many places, probably. But was there some fatal fork where I had turned left instead of right and lost my way?

I waited for the suit, because it seemed that anything beyond the suit was lost to me. It became everything that I would never have again.

On the day I was supposed to pick it up, Beau texted me:

They're fumigating the building. I have to take everything home. Come by next week?

And then he gave me a few dates.

I didn't have another week. I had been lucky so far. Maybe whatever precinct Barry's mother had reported him to hadn't gotten the West Village cops on the phone yet, hadn't put two and two together. Maybe it was another instance of misplaced priorities—perhaps the hunt for Pip Miles, or any other number of investigation and enforcement activities, occupied resources that should have gone to looking for people who mattered more, to me. I knew I should be grateful, and hated that I knew it.

I couldn't push this kind of luck any further than I had. If I had been looking for a sign, this was it.

This time I dumped the tubs not into plastic storage bins but into whatever vessels I had been able to find in the neighborhood recycling: Ball jars, artisanal yogurt tubs, wine bottles I corked with my collection of saved Scotch tops. All of it fitted neatly into boxes from the local coffee shop, the local liquor store. I would distill it when I was safely out of the city.

Half of Giovanni had already gone into the fridge. Along with his fellows, I transferred him to a cooler with a couple of cold packs.

I didn't take much else. My favorite books, my dented moka pot. The bed linens made handy covers for the boxes of oddly colored alcohol in assorted scavenged containers. My clothes all fit into my hamper. Everything would stack easily into the Corolla, which had a roomy trunk.

By the time night fell, I was uptown with my keys in the ignition. Ten minutes later I was parallel parking fifty yards from Iolanda's front door. Within an hour, the car was packed.

There wasn't much alcohol left in the basement—just a couple of nearly empty drums. But there was a natural gas line that, for tonight's purpose, made the alcohol redundant.

I dragged Iolanda and Barry and Giovanni as close to the heart of the expected blast as I could, in the cramped firetrap of the basement. For a moment I stood over them and breathed in the stinging fumes of alcohol, feeling a sense of vertigo. As if the earth beneath me was not horizontal after all, but sloping away, its angle increasing every moment.

How had I gotten here? How had I slid so far, so fast? How much further did I have to go?

The valve on the gas line was corroded so badly I worried I wouldn't be able to open it up. But it finally gave with a startling crack that had me worrying—too late—about sparks. If I had caused one I doubt I would be relating this now.

I didn't open it all the way. I didn't want to napalm the block. Just enough to fill the air with sulfur stench. Then I turned on my stove and left a pan of rotten leftovers over a high flame. The combination of scents was unique, and not particularly pleasant. I think you'll agree. I didn't stick around to savor it, and I've built this so the hint of it passes quickly in favor of springtime city street at night: pollen, pear tree, idling car exhaust.

Locked inside the Corolla, I waited with clenched fists. Bated breath. Whatever physical expression of tension and terror feels most natural to you. Anxiety shits? Sure. But even as my guts turned somersaults, I heard a strange rippling sound through the windows of the car—like fabric tearing. Flames leaped from the basement windows like hungry fish from dark water, straining for something just out of reach.

Don't worry—the upper windows of the house were dark. I'm sure floors two through four were busy earning minimum wage at their various dead-end jobs, flirting for tips, or desperately studying in the library hoping yet another degree would give them a leg up over their peers. The neighbors would no doubt make nice insurance claims. And all I cared about, really, was that everything in the basement burned to a crisp. They would have to identify my assistant, my landlady, my friend, all by their dental records. I'd had time, if I wanted, to pry their teeth out to prevent it. But it didn't seem worth the effort. By the time New York's finest solved this puzzle, I would be well away.

I thought briefly of all the teeth I had buried upstate, which would never be found or identified. And then I thought about Jane, teeth catching her lip, or caging her tongue. The red marks her bites left on my skin.

I stayed long enough to make sure the fire caught, but left before the first responders arrived. By then, other people were beginning to move their cars as well. My Corolla blended in nicely with the exodus, and soon I was off my block and across the bridge, slipping into the night at a speed just slightly above the posted limit—to follow the rules too closely would be as suspicious as ignoring them altogether.

35

Notes de Tête: Lilacs
Notes de Cœur: Warm Cotton Sheets, Paint Dust
Notes de Fond: Sweat and Blood

I almost didn't stop. I knew I shouldn't. It wasn't even in the right direction. But I crossed the Harlem and East Rivers and drove through Queens into Crown Heights. The directions written on the back of my hand were smeared almost into illegibility, but they were safer than GPS.

I had left my cell phone and my laptop behind to burn. Safer that way. I had backed up both to an external hard drive, which meant I still had all my contacts, all my photos, all my texts. A slightly more practical version of Dickie Greenleaf's ring. My one indulgence, my one risk in this endeavor. Except what I was about to do.

On the way, I justified my actions to myself. I pretended that this was not a desperate, last-ditch attempt at reconciliation. Or at whatever I could get. I could not tell myself this was a whim—I had looked up how to get there long before I set Iolanda's house on fire. I had known where I was going, before I left New York for good.

It was not just for a suit; I could not fool myself that far. It was more that I regretted the necessity of my actions. I regretted even more that Beau and Jane didn't know what had happened to their friend, nor that

I had sacrificed him for their sakes. If I left now and didn't tell them, it felt like a true break, a betrayal. I had already splintered our confederacy when I killed Giovanni—to leave them in ignorance now would mean they were no more than my tools.

Which they had been, long ago. I had not meant for this project to become a collaboration. I had meant to delegate, not draw in.

If it had been only Beau, perhaps I could have run away with my secret. He was not the kind of person to delve too deeply when it hurt to do so. I was his friend. Giovanni had been also. When we were gone he would mourn us both and move on. Or he would have, if he had not had Jane like a bur in his side reminding him, reminding him. She was the kind to hold a grudge. I knew because I was the same.

Jane . . . Jane would dwell on it. She would turn it over and over, poke and prod at her suspicion. I could not bear to leave her alone with those thoughts. Every day that I was gone, I would wonder if they had festered into anger yet.

If she hated me, I would much rather know for sure. And if I told her now, and she hated me, it would be a sudden, cauterizing fury. It would help me leave, cut me away cleanly.

I would not let myself entertain the idea that desperately wanted to be let in and chatted up: that Jane might make the bad choice. *You* put the blood on her hands, I told myself. And then, devil's advocate: Ah, but she held them out for me.

No. Jane valued bread over roses. She had proven it again and again. I was only taking this detour for closure. And anyway: I *did* want to pick up my suit.

Parking under a broken streetlight, I looked up and down the empty thoroughfare. No dog walkers, no drunk teens. It was late. Jane would be done with work by now, and home. Unless Beau was out at a party, client hunting, he should be home too. They should be in bed together, warm together. Wrapped in grief, together.

The car wasn't cold, but *I* was. Shock, probably. Or poor circulation. I turned off the engine and sat, staring up at the dark windows. But even as I watched, a light flipped on.

A midnight snack? The image was so strong for me I could almost smell the freon fog of an open refrigerator, the toasty crumbs of matzo cracked in half.

Out of the car before I realized I had moved, I found myself halfway to their door, staring up the stoop.

This time I knew which doorbell to press. Nothing happened at first, so I pressed again, leaning into it and letting the imagined sound of the buzzer go on and on inside my head.

My insistence was rewarded with the gentle shudder of the downstairs door as the upstairs door opened. I realized I had leaned in to the scarred wood, close enough to feel its vibrations through the fine hairs on the skin of my cheek.

Footsteps on the stairs. When they stopped I realized my inner monologue was hovering on "fourteen." I had not even realized I was counting. The door quivered when the mechanism turned, and I staggered back in time to straighten and face my ill-considered confrontation with a little dignity.

"What the fuck?" said Beau. He wore pajamas, silk striped in red and white, unbuttoned as if he had thrown the shirt on quickly. The pants were slung dangerously low, tie snarled in a crooked knot that rested in the divot of his hip. He smelled like warm sheets, sleep-sweat. He smelled like Jane, and like himself, and like paint dust from their apartment, which I had cataloged months ago and forgotten that I knew.

"Can I come in?" I asked.

"It's three in the morning!"

I nodded, and stepped across the threshold before he could stop me. "I need to talk to Jane." I heard myself half a beat too late. "And you. Together."

He stood in the doorway for a moment, as if I were still in front of him. Then turned on his heel, the sole of his bare foot hissing on the decorative tile of the vestibule. They don't build houses like they used to.

"It couldn't wait until tomorrow?" he asked.

I shook my head and started up the stairs. He hurried to follow, and I wondered if he was afraid of me. All five foot five, one hundred twenty-five pounds of me, half his size. Then I thought, He should be.

The upstairs door was open, and Jane was already leaning through the gap, looking bleary. When she saw me her eyes cleared and widened.

"Hey," I said. "Can I come in?"

◆ ◆ ◆

The kitchen overhead at night was as unforgiving as I remembered. It still showed dark circles beneath Jane's eyes, and didn't do Beau any favors. I wished briefly that he were not here—his presence disrupted the symmetry of this with every other difficult conversation Jane and I had had across a table in the last six months.

I thought of the suit he had made me, and hated that I wished this.

"What's going on?" asked Jane. This sanguinity came only after I assured both of them we were not all in immediate danger of arrest.

"I'm leaving the city," I said.

"Okay, Didion." Beau crossed his arms. "So you just dropped in to say goodbye?"

Jane's hand moved as though she would have reached out to touch his arm—a placating, silencing press of her palm. But the motion died before her fingertips had even lifted from the table.

"Yes," I said, and when he started to roll his eyes, I added, "No. Not just."

"You wanted to pick up your suit before you went?" he asked, and the hostility in it left little doubt that Jane knew what I had done and had told him so. He had held his fury in check to deal with me professionally,

I realized, and more than anything, that hurt. I was a customer now, a client, and not a comrade in arms. I was the kind of person he would kill for complaining, and right now he had no reason to treat me with even the thinnest veneer of courtesy. I needed to tread carefully.

"I hadn't thought of it," I lied.

"Vic," said Jane. As I had so often made the single syllable of her name mean *please, stay, I want you, I'm sorry*, she managed to convey weariness, distrust, disappointment, and warning. But maybe, also: pain. And that was the note that sang in my heart because it meant regret. It meant *wanting*.

I hated to have disappointed her, ever. And I refused to go on doing so now.

"I wanted to . . . I need to tell you something," I said. "Before I go. I didn't want to leave you wondering."

Jane tensed in her chair—she knew what was coming and didn't want to hear it. And that too emboldened me. If she did not want this truth from me, it meant there was some part of her that still wanted what had hung between us, insubstantial but arresting as the scent of linen and lilacs. She wanted that, but not the harder, colder truths at the base of who I was.

Perversely, this strengthened my resolve to tell her. A perfume without base notes has no staying power. If she wanted the beauty, she would have to take the filth as well. And Jane . . . I believed that Jane could learn to love it.

"Well come the fuck on," said Beau. "If you're in such a hurry to get out of town."

This time she did reach out, sightlessly, to spread her open hand across his ribs. "Beau, please." It was not a request. Of all of us, it seemed only Jane knew what was unfolding. I wished I had any of her poise. I still felt like I was barreling downhill, and wished I could pinpoint the moment my momentum had started, inexorably, to build.

Would I have stopped it, if I could?

"Go ahead and say it." Jane clasped her hands in front of her, and the illusion of competent stillness was nearly complete, except for the white skin where the pressure of her grip drove blood away from the surface. If she had laced her fingers any more tightly, she would have had the appearance of a woman in desperate prayer. "If you don't say it now, there's always going to be a part of me that wonders if it isn't true. And I can't live like that."

It felt like a shining blade was poised to fall between us, so brightly polished that it was as good as a mirror. I would rather end this now, and so would she: a clean wound. A sharp and sudden break between this chapter of our lives and the next, in which neither would feature in the other's biography except as painful memories.

Or perhaps not a guillotine. Perhaps a scalpel, making a skillful cut that could heal cleanly. A graft where two separate pieces could grow together as one.

"I killed Giovanni," I said, and let the razor edge come down.

◆ ◆ ◆

"You motherfucker," said Beau, like the wind had been knocked out of him. Jane would not have kept this secret from him, would she? Even now I felt a twinge of admiration that she might surprise me. But whether he had known or not—and I expect he had—hearing it aloud, stated with such calm and clarity, undid a knot of fury he had so far held taut.

"I can tell you why, if you'd like to hear."

Jane shook her head.

"'Cause you didn't want to go to prison, I bet," said Beau. "Jesus *Christ*, I've known him as long as I've known Jane."

"I didn't want you to go to prison either," I said, looking at her and not at him.

"Sure," said Beau. "Because you give a single *fuck* about anyone besides yourself."

"Beau," said Jane. A note of pleading had entered her voice, though she didn't raise her eyes to his. This was not the clean break she and I had wanted. And now I realized my brief hope of a surgical incision, a clean graft, was a fantasy. Perhaps foolishly, neither of us had anticipated his reaction.

"Don't," he said. "Just don't."

She had expected acquiescence, and this caught her off guard.

"You got taken in just like me," he said. "The only difference is you're too fucking *cool* to admit it. You think you're above it all. You've made sacrifices nobody else would *dream* of making, and you're only grubbing around down here with the rest of us because of some cosmic injustice. But you're not special." He was glaring at me as he spoke—I think he had forgotten Jane was lumped into his tirade. But when I glanced at her she had gone green around the lips, mouth crooked where she had dug into the inside of her lip with her teeth.

When I looked away, Beau had come closer. Nearly close enough to touch.

"We're supposed to be in this *together*," he said. "But you know what it's like out here and you're *just as bad as them*."

"Beau," said Jane, in a strangled voice I had never heard her use. I took my eyes off him for just a moment and caught a glimpse of her open mouth, the pink of her tongue.

I heard Beau say, "Actually, I think you're *worse*."

And from there, the bottom went out of it all.

Jane shouted his name once more when he lunged. It didn't even give him pause. He was much bigger than me, but I had taken on big men before and won. Usually I had the element of surprise, but sometimes I lost it too early. I had learned to wrest the advantage back from all kinds of opponents.

Jane was talking, in the background. Not at volume, not after her first outburst, but a sort of panicked, monotone stream of exhortations. I caught maybe one in five words, but the tenor of it was clear. She wanted us to stop. But I wouldn't stop unless he did, because I had come this far and damned if I was going to die here, on the same floor where I had spilled a bag of frozen peas.

He was heavy. His weight forced nearly all the air from my lungs. He had hit me several times before I got my metaphorical feet under me, and now my head was spinning and my vision had begun to go yellow. In a more rational state perhaps I could have pulled my blows, but I was half-way to unconsciousness already and not keen to complete the journey.

I got a thumb in his eye, not hard enough to puncture the sclera but hard enough he reeled back, blind and cursing. He came at me again, but clumsier, and I chopped at his neck with the back of my hand where it met the hard edge of my wrist. The sound and feeling were familiar. There was no coming back from that crunch.

He rocked onto his heels, making abortive sounds and grabbing at his throat as if it had betrayed him.

"Oh my god," said Jane. At some point she had stood up from her chair, and now she fell to her knees and held her hands out inches from his skin, as if afraid to break him any further. "Oh my god."

There was nothing I could do, and I didn't know what to say. So I just sat there and watched him die.

◆ ◆ ◆

"What did you do?" she asked, and I couldn't tell if the question was for me or him. She was staring at her own hands, still at last, pressed into the dark curls that covered Beau's chest. Maybe the question was for herself.

What was the last thing he had said to her? *You're just as bad as them.* He hadn't meant to—he thought he was going to win this fight. And anyway, he had been talking to me. But that wasn't what she had heard.

I knew she wouldn't want to hear *I'm sorry*. She never wanted apologies—she only wanted the problem solved. And this one couldn't be.

"What am I supposed to do?" She closed her fists in his chest hair. I saw a glint of silver in the black. "I can't call the police. I can't . . . if they ask me any questions I . . ." She shook her head.

"Come with me." I spoke before I could think. A desperate bid to stitch together what I had torn apart. A hope that our bond, whatever it was based on—hatred, anger, pheromones, aesthetic—would bridge this ever-widening gap. That the thing in me that *wanted* would reach out toward the thing in her that *wanted* too, and that this wanting would be enough to eclipse every consequence of its own greed.

She looked up at me and blinked: a camera flash, uncomprehending. "What?"

"Leave with me," I said. "Grab the cash. Put on some clothes. I can make room in the car."

It was like waiting for the gas explosion back uptown. I imagined the smell of asafoetida thickening in the air: the only tangible measure of the growing threat. It always appealed to me, that this invisible danger had been marked purposefully with scent.

Her anger, when it came, exploded out of her so forcefully it should have broken windows.

"Are you fucking *crazy*?" She crossed her arms over Beau's chest, as if I would take him away from her again. "Why? Why would I? Jesus *Christ*." She said it with the same emphasis he had, and I remembered meeting Beau for the first time, seeing the crook of his eyebrow that he had so obviously learned from her.

His last words lingered like the cooking smells that still stuck in the corners of the kitchen. His cruelty had not been meant for Jane, but that didn't matter now. She had heard them, and knew at least some of them were true.

I wondered if any of the things I could say would soften the blow, or if they would only land it harder: *You loved him because he made you feel*

*like you knew what you were doing, and the responsibility was exhausting.
He was right about you: you thought you were better than him. You needed
that. It made you feel competent and in control.*

She had made the sacrifices, yes. He was right in that. She had sacrificed everything beautiful, and chosen to live on bread alone. Beau had
tried so hard to be her roses, but she had never trusted him to deliver.
He had offered her the precarious chance to pursue her passion. Over
and over again, he promised he could make another life possible: *You
don't have to go through with this . . . I can find a job. We'll make it work.*
Perhaps he truly believed they could. And every time she told him no.

Can you imagine the agony of refusing your dearest wish, daily? I
would never put her in that position, because I would never offer her
hope.

Hope is cheap. I wanted to believe that she had better taste.

Jane got up slowly, moving Beau's body from her knees with effort
and trying to prevent him thudding to the floor. She couldn't, and
winced. I wondered if the downstairs neighbors had woken up. I didn't
think that was why she was wincing.

I did not get up to match her, but watched her waver between several decisions—all opaque to me. I could read only the ripple of her body
as her weight shifted from one foot to the other, the flicker of her silver
eyes from right to left. As she moved the air moved around her, and I
caught a fleeting few scraps of sun-warmed hay, horse scent, the breeze
along Central Park South.

I thought for a moment I smelled lilacs.

She came down a step away, weight on her heels, and turned toward
the counter. Toward the knife block. I heard the blades rattle in their
wooden housing as she drew one out. Her hands must have been shaking.

"Jane," I said, in the same way she had said Beau's name. She refused
to hear me, just as he had her.

She held the knife not like a slasher-movie villain but like a woman
considering a supermarket chicken she intended to break down. Like a

tool, and not a weapon. Like she was going to ask me to tear up leaves for a salad, or peel a carrot, or mix her a drink.

I didn't see the movement coming—nothing telegraphed it, except her obvious intent. She was utterly still, staring at me, and then the knife was at my throat. I never had time to raise my arms or flinch away.

She had meant to slash me open but calculated the angle wrong—these things are always more difficult than they seem. Instead the blade bounced off a tendon and clattered across the tops of my collarbone. I stumbled back, too late, blood welling and pain following in its footsteps.

I didn't let her land a second blow.

"I don't want to do this," I said. "I don't want to." But we all do things we don't want to do, just to get by from day to day.

Just as I had known what she would decide, she had known what I would choose when she made her decision. She had seen my last night with Jonathan. She knew the lengths to which I would go to pursue my art. But I understood, by then, what I had lost that night. The idea of losing it again almost staid my hand. Almost.

Her smell was in my nose the whole time, pungent with the sweat of fear. Her skin was soft—I had held her throat like this in other intimacies, kissing her breathless mouth until her fingernails bit into my skin and she thrashed to be free. Then, I had let her go. Now, I could not afford to.

I knew she could kill—I had taught her how. And more than that, I had seen her follow through. There was a discipline in her that not many people had, to do the things that needed to be done. To make sacrifices nobody else would dream of making.

Jane knew how I cleaned and cured a corpse. What would she do with me? Nothing. She would call 911 when it was done, or the police, maybe. Or maybe not. Maybe she would take her cash and her coat and she would run alone. That I could almost respect. But I had *made* something out of my murderousness, and I refused to fall to someone who would waste that talent. Waste *me*.

I wondered if Jonathan had suspected in his last moments what I would make of him when he was dead. Now that Jane knew, did she hope I would do the same for her?

She tried, at one point, to scratch at my eyes—like I had done to Beau—but she was losing strength by then. Her nails left shallow cuts on my cheek. When it was all said and done, I reached up to touch the swollen welts around the broken skin. My fingers came away wet and salty, streaked with rusty pink.

The color reminded me to take my suit from the wardrobe.

EPILOGUE

There is, perhaps, a scent that's missing from this collection: the night of my flight from New York.

The details aren't exactly tedious—I was terrified the entire time, soaked in my own blood, certain someone would see me as I rearranged the contents of my trunk. I had told Jane I could make room in the car. It was true. Except instead of making room for a passenger, I had to clear cargo space.

The weather was too warm. The AC in the Corolla worked, but it wheezed and smelled like fish sauce. I had brought no perfumer's alcohol with me, and the problem of how to acquire more presented a challenge. But by now you know me—I'm a problem solver.

None of this is to the point. The additional logistics, the dawn arrival in the gravel driveway of my rural bolt-hole, the scramble to unpack everything before the sun came up . . . these I'm sure you can conjure for yourself. There is nothing *personal* about them that I need to convey.

The house, of course, is squalid. And still not as cheap as Iolanda's basement. Upstate doesn't mean cheap anymore. The only people who can afford to leave the city are people who could afford to live there to begin with.

There is no internet, no phone line. Poor service on my prepaid burner, not that I've used it for much. The bedroom is drafty, the kitchen and bathroom dull with indelible grime. The cellar has no running water—an inconvenience, given what was necessary when I first arrived.

I will not stay here too much longer, I don't think. Because things will go badly in the city and my name and deeds will be dragged into the light. Or because I will need to start a new life no matter what. I cannot stay in this crumbling house forever, subsisting on processed foods from the truck stop off the highway.

I have been buying newspapers there—the sorry excuses for groceries are almost an afterthought. These newspapers are the most vivid thing in my life: their slippery heft, the sounds they make, their thirsty texture. And their smell, of course: burnt paper, cheap ink, stale air.

I never read the paper, before now. Who in my demographic does? But if I need to run, I need to know when to do it.

The relevant news items are few and far between, and their prominence depends on the publication. I wish I could get local papers from the hometowns of my dead tycoons—I'm sure for lack of stories they are devoting lots of coverage to the disappearances of their successful sons. But I make do with what I can find, and wait for it to get worse or to disappear.

In the Real Estate section of the *Times* last week I read a profile of the brains and money behind the development in Giovanni's building. There was no mention of his name or shop, but there was a snapshot of the lead developer—blond and tan and not as young as he looked—sitting sidewise in a barber's chair. My chair. The last one before the door. Behind him, tastefully blurred by a shallow depth of field, a yawning dark void where the bathroom and the office had once been. The caption identified the space as the newest outpost of a trendy chain.

I have not seen a barber in some time now. My hair has grown out badly. In some places, I have noticed threads of silver. I imagine I will let it go on growing—the shimmer of grays is appealing, and length will go a long way to disguising me when paired with a new ID, a new name. Or rather, a very old one, which I shed after dropping out of school and into which I will now squeeze, like a crustacean forcing itself into an old shell.

When the time comes—or even if it doesn't, because I must be so very cautious now—I will disappear into a new life. I will work in a small boutique, perhaps, in a town that is just turning the corner from depressed to trendy. Or I will start an Etsy shop selling "natural essences" to women who worry about chemicals in their perfume. The kind of women who wear mineral-based powder makeup and spend seventy-five dollars on eye cream. Or I will take a menial receptionist job at a small law office or local real-estate firm, where these same women will discreetly recommend their stylists to me when they notice that I do not dye my hair.

I will never wear the suit Beau made for me. To put it on would mar the careful illusion I've created. My watch, which you have noticed—yellow gold, showing brass where the plating is worn away—is already too daring, too obviously out of character. But if anyone asks, I will call it a family heirloom. An antique. This is not so far from the truth.

Vic Fowler's life is over, as surely as Jane's, Beau's, Giovanni's, Jonathan's. I—whoever I am, and no, I will not tell you that—will live this new one now. It is in no way the life I envisioned for myself, but who among us is so lucky?

I came close. That should be enough.

That, and my work. No matter what, I will always have my work. And this is my masterpiece. Eleven soliflores and a series of thirty-six scents in succession. Created not only for myself—isn't all art created for its artist first?—but for you.

Think of it as a self-portrait, but a self-portrait from which you, the viewer, look outward. A self-portrait that re-creates the subject's surroundings so exactly that you, inhabiting the canvas, experience my likeness entirely from context.

The mildew of a basement studio. Steaming egg-yolk buns. The searing swirl of Scotch in a Glencairn glass. Burnt coffee. Jonathan's rain-soaked cashmere coat. Proraso and Barbicide. Ambergris. Prosecco steam curling from the surface of a zabaglione, still warm. Sweet green hay, horse sweat, dry shampoo. The smell of Jane Betjeman's neck, just behind her ear.

For me, this collection of scents is nostalgia, reminiscence, recollection. For you, it is an experience in radical empathy, or at least an adventure in voyeurism.

But for Vic Fowler, the persona, it is a reanimation. A raising from the dead.

When I wear these perfumes, I am me again. And when you wear them, you're me too.

ACKNOWLEDGMENTS

There are so many people to thank for this book, for so many things. *Base Notes* got off to a rocky start, but there were some people who saw where it was headed before I did. Diana Pho knew from a half-assed pitch that the story had legs, and Connor Goldsmith said, "You've captured lightning in a bottle with this one," which gave me the idea that I might be on the right track. Caitlin McDonald saw what the half-finished manuscript wanted so badly to be, and believed in it. Her feedback convinced me there were readers who would understand *exactly* what this gruesome, angry book was all about.

Long before all that, John Joseph Adams and Wendy Wagner published a reprint of "The Dirty American" in *Nightmare*. Before that appeared *The Orange Volume*, an anthology my Clarion class (2012) put together to raise money for the workshop.

But even before *that*, the idea was born when I read Jude Ellison Sady Doyle's "My quest to find the great American perfume," published in *The Guardian*. Without that exploration of the unpleasant in perfume, you wouldn't have read this one.

I did a lot of research for this book—and leaned on a lot of other people's expertise—but ended up ignoring most of it in favor of telling a very strange story. All mistakes are my own, as are all the flights of fancy.

Thank you to the staff at Perfumarie, especially Rachel Ann and Madison, and to Andrea Bifulco of Nose University. Twisted Lily (*requiescat in pace*), with its generous sample policy, was an invaluable resource and will be sorely missed. Speaking of samples: thank you to everyone on the Dry Down Slack who swapped with me.

There are many small business owners to thank as well, and we'll start with the perfumers:

Chris Rusak (Chris Rusak), Carter Weeks Maddox (Chronotope Perfume), and Daniel Jones (Dandy Parfums) all generously offered their time, attention, conversation, and advice on the technical and professional aspects of niche perfumery. Thanks also to Sixteen92, Nasomatto, and CB I Hate Perfume, who were gracious enough to consent to the use of their copy.

Several consulting tailors offered sound advice on just what exactly would make them homicidal: David Reeves (David Reeves Bespoke), Jean-Francois Rodrigues (Cad & the Dandy), and Nathaniel Adams (Natty Adams). Actually, Natty would insist (rightly) he is a *designer*, not a tailor, but he still had a bone to pick with contrasting buttonholes.

A tip of the hat to tonsorial rockabilly Michael Haar, of the eponymous Haar & Co., who throws great parties, makes great playlists, and once let me smell his Barbicide. (It smells like salicylic acid, if you're wondering.)

Then, there are the readers.

Ella Dawson read and loved *Base Notes* before anyone else other than Caitlin. Leah Zander introduced me to Tarquin Winot when he was most needed. Andrew Keahey provided invaluable advice on creeping this book up. Molly Majumder and Ryan Douglass were more than game for quick turnaround and gave thoughtful feedback. Jackie Kay was my cavalry, coming in at the last minute with some refreshing thoughts about cantaloupe, among other things.

I have Micaiah Huw Evans, former pathologist, to thank for the alcohol enemas, as well as many facts about rigor mortis. He also gave some great late-stage pep talks about craft, perfume, and classical music that honestly got this book over the finish line.

I cannot overstate the value of Rachel Sobel's friendship and advice. *Base Notes* would not be itself without her. (Sorry, Rachel, I'm not even softening this with sarcasm or a snarky aside. You will just have to suffer through my sincerity.)

There are friends and family too who may be reading this for the first time and realizing in horror what their support helped me accomplish. Michael Jaoui did some emergency wrangling of chemist recommendations in the final weeks of edits. Then there's everyone in the Pub, of course, especially L. X. Beckett, for the cherry on—or down, as it were—the top and many other excellent pieces of advice; Jay Wolf, as ever, for having all the good ideas; and Tessa Fisher, who helped me murder Giovanni.

Thanks, Dad, for Trumper and Süskind, and Mom, who brought me the last drops of Dali to smell when all I could remember was "the bottle shaped like a nose." And Eliot, of course, who sat over my left shoulder most evenings I was drafting and suffered many moments of my spinning in my office chair and steepling my fingers like a Bond villain, saying, "so," and sticking him with a thorny plot problem to solve.

A final thank-you to Holly Black, who said at Clarion that in real life, it's bad not to tip a waiter; it's worse to cheat on your spouse; murder is the gravest sin. And then said it's pretty much the opposite in fiction.

ABOUT THE AUTHOR

Photo © 2020 Eliot Routh

Lara Elena Donnelly is the author of the Nebula-, Lambda-, and Locus-nominated trilogy the Amberlough Dossier. She has taught in the MFA program at Sarah Lawrence College, as well as the Catapult classes in New York and the Alpha SF/F/H Workshop for Young Writers.

In the summer, she wears The Cobra & the Canary. In the winter, Nudiflorum. And some others in between, to keep things interesting.

Corporeally, she lives on the grounds of the old Hamilton Estate, with a screenwriter and a small mask-and-mantle tabby pretentiously named after a bitter Italian aperitif. Digitally, you can visit her at www.laradonnelly.com.